AT THE MERCY OF MRS. WU

"I know Mrs. Wu has been arrested," the general stormed. "I know that she is in custody. Why did you lie to me?" he demanded angrily.

"Because she said she would have me killed if I told you," I cried, blurting out two or three words at a time between hysterical sobs. "I was afraid she would kill me."

He was silent for a time. "She wrote some letters to my young officers," he said, indicating several on his desk. "She told them to have nothing to do with you."

For a long time there had been no walks in the garden, no mah-jong games, no dancing. So that was the reason.

"She said she picked you off the street working as a prostitute and warned them to beware of you. She threatened that if they continued to see you their positions would be endangered, their careers ruined."

"How could she do this to me?" I wailed. "How could she?"

GENTLE TIGRESS

C.O. Lamp

LEISURE BOOKS • NEW YORK CITY

For Dorothy Yuen Wise, in gratitude for the countless hours she spent telling me her story; and for the other survivors who helped me by verifying conversations and facts.

A LEISURE BOOK

Published by

Nordon Publications, Inc.
Two Park Avenue
New York, N.Y. 10016

Printed in the United States of America

Chapter One

Like chicks popping out of their shells, on the first bright Saturday in the spring of 1933, dozens of my friends poured out of the giant brownstone incubators along New York's Thirteenth Street. We began to skate ringalevio on a pavement glowing white under a dazzling sun. Within an hour we tired of our hide-and-seek game and a few of us rolled down to the corner to instigate something more exciting. We started a fire in the street. I was nonchalantly fleeing the scene, jumping rhythmically, left foot then right, when I heard the whir of skates behind me.

Whack!

A bratty kid hit me on the back as he flashed past, taunting, "Chink! Chink! You're a kinky Chink!"

Breath exploded from my lungs. "Ow!" I cried in response to pain searing across my spine. In an instant I caught my balance and went streaking after him, closing the distance, punching him in the kidneys. Veering into him with my skates, I caught him off balance and he tried running clown-crazy till body English telegraphed along my stiffened arm and sent him catapulting over the curb and sprawling into Thirteenth.

"Pimple face!" I screamed at him as he tearfully struggled to his feet, rubbing a pained knee, glaring at a bruised and abraded elbow.

"Dirty Chink!" he spat at me, red-faced, infuriated that he could be humiliated by a skinny girl not quite eleven.

If there was anything I hated it was being called a Chink. Besides, I wasn't a Chink—only half a Chink.

A glistening red NYC fire truck clanged its bell and the shriek of its siren ripped the air as the driver began racing the heavy engine and spanking the horn. Vaulting up the steps, I lingered on the stoop to watch the hook and ladder make a lumbering turn. A polished silver headlamp winked like a mirror in the sun before the rig straightened out on Second Avenue and disappeared from view.

"You shoulda seen the bonfire," I told my younger sister Edna. "We piled boxes and crates and paper and stuff in a big pile and set it on fire. The fire truck came screaming. You shoulda been there!"

Removing a braided loop from around my neck I took the key it held and cranked off my skates.

"Dorothy," said my younger sister. "Don't go up yet. Mom and Dad are talking worried talk."

"What about?"

"You know—"

"Edith Tong?"

Edna's eyes widened. "Yeah."

In our family no name was as certain of triggering a violent reaction as that of Father's long-ago, left-in-China girlfriend, Edith Tong. Once Mother accused Father of seeing another woman—women, actually. Father listened with characteristic patience until Mother mentioned Edith Tong. Then the sleeping tiger of his terrible temper came roaring out of the depths, slashing through the pervasive calm that comprises an essential part of the Oriental mystique. With his bare hands Father annihilated a chair, reducing it to many-splendored kindling.

Mother jealously resented the very mention of Edith Tong, the girl the Yuen and Tong families had selected to be Father's bride before he came to America. Why then, when I was born, had Father named me Edith? According to ancient Chinese custom that was his prerogative, but I had seen the hurt clouding Mother's eyes when the name had to be used, like when she registered me at school. Fortunately, I had other names such as Dorothy and Lillian, Mother's name, so I became Dorothy.

Borrowing Mother's name for my third name hadn't gotten Father off the hook. How could he have been so insensitive of Mother's feelings? Maybe Father didn't realize the implications of his choice until it was too late. Once he made his selection he would have lost face had he changed it. However, when he became aware of the pain it caused Mother he scrupulously avoided calling me Edith. Nor could he mistake how *I* felt about "Edith." I hated the name with every fiber of my being.

Surprisingly, the few times I was called Edith occurred

when Mother's patience reached the teutonic breaking point. Then she yelled, "Edith Dorothy Lillian Yuen—you get in here at once!"

Sandow and Lillian Yuen were an exciting couple in those halcyon days between wars. Tall and ax-handle lean, my father devoted himself to physical fitness. Clad in blue trunks, his early morning jogs constantly embarrassed Mother. To her, Sandow was more than a sad-eyed inscrutable Oriental; he was a man who was different and it was precisely this difference that made him fascinating.

A relentless will of iron, said by Father to spring from Mother's stubborn Swedish background, frequently caused her clear blue eyes to flash in dark defiance. Set in deep sockets, her eyes appeared haunting, the spectral effect mostly overcome by her warm outgoing personality. Soft golden curls cascaded to her shoulders, accenting a "Lady Esther" complexion. One of the most popular and gregarious women in the neighborhood, not only Father found her attractive.

Neither of my parents paid the least attention to the fact that they were involved in what polite society called "a mixed marriage." It was we children who suffered the onus of being Chinese-Swedes, or rather, Swedish Chinese, for in New York it was the Oriental half that made us unacceptable.

Yet, being part Chinese had not been the most devastating crisis in our lives. My sister, Edna, suffered through a mastoid operation after we returned from spending a year in Detroit where Father studied engineering at the Ford Institute. Infantile paralysis laid low my younger brother, Jack, but he miraculously survived without any trace of lameness. Baby Gloria scratched her way through chicken pox and German measles and I survived a bout with scarlet fever.

Unscathed by childhood diseases, my Swedish-Norwegian half-brother, Robert, five years my senior, found more to protest than any accident of birth involving ancestry. Mother's son from a previous marriage, Bobby had never seen the father who marched off to France to battle the Kaiser and now slept in Flanders. Acquiring a Chinese step father at the same time he encountered the trauma of his first teacher, in characteristic fashion Bobby decided to accept only one of them. He selected Father and rejected teachers for all time. Eluding a truant officer became a way of life. Now sixteen, Bobby worked part time at the RKO-Orpheum and spent the rest of his time watching the latest Hollywood epics or making stink bombs out of celluloid bits discarded by the projectionist. When rolled in a scrap of paper, ignited, quickly extinguished and flipped into the doorway of a restaurant, the smouldering segment guaranteed the sudden exodus of the patrons.

"Dorothy, it's something real important," Edna said as we trudged up the four flights to our fifth floor apartment.

"How can you tell?" I asked.

"It's worried talk," Edna said again.

We crept in quietly and hid around the corner to listen. Father's voice was louder than usual.

"There's no point in waiting for money from China," he said.

"No," Mother agreed. "Your uncle doesn't even answer our letters now."

Father's uncle managed the factory Father inherited in Shanghai. For a time Uncle sent us money but the money had stopped.

"He's stealing my factory," Father said angrily. "I know it."

"Maybe they're having a depression in China too," said Mother. "Hard times—"

"No. He's stealing from me. Otherwise he'd answer."

"Meanwhile we're not eating right."

"I can't make it here with two jobs," Father said, defeat crippling his voice. "I'm a chauffeur. I'm a cook. Still I can't make it. What am I going to do?"

Father had a long thin face and when he was sad it had to be the longest face in the world.

"It's the children who take the money, Sandow," Mother said. "You have four children to provide for, otherwise it would be easier."

"Five," Father corrected.

"Yes. With Bobby. I know you love him . . ."

"There's no future for me here. Unemployment remains high. If I lose just one of my jobs—" He shrugged helplessly and left it there.

"So you're going home. You've decided."

Father nodded. "My future is in China," he said firmly.

Mother placed her hands on her hips, her eyes a defiant blue, and regarded him levelly. "You're not leaving me here with five kids and no job. What do you want me to do, go on Relief? Well, I won't. I'm not going to do it."

"Sweetie—" Father said blandly, his face persuasively serene. "I've thought it over." He spread his palms prayerfully. "Of course Bobby will stay with you. Gloria is too small to travel and must remain here. You'll need help with her. Dorothy is almost a woman and can be a big help to you. So Dorothy will stay. I'll take Jack and Edna with me."

"Me?" Edna squealed, bounding out of our place of concealment. "You're taking me with you to *China*? You're taking me?"

"Yes," Father said quietly. "But try to act more like a lady. In China you will have to be a little lady."

Seeing my crestfallen look he came over and took my face in his hands. "Don't worry, Dorothy. I'll send for you as soon as I can. And I promise that when you come to me, you'll be travelling first class." He turned to Mother. "I promise that, Sweetie."

"I heard you, Sandow," Mother said.

In the days that followed Mother and Father were very loving and Mother teased that if he didn't stop the family might get larger than it already was. As the time for his departure drew near, Mother became withdrawn. It was as if she considered him already gone . . . like mourning the death of a loved one.

One afternoon I overheard Father say, "I'm surprised that you haven't mentioned *her*."

I knew he meant Edith Tong.

"She's probably married and has ten kids by now," Mother said hopefully, unable to mask the icy tension in her voice. "Why should I fuss? What good would it do? It's settled. You're going."

"You're right, Sweetie."

"Remember two can play at that game," Mother said, having the last word.

At first I'd been a little depressed but as the days grew fewer and fewer before it was time for Father, Edna and Jack to leave, I grew increasingly sad. Pain and loneliness filled my heart.

On an occasion when Father and I were alone I ran to him, hugging him about the waist, burying my head in his chest. Tears started in my eyes.

"You're not going to forget me, are you?" I sobbed. "Will I ever see you again?"

"No, I shall not forget you, firstborn child of my heart. How could I ever forget you? Of course we shall see each other again. But for now you must stay and help your mother. When I have recovered my birthright I will send for you all."

"Will it be long?"

"Not long."

"How long?"

"No longer than it takes to get the money." He gently ran a fingertip across my eyelids. "There now. I have squeezed out the last bitter tear. No more tears now. Give your daddy a big smile."

I blinked through my tears. "Will it be more than a year?"

"How long does it take a bluebird to reach the tallest limb of a cherry tree? That's how long it will be."

"Oh . . ."

"The rewards for your patience will be very great. You will be coming to China in style. Not like us . . ."

"I love you, Daddy."

"You are the joy of my heart."

"A fine pair you are," Mother observed as she came in carrying a single bag of groceries. "I can't turn my back on you one minute."

Father, Edna and Jack took a bus to San Francisco and sailed away to China in search of a birthright usurped by a wicked uncle. The money Father saved by traveling steerage had been left with Mother but it was soon gone. Forced to abandon our fifth floor apartment, we found a place on Eleventh Street near Stuyvesant. There were no bannisters to slide down but it was easier walking up one flight than it had been struggling up four. Mostly I lived in the streets, rolling amazing distances on my skates.

"Be sure to look both ways before crossing the street," Mother warned. "Traffic is getting something fierce."

Now and then a Model-T Ford put-putted past and sometimes a Model-A or a Model-B. Mike, our policeman, hardly ever directed traffic.

Mike pounced on me one afternoon as I squatted in the street and slowly turned a skewered potato over a tiny bonfire.

"What are you doing, young lady?" He grabbed me by the ear. "Let's have a talk with your mother."

Without releasing my ear he rang the bell for our apartment. Mother popped her head out of the second story window.

"Is this your daughter?" Mike called. "I caught her making a fire in the street. What do you want me to do with her?"

"Whatever you want. Take her in."

"Oh, please don't," I cried. "Please don't."

At length Mike released my ear. With a withering look he warned, "Don't ever do that again. Next time I'll run you in."

Mother didn't scold every time we got into trouble but she fussed if we didn't look neat. "Cleanliness is next to Godliness," she said as she supervised my getting into the third dress of the day. "You're going to the Hungarian Catholic Church again? That's nice."

Accustomed to playing hide-and-seek in its many shadowed pews, a number of us learned of the frequent bazaars and parties held in the basement. Usually street urchins were quickly expelled but I discovered a confident smile and a party dress would go a long way toward getting me the cake, ice cream or lemonade I wanted.

Wearing my special pink dress with white collar I inched forward in line.

"Isn't she cute?" a church lady clucked as she served me a wedge of sweet angel food. "She must be the daughter of somebody's servant."

"I just *love* their big almond eyes, don't you?" gushed another as she handed me a half glass of milk.

Seething inside, I sat with the equanimity of an Oriental princess until I finished my cake. Then I ran home and confronted myself in a mirror. My eyes didn't look anything like almonds. They were more like hazelnuts. I hated being called almond eyes. Still, it was better than slant-eyes, a name used by hateful boys at school. I hated slant-eyes most of all.

The name calling would end, I told myself in fist-clenching fury, just as soon as Father sent for us. In China I wouldn't look any different . . .

We hadn't heard from Father but we kept hoping, especially when our money ran out. Without money the festivals at the Hungarian Church became more important than ever. Several times Mother put on a party dress and joined me. During that bleak period, as Mother and I walked past shop windows emblazoned with large blue N.R.A. eagles, she sneered, "No Relief at All. That's what it means."

But we did go on Relief and became rather adept at it too. "Get in the milk line," Mother said as she edged into the line for bread.

With the arrival of autumn I skated to school in Greenwich Village. Frequently I hooked onto one of the slow-moving green electric trucks bearing the red diamond emblem of Railway Express.

Two weeks into the semester a letter bearing unusual stamps arrived from Father. Mother let me read the first page.

Sweetie,

No wonder we weren't getting any money from King Chung Engineering. My uncle has two wives and ten children, two of whom have been living with show girls on my money. I have asked Uncle to cut their big allowances but I cannot reason with him whatsoever. He is used to high living and also smokes opium. I have filed a lawsuit to get back what is rightfully mine as the oldest son. Please be patient. I am sure good fortune will soon smile on us all. Tell Dorothy that I have not forgotten my promise that you shall all travel first . . .

Mother said the next word on the second page was, "class," but she wouldn't allow me to read any more. She wrote Father telling of our urgent need for money, asking that he send some, even a little, as soon as he could. I put in a letter of my own, telling Father I longed with all my heart to come to China to be with him.

Before any money arrived, there came a day when I returned from school and found that mother had gone. I ran about the neighborhood calling her name and received no answer. No one had seen her. Had she deserted me? Worried and frightened, I sat in a darkening room feeling utterly alone. No father, no mother, what could I do? At long last Mother returned.

"I got a job with Alice Brady," she exclaimed.

Of course I had no idea who Alice Brady was but I soon learned Miss Brady starred in World and Realart Films—silent pictures—before and during the war. A victim of "mediocre stories," her career had waned until recently when she'd been rescued by Selznick. Now her career was zooming again; she'd completed a half dozen talkies and had a contract for several more.

Mother thoroughly enjoyed working for Miss Brady and came home with copious quantities of hand-me-down clothes—high fashion gowns decorated with spangles, fur and beads. Miss Brady also gave Mother a pair of sequin-studded shoes.

How nice Mother looked in her newly acquired finery! She accepted an invitation from Riley the Undertaker, a friend from our old apartment building. As Mother walked down the street on Riley's arm, her blue eyes filled with mirth and long golden curls bouncing, I thought she looked more like a movie star than the full-cheeked, dark-eyed Alice Brady, even if Mother's mouth was a straight little gash and not a perfect cupid's bow.

Mother couldn't have been happier. In her Alice Brady gowns she continued making the rounds of parties with her friend, Riley. Late one evening they came tripping in, unaware they'd wakened me. Padding quietly in my bare feet to Mother's room, I caught them. Mother turned her face unexpectedly and our eyes met fleetingly before I hurried back to my own bed. Nothing was ever said by either of us but I didn't like Riley the Undertaker after that.

Mother continued to see him. I think she wanted the gay mad whirl to go on forever, but she could see the end coming. Perhaps that's why she kept it up to the last.

News from China encouraged us and gradually money arrived. Father wrote that he'd been successful in his lawsuit and had control of King Chung Engineering. By Easter I knew we'd be going to meet him as soon as the term ended.

"What can I take along?" I asked Mother. "I want my skates."

She smiled indulgently. "Certainly you may take your skates. But we can't take any 'Made in Japan' junk. Your father won't allow anything in the house that's made in Japan."

"Why not?"

"Ask your father when we get there. It's something the Chinese have about the Japanese." She blotted the beet red lipstick she'd taken to wearing since going out with Riley and put on her hat. "Now you take care of Gloria."

"Yes, Mother. Where ya going?"

"Down to get my passport. I'll be back as soon as I can."

Three hours later she burst in the door, red faced and breathless. "Damn government!" she exploded. "They wouldn't give me a passport."

Before I could say, "Why not?" she raved on. "Here I am a citizen—born in the United States—now they tell me I have to go through *naturalization* to get a passport! Just because I married a Chinese National. Bitches!"

Usually fastidious, Mother's hair appeared disheveled and the seams of her stockings slanted across the back of her legs. "Damn!" she said as she collapsed in a chair. Kicking off her pumps she unhooked her garters and rolled down her hose.

"I thought Roosevelt was going to straighten everything out but he hasn't. It's worse. Now there's a bureaucrat sitting behind every government man thinking up new forms. Of all the damn red tape! I never saw anything like it."

She inspected her hose for runs and found none. "Still," she paused, a sigh escaping her, "I suppose it helps some guys get jobs. But it makes me mad. Do they think the Chinese are any different? It's a damn insult, that's what it is!"

"I know I'll be glad to get to China," I said. "Then they won't call me slant-eyes any more."

In China Mother's spun gold curls would stand out; she'd be different. But that wasn't really a problem. Adults didn't call each other hateful names. Parents never encountered any problem by being different.

Mother sat down at the table and began to fill out the many forms. As it turned out, she had no real difficulty with Immigration and Naturalization. She only had to complete the forms. The day she obtained her passport she bubbled with happiness but underneath the hurt remained.

"I think they were glad to get rid of me," Mother said.

In spite of our joy we worried about a separation.

"Isn't Bobby going with us?" I asked.

"No, dear. Your father didn't send for him. In the first place, Bobby doesn't want to go. He wants to stay here in New York."

"But there won't be anyone for him to live with," I pleaded. "Not when we're gone."

"He's going to live with Peter, his Filipino friend."

"But he'll be all alone—"

"Alone? What do you mean, alone?" Mother retorted. "I've been on my own since I was sixteen. Bobby is seventeen and he's a man. It's time for him to roll out of the nest. Don't worry about Bobby, he'll get along all right."

Despite her insistance, I think Mother was trying to convince herself. After we'd talked about it she seemed more contented.

Bobby appeared happy with his choice. We helped him move his things to Peter's and said goodby to him there because, as Bobby insisted, "It will be better." He didn't like sentimental scenes and if the early farewell wasn't better, it was easier. Trust Bobby to find the easiest way.

On the day we were to leave I sat in the kitchen with our bags and waited for a taxi to take us to the bus station. My eyes came to rest on a calendar that still hung on the wall. I gave it a long hard look, wondering, would I ever forget the twenty-first of June, 1934? In my mind I played a scene as poignant as any "Ma Perkins" or "Stella Dallas" soap opera. Could any day rival the importance of the day I finally left New York? Can a poor half-breed Chinese girl find happiness in the mysterious far-away Orient? "Oh, yes," I murmured in a frenzy of rapture. "Yes!"

A foolish and sentimental act. Had I known what adventures were in store for me, I would have taken little notice of the day—or the month.

A Greyhound bus carried us out of the city, beyond grape

country, past smoky factories, through miles of waving grain, across endless dry plains further west, over mountains and to the sea. Somewhere in another time and place a venerable Chinese sage opined, "As a bird flies so it rests in the nest." The adage is said to mean that the joy or sorrow of a visit can be divined or predicted by the hazards encountered in the journey. What happened to us in San Francisco was in no way foreseeable when we left New York, but a Chinese philosopher might have used the circumstance to predict future events.

The man in the office of the President Lines shifted nervously. "I'm sorry, Missus Yuen," he said. "This strike has us tied up completely. We can't move." Sweating profusely, large beads stood out on his forehead and great wet blotches spread at his armpits. He turned up his palms helplessly. "Our ships can't get out of port."

"Well, what do you expect us to do?" Mother demanded. "Sleep right here?"

"No, Ma'am. No, Ma'am," he said, sponging his brow.

"You could allow us to go aboard. We'd at least have a place to stay while we wait."

"I can't do that." He rubbed his hands on his trousers.

"That doesn't make sense." Mother's voice rose. "If we're allowed on board we'd have a place to sleep—a place to rest."

"I-I can't . . ."

Other disgruntled passengers crowded around.

"Yeah, let us aboard," said a chubby white-suited man with a large cigar.

The harried clerk snapped his pencil. "J-Just a minute. Just a minute. I-I'll see what I can do. I'll see if the superintendant has anything . . ."

"You tell him we're not leaving," Mother said. "We came all the way from New York and we're going to camp right here. This is some way to treat first class customers!"

"You tell 'em, sister," piped up the fat man.

After a while the clerk came back, less tense but still sweating profusely.

"We've chartered a bus—at our expense—to take you to Los Angeles. We're putting some of you aboard the *President Polk*."

"Now *that* makes sense," said Mother.

Soon a bus arrived. We spent a day speeding down the California coast. Inspired by other passengers, Mother continued talking and joking. By the time we boarded the *President Polk* everyone was friendly and the incident largely forgotten.

A carnival atmosphere prevailed as the big steamer prepared to put to sea. Actress Helen Hayes came down to see her mother off. People were drinking champagne and laughing, throwing confetti and colored paper streamers. Horns, bells and whistles added to the din of giddy voices. When the liner emitted a slow, melancholy foghorn sound folks hurried ashore and we slowly moved out of the harbor.

Our stateroom was one deck down, outside, and very comfortable.

"Look at the fruit," Gloria cheered, attacking a bunch of grapes from a complimentary fruit bowl. The steamship company sent a beautiful new bowl to our quarters daily.

The party atmosphere continued unabated, barely slowing as passengers darted to and fro, debating whether or not to dress the first night out. Half did and half didn't, but on the second night everyone wore their finery.

"These Alice Brady dresses are certainly coming in handy," Mother said as we made our way to the main dining room. Somehow she managed to get us seated at the Captain's table. The way people reacted I'm sure they thought Mother was someone important.

"What does your father do, my dear?" cooed an old dowager who reminded me of a lady from the Hungarian Church.

"He owns a factory," I answered, just the way Mother instructed.

The old lady nodded, saying, "Eew," instead of "Oh."

After dinner Mother put us to bed early so she could go dancing. I waited until Gloria was sound asleep, then I slipped out of the cabin to renew my friendship with several room boys, all of whom were Chinese. They took me to the kitchen were I met the chefs. They were also Chinese and we became good friends, especially the number one chef and I. A middle-aged man with an audible smile, he chuckled as he gave me an endless variety of treats. I marveled at his room-sized refrigerator and for the remainder of the trip I had everything I could possibly eat.

One of the room boys acted as look-out and when Mother left the ballroom I raced back to our cabin, jumped into bed and pretended to be fast asleep when she arrived. We repeated the performance for several days.

In Hawaii, grass-skirted hula girls came down to the wharf and danced to syrupy rhythms. They placed flowered leis about our necks and made us welcome. According to tradition we were to cast our leis off the fantail and if the leis drifted toward shore it signified that we'd visit the islands again. I didn't wish to give up my beautiful leis but I had so many that I joined the crowd and tossed just one of them into the sea. We stood there, happy-sad, watching the leis floating toward the beach as Diamond Head faded in our wake.

On my twelfth birthday the President Line sponsored a party for me. In gratitude to the captain I promptly came down with the mumps. The ship's doctor traced the disease to Panama where the ship had recently docked but his pronouncement didn't prevent me from looking like an enormous golden grapefruit. I felt absolutely miserable.

By the time we docked in Kobe, Japan, little swelling remained. Mother and the captain discussed my situation in hushed voices. After their conversation Mother informed me, "You're going to remain on board while the rest of us go ashore . . . so the ship won't be quarantined."

She ordered me to stay in our cabin but when everyone had gone I ventured up on deck.

"What are you doing here, young lady?" my quartermaster friend asked.

"I can't go ashore. Mother says they'll quarantine the ship."

"Oh hell," he sniffed. "You look all right to me. Come on."

The quartermaster rented a ricksha and we rode all over Kobe.

"Let's celebrate your birthday again," he said.

In one of the fantastic shops he bought a magic box and a perfectly divine string of iridescent crystalline beads that flicked blue and orange rays in the sunlight. Never had I had such wonderful gifts.

As we returned to the *President Polk* we saw Mother

frantically running along the deck searching for me.

"It's time we got you back," the quartermaster said.

"Where have you been?" Mother scolded. "I've been looking all over for you. I told you not to leave the cabin."

"It's my fault," the quartermaster spoke up. "When I saw she was here alone I took her with me. If there's anyone to blame it's me." With a disarming grin he stared at Mother in a funny way, looking her up and down. "Is there anything I can do to make it right?"

"No."

"Well, I want to apologize."

"No harm done." Mother swallowed, her cheeks pinking under his insolent, penetrating gaze. "Perhaps I should thank you—for looking after her." Avoiding his disrobing eyes, she fumbled with my gifts.

"Aren't they positively precious?" I asked.

"Yes, they are. But you won't be able to take them ashore in Shanghai, you know."

"How come?"

"Remember what I told you about Father and 'Made in Japan' junk? You'll have to get rid of them."

"Oh, no," I cried, heartbroken. "That isn't fair." Tears welled in my eyes. "It isn't fair!"

At first I thought Mother was punishing me for leaving the stateroom but I remembered her telling me in New York how Daddy felt about anything Japanese. In despair I realized I'd have to part with my newly acquired treasures.

As the ship plowed closer to China I fingered the beads lovingly. How I longed to keep them. Finally, when we were already in sight of land, I gave the beads and magic box to a girl who'd become my best friend on the voyage.

The *President Polk* anchored in the bay, unable to moor at a dock because the harbor in Shanghai is too shallow. We rode in on a tender. I could feel the chug of the tender's engine vibrating beneath my feet. Around us sampans dropped their bat-wing sails and coasted silently toward many-fingered piers extending from shore. Pungent smells of fish, brackish water, oil and sweat mingled in my nostrils.

Round-eyed and eager I peered at shore, looking for my father. Suddenly I spied him leaning against a Model-T, looking dapper in a white linen suit. A wave of euphoria flared in my breast. Was there ever so grand a day as the Thirteenth of August, 1934? Here I was, on the threshold of a glorious new life. Unable to suppress my eagerness, I waved enthusiastically, yelling, "Hi, Daddy! Hi, Daddy!" until I was close enough to see his face. A hint of censure in his expression told me I was behaving too exuberantly so I abruptly dropped my arm.

The tender thudded against the dock, backed off and nosed against the planks again. Sailors flung out hawsers with large loops.

"We're here," I said. "And we arrived first class!"

Father had kept his promise.

Chapter Two

The moment the gangplank dropped into place I surged forward, pushing my way through the crowd.

"Oh, Daddy, I'm so glad to be here," I cried, flinging myself into his arms. He wrapped me in a hug.

Father was not alone. Two ladies waited a respectful step behind him. "This is Auntie May," he said, indicating a lady with big beautiful eyes.

Mother came gliding through the crowd, her left hand on her Alice Brady hat, just as Father turned to a chubby woman with a pleasant face. "And this is Auntie Ying."

"We are happy to meet you," said Auntie Ying.

"Charmed," Mother said, imitating a lady we met on the *President Polk*.

Six years in the future I would remind Mother that the first word she uttered on reaching China was, "Charmed," and she would erupt, "Damn! Was there ever a more stupid remark?"

As we stood there on the dock, reunited, I watched a beautiful smile spread across Mother's face. "Sandow—" she murmured, her lips parting as Father reached down and swept her off her feet, closing her mouth with his own. Mother's hand came off her hat and she embraced him warmly. Auntie May and Auntie Ying giggled politely in the background.

We were on the Bund, the international section of Shanghai. Parallel lines of English, American and boxy French cars inched along the boulevard in opposite directions, separated by a single row of cars parked side by side in the middle of the street. A hundred coolies drawing rickshas darted in and out of traffic. Statues dotted the grass-lined avenue. In front of a commercial building two enormous bronze tigers lay on their stomachs, undisturbed by the workmen who would flick out their hands in passing, giving them a rub, causing the extended forepaws of each tiger to glisten gold.

The Yuen family. (Left to right) Back row: Gloria Yuen, Jack Yuen. Front row: Edna Yuen, Colonel Sandow Yuen, Lillian Yuen, Dorothy Yuen.

"The workers believe touching a tiger gives them strength," Father explained.

People minced in all directions, carrying produce suspended on bamboo poles or lugging baskets heavily laden. Merchants in ankle length gowns, vests, and tight fitting caps chattered heartily as they bartered their wares, apparently convinced that the ancient philosopher Lao-tze spoke verily when he advised, "Without a smiling face, do not become a merchant."

There were no painted signs with rows of winking light-bulbs as in New York. The street was a sea of garish red and gold rug-sized banners with huge black Chinese characters. Unfurled from rods at the tops of buildings, they fluttered down to eye level, blotting out the horizon unless one happened to be standing in the middle of the street.

Slowly our car moved past mounds of baskets and bird cages, past tables of sleepy letter writers, old men waiting for the many illiterate to come and ask them to read or write a letter. A lady in a straight-bottomed knee length vest, her hair in a queue that trailed to her waist, bent down and picked up a basket of vegetables. She thrust the basket at us as we drove by.

After a time Father directed the Ford down Scott Street in the Chapei section and halted at the door of a three story western style house with assorted split levels.

"We are home," he said.

Mother and I had speculated whether the house would have flush toilets and the discovery that it did would stand out as a significant experience—one of the last basic joys we would experience for years to come.

As we entered the home I was attracted to an ornate display of chinaware in a position of prominence. Inspection revealed it to be a Japanese tea set. *A Japanese tea set!* In my father's house? My brain reeled. "What?" I cried, shock and dismay giving way to anger. Wheeling on Mother I cried, "I thought you said no Japanese stuff!" Still heartsick over giving away my beautiful necklace and magic box I was completely crushed.

Mother swallowed. "Well, I didn't expect it. It's a surprise to me."

"Oh! How could you?" I stormed, absolutely furious.

"You should have *known*. You didn't have to make me give everything away. It was stupid."

"Use restraint," Father said coldly, his face without expression. "Try to act like a lady."

"We should have tried," I muttered. My grief was inconsolable.

Father gave an order to one of the maids hovering about and presently an old lady came stumping on the scene. "This is your grandmother," he said.

Grandma smiled warmly and said something I couldn't understand.

"What did she say?" I asked. My eyes raced to her tiny feet, hardly more than five inches in length as a result of having been tightly bound. Her insteps were horribly misshapen but her ankles were quite thin.

"She said hello."

"Hello," I said.

When we were in New York we had a decorative glass slipper on the mantel and Father had often remarked that Grandmother's foot would easily fit into it.

"You were right about the glass slipper," I reminded Father. In New York he talked about Grandmother's little feet and the glass slipper frequently and with enthusiasm. Now he merely shrugged and looked away.

The house was a pavillion of many people. Besides Grandma, who pegged around giving orders in Chinese, Auntie May and one of her daughters were staying with us. Two maids moved about noiselessly and unseen and cook presided over the kitchen. Father had his own private ricksha and ricksha coolie. There were enough people for a party but a party it was not.

At dinner, Father sat down at the head of the table. Far down, directly across from him, Grandmother seated herself with elaborate ceremony. Brother Jack and sister Edna, who had been here a year, paraded in like wind-up toys. Because the table was long and narrow the maid brought two large bowls of everything and placed half at each end. Only Mother was given a knife and fork.

"What's this?" I asked, staring at the chop-sticks near my plate. "I don't know how to use them."

"You will learn," Father said quietly.

Edna and Jack sat there like stuffed China dolls, silently moving their chop-sticks with ease and facility, only a hint of amusement reflected in their faces. At that moment I hated them both. It would be some time before I realized they had a critical headstart in the mastery of Chinese. In fact, I would never catch up. Being young they took to a second language with the ease of most small children.

"Your thoughtfulness is appreciated," Mother said. "I never realized eating with a knife and fork made me an outcast. I feel like a stranger at my own table."

Father made no reply. Conversation was stilted and extremely inhibited. It was as if everyone had received bad tidings.

"Doesn't anybody say anything?" Mother asked.

"Mealtime is a time of dignity and contemplation," Father said.

"The captain's table on the *President Polk* was dignified. But it was a helova lot more fun than this," Mother said.

"It sure was!" I chimed in, still upset about being forced to relinquish my beautiful Japanese necklace.

Father silenced me with a cold steely look. I realized that from this time forward I was expected to be a little lady, a Chinese kewpie doll, as inhibited as if I'd been constipated for two weeks. Anger flowed up my spine, almost blinding my reason. I suppressed a sudden urge to dip a spoon into my rice and snap it *kersplat* into their faces. I had never done anything like that, nor would I had I a spoon, so I choked down my protests under Father's frosty gaze and attempted to work the chop-sticks. But he couldn't stop my thinking they were all crazy. My eyes met Mother's and when she realized that I was reading the same sorrow and disappointment in her face that she detected in mine, she quickly averted her gaze.

At bedtime, which Mother and I sought early, we listened to Father make room assignments. Only when everyone else had been provided for did Father turn to me and gesture toward a split-level bedroom off the second floor. "You will be sleeping with Grandma."

With that crazy woman? I thought bitterly. Oh no!

Mother preceded me into the washroom and encountered a problem. "No hot water?" she fumed.

"The maid will heat some for you," Father said. His voice took on an edge. "Any time you want it."

"You mean every time I want hot water it has to be heated?" Mother said in a shrill voice. "Well, that's a change, but I suppose I can get used to it. I'll have to make a schedule—" Mother entered their bedroom.

Lingering on the threshold before going in with Grandma, I observed a maid padding along, carrying a basin. She approached my parents' bedroom and went in without knocking.

"What's she doing?" Mother screamed. "She's touching me."

"She came in to wash your feet," Father said.

"To wash my *feet*?" Mother exclaimed in total disbelief. "Sandow, tell her to get out of here! Tell her to *get out*!"

"No," Father said quietly. "When in Shanghai, do as the Chinese do."

Mother suffered what she thought an indignity of the highest order. It became the custom at bedtime for a maid to come in and wash our feet, and in the case of the little children, to bathe their entire bodies.

Alone with my Grandmother, her full round face happily animated as she chattered 'ho-talk,' I inspected the four postered bed. It had no mattress. For summer coolness a mat had been flung over a network of ropes making the bed hard, unyielding and uncomfortable.

Feeling completely rejected in this strange and foreign place, where I couldn't even understand the grandmother with whom I shared a bed, I was suddenly overcome by homesickness. Waves of loneliness washed over me, body and soul. I thought of my brother, Bobby, back in friendly old New York, having a wonderful time with his best friend, Peter. Slowly, deliberately, restraining no animus, I muttered aloud, "Bobby Roloson, you lucky dog. You're really the lucky one." It took all the determination I could muster not to cry myself to sleep.

Mother threw up her arms in disgust. "This isn't my house. I feel worthless. I keep falling over servants. There's nothing for me to do in this—this house of many servants." She waved her arms again.

"I'm surprised," Father said, perplexed. "In America it was almost a national pastime for women to dream of having servants. I can remember that you said—"

"Maybe I would like it better if I could communicate with them. I can't even give them orders," complained Mother. "I'd rather do the work myself. At least then it would get done the way I want it."

"We're not getting rid of the servants," Father said firmly. "A man of my position is expected to have servants."

Perhaps Father thought Mother was discontented because of her encounter with 'the complaint' resulting from a change in food and water. It should have been obvious that it was something else.

"I don't understand you," Father said impatiently. "I thought you would enjoy servants after all you've been through. Having to work in New York—sitting around the apartment—"

"Sitting around the apartment?" I blurted, unheeding of where my words could lead. "What about the parti—?" I closed my mouth and broke it off before completing the plural.

"What party?" asked Father.

"Oh, just a party they had in our old neighborhood," Mother interjected, glaring Swedish daggers at me. "Everybody in the building was invited."

Shrugging, I made a hasty backward step and went slinking off. I was angry at myself and expected Mother to rage at me, "You keep your mouth shut, young lady," but she said not a word.

It might have been better if she had, for it would have cleared the air between us. Then Mother would have known where she stood with me. I had no intention of saying anything about Riley the Undertaker. But Mother couldn't know that. I wanted to wipe the entire episode from my mind. Apparently Mother could not. Friction between us grew as Mother took to cutting me down in the presence of my father and she began punishing me for things I hadn't done. I sought the solace of my father and our relationship became very close.

"Your mother isn't feeling well," Father explained.

"We—all of us—need to be more understanding of her. She really feels miserable."

"I know—"

"Many of our customs are strange to her and she is having trouble adjusting. Her stomach is giving her no peace. Once her stomach gets in shape she will be okay."

"She's been sick ever since we got here. She isn't getting any better. How long will it last, anyway? It isn't fair the way she picks on me."

"Being sick all the time isn't fair either. Why don't you stay out of her way? If she doesn't see you she won't punish you. Why don't you spend more time with Auntie May or Grandma?"

"I'll try, Daddy."

"Good. That's my girl."

Mother came bearing down on us. "What are you two doing?" she demanded, her face malevolent. "Scheming against me again?"

"Why no, Sweetie," Father said. "We were just having a talk." He waved me away. "How are you feeling, Sweetie?"

"Lousy," Mother said.

Hastening from the scene I heard no more. As a consequence of Father's suggestion I became better acquainted with my relatives and began to develop an appreciation of their views. How strange Mother and I must have seemed with our Western ways. A year earlier, when Edna and Jack arrived, they were mere children and any idiosyncracies they might have displayed were probably dismissed as childish behavior. Mother and I were adults—I already towered over my relatives—to be clucked over with surprise if not with amusement.

Grandma's talkee-talkee went past me without comprehension but Auntie May could speak English so I learned much about Grandma from her. Formerly Buddhist, Grandma had switched to Christianity in her sixties, an event growing out of a serious illness. She had recovered and was now a devout Baptist who spent most of every Sunday in church, fasting. There was a large portrait of a Caucasian Jesus in her room and despite her devotion Poh-poȟ—as we called her—never scolded any of us for not attending church.

It was Grandma who stumped around giving orders to the servants, bobbing her head, a smile on her happy jack-o-lantern face.

A few days later Mother accosted Father again. "I can't stand this house anymore," she stormed. "Servants and relatives. People, people, people! Sandow, I want a house of my own where we can be a family again."

"I've already decided about the servants," Father reminded her. "We are not getting rid of the servants."

"But all these relatives," Mother said. "It's your house with Grandma's servants and Auntie May's room. What do I have? There's nothing for me to do. I'm unneeded. Unwanted."

"I need you, Sweetie."

Mother pretended not to hear. "Your daughter has more prerogatives around this house than I do. Every time I try to discipline her—Lord knows she needs it—she runs to you. You're thick as thieves—"

"But, Sweetie—"

"Well, I've had it," screamed Mother. "And I mean it!"

"But Dorothy needs understanding."

"*I'm* the one who needs understanding," Mother insisted. "Either she goes, or I go. And that's final!"

As a result of Mother's ultimatum, Father banished me to the home of his wicked uncle, the man who had usurped his authority and for a time diverted the profits of King Chung Engineering to his own purposes. Although disgraced within our family, everyone took great care to keep the matter secret. Had knowledge of Uncle's defalcations become public not only Uncle but the entire family would have been dishonored. Uncle had been allowed to remain at the factory and received wages according to his labors.

Despite internecine conflicts, Chinese family ties are securely welded and great lengths are taken to maintain honor. Allowed to save face, Uncle now owed Father a debt so that when Father decided to send me away all he had to do was ask.

"It's really for your own good," Father said as he drove me to the Chen-ju section of Shanghai. "You've been too long out of school. Jack and Edna are attending and it's time you did too."

"Yes, Father."

We were silent a long time. Both of us found parting difficult. A sad expression came over his face. Until then I hadn't realized how painful the decision had been for him.

Presently he gestured toward a country house, a traditional one-story structure without central heating or indoor plumbing. The house sat on the edge of a compound within an enclosure that suddenly looked like a prison.

A great outpouring of people greeted our arrival— Uncle, his two wives and most of their ten children, some of whom had birthdays scant weeks apart.

"This is Grandfather," Father said, introducing me to my great uncle. Titles among family members are often based on status or respect rather than biological fact. Father presented me to his cousins, saying, "This is Fat Auntie; this is Tall Auntie; this is Happy Auntie—"

Father bowed. "Grandfather" bowed and I was formally in my new home. In a few days I started school, enrolled in fourth grade, unable to understand a word. Only mathematics made any sense. Quickly bored, I became more unhappy in school than in Grandfather's house.

Grandfather belonged to another era. He wore old fashioned gowns that came to his ankles and padded about in traditional Chinese slippers, searching for a dream world. I couldn't approach him with my school problems.

Lonely and miserable, I don't know what I'd have done if Happy Auntie hadn't come to comfort me. Happy Auntie's real name was Sun-sue. A pleasant young lady nearly my own age, Auntie Sun-sue liked to wear bright red clothing and the high collars of the late Ching dynasty. I could understand why she preferred red. Red is the color of joy and great rejoicing. The brilliance of cherries certainly fit Sun-sue's personality. She attempted to teach me Chinese and I taught her English. Most of all she instructed me in old world customs and traditions. I learned that twins or pairs are good luck symbols. Thus, for a birthday one does not give a single coin but two identical coins placed in a red box or wrapped in red paper.

While yet in the first week of school I complained to Auntie Sun-sue. "The other kids are making fun of me. They point and laugh. I know they're calling me names." I repeated what I could remember.

"It's because you are different—because you're not Chinese," Sun-sue said. Although she was serious a trace of amusement lingered at the corners of her mouth. "Perhaps I shouldn't tell you—they call you a white devil."

"Not *Chinese*?" I cried, aghast. "In New York I was too Chinese and here I'm too white. I don't want to be a white devil. I'm not going back to that school! Everybody hates me."

"No one hates you, Dorothy. They laugh and tease because you are different. You're so wonderfully tall. Little children can be unkind. It will pass. When they know you better they will be your friends."

"No! I'm not going to school. I'm going to speak with Grandfather about it. Right now."

"I wouldn't," Sun-sue said soberly. "It would not be wise to intrude on him at this time."

In her way Sun-sue had told me that her father was smoking opium again. Several days earlier, as I stalked through the house, I observed Grandfather and his second wife lying crossways on a bed. Between them on a small table a flame flickered in a cloisonné burner. Grandfather dipped a long-handled spoon into a flat round jar containing a thick syrup. Twirling the spoon he brought it over the bowl of the pipe, tilting the bowl into the burner's flame. The opium played a sizzling, bubbling tune in the flute-shaped pipe as Grandfather alternately fanned and puffed.

Remembering what I had seen, I knew Grandfather could not be disturbed in his world of dreams.

"I'm not learning anything in that dumb school," I told Sun-sue.

"Going to school is the wish of your father," Sun-sue reminded me before she left me to sulk.

Happy Auntie had made a point. If something was to be changed, the order would have to come from Father. However, asking Father was out of the question. Fear boggled my tortured mind. I couldn't do it. Why, I demanded of myself, could I not ask him? What was the source of the fear that gripped me?

I flung myself across the bed in desperation, seeking an answer, hoping to sort my way through the maze of sorrow that engulfed me. Going to Father about my school problems was not like sharing a happy moment or asking him to intercede on my behalf with Mother. More than a routine request, asking to leave school meant confrontation, a direct challenge to an order he had given. Despite Mother's accusation that we were thick as thieves, I remembered that most of the times Father and I talked privately had occurred during a rift between him and Mother or when tension ran high between them. Then it was Father who sought my company and initiated conversation. I realized that basically I was afraid of him. I dared not risk his displeasure. Not now. Not when he was the only person in the world who understood me, the only person who cared deeply for me.

Cast out by Mother, living under the roof of a distant Grandfather who didn't understand or care, was there no place for me to turn? I swallowed a knot in my throat as my eyes became misty. In New York kids hated me because I was a Chink. Here I was a white devil. "Oh God," I sobbed. "Is there no place for me? What am I, some kind of freak? A misfit?"

I blew my nose and continued to sob. "What am I? Who am I? Someone tell me. I don't know. School, I hate you. World, I hate you. Edith, I hate you—"

Calling myself Edith made me realize I had sunk to the lowest possible level. I blew my nose again and broke off crying, shutting out the pervasive sadness by escaping into sleep.

Languishing as a martyr, the year I spent in Grandfather's house nevertheless had a positive effect. Unable to break out of the cocoon of my inferiority, I became aware of an ability to think deep thoughts. Unlike Grandfather, my deep thoughts had nothing to do with opium. I found solace and strength in contemplation and meditation.

The days scudded past, an endless procession of gray clouds, uninterrupted except for a sunburst of interest that began when officers pounded on the front door and demanded to see Grandfather.

"We're here to search for opium," announced the captain, a stiff imperious young man.

Grandfather appeared. The men exchanged bows. After a profusion of conversation, Grandfather made a sweeping gesture of acquiescence, ushering the search team to their duties. He remained at the door, head slightly bowed as if in prayer.

The officers made a thorough search. They found nothing.

"You know that smoking opium is against the law," charged the captain. "You know that."

Grandfather swallowed. "Yes, I know."

The haughty young officer snapped in and out of a brittle bow. He wheeled and marched off at the head of his unit, his back stiff with anger.

As the clop-clop of marching feet faded in the distance, Grandfather's feet rolled into motion. He made straightway for his bedroom. "What happened?" he asked dumbfounded. "Why didn't they find it? I don't understand—"

A maid stepped forward timidly and bowed low. "When the master was speaking to the police I placed everything in the commode. They did not lift the lid."

"Well done," Grandfather exclaimed, pleased that his contraband had not been discovered in the toilet. For once he made a small bow in return.

There was no more excitement, no further visits from the police. I was happy the school year was finally drawing to a close. The most glorious moment came the day after school ended, the moment I saw Father driving up in his Ford. No one had told me he was coming.

"I have come to take you home," he said.

I wanted to cry out in ecstasy, throw myself into his arms, whooping for joy, hugging him tightly. Instead I made a four inch bow, fitted an "ah so" expression on my face and waited for him to explain.

"Auntie May's husband came home so she and your cousin are no longer living with us. They have a place of their own. Grandma has gone to live with them. We have the house all to ourselves—except for the servants. We can be a family again as your mother wishes."

"Daddy, I'm so glad you are letting me come back," I said.

"I never wanted you to leave," he said wanly. "It was your mother. She has been so unhappy. I had to do something—"

"Will she allow—*want* me to come back?"

"Of course. She loves you. We must try to understand

Dorothy Yuen (Shanghai)

your mother. She has been constantly ill which makes her irritable, striking out at whomever is near. Also, I think she's approaching the fullness of life when women have problems. Will you try to be patient with her?"

I nodded. "Will she be patient with me? I've been so terribly unhappy too."

"I knew you weren't happy, Dorothy. That's why I have come." His eyes opened wide. "I have a surprise. We're not going back to the old house. We have a new home at the end of the road."

He started the Ford and we drove off. When we came to our old house, Daddy waved as we passed, a silly gesture that expressed his joy at being well rid of the place. He was in an exceptionally good mood.

I smiled happily, overjoyed that my exile had ended.

Near the end of Scott Road, Daddy halted the car. "This is it," he said. "How do you like it?"

At that moment I didn't care how the new house looked. Thrilled to be home, I jumped out and raced to meet the family.

"I'm home," I cried. "I'm home!"

"We can see that," said Mother. A short laugh escaped her. "Heavens, I think you've grown another two inches. I've missed you, Honey."

"I've missed you too." We hugged each other with enthusiasm.

I hugged Edna, Gloria and Jack.

"How come I was last?" Jack asked. "I'm older than Gloria."

"I saved the best for last," I said, giving him another hug.

"Whoopee," cried Jack.

Things were certainly more relaxed than I remembered. The atmosphere was more like it had been in New York. Mother went to the kitchen to help the cook prepare dinner. There was no doubt that Mother was in charge. Obviously she was feeling better. I told her how miserable I had been.

"I had some rocky times too . . . when I first got here," Mother confided. "I just couldn't accept things the way they were. In his letters your father promised I'd have a home of my own—that it'd have gold on it. He said we had a Simmons bed. After walkup apartments in New York I expected what I'd been promised. That ain't what I got. I didn't have a home of my own. I had a house full of relatives and servants, and the gold was only cheap gilt. I thought my heart would break." She placed her hands on her hips and sighed wearily. "At least we have a Simmons bed."

"Daddy told me Grandma went to live with Auntie May—"

"Yeah. Auntie May never could get over the fact that I didn't smoke. She thinks all American women smoke. I guess she read that in some pulp magazine."

Mother stopped slicing carrots and made eye contact. She decided to trust me further. "I got so distraught I almost came to live with you. Uncle invited me." She shrugged. "Instead I went to the American consulate. I told them I wanted to go home and take my children with me. I ran into a brick wall. They said I could take you and Gloria but not Jack or Edna. Jack and Edna are entered on your father's passport. That puts them in his custody. Damn bureaucrats! I decided if I couldn't take all my kids I'd stay here. That's what I've done. So far. Don't tell your father what I said."

"I won't."

"You've really grown up. It sure is nice having you here—having someone I can let my hair down with—someone who can speak English."

"Gee whiz! If it hadn't been for Auntie Sun-sue's English I don't know what I'd have done."

"There's an English-speaking family down the end of the street. The Changs. They're well educated. They've got enough graduation certificates to plaster a wall."

"I'm so happy that we're together again!"

"I'm glad you're home. Now that you're here, make yourself useful. Hand me that bread—"

Mother and I got on famously for a time. I should have remembered that a new lair does not a contented tiger make. Her special kindness lasted two days. Then she was after me again.

With just our family in the new house it was difficult to avoid Mother except when I went horseback riding with Father. Early morning rides became a habit with us. During one of these rides we encountered Amoy Chang, a boy from the end of the block. Before long, Amoy and I were riding alone.

A year my senior, Amoy had a handsome intense face, a face scholarly in repose but so mobile and expressive it displayed the entire gamut of emotions. He reminded me of an idealistic young professor. I knew he'd studied English with a British tutor.

In a short time his speech became sprinkled with idioms such as "It's a doozy," borrowed from me.

"Amoy, if you use that kind of English around the house your parents won't let you see me. You're starting to sound like a kid from New York." I knew about family taboos. Father hadn't wanted me to visit the Portuguese family who lived down the block.

"Speaking of English," Amoy said didactically, "I've been wanting to speak with you about your predeliction for English. Do you know that you're an escape artist? You've been in China a year. You should have learned Chinese. If you continue to take the path of least resistance and gravitate to people who speak English, you'll never learn Chinese. I should say Shanghainese, which is the preferred dialect. Accordingly, I shall speak to you mostly in Shanghainese."

The truth of his words stung me. I would meditate on them later.

"You're a scream," I said. "Sometimes you talk like a textbook."

"I'm not aware that I was screaming," he said, tilting back his head, pretending to be aloof.

With each meeting Amoy became less and less the little professor and more and more a friend. He had a competitive nature and we became friendly rivals in a dozen sports.

It would have been better if I met Amoy Chang a year earlier. Then I'd have known more Chinese. When I started school again Father spoke with the headmaster. The nonsense of being in the fourth grade, unable to function, ended. The headmaster placed me in kindergarten with children less than half my age, less than half my height.

Understanding a smattering of Shanghainese, I quickly realized the kindergartners called me "the great white ghost."

The brats! Having been kicked in New York in no way

lessened the pain when kicked in Shanghai. Stung by their insults, I felt ashamed of being a giant in kindergarten. I hated school with a passion. How I longed to be in Greenwich Village and ninth grade! Everything within me cried out to return to New York.

Out of the intensity of my desperation a strong bond grew between me and Amoy Chang. I constantly looked forward to meeting him.

Horseback riding gave way to racing. Our mounts were race-horses recently retired from the track and they loved galloping headlong down the Scott Road Extension. I reined up and Amoy's expression told me I was about to be teased.

"My brothers were riding on top of a double-decker London bus," he began. "They were able to see over the school yard fence. They observed you doing exercises."

"What?" I screamed, completely mortified. "They saw me doing calisthenics? Oh no!" Digging a heel into my pony's side I went racing beyond the Extension. I had to get away.

Amoy followed, giving his mount his head.

"Hey," he called when I reined up. "That was fun. Your calisthenics had a salutory effect."

Pink warmed my cheeks. How humiliated I was that his brothers had seen me! "Amoy, you're the berries!"

He switched to Shanghainese, but not before he asked a serious question. "What does it mean? You're the berries?"

After I explained I urged my mount forward. Amoy followed. We had a trust relationship, Amoy and I. We shared each other's confidence.

"I'm beginning to understand the conflict between you and your mother," he said. "It's not because you are so different but because you are the same."

"I don't believe that."

"It's true. Precisely. Dorothy, you're irrepressible."

I didn't want to admit that I didn't know what 'irrepressible' meant. "Twenty-three skidoo," I called in farewell.

"Twenty-three skidoo," he responded.

When I reached home and questioned mother about the meaning of 'irrepressible' she laughed. "That means you're a tomboy."

I went to the dictionary that was becoming more and

more a companion; I so wanted to learn. Little by little I improved my vocabulary.

In the same gradual way Father became almost as strict as Mother. Seeing me tap-dancing and jigging about the house he ordered me to stop. "That's unladylike."

He insisted I have dancing lessons. I never dreamed that becoming an accomplished dancer would be valuable in the years ahead. Father continued to insist that I not associate with the Portuguese family down the block because he considered Portuguese low class. One of his stranger ideas, it met with total resistance from me. I frequently appropriated Father's ricksha and sneaked over to see them. Eventually caught, I responded with copious tears until Father relented.

Although I didn't realize it then, the two years we lived at the end of Scott Road were the happiest days I spent in China, days about to come to a sudden and dramatic end.

"The Japanese are getting too aggressive," Father said as he put down his copy of the *Shanghai Evening News and Mercury*. "They're making the International Settlement an armed camp. I don't like it."

Chapter Three

Father arrived home from the factory early, his shirt soaked with perspiration. A rush of words and the anxiety in his voice assembled the family without being summoned. "War is coming to Shanghai," he said, his voice charged with emotion.

The drawn and haggard look which haunted his face in recent days had been replaced by the relief that follows the difficulty of decision. "We have to move," he said, gesturing with both hands. "The situation is getting serious. Japanese troops have landed in Woosung, less than ten miles from here. Our troops are fighting back—"

"Move where, Sandow?" Mother said.

"The International Settlement. It's our only chance. If the Japs respect the sovereignty of other nations we'll be safe even if we lose the factory. I can't see the Japs risking a war with the British—the French—everybody."

"Lose the factory?" Mother gasped, eyes widened in dismay.

Father nodded, his face grave. "It sits there close to the river. The Japs are moving in more warships all the time. Little Tokyo is an armed garrison. Once the battle begins, the factory won't last long. I've rented a house in the British sector—a mansion really. It's more than we can afford—frightfully expensive as the British say—but it's the only place I could find. People have started moving into the Settlement, at least the smart ones. I want everyone to start packing. Tomorrow some of the workers from the factory will be here to help us move."

"Tomorrow?" Mother protested. "We can't possibly be ready tomorrow. We need at least a week."

"No," Father said firmly. "Tomorrow is Thursday the Twelfth. The next day is Friday the Thirteenth. We're going to be out of here on the Thirteenth. If we aren't, it'll be too late."

"All right," said Mother.

We all knew Father was superstitious, especially about the number thirteen. For him, thirteen was the worst of bad luck symbols, and with hostile troops less than ten miles away he wouldn't risk our safety. It made sense to flee to the International Settlement.

Tales of war had long been with us. Ever since we came to China a battle raged somewhere. One warlord attacked another. Communists fought the Kuomintang. Tension between the Chinese and Japanese ran high. By now everyone knew about Marco Polo Bridge, thirty graceful arches and twin rows of three hundred marble lions seated on short columns, the place where the war began.

On the evening of July 7, 1937 Japanese troops were on maneuvers in an international zone near Lukouchiao, a railway station on the Yungtung River, fifteen miles west of Peking. Across the river stood the walled city of Wanping. When one of his soldiers was reported missing, the Japanese commander demanded to enter Wanping to search for him. His request denied, the Japanese retaliated by firing on Chinese troops at the Marco Polo Bridge. The fact that the missing soldier later appeared—it had all been a Japanese hoax—a deliberate provocation—made the night of the 'double sevens' all the more infamous.

For weeks Shanghai newpapers openly exhorted the nation to war. If the editors were happy to see a war, I was not. My world was turning upside down. What had begun at distant Lukouchiao now oozed across the face of China, trapping us like flies in tanglefoot. With a heavy heart I prepared to leave our home on Scott Road. I packed my rollerskates.

At dawn, workers from the factory arrived to help us. A burly six-foot carpenter with a red nose was soon bathed with sweat. He and the others loaded the car until the back tires nearly went flat. When Father started the Ford two men leaped on the back bumper and clung precariously to the load. I sat up front.

"The Japs are getting hungry," Father said as we drove through a corner of Little Tokyo. "Our stevedores refuse to unload Japanese ships. They're running out of food. I'm sure they're going to attack. Look. The entire Honkew area is an armed camp. See the equipment, all that armor?"

"Yes." I saw several large guns, mounds of military supplies. Japanese troops spilled out of crowded barracks and filled the parade grounds.

Continuing south, we crossed a bridge over Soochow Creek and drove past a contingent of Americans. Further on, in the British zone, a company of unarmed men marched to a clipped cadence.

"Notice the difference?" Father asked. "Can you see why I'm worried? The Japs are getting ready to attack. It's not just Friday the Thirteenth I fear—I heard you and Mother talking."

Crimson rushed to my cheeks. "I understand," I said. "I can think deep thoughts."

"Yes, Dorothy. I'm aware of that."

He pulled into the driveway of our new home and parked. In a few minutes the car was unloaded and I was ready to make another trip.

Father shook his head. "Now that you're here, I want you to stay, please."

My mouth opened in protest but Father raised a silencing palm. "I observed the evil looks the Jap soldiers gave you. We shall not risk that again. You will stay, please."

As I watched him drive off it occurred to me that Father had chosen not to risk the entire family on any one trip. I never saw the Chapei section again. The next day, the Thirteenth of August, the Japanese overran the area surrounding our old home.

Overhead, planes droned and whirred, engaging each other in dogfights, their guns stuttering as they tilted at each other. From the distance the rumble of cannon punctuated the *blat-blat* of nearby small arms fire. The Japanese battleship *Idzumo* moved up the Wangpoo River and anchored opposite the Settlement. With a great thundering *boom* it lobbed shells into the hills beyond.

"They're trying to knock out the Shanghai-Hanchow Railway," said my brother Jack.

We viewed dogfights overhead as one watches a movie, with a sense of unreality, as if the participants were make-believe people and death was remote, beyond the next hill. Presently Mother shooed us inside.

"It's Friday the Thirteenth," Mother said. "Your father

was right. It *is* an unlucky day."

"It's lucky for us," I insisted. "See how lucky we are to be here in the British zone."

Saturday morning Mother put on her Alice Brady hat. "Dorothy," she said. "I'm going downtown. We've already been contacted by the American Consulate and I'm going to have a talk with them. I want you to come with me so you know how things are—what to do in case something happens to me."

She said it so calmly, so matter-of-factly, that I barely grasped the impact of her words before she switched to another topic.

"We need to do some shopping. With a war on, food'll be scarce. The time to stock up is now."

First we stopped at the Consulate. The representative advised us to return to the United States as Mother predicted. She said she'd think it over. As we exited, Mother said, "The British aren't as jittery as the Americans."

Downtown streets were jammed with refugees.

"There must be a million people here," Mother exclaimed. She pointed to a group, obviously farmers from beyond the city, people moving in, bringing their possessions, including a trussed squealing pig. Cars threaded bumper to bumper along clogged streets. Our ricksha driver halted, his path blocked by a coolie lugging a crate of ducks. The men traded insults before we began to move.

Horns tooted and the chatter of the crowd blotted out the distant rumble of guns. Planes churned in dogfights, darting and zooming. A number of people turned up their faces to watch, some with casual disinterest. The *Idzumo*, anchored in front of the downtown district, spoke up with her mighty guns. A Chinese pilot in a Northrup bomber came over, intent on dropping his bombs on the *Idzumo*. Japanese fighters bore in on him, their guns hammering. The engine of the Northrup faltered, caught hold, faltered again, then sputtered uncertainly as two Chinese fighters sped to its aid. As the Japanese fighters dispersed, the bomber pilot attempted to get his wounded plane back to the Hungjao airdrome. Suddenly two bombs dropped. They came whistling down on the plaza and exploded with a deafening roar. My ears rang, and rang again with the screams and cries of the wounded. A surging crowd upset our ricksha. Mother and I tumbled out and started running. We heard the sound of shattering glass. Windows in the hotel fell out. A woman with a window-glass spear protruding from her back ran past screaming. More screams. I saw a leg with no body . . . a severed hand instantly trampled. Someone shoved me and sent me sprawling. Before my eyes a clump of flesh quivered, pulsated, still alive.

"Mother," I screamed. *"Mother!"*

I felt her hand in mine, pulling me to my feet. I saw two men stripped naked by the concussion. One sat on his haunches crying. The other, soot-stained and bloody, staggered to his feet.

We ran past a car. The chauffeur sat rigid in death, blackened hands clutching the wheel, his face charred, clothes burning. Flames from his shoulder licked up around his ears. I glimpsed a lifeless passenger, also charred.

A car upset and burned. The gastank exploded. Another car veered and crashed into a building. Mother pulled me along. I pulled her along.

The screaming became tortured now. Cries of pain stabbed out behind us, accompanied by moans of those in shock. Flame seared my lungs. Gasping, I stopped, completely out of breath. I tried to speak and could not.

"Are you all right?" I heard Mother say. "Are you all right?"

"Yes. Yes." I tried to talk. Words failed me. I shook my head. I turned—

"Don't look back," Mother said.

Her warning came too late. My eyes swept the awful carnage. I saw an escaped hog go chomping up to the battered body of an infant. A man yelled and struck at it but missed. The boar clamped its jaw over the baby and ran shaking its prey up and down like a rag doll.

I started running again. Mother soon caught me.

"Now don't frighten Edna, Jackie and Gloria with a ghastly account of all this," Mother said. "Still, I suppose they'll have to know. My God! Bombed by a Chinese pilot—one of our own—not even one of theirs! We've got to get home. If the kids hear this on the radio, they'll be worried to death."

She continued to chatter in reaction to shock.

"Mother! You lost your Alice Brady hat."

Her hand went to her head. "I did, didn't I? I wonder if my other hat will match this outfit?"

We stared at each other in disbelief, surprised at our idiotic conversation.

"We're safe," I said dumbfounded. "We're all right."

"It's a wonder."

Early radio reports set the death toll at 2000. Later the figure jumped to 2500. The stricken bomber, it was said, was attempting to jettison its bombs safely on the race track but miscalculated. The Chinese government regretted—regretted all of Black Saturday.

The Japanese consolidated their positions in the Honkew area and soon controlled everything north of Soochow Creek. They discharged the International Police—bearded, turbaned Sikhs—who came across to the American and British side to help control crowds. One and one-half million refugees poured into the area. The British asked that the entire city of Shanghai be made a No Man's Land and excluded from the war. High-ranking sources speculated this might be accomplished. At any rate, the integrity of the British, American and French Concessions would certainly be respected.

Horrified by the downtown bombing, Mother considered it an isolated incident. Reluctant to follow the advice given us at the American Consulate, she still remembered they had denied her exit visas for Jack and Gloria. Two days later, when a large piece of shrapnel crashed through a section of the arm of a chair in which Edna was sitting, Mother changed her mind.

"This is impossible! We're getting out of here. We're going back to the States—" She broke off to stare at Father who had come running into the house, battered and bleeding, his clothes in tatters.

"The factory is lost," he said.

Mother dipped a towel into warm water and sponged his face.

"The Japs came ashore and took over the Chinese Concessions—all of the Old Chinese City, South Station—Nantao too, I think. I barely made it to the French

Concession. The Japs are looking for me right now."

Mother mumbled an oath. "We've got to go home. There's no reason to stay here now."

"No," Father said and fell silent. At length he rose from the chair, wearily, as if his pockets were filled with lead. He stood hunched over, directing his sad basset face toward the horizon, seeking something that was not there, dreaming of things that could not be. A dark question crept into his face, foreshadowing a series of events he was powerless to prevent, most of which he could not have imagined. With a determined look he turned and paused, as if listening for an echo. We were startled by someone calling his name. In a rising murmur of angry voices we heard his name called again. We crossed to the window and looked out.

In our front yard milled a crowd of forty men, women and children. I recognized some of the workmen from Father's factory, the six-foot carpenter with a red nose among them. Having helped us move a few days earlier, they knew where we lived. Father went out on the porch to speak with them.

"We want our money," a man shouted.

"We have worked for you many years—"

"Severance pay," demanded another.

Father raised his hands to quiet them. "Friends—friends. Please. There is no question that I owe you the money. But I *have* no money. Hours ago I barely escaped with my life. Just like you. All of my money is invested in steel... parts for repairing ships. We're supposed to be paid when the job is completed. The Japs have seized those ships, the factory, everything. Who knows if our contracts will ever be completed?"

"Our troops will soon recapture the factory!"

"In what condition? You know the Japanese destroy everything."

"We want our money," retorted an angry voice. The crowd, already surly, threatened to lose control. They advanced...

Father turned and shot me a look calculated to send my feet indoors. However, I stayed.

"Wait. Wait," Father shouted. "I'll try to get your money. Perhaps I can collect some old bills. You've known me—some of you have known me many years. I do not run from you. Here I am. Do with me as you will." Head erect, eyes forward, Father strode down the steps and walked directly to the six-foot carpenter and stuck out his hand. The carpenter hesitated, reached out and shook it.

In a moment angry sounds subsided and I heard several say, "We're sorry, Mister Yuen." They started cursing the Japanese.

Our front yard became a camp for refugees. The workers raised a wood and canvas leanto and set up a tripod from which a kettle dangled. Small fires banked with bricks appeared in several locations. The crowd broke up into small groups and the workers' wives began cooking the evening meal. After they had eaten, most of the wives and children moved into the first floor of our home. We had already moved upstairs.

Mother regarded Father with incredulity. He shrugged, spread his hands and said, "It is better to be kind at home then burn incense in a far place. Sometimes it is easier for a poor man to share what he has than for a rich man to give a trifle."

"You're a good man, Sandow." Mother gave him a hug.

Father forced a smile. "It is harder to be poor without murmuring than rich without arrogance."

Daddy was drawing on an ancient philosophy. Despite Mother's display of affection he could see a chasm widening between them. She wanted to return to New York.

A dark wave of melancholy washed over him as he realized that if he honored Mother's wish it meant turning his back on China. If he remained, it meant separation from Mother and the family.

"This will all blow over, Sweetie," Father said. "It's a temporary setback. I'll find something new. Remember in New York I was a cook and a taxi driver. Okay. With all these people there are bound to be opportunities. People mean opportunity."

"People! Hmmpf!" Mother sniffed deprecatingly. "We're no longer people. We're a mob fleeing for our lives."

Father's voice went low. "I have my savings. There's enough to start another business. I didn't tell the workers because they ought to be paid from company funds . . . not my private savings. We can move to another city—"

"Yeah. New York City."

"Inland," Father said. "Already people are moving to the interior. Cities will rise. Whole new cities."

"The Japs'll bomb them just as fast."

"Wide streets, factories, new homes. People will unite. We'll push the Japs back into the sea. We'll build a new China."

"I'll watch it from the outside." Mother's voice raised. "I don't want the children stranded here, surrounded by Japanese. The Settlement is an island. That's what it's become." Her chin came out. "I'm sorry. We're leaving."

"I'm sorrier still," Father said. He must have known the picture he painted was a pipedream.

The tense voices of my parents continued to be heard in their darkened bedroom long after we children were supposed to be asleep. Finally Mother shouted, "We've been over it ten times. No! Goodnight now!"

In the morning each of my parents set out on a mission. Father returned with money for his workmen. Although he never said, Mother suspected that he borrowed it from a rich friend. Mother came home with instructions from the American Consulate for our evacuation.

All afternoon Father repeatedly attempted to get Mother to change her mind. "I know there has been trouble, Sweetie," he pleaded. "But if we stay a family, we can face the trouble together. I think the Japanese will respect British territory. Japan doesn't want a war with Great Britain. Between us there is an age old rivalry, yes. With Britain, France, America—no. Please change your mind and stay with me a little longer."

"No. I'm not going to let the kids be killed by mistake—killed because a bomb gets dumped on a busy street—killed because shrapnel as big as your head falls out of the sky. No, Sandow, we're getting out. And that's final."

"Oh-h . . ."

"Why don't you change your mind and come with us?"

Father shook his head. "One foot cannot stand on two boats. I cannot desert my country in her hour of need."

"What are you going to do, Sandow?"

"Chiang Kai-shek has asked all former overseas students to volunteer. Commissions are being offered. I've already spoken to some of my men. Several have expressed an interest in joining my unit if I can be their commander."

Father slumped into his favorite chair, utterly defeated, quietly weeping as Mother and I ironed clothes and packed. From time to time he reached out to hold my youngest sister, Gloria, and patted her lovingly.

We labored far into the night getting things boxed, wrapped and tied. At three in the morning we completed the task and were able to get brief moments of sleep. August 21st, eight days after the Japanese occupied the area around our old home, we sat on the Bund waiting to leave.

Tears welled in Father's eyes and in my own.

"Dorothy, be good to your mother," he said. "Take care of your brothers and sisters. You're the oldest. I must rely on you."

"Yes, Father." I had to look away. I could no longer bear to see him this way.

A small group gathered on the dock and the tender had to make several trips to the American destroyer. On board, the sailors passed out candy and black olives while we waited. At length the destroyer took us down the Wangpoo River to the *President Hoover*. Three days later we landed in Manila.

On our arrival in the Philippines we were placed in the care of the Red Cross. Although grateful to the Red Cross, the manner in which they treated us generated bitterness in our hearts, a bitterness that grew with the passing of time. Caucasian families received preferential treatment and were billeted in first class hotels. The rest of us, those with mixed Oriental blood, were placed in third class hotels recently splashed with paint. The paint allegedly brought the hotels up to an acceptable standard.

Thoroughly miffed, Mother complained, "The rich-bitches get grade A hotels. I'm as white as they are. You can't get much whiter than a Swede. I was born in the United States and I'm a citizen. Twice already." She continued to rave. "Every day I'm down at the Red Cross rolling bandages. Who do you see volunteering? Just those of us from Oriental families. Not those other—*ladies*." She grimaced, shaking her head in imitation of some haughty nose-in-the-air type.

Sadness settled over our hotel. Every day families departed and those remaining lined up to sing "Aloha" and make tearful farewells. The Kim family—four children whose parents had sent them out—waved goodby. Nearly everyone headed for the States.

Mother developed a wait-and-see attitude. She missed Father and no longer spoke of returning to New York. Some predicted the war would be over in a couple of weeks. "The Chinese Army will soon reverse the tide."

In the interim of fleeting friendships I became fond of a delicate black-haired young woman, the mother of two small children. Maggie had a gamin face, large expressive eyes and a mobile mouth. She spoke with a British-Portuguese accent reminiscent of Macau.

Aware that we were growing close, Mother became sharply critical of Maggie, the way she did whenever I made a friend outside the family. "Why do you hang around with that street girl? She's no good."

"What do you mean, street girl?"

"Never mind," Mother snapped. "We're not going to talk about it. I just don't want you hanging around some chippy."

The next time I saw Maggie, I stupidly asked, "What's a chippy?"

"Did your mother call me that?" Maggie shot back, frowning.

I had not the presence to deny it. Besides, my face betrayed me.

Seeing my confusion, Maggie smiled her pixie smile and said, "A chippy is a girl who spends too much time on the street."

I knew as much as I did before. There was a great deal more to growing up, I learned, than being able to think deep thoughts, to analyze, accept responsibility and make decisions. The physical side encompassed more than growing another inch and standing tall. As the lotus is the emblem of fruitfulness and betokens perfection and purity because it grows out of the mud and is not defiled, I thrust my head out of the quagmire of ignorance into the presence of a woman many would scorn. Fortunately I knew of no reason to be contemptuous of Maggie and reaped the benefits of her knowledge.

One afternoon when Mother was rolling bandages an emergency sent me running to Maggie in a frenzy. "I'm bleeding," I cried. "And I can't get it stopped!"

"Where?" she asked.

"I think I hurt myself climbing a mango tree," I blurted. "But I can't remember injuring myself."

"Where? I don't see any—"

Anxiously I indicated my pubic area.

Her eyes widened. "Are you kidding me?"

"No. I wouldn't kid about bleeding to death."

"Hmmm. I can see you're not kidding. Well, you've just become a woman. Situation normal, there's nothing to worry about." She stifled a pixyish grin. "It's called a period and you'll get it every four weeks. If you're lucky."

"Lucky?"

"Didn't your mother tell you anything? I can't believe you don't know anything about it. You couldn't possibly be that dumb. On second thought, maybe you could." A sigh of disgust escaped her. "Somebody's got to take you in hand. C'mere."

Maggie helped solve my immediate problem, then sat me down and gave me some advice.

"How old are you, Dorothy?"

"Fifteen last July."

"Good God! Fifteen! I can't get over you being so damned dumb. I got mine when I was twelve. By the time I was fifteen—but let's not talk about that. If you don't know about periods, you don't know anything. Now the first thing to remember, when you have your period, don't put your feet in cold water. And don't eat onions. Got that?"

I nodded.

"You can have babies now, so when you're out with a man don't let him touch you above the knee. Or below the shoulder. If they try, you make them stop. Right now. I don't want happening to you what happened to me."

"What happened to you, Maggie?" I had to know more. It has long been said in China that to raise a son without learning is to raise an ass; to raise a daughter without learning is to raise a pig. I didn't want to be a dumb pig.

Maggie shrugged. "It's a sad story. You don't want to hear it."

"Yes, I do."

A smirk sent Maggie's cheek up and spread her mouth across her lean little face. She inclined her head, looked far away for a moment, then directly at me. "Might as well. In the beginning my mother was sick. We were alone. I had to get money. There was one easy way—from men."

Maggie told me more than I could understand but gradually it became clear.

"After living on the street I met this American sailor. He knew what I was—married me anyway." Concern clouded her face. "I haven't heard from him for a while. I hope he hasn't deserted me. His folks live in Arkansas. I was going there, but I can't. I'm afraid—"

"But why, Maggie?"

"They might not like me. My husband didn't talk about them. They might not even know about me—or the kids."

My heart went out to Maggie. I thought deeply about her problem but failed to find an answer.

The Red Cross learned that a number of us were not ready to return to the United States and relocated us near the exclusive Wak-Wak Golf Club. Maggie moved with us and when Mother got to know her better she stopped saying mean things about her.

Shortly thereafter one of Daddy's letters arrived. Now a full Colonel in Generalissimo Chiang Kai-shek's Army, he told us eight of his former employees had also joined the Army and were in his command. "I miss you all very much. I wish you could return to Shanghai."

Mother read the letter and scoffed. "That's easy for him to say. Before I return to Shanghai, I'll go home to the States."

"Daddy is so unhappy," I said. "He misses us . . ."

"It isn't safe in Shanghai," Mother said and went about her work.

The letter from Father, and something Mother had said to Maggie earlier—"I know the grandparents would like to see those kids,"—gave me an idea.

"Maggie. Maggie," I said excitedly. "Send your husband's parents a wire. The telegram will be your introduction. Ask if you and the children can come for a visit." I repeated what Mother had said.

"Ah, grandchildren," Maggie said with rising spirits. In

China grandchildren are greatly revered. "It might work. At least I'll know if they want to see me. I'd simply die if we got all the way to Arkansas and they didn't want to see us."

"They won't say no."

"I hope not."

We spent the entire morning writing and rewriting the message. Mother learned what we were doing and lent her advice. "Have the Red Cross send the wire. That'll make it official. Besides, that's what the Red Cross is for."

"Thanks, Missus Yuen. I hope it works."

Maggie dressed her children and set out for the Red Cross office downtown.

We paid little attention to the weather until an overcast sky turned prematurely dark, as if a big bag had been pulled over the landscape. A liang wind gathered force; shutters clapped back and forth against the house, shattering the fragile shells in the shoji screens. The wind increased from a moan to a howl to a shriek, to the thundering roar of a locomotive. By this time papers had blown around the house and a lamp crashed. Rain started sheeting down.

Peering over the window ledge I saw a nearby thatched roof rip off and whirl away. Palm trees bent down to kiss the earth before the typhoon's power.

"Get down," Mother screamed in my ear as she pulled me back.

Old boards creaked. Something thudded, jarring the house. I feared the house would shake loose from its foundation and go tumbling across the yard.

"—be crushed here—" I heard mother yell.

A raging sea poured in the windows, drenching everything.

Holding each other's hands we rushed out into the gale, were caught, and carried along. A tree cracked like a rifle shot and fell. A mango had been upended, torn out by its roots. We flung ourselves along its trunk.

Blinding torrents ripped over us, rain so dense we were unable to breathe. We hugged the earth, cupping our nostrils in our hands, gasping for breath as mud splattered our faces. Lying in a low area, the sudden rush of water caught us off guard. Ice cold, it chilled our bones. Mother lost Gloria and went plunging after her. They staggered and fell. Mother's mouth opened in a scream lost in the roar of the storm. Mother lifted Gloria to her feet. They struggled to safety. Edna and I pulled Jack along between us. A crevasse from a recent earthquake opened at our feet and we leaped across. We fell on our faces. Edna was crying, choking. Gasping for breath, Jack cupped his hands around his mouth, his nose almost in the mud, attempting to suck in life, like some ravenous bottom-feeding scavenger fish.

At length fury went out of the typhoon. The wind subsided, leaving only a hard rain. Ringed by devastation, we saw at least two dozen mango trees uprooted. Roofs were torn off a dozen housetops . . . many buildings destroyed.

Jack rose unsteadily and spread his arms, caressing the rain, allowing it to wash the mud from his body. All of us followed his example.

A man called, "Hey, are you all right?"

"Yes," we replied.

"I must look a sight," Mother said. "With my hair all straggly and matted down."

"We forgot all about you folks down here," the man said. "It's a wonder you weren't killed. We want you to come up to the club where you'll be safe."

Sloshing toward the Wak-Wak Club we encountered a farmer we'd seen in the area from time to time. "Are you going to town soon?" Mother asked.

"Yes," he nodded. "First thing in the morning. If you get up early you can ride with me."

"Thank you," said Mother. "I'll take you up on that."

In the Wak-Wak Club we were made comfortable. They provided us warm clothes while we hung ours up to dry. I saw Maggie and ran to join her.

"Maggie! I'm glad you're safe."

"Me too. The Red Cross wouldn't send our message," she said after we talked about the storm. "At least not the way we wrote it. The director said they'd contact my husband's parents, but in their own way. He was busy with someone else. He didn't even want to talk with me. I was so mad I went across to Western Union and sent it myself."

Hard lines formed around Mother's mouth. Her jaw came out.

"The money came out of my allowance," Maggie said

quickly. "I'd been saving—"

Maggie had misinterpreted Mother's stern rebuking look. Whatever Mother was thinking of had nothing to do with how Maggie might have obtained the money. Mother's eyes seemed to be fixed on something distant.

We awoke at first light. Before the farmer arrived Mother asked me to accompany her to the city. Whatever had been on her mind the night before remained there. It had to be something important but she gave no inkling.

In town, the farmer dropped us near the Red Cross building. Mother was silent as we entered.

Marching past protesting secretaries, Mother made straightway to the commanding officer's desk and waved a scolding finger in his face. "We've stayed in your fleabag hotels. We've rolled your bandages while the upper-crust women sat on their asses and smoked cigarettes. Do you know that?" There was the quiver of a raw touched nerve at the corner of her mouth. Her voice shook. "We've been shuttled out into the country where all the kids would have drowned if it hadn't been for the people at the Wak-Wak Club. Water in our cabin is deeper than a broomstick."

Mother stopped momentarily. "I still don't think I've got your attention," she yelled. "Well, maybe there's a way to get it." Leaping forward she stretched out her arm and raked everything off his desk. Papers, a glass holding pencils, a flower-filled vase, a telephone and a portable typewriter crashed to the floor. "We're *Americans*. All of us. We were born in the States. I was born in New York. Now, I'm more than fed up with your gahdamned prejudice and if you don't get on the ball I'm going to call President Roosevelt!"

Mother had a temper but this was the first time I had seen her violent. I stood with my mouth agape, eyes wide, intensely proud of Mother. What she said had needed saying for a long time.

The Red Cross director threw up his hands as if to shield his face, repeating, "Yes, Ma'am. Yes, Ma'am. Control yourself!"

Mother finally calmed down and the Red Cross put us in a nice hotel. Still there was prejudice: the hotel catered to Chinese.

Another letter came from Father telling us of his

assignment to Canton. Again he begged us to return to Shanghai—or possibly Hong Kong because Hong Kong wasn't far from Canton. As a consequence, Mother immediately prepared to return to New York. "It'll be nice seeing your brother Bobby again and his Filipino friend, Peter."

"I don't want to go to New York," I said. "I want to be in Canton with Daddy."

"It isn't safe there."

"I don't care. That's where Daddy is. If it's safe enough for him, it's safe enough for me."

"Well, I'm going to New York," Mother said.

"And I'm going to Shaghai," I said. "I'll go alone."

"What are you gonna do in Shanghai alone?"

"Wait for Father to send for me."

"Your Father is out in the field with his troops. You can't be with him."

"I can too."

"You don't know what you're saying. What if you're captured? You know what the Japs do to women."

"Well, *you* certainly never told me," I retorted, bitterly remembering that Maggie had to tell me the facts of life.

Mother shook her head and scowled. "No."

"I want to be with Daddy."

"You always were thick as thieves," Mother scolded. "I can't let you do it. It's too dangerous. You know that. Can't you remember how we almost got blown up?"

"I don't care. If Daddy gets blown up I want to be blown up with him. I don't want to go to any old New York."

"You're crazy, Dorothy."

"I'm not crazy," I cried. "A family should stay together."

"Well, we're going to New York," Mother shouted. "And that's final!"

"It ain't either final. You can pull that stuff with Daddy but I'm not Daddy. He stops when you say, 'That's final.' Not me. If you try to take me to New York I'll jump over the side of the boat and swim to China." Tears streamed down my face.

Mother yelled, "Keep that up and I'll throw you over. And don't stamp your foot at me!"

I kept insisting. We were at each other's throats for days. Finally mother gave up.

"All right. If you go back, we'll all go back. A family should stick together. We'll go to Shanghai as your father wishes. Just remember what Governor McNutt said. 'All Americans who refuse to go to the United States and elect to return to China do so at their own risk.' Remember that."

February 3, 1938 we left the Philippines. I thought of the Chinese double good luck symbol. Happiness twice warmed my heart. A week before Maggie had sailed for the United States to be with her husband's parents in Little Rock. Now I was on the way to China to be with Daddy.

Chapter Four

Returning to Shanghai, I thought our visit would be brief before we continued to Canton and Father. Had I known that we would remain there for sixteen months before any attempt was made to journey inland, my spirits would have been considerably dampened.

Mother acted resigned. "Dorothy, this is a bad decision. Still, I suppose we'll meet some of our old friends."

"I hope so."

No bombs fell now. Streets swollen with crowds during the initial attack were virtually deserted, business at a low ebb. We sensed a tense expectance among those who remained, as if they'd heard a shoe drop in the apartment above and waited for the second. Would the Japanese suddenly swarm across the British, French and American zones? The British seemed only mildly concerned, as if they didn't care whether the second shoe dropped or not.

We spent the night at a hotel and set out for the mansion that had been our home for little more than a week before we fled to the Philippines. The house stood vacant now, the rooms bare.

"Where's our furniture?"

"Did Father take it to Canton?"

We heard Jack calling for us to come out back. "It's all here in the servant's quarters," he said.

We were happy to have our things.

"We'll move it as soon as I find a new place," Mother said.

Knowing that the rent for the mansion had been exorbitant, Mother never bothered to seek the owner. That same day we moved into a smaller house at 1412 Yu Yuen Road, near Jessfield Park.

"I'm surprised how cheap the rent is," Mother said. "With people fleeing the war I guess a lot of homes are empty. No, Jackie, not there. Bring that chair over here."

Mother was happy to be doing something. She went about renewing old friendships—those few she could find. I came across the Portuguese family that formerly lived on Scott Road. They told me that the Remedios family, mutual friends, lived near our back door.

I remembered the Remedios brothers. The younger one had been particularly offensive. One day, more than a year ago, I remarked how obnoxious he was, little realizing I was talking to his older brother. Carlos dos Remedios promptly went home and beat up his brother. For such acts and others equally belligerent, Carlos earned the nickname "Tiger."

We soon met Tiger and he accompanied us whenever we went to Jessfield Park.

"That's good," said Mother. "You'll be safe as long as Tiger is with you."

From time to time we heard how cheeky the Japanese were getting. "Cheeky" is a British expression used to denote a breech of good manners, like when a Japanese soldier removed his uniform, masqueraded as a taxi driver and carried some girl off to the Honkew Area north of Soochow Creek.

Manners indeed!

If the British are masters of understatement, employing polite euphemisms when a girl was raped, mutilated and her disfigured body thrown back across the line, it cannot be gainsaid that the Chinese are masters of the rumor. The Chinese may not have invented rumors, but certainly they ought to be credited with perfecting rumor-mongering to a high art. It didn't matter if a newsman snatched from the streets was seen again in his office two days later, the report that he had been beheaded persisted to be further embellished. Certain features of the rumors were always the same. With girls, the Japs raped them and cut off their breasts. Boys could expect to have their penises slashed off.

Rumors became facts. Horror etched the faces of young people as they told of atrocities. In the days ahead I would see a young girl's nude body, her face slashed as if she'd been in a tiger's cage, her chest gouged where breasts had been. I saw men hung from lampposts and once a head rolled in the gutter, no body attached.

Of course, these acts were unofficial. The Japanese government announced, "We take no responsibility for cutthroats, brigands and roving desperadoes. We respect the neutrality and sovereignty of the British, Americans, French, Italians and Portuguese. Otherwise, would we have posted sentries at Garden Bridge in an effort to control the violence?"

Theoretically it would have been possible for the various nationalities—except the Chinese—to cross over into that part of the International Settlement north of Soochow Creek under Japanese control but I never heard that the British or Americans ever did so. Each nation seemed to be taking pains to keep its troops in its own area.

We wrote Father of our arrival and I urged, "Please send for us at once." Weeks passed while we waited for his reply. Nothing he might have written could have triggered such a dramatic or violent reaction as a packet of letters he had left behind. Neatly tied in a pink ribbon, Mother found them when she cleaned his files. In Father's hand, the letters had been returned because the addressee moved. Why he saved them I'll never know. They were addressed to his long-ago, left-in-China girlfriend, Edith Tong.

"The minute my back is turned," Mother shouted, her face livid. "He writes to Edith Tong!" She spat the words as if Edith Tong was lower than the serpent that defiled the Garden of Eden. In a blind rage she flung Father's letters at me. "Look at them. See what your father has done! See how little he cares for us! We mean nothing to him!"

I picked up the scattered letters and began to read. They were tenderly written. Edith's husband had died—Father's letter didn't mention how. In an earlier letter Father sent condolences. Expressions of sympathy brought back fond memories, memories of shared moments begging to be recaptured. A long-smouldering passion within my father fanned into flame. No doubt about it, I was reading love letters.

Mother raged not only because of what she read, but for the reason that Father had never sent this type of letter to her. In a few moments curiosity overcame anger.

"What does he say?" she said. "Let me read some more." Still seething, Mother forced herself to finish them.

Anger had not yet run its course. "I'll fix him," she stormed. "I'll make your father choose who he wants—*her* or us. He's got to make up his mind. I'm going to Canton and have it out with him. If I can't get things ironed out, we're going back to the States!"

Already at odds with China, its language and traditions, Mother now declared war on Father. I trembled at the thought of what she might do. I certainly didn't want to go to New York.

Mother rushed off to distant Canton leaving an old Chinese gentleman to care for us during the day and our friend, Tiger dos Remedios, to watch out for us at night. By the time we went to bed, Edna and I had so frightened ourselves with atrocity stories that neither of us could sleep. It was comforting to know Tiger was downstairs. Before the Japanese could get us, they would, Tiger promised, "have to cross my dead body."

A month went by before Mother unexpectedly walked in the front door.

"Are we going back to the States?" I demanded at once, preparing myself for a dreaded answer.

"No," she said. A hint of a smile formed on her little gash of a mouth and I knew things were right again between her and Father.

I watched her burn Father's letters to Edith Tong, a look of triumph on her face. Why hadn't she taken them to accost Father? I had no answer and didn't puzzle over it long. It was enough to know that she wouldn't be taking us to New York.

"When are we going to Canton?" I asked.

"Yes," Edna said. "When are we going?"

All of us had gotten restless during Mother's absence. None of us attended school. Our education was being completely neglected.

"The situation in Canton needs clarification," Mother said, sounding rather like a British correspondent. For a moment I thought she was speaking about her relationship with Father, but when she added, "It's too dangerous in Canton right now," I realized she meant the war.

The situation "clarified" on October 21, 1938—the day Canton fell to the Japanese. All of us feared for Father's safety. Tension mounted each day that we didn't hear from him. Finally a letter arrived telling us that he was safe in Kukong. Edna and I answered at once, telling Father, "We love you and want to come to Kukong to be with you."

"We're not going to Kukong," Mother objected. "Not unless he can assure us it's safe. I don't want to find myself in the middle of a retreating army."

Apparently Mother wrote Father in the same vein because in his next letter he assured us he wouldn't send for us until it was safe. We continued to wait, not attending school, expecting Father's message to arrive any day. The British school was some distance away and Mother was afraid a band of roving Japanese might capture us. Atrocities mounted. No one dared take a taxi for fear the driver would spirit him across the bridge on Soochow Creek. We heard that one British officer drew his pistol and pointed it at the back of the driver's head every time he took a cab.

Dark days of waiting stretched into months, brightened only by the coming of spring and a visit from my best friend, Amoy Chang. In good spirits, ever the little professor, Amoy insisted that I enter a skating contest, an all city event sponsored by leading citizens to boost morale, to show the Japanese we couldn't be intimidated. Shades of New York's Thirteenth Street! I won the speed skating championship and came home with a magnificent trophy.

I enjoyed the trophy but a few weeks. In July Father wrote, "It's no longer safe for you in the International Settlement. I'm sending a steward to guide you inland."

In a few days, a precise, intense, jittery little man appeared in our doorway. A suggestion of weight at his middle and the fact that his hair had begun to recede made me guess him to be about forty.

It didn't seem important when he emphasized that he was Ah-Chen, accenting the first syllable. Not until Jack blurted, "Are you an officer?" and his eyelids raised in disclaimer, "No, my name is *Ah*-Chen, young master," did I suspect the truth. Several times the steward insisted on the diminutive prefix "Ah," normally reserved for servants. As an officer, nothing would be more important to him than keeping his identity secret. The Japanese would have loved to capture a Chinese officer.

Father's last letter included a request for butter, jam and his favorite teakwood chairs. We packed some of the things he wanted but Mother thought the chairs were too heavy.

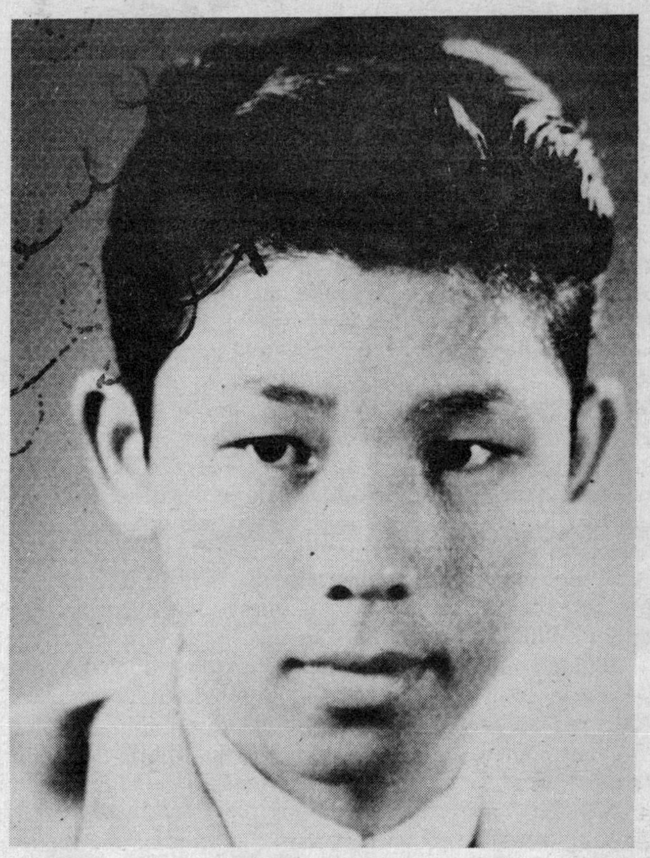

Amoy Chang, student dissident and Dorothy's friend.

Constructed like beach chairs, they had canvas seats and armrests that could be pushed forward, allowing Father to dangle his leg over the arm. I remembered him sitting in this totally relaxed position, a smile on his face. I insisted we take the chairs.

"No," said Mother.

Mother and I compromised. There were four chairs. We took two.

Ah-Chen gave us boat tickets and helped us secure our supply of furniture, bedding and canned goods for the seven-hundred-mile voyage down the coast. It would have been easier to have landed at Hong Kong and taken the train to Canton, and another train to Kukong, but Canton had been in Japanese hands for nine months. Thus far, Chinese troops had been unable to retake the city. Accordingly, we planned to put in at Swatow and journey upriver to Liu-huang where Ah-Chen promised a truck would meet us.

The moment we arrived in Swatow our plan disintegrated. The city was preparing for a siege. Officers barked orders, men scrambled to obey. Barricades, sand bags and barbed wire entanglments were everywhere. Soldiers placed heavy guns and dug in.

"Too dangerous," Ah-Chen said nervously, after he talked with an officer on shore. "Too dangerous to stay here."

By now he addressed his remarks only to me because Mother couldn't understand Chinese. She became very upset. "What's he saying?"

"We're going upriver, Mother," I explained.

Ten or twelve miles inland we stopped at Chaoan and secured lodging in a three-story hotel.

"Where's Ah-Chen going?" Mother asked with an anxious look.

"Upstream. To see if the truck arrived at Liu-huang where it's supposed to meet us."

"I wonder how long he will be?" It was the first sign I had that Mother accepted the fact that life moved slowly in China. In New York Ah-Chen would have been gone perhaps an hour. Here we might not see him for weeks. In wartime China we lived with uncertainty.

"Ah-Chen will be back in three days," I told Mother. "We are to stay here. He says there are no decent accommodations further upriver."

"This place is bad enough. Look at this bed!" She scowled, waving her hand at the platform of boards covered by a thin pad. "If I'd have known this, I'd have brought my Simmons."

Sweltering in the night, my body clammy and sticky, I found the floor an unyielding bed. After repeated attempts I finally dozed off. Some time later I awakened to the sound of chaos and panic. People shouted and screamed in the street below. A truck squealed meshing its gears. It could mean only one thing. The enemy! We had to escape!

I rang for the room boy and yelled for everyone to get dressed. The room boy responded, his face drawn and white. "The Japs landed in Swatow," he said excitedly. "Phones are out. The railroad is destroyed. Bridges have been dynamited. The river boats are gone. They're not coming back."

Mother and the children were crying and hysterical. Stories of rape and butchery flooded my mind. There would be no mercy for the family of a Chinese Colonel. None. The Japs would enjoy their fiendish torture. I had to get us away. It was up to me. Cries of terror and confusion swirled up from the street.

I shot a question at the room boy. "What's the quickest way out of town?"

"The river."

Quickly I spread my map. "We're on the way to Kukong." I shouted. "If you help us I will pay you well. My father is a Colonel in Chiang's army. He'll find a job for you if you get us out of here safely. He's a man of great importance—"

The boy quickly nodded agreement. "Yes, Big Miss. I want to get out too. I'll try to get a boat. There's a missionary compound up the street a couple blocks. Why don't you try that?"

As the boy ran to the river in search of a boat I started for the mission. Terrified shopkeepers nailed shut their doors. Men and women with children on their backs rushed about in panic. People with bamboo poles slung across their shoulders, a few precious belongings dangling below, fled for sanctuary in the countryside. Soldiers quickly spread barbed wire barricades and set up machine gun emplacements. Looters moved in to steal anything of value.

At the mission a French priest answered my knock and listened patiently. "We are not leaving," he said. "You and your mother—all the children—are welcome to stay here with us."

Out of the question. The Japs might respect a French priest, even the French nuns, but a glance would tell them we weren't French. They'd learn Father was a Colonel in the Chinese army.

"No," I said.

The kindly priest offered, "I can send a message on my wireless telling your father where you are."

"All right."

My message was terse and somewhat cryptic. "We are leaving this area—coming toward you the best way we can."

The best way was by river. Father would know that. I was counting on the room boy getting a boat. Thanking the priest, I started back, working against the surge of traffic. In the distance artillery thundered and flashed against the night sky. I saw a large glow. Swatow was in flames.

The room boy returned, all hope drained from his face. "It's no use," he said sadly. "The military took over all the sampans to transport the wounded."

I explained our plight to Mother.

"They've got to let us aboard," she said, urgency in her voice. "Maybe this'll help." She held up a picture of her and Daddy taken during her recent visit.

Gathering our luggage, we pushed our way through the desperate crowd streaming toward the river.

Without hesitation Mother attempted to board a junk. An officer yelled at her, ordering her to halt. She waved Father's picture in his face. "My husband is in the Army too. Let us aboard."

The officer, not understanding a word of English, was at a loss. Mother's voice took on the sharp edge of indignation. "Look. This is my husband's picture." She furtively waved us aboard.

Carrying our crated pots, pans, canned goods, and

Father's chairs, we struggled aboard.

"I can't understand what you're saying," the Chinese officer said in a loud voice.

"Look at the picture," Mother shouted in English.

"You can't get on an official hospital ship," the officer shouted back.

I was tempted to step in and interpret but wisely held my tongue. Confusion clouded the officer's face.

Behind us a voice of authority boomed. "What's holding things up? Move!"

"We can't hurt a white woman," I heard the officer say as his face snapped back and forth between Mother and his superior. He muttered something about Chiang Kai-shek.

Meanwhile Mother boarded.

Had the officer mistaken Father's picture for Generalissimo Chiang? The two looked a great deal alike. Or was he preparing an excuse for his Commander as to why he had allowed us aboard? It didn't matter. I was glad we were on our way, fleeing the onrushing Japanese.

The room boy, Ah-Lau, beamed at his good fortune. Room boys are notoriously poor and Ah-Lau was happy to be with us. "We go to your father now, Big Miss," he said.

"Yes," I nodded.

A junk is a flat bottomed vessel, the largest of sampans, usually powered by battened sails. However, when there is no wind, men bend their backs against ropes leading to shore and slowly trudge along well-defined trails. We were using a third method—the power of eight polesmen, four on a side. In unison they plunged their poles into murky water, leaning forward, straining mightily as they slowly walked along a narrow catwalk on each side of the junk. As the vessel moved forward they ran back, thrust in their poles and repeated the effort. In happier times they would sing. Now they only cursed.

The moon provided an eerie half light in which we could barely see the forms of wounded men lying on deck. Their moans and cries prevented sleep. We huddled and waited.

Through the dismal gray mist the sun came peeping, raw and red. Mother rose and moved among the wounded, comforting them. She tore up an old dress for bandages.

Some of the men tried to touch her. Others merely reached out to touch the hem of her dress. Were they delirious? Imagining they saw an angel? Then I realized that some of them hadn't seen a white woman before. They ascribed mystical powers to the blond-haired white woman. During the long years of the war peasants along our way would beg for Mother's touch and women would bring children to be touched and cured. This made a deep impression on Mother—indeed, on us all.

By the first full light of dawn we had already been discovered by Japanese aircraft. Like the symbols on their wingtips, they came at us out of the rising sun, eagles screaming down on a river clogged with sitting ducks.

We scrambled below deck. Some of the soldiers carried planks and placed them port to starboard, balancing precariously above the foul-smelling water of the hold. Gloria sobbed; Mother began to pray.

As we huddled, terrified, a bizarre thought entered my mind. I remembered the Festival-For-Flying-Kites-On-High, when kite and lantern shops were filled with every manner of kite. One young man had a fantastic black cat kite. Perplexed why I was thinking of a black cat kite at what might very well be my last moment on earth, I remembered that for Occidentals a black cat is a symbol of bad luck. In China the cat needn't be black; *any* strange cat entering a house means bad luck and approaching poverty. Misfortune is said to follow the theft of one's cat. It would be safer, I concluded, not to have cats at all. Then there could be no strange cats, no stolen cats. It would also be safer if there were no Japanese planes. I noticed that as the planes made their power dives they sounded like whining cats. "*Me-e-e-e-e-e-oww*!" they cried as they pulled out, guns spitting.

"Can't they see our Red Crosses?" Mother said bitterly.

Large Red Cross emblems were fastened to each side of our junk and a Red Cross banner had been raised on our sail.

I heard a big "*meow*" and machine gun bullets stitched across the deck, splintering timbers over our head. Edna screamed—all the children were crying now. A wounded man jerked and lay very still. Again and again the Japs strafed us. The Red Cross emblem was a virtual beacon.

Some of the wounded fell off their planks into the water of the hold. Mother leaped in to rescue a disabled man and held his head above water.

I scampered up on deck. Thin planks overhead were no protection whatever against marauding planes, I told myself. If I was going to get killed I wanted to see the plane that did it. Countless sampans clogged the river, bucking the current, all of them under sail now, hoping to capture a bit of the breeze. Except for sporadic small arms fire from a few sampans we were totally unprotected. When the Japanese planes ran out of bombs they returned to a nearby airfield. Within an hour they were back.

A couple of big bombers joined them. I saw sampans blown out of the water, men and bodies flying. As men died, others stripped off their clothing and eased them into the river. One corpse was treated in a most cavalier manner, heaved in completely without respect. The men assigned quickly grew accustomed to their grisly task. Either that, or they hadn't liked the late lamented. I was glad Mother wasn't on deck. She wasn't ready to witness such horror. I prepared her at the first opportunity and explained why it was necessary to dispose of bodies. "Our ship is heavily laden. It's riding so low in the water we can hardly maneuver. We have to lighten the load."

I'm glad she didn't ask how I learned that. My knowledge came from watching survivors of other boats swimming toward ours, only to be beaten away with poles by our crew. One gasping man, rapped on the head, slipped beneath the surface. Seeing my look of horror and outrage, an officer explained we were in danger of swamping.

In late afternoon, after a particularly terrifying raid, Mother said, "I can't go on. We'll all be killed. We've got to get off this boat."

"Yes," I agreed.

We pulled into a harbor of sorts. As we neared the dock we heard a voice calling, "Jack Yuen. Jack Yuen. Jack Yuen."

My brother was delighted to hear his name called. It was Father's man, Ah-Chen. He came aboard at once.

"How ever did you find us?" I asked.

"Easy." Ah-Chen smiled. "I kept asking for a boat with

foreigners aboard. I was directed to this area." His expression became grave. "You can't go on," he said nervously. "It isn't safe."

"We already decided to get off."

"The only way to Kukong is overland but trucks from Kukong can't get here to pick up your supplies. The bridges have all been destroyed. Your cargo must continue upstream."

Ah-Chen—he was now Captain Chen—and I talked with the room boy, Ah-Lau. He agreed to stay with the junk. Hopefully it would reach a point where a truck would have access to a dock. Captain Chen explained that one of Father's trucks would meet him.

"When you reach Kukong my father will reward you," I promised Ah-Lau.

"Yes, Big Miss. Do not worry. I will see that your things get there safely."

"The Army destroyed all bridges trying to halt the Japanese," said Captain Chen. "The only thing we can do now is walk."

I told Mother the bad news.

"Not till morning," she said, near collapse. "Not till morning."

We spent the night in a hardboard inn. At dawn, with Captain Chen leading, we set out. Each of us carried a single change of clothing and a tiny umbrella. We left the rest of our clothes behind. Jack looked rather silly in his British cork helmet, clutching a red tin of biscuits. Edna and Gloria each carried a thermos of tea. We knew mountain stream water wouldn't be fit to drink. I lugged a satchel filled with inflated Chinese currency, Father's savings from Shanghai.

We stumbled over rough and rocky roads. Where bridges were dynamited we waded streams. Before long the children's feet were bleeding. Mother grew weary.

We encountered a man trying to start his car. "You can ride with me," he said. "That is, if I can ever get it started."

He had the gas line off and after blowing through it the old car putted to life, emitting a cloud of smoke. We went as far as a dynamited bridge. Several planks remained intact. I helped Captain Chen lay them across the chasm and after checking that they were spaced like the wheels the man got into his car and slowly drove across. The planks sagged and groaned and nearly broke but the car made it safely across. With all the destruction we constantly doubled back, using four times as much gas as we should have for the distance. When the tank ran dry we bade the man farewell and continued on foot.

We came to a congested road. Soldiers stopped to stare at Mother. Some came over and touched her arm or her dress. I hated being on the roads, not because of the way soldiers worshipped Mother, but because we became prime targets. Japanese aircraft strafed the roads constantly, guns spitting, sending lethal dots racing down the highway, kicking up lines of dust. Always men screamed, twitched and died. Too terrified to cry, I wondered when I would be dotted with death. Sometimes death came zipping down the middle of the road, sometimes gunners missed the road and killed those cowering in ditches. The moment we heard aircraft—they had to be Japanese—we hadn't seen any of ours since the early days in Shanghai—we attempted to hide.

Crossing a paddy of waist-high rice, Captain Chen heard planes. "Get down," he warned.

"Scatter," I cried, flinging the money-filled valise.

We fell on our faces, digging our fingers into the mud, praying for life. The planes fired a few short bursts and continued bush hopping down the valley. When we were sure they had gone we staggered to our feet and began to scrape off mud.

"Where's the money?" Jack cried.

"Oh my goodness! I threw it over here somewhere. I think—"

A new fear boiled up in me. A voice within me shrieked, "I can't find it!"

We searched in an arc and eventually found the satchel nestled in some tall plants.

"I knew it was here all the time," I said.

"No, you didn't." Jack chose not to believe me.

We came to a stream and bathed, removing our flimsy dresses, the only garments we girls wore. We rinsed them, shook them out and crawled back into them. Before we had gone thirty steps Mother faltered and fell. I don't know how many times she fainted in the following days.

During the night we encountered a new enemy from which we couldn't hide. Swarms of mosquitos attacked with relentless fury, robbing us of sleep and energy, raising welts which we scratched into infected sores. With our tea gone, we drank mountain water. Most of us broke out in a rash. We cursed the cold night air, the mosquitos, our misfortune and most of all the Japanese. "Some day," I vowed, "I'm going to get even."

Our feet bleeding and swollen, we stumbled on. Some peasants shared their food with us. None would accept any money.

In every village Captain Chen checked with authorities to see if they had a message from Father. When they did not, he left a message of his own in case Father inquired, telling him that we had passed this way and were proceeding toward Kukong.

Mother's fainting spells became more frequent. Edna and I suffered a terrible illness. We came to Hsingning, a town devastated by bombs. Only steel reinforced structures remained. A small hotel had the lower two stories bombed out but the upper two floors miraculously hung there.

Feverish from polluted water and insects so thick that a well-placed slap would kill hundreds, we neared complete exhaustion.

"I can't go another step," Mother groaned.

We dragged each other up to the fourth floor and collapsed. We didn't stir until the following day when the police told us a raid was imminent. On their order we ran into the country. A little later we rushed out of the village a second time.

The police refused to honor the passes given us by the Embassy, passes that stated we could go anywhere. Mother's temper reached the boiling point.

"I've got sick kids," I translated for her. "If there's another raid I'm not leaving the hotel." Dizzy and debilitated, I doubt if her anger appeared in my translation. Couldn't the police see it on her face?

The next day when the manager came to warn us of a raid—he had some official connection—Mother remained seated on the bed and refused to leave.

"Oh no!!"

"You must go to the country," he said. "You can't stay here."

"We're not moving," Mother said.

I found myself in the middle of a shouting match.

"You've got to go. That's an order."

"We're staying right here," Mother shouted back. "This place is just as safe as anywhere. I've got sick kids. We're too weak to move."

I agreed with mother. Too sick to care, dying seemed merciful.

"We'll lock our door from the inside," Mother told the man. "You lock the hotel from the outside. If anything happens you can say you thought we went out. That way the gendarmes can't hold you responsible. We're not leaving!"

The manager shrugged helplessly and left.

Planes droned overhead. In my fever-distorted mind I barely heard the strafing. A bomb landed close enough to shake the building. How many hours went by? My brother found it difficult to remain quiet. Strangely, neither Jack nor Gloria contracted our illness.

"Jackie, will you stop that running around," Mother scolded.

"But there's a knock at the door."

"Don't answer it. It's the police."

The knock became insistent. A voice called, "Yuen family? Is the Yuen family in there?"

I heard Jack chattering in fluent Shanghai-Cantonese. "Dad is here," he cried.

We opened the door. It wasn't Father, only a manservant. He bowed and said, "Wait, please."

In a moment Father appeared. "Daddy! Daddy!" I cried, attempting to see him through tear-blurred eyes. "How did you find us?" I threw myself into his arms. "I'm so glad to see you!"

"Sandow," said Mother. "You're a sight for sore eyes." She rose unsteadily and went to embrace him.

"How ever did you find us?" I asked again.

"I got your message from the missionary and set out. I hoped you'd left the river at Liuhuang. Every time I came to a village I sent my chauffeur or orderly out to look for you. The police here had Captain Chen's message. My chauffeur is looking for Captain Chen now."

All of us hugged Daddy to make sure he was real. He issued a command. His orderly and another man carried Mother, Edna and me to a panel truck and carefully placed us on tables.

Mother raised her head. "Sandow," she whispered. She put her head down, a smile on her drawn haggard face. "I'm glad—"

Father smiled. "Truly this is a day for sending up rockets."

Of course there were no rockets. Every bit of powder was needed to make war. The Diamond-T truck bounced and swayed but I scarcely noticed the bumps. We were a family again.

Chapter Five

oldiers swarmed over our Diamond-T truck like ants on a iece of candy.

"It's too dangerous refusing them rides," Father advised is chauffeur as we inched along the refugee-clogged ighway.

Uneducated, ill-clad, ill-housed and frequently unpaid, he gaunt men of the Chinese infantry were never more than hairbreadth away from becoming a mob. Every now and hen the chauffeur stopped at an intersection, indicating with gesture, "That's your road."

The ragged troops would scramble off and start trudging n the direction of our driver's point. Of course, it wasn't heir road, merely a ruse to get them off the truck. Who knew he location of their scattered units? Almost at once we cquired a new group of riders.

I sat up to watch the progress.

"Ah, you're feeling better," Father said.

"Yes. The food your orderly prepared calmed my aching tomach."

"Chinese cooking," Daddy observed. "That's what gives you strength. My orderly is a wonderful cook. He's taken good care of me."

"Yes," I agreed. Despite being thinner Father looked well.

"How come so many of the soldiers are carrying puppies?" I asked. "Everyone has a little dog."

"They have a great fondness for dogs," Father said. He glanced back to see if Mother was resting and added in a low voice, "When things get tough they eat them."

"Really?"

"Yes. It's been handed down from the ancients that a man draws great strength from eating the meat of a dog. Nothing wards off the cold as well as dog meat. The soldiers are often cold."

"I know I wouldn't like it."

Daddy smiled. "You *are* feeling better."

Indeed I was.

When we arrived in Kukong I saw an expanding city. A railway stop on the Canton to Changsha run, in a province compressed by war, the city assumed a new importance. To accommodate the flood of refugees, flimsy houses spring up on every side. A frequent target of Japanese bombers, the center of the city remained reasonably intact. Downtown streets were paved—a modern touch—but the quaint way roofs of business places extended over columned arches to shield the sidewalk reflected an older order.

We continued several miles beyond the city. My heart gladdened and I remembered my journey from the Philippines had begun with a feeling of exceeding joy. Again I thrilled to the occasion of a double happiness. I was home at last and it was my birthday.

"I can't believe that I'm seventeen."

"Well, you are," said Father. "Congratulations and welcome home."

The truck stopped. Mother took one look at the mud hut with thatched roof and earthen floor and muttered, "In the States pigs live better than this."

"It's a peasant's house," Father explained. "It's only temporary. I'll have you out of here in a few days, Sweetie. I promise."

"Remember when we went to Detroit? All those red barns with white trim. I wish I had one of them now. We could use a little civilization over here."

"I promise," Father said again, his face unable to conceal his injured pride.

Mother's chin rose. "I'm raw on the inside—covered with bug bites on the outside—soldiers pawing me wherever I go—living in a mud hut with no floor—it's enough to try the patience of a saint." She looked heavenward. "If someone's preparing me for sainthood, I quit. And that's final."

We moved out of the peasant's mud hut before the room boy, Ah-Lau, arrived with our household goods. About two weeks after we reached Kukong he and one of Father's trucks made a rendezvous.

"Am I glad to get these," Father declared when he saw his chairs.

As I'd promised, he gave Ah-Lau a job.

By this time Father's soldiers had built us a new home. A couple of the men who had come with him from Shanghai were carpenters by trade, the six-foot man with a red nose among them and it only took them two days.

The main room was constructed in the shape of a pentagon with a small bedroom added at the rear for my parents. Beds for Edna, Jack, Gloria and me were hinged to the walls and folded out of the way during the day. Woven straw mat windows were pushed out at the bottom to admit sunlight. Outside, a small fire for cooking flickered in the arc formed by the union of the two rooms. Under the thatched roof, the crowning glory of our new house was the wooden floor.

As prestigious as a wooden floor might be, I learned to hate each plank with every fiber of my being. Mother made me scrub the floor daily. On my hands and knees, doing the work of the lowliest coolie, I seethed with indignation and felt sorely ashamed. *Is this any way to treat the daughter of Colonel Sandow Yuen, Army of Chiang Kai-shek, the man in charge of maintaining all the mechanized equipment in Kwangtung Province?*

Known as the Fifth Repair Factory, Father's unit consisted of a fleet of Diamond-T trucks and busses equipped with jutting torches, welding guns, lathes and presses used to design and fabricate spare parts. Mostly the men repaired broken-down vehicles and those damaged by bombs. Early on, the army realized the dire consequences of losing technical equipment and gave Father free-wheeling authority. Apparently Japanese Intelligence knew of the mobile factories because they were sought-after targets of enemy aircraft.

Our home was more than an hour's drive north of Kukong. In future days, as the emphasis of the war shifted, Father would be ordered to relocate and another home would be built for us approximately the same distance south of Kukong. A Japanese breakthrough would force us to abandon the house; we'd burn another in the face of oncoming invaders. Constructed on the same plan, all of the homes were located in a wooded area to provide cover and firewood. The cooking fire had a voracious appetite and we were constantly short of fuel. A nearby stream supplied our water.

After a few months, the joy of being together in our first home faded with the monotony and agony of war. Father showed the strain of his daily hide-and-seek games with Japanese aircraft and Mother's health failed. Worse, the relationship between my parents disintegrated to the breaking point. It was as if the shadow of a strange cat had come between them. Mother began to abuse Father at every opportunity. Father became completely withdrawn. As unrelenting as they were unreasonable, Mother's attacks more and more centered on the distant past.

I could tell by the fire in her eyes, the slashing movement of her hand that another battle was imminent.

"Phyllis. That was her name," Mother said, her voice high and thin. "Nineteen twenty-two. I'm sure that was the year."

"A river has gone to sea, evaporated and kissed the earth as rain since then," Father replied.

"If there was any kissing done," Mother snapped, "You did it. Nineteen twenty-four. Mabel. A red-head. I caught you having lunch with her."

"That was business."

"Yeah, funny business."

"Why do you torture yourself this way, Sweetie? There is no need—"

"No need?" Mother stormed. "You don't want me to remind you, that's all. Whatsamatter, can't you stand the truth?"

"It *isn't* the truth. You're imagining things. You're only making yourself ill." Father's face took on a wounded dog look.

"Alice Fan. *There* was a floozie. It took you six months to get over her. Nineteen twenty-five; nineteen twenty-six."

"Please, Sweetie, the children—"

"What about the children? It's high time they knew what kind of father they have. Alice Fan—and that—what's her name? A real weird broad with a real weird name. Phoebe! Yes, Phoebe. Nineteen twenty-nine. Nineteen thirty. God, I forgot Stella! Back in nineteen twenty-four!"

"Sweetie, I-I—" Father shook his head. Tears welled in

his eyes as Mother continued to rave. He spread his hands helplessly. "I've never heard of most of those women," he got out over a choked sob. "She's out of her mind. She doesn't know what she's saying."

"Liar," Mother screamed. "I know exactly what I'm saying. Liar! Liar!"

Father's face paled. His hands shook. "I've been disgraced in front of my children," he cried. He ran out of the house, his body racked with sobs. We barely heard, "It's more than I can bear."

I stood transfixed, staring at Mother. Cold blue eyes glaring, mouth an angry slash, she continued to spew venom. A sudden urgency pounded my brain. A terrible thought—*oh no*! Frantically I kicked myself into a run.

Father stood in the cooking area, head bowed, holding a sixteen inch butcher knife in both hands, eyes glazed, his face frozen in a trance, ready to plunge the knife into his abdomen, falling forward—

"Daddy! Daddy!" I screamed at the top of my lungs. "Stop. Don't do it. Don't do it! Don't! I love you!"

At the last moment he hesitated. He straightened. His face thawed. Life came back into his features. "I'm all right," he got out.

Sliding my arm along his I took the knife from his hands. "Are you—?" I placed my arm around him.

"I'm all right," he said with emphasis.

My eyes met his fleetingly and in that tense instant there passed between us all the hurt, pain, misery and sorrow of life. I was filled with compassion. I knew he had to get away. "You will want to think deep thoughts now," I said.

"Yes," he whispered.

To show I had confidence in him I placed the knife back on the chopping block where he could easily get it. He watched—I hope he understood. I turned away.

Mother had been watching, her face chalk white. "I-Is he all right?"

"Yes!" I snarled, glaring at her with the fury of a thousand tigers. "No thanks to you!" A quick flood of tears washed my face. "If you ever do that again," I screamed, "we will all leave you!"

Her mouth dropped in surprise and closed quickly. In the

future she had many arguments with Father, some heated, but never again like the terrible one we'd just witnessed.

Father never uttered a word critical of Mother, nor would he allow his children to speak unkindly of her. He was now more aware of the problems I faced with Mother and a new understanding grew between us.

After Father's transfer to headquarters we became socially active. Many invitations arrived at our new home. Mother accompanied him to the military parties several times, but unable to understand the language or customs of China she soon refused to go. With increasing frequency Father asked me to attend in her place.

At the home of a high ranking officer I saw many new faces, mostly Air Force officers. During the past months we'd seen more and more Chinese planes. Their presence halted the Japanese advance and stabilized our position in Kukong. A dashing lot, especially the air aces, none commanded a fraction of the attention of a diminutive young woman barely five feet tall. Wearing a stunning red and gold cheong-sam, the form-fitting high-collared gown petite girls can wear with devastating effect, she obviously enjoyed the attention of men.

"Don't stare," Father whispered. "That's Cheuk Sung-hai. Miss Cheuk is very influential."

With my head down, I glanced at her from time to time, studying her. Darker than most Chinese, she looked like a motion picture actress. Thinly plucked eyebrows arched over eyes like dancing coals and a smile came often to her red splash of a mouth. Dark ebony curls framed a tiny oval face. If a flaw could be found there, it had to be the nose. Her nose was too wide. However, I doubt if ever a man noticed that. The eyes of the men never left her. They hung on her every word.

A social leader—my mind leaped to a newspaper account of an Elsa Maxwell party in New York. The notion that Miss Cheuk might one day be fat and wrinkled like Elsa Maxwell made my face light up in amusement. Had I known the influence the diabolic Miss Cheuk would have on my life I definitely wouldn't have been amused.

After we had eaten, officers crowded around Miss Cheuk,

Intelligence Agent Cheuk Sung-Hai (also known as Mrs. Wu).

often with the pretense of introducing their ladies. Miss Cheuk gave the ladies a half smile, her eyes meeting theirs but fleetingly, as if she didn't see them at all, bestowing her full attention on each officer, bathing his face with a smile. None of the women reacted to the affront; most tittered at the privilege of being granted an audience.

As we drew near, Father said, "She has friends in high places."

No wonder officers fawned over her.

"Miss Cheuk, this is my daughter, Dorothy, from New York."

"America," Miss Cheuk exclaimed. "Ah, then you speak English. I'm happy to see you here."

"Yes, I speak English," I said, reverting to my favorite language. "But there aren't many people here who do. We are the only family—"

Her little brows knit in puzzlement for a split-instant, replaced by a confident smile. "Well, I do not," she said with a throaty laugh, continuing to speak Cantonese. "However, I have a sister who does." She turned to an aide. "Have Connie come here, please." She faced me again, glancing at me from head to toe, observing me as completely as if her dark little eyes were the lens of a camera. "We're proud your father has come back to China. It's men like your father who are building a great new China."

No longer uneasy, I smiled. "I'm proud of him too."

The sister whose presence had been commanded appeared.

"Connie, I want you to meet my friend, Dorothy Yuen. Dorothy is from America. You will have an opportunity to practice your English."

I was overwhelmed. Miss Cheuk had taken special notice of me. I offered Connie my hand.

Nearly my own age, Connie had none of the aura of her older sister. An unpretentious girl, she immediately became my friend and invited me to spend the night. Father granted permission without hesitation. On my second visit to the Cheuk home I again encountered Cheuk Sung-hai.

"I've been watching you," Miss Cheuk said. "You're a bright young lady with a fantastic future. . .if you choose wisely among the roads spread before you. Connie tells me that you speak English with excellence." There came a momentary pause as she frowned, a frown softened by the upturning of her broad, generous mouth. "Your Cantonese is that of a child—but we can work on that. Your Mandarin too."

Flame rushed to my cheeks. I was greatly embarrassed by my lack of education. My eyes sought refuge in my sandals. I felt so stupid.

"Modesty becomes you," she said. "Men like that. I will come directly to the point. How would you like to come to Chungking with me? Many important events are happening in the new capital, important people are gathering to map plans for our nation's future. I'm sure we'll be able to find a job for you. Connie mentioned that you have no employment. For a friend of Connie's I'm sure we can find something to suit your talents."

My head snapped up in surprise. I remembered to close my mouth but failed to hide the sudden reaction on my face, the happiness that glowed there. I managed, "I-I will have to seek the permission of my father."

"Of course. Have him come see me."

"I will," I bubbled. "I will."

Miss Cheuk touched her finger to her lips pensively and remarked in afterthought, "You're so wonderfully tall. Sometimes obvious things are the most difficult to see."

At the first opportunity I spoke to Father and received his tentative permission. Miss Cheuk's request that he visit her, I knew, had nothing to do with permission, but concerned financial arrangements. In China there were always arrangements, fees and kickbacks which the British called "the squeeze." A servant charged with shopping for a family was expected to squeeze out a little for himself.

"We have several days to consider," Father said after he'd spoken with Miss Cheuk. "I'm pleased the only expense involved is your ticket to Chungking."

"Really?"

"With the war on," Father said, "many families have abandoned celebrating Chiao Nu Chieh." He was speaking of the festival of the double sevens held the seventh day of the seventh month, when marriageable girls displayed their skills in cooking, sewing and housekeeping. "Because you do not have an interest in marriage it would be prudent to acquire other skills." He held up a warning finger. "Wisdom dictates that a proper time be selected to tell your mother."

In a short speech Father had given me much to consider. He pointed out that I was not interested in marriage—we had talked about this many times—and he reminded me that I had turned eighteen near the time of the traditional double seven holiday. He'd also told me how to approach Mother.

In the months since my birthday, Mother had harangued me on a theme as constant and unvarying as Father's alleged transgressions with other women. When she mounted the horse of diatribe she usually rode it to death. I didn't have long to wait; she started a new ride that same day.

"When are you going out and get a job? Eighteen years old and lying around the house. What are you good for? When I was sixteen I was out on my own. I've been on my own ever since."

I realized the time had come to tell her.

Mother continued to scold. "It's high time you got out of here and went to work."

I grimaced. What did she think I was doing—rising at dawn, scrubbing the wooden floor, spending the rest of the day laundering and ironing.

"As you wish me to do," I said. "I've been looking."

"You'll have to do more than look. Work doesn't get done just by looking at it."

"I know, Mother. I've been speaking with Miss Cheuk."

"I never will forget the first job I had. Thrown out at sixteen, I went to work for a family. I had to wake up before they did and get the fire started. I had to chop wood—"

"Father says you're right. It is time for me to find a job. That's why he's allowing me to go to Chungking with Miss Cheuk. To find a job . . ."

Mother's head came up sharply. "Chungking?" She recoiled. "You're going to Chungking?"

"Yes," I said timidly.

"Already cleared it with your father, eh? I might have known. You always were thick as thieves. Well, good. It'll be a pleasant change not having you underfoot. You'll learn what it means to be out in the world. You'll find out life isn't a bowl of cherries. It's time you learned. It's none too soon."

She continued preaching about the hardships of life when she was sixteen. As the day lengthened her enthusiasm at getting me out of the house waned. Her gramophone record finally ran down. Up to now there had been no peril in her position. She could cajole and scold me for not having a job and be safe in the knowledge that I'd be unable to find one. There were no jobs in Kukong. How could she have foreseen that I would seek a job in faraway Chungking? As she thought about it I'm sure she realized that not having me underfoot also meant that she was losing a number one servant girl. Who'd scrub the floor, do the washing and ironing? My sister Edna? That was a laugh.

Because she'd been raving about my leaving home, there was no way Mother could withhold consent, but as realization dawned what my absence meant, I knew she'd find some way to throw a stumbling block in my path.

Two evenings later, bustling about, I planned what clothes I would take. "How am I going to carry my things?"

"You can't take my suitcase," Mother said abruptly. Among the household goods that Ah-Lau brought upstream was a nearly new suitcase.

"I don't want to wrap my clothes in a jacket like a coolie."

"You're not taking my suitcase," Mother insisted.

"What harm would it do?" Father interjected. "You haven't used it in a year and a half."

"I did too. Every time the Japs break through and we have to run I use it. They're liable to breach the line any time and I want to be ready."

"That's not going to happen," said Father. "We've turned the tide. One of these days we'll mount an offensive."

"The suitcase is mine," Mother said stubbornly. "And I'm going to keep it."

"It wouldn't hurt you to be more generous," said Father.

"I don't want to tie my clothes up in a bundle," I said. "I'd die if Miss Cheuk saw that. If I can't take the suitcase what am I going to do?"

Mother wheeled to face me, hands on her hips. "Stay

home then. If you're too ashamed to go out in the world at eighteen, after all Father and I have done for you, why you can just stay here."

"That's what you'd like, isn't it?" I charged, tears coming to my eyes.

"Somebody has to help with all this housework," Mother shouted. "The way work piles up around here I could use ten servants."

Father shook his head. "That makes a circle." Patience exhausted, he waved his arm in a downward "go away" slash. "I'll settle it once and for all. Dorothy takes the suitcase . . . and I don't want to hear any more about it."

Father arranged to have military business conducted about the time my train was to depart and dispatched a driver. Extremely conscious of wasting gasoline, the men in his unit sometimes criticized him for it. Heedless of the criticism, Father frequently said, "Every ounce of gasoline is like a drop of blood for China."

His driver dropped me at the station.

I glimpsed the lovely Miss Cheuk and had a disquieting thought. The night before, when I'd gone to say goodby to Connie, she'd pointed out that officially her sister was known as Mrs. Wu. Why had Connie taken pains to tell me that? What did officially mean? And who was *Mr.* Wu? An increasingly mystifying puzzle, the only things I knew about Miss Cheuk—I gave an empty shrug.

Why had I leaped at this opportunity to seek an undescribed job, when in my heart I knew I was qualified only for scrubbing floors? I should have been more cautious.

"Ready to go, Dorothy?"

"Ready," I said.

Chapter Six

The engine coughed lustily and our car jolted forward to the rush of steam, the shriek of wheels spinning on steel rails. Miss Cheuk's hands came up to catch me as I lurched out of my seat. The engine puffed again; slack came out of the couplings and a large tremor went snaking down the row of cars in aftershock.

"We must have an American engineer." Miss Cheuk laughed as the train inched forward.

I smiled back, too supremely happy to make anything of her remark. Here I was, leaving home, on my own at last. The painful scenes with my mother behind me, the interminable scolding, Mother's brittle voice screaming, "When I was sixteen, I was on my own . . ." the recrimination about the suitcase—all behind me.

We were on the way to Chungking and we were traveling first class. Certainly the stateroom was first class, and when I thought how important it was for Father to travel first class, I also remembered how much I loved him, how difficult it was to leave him. I became morose. I visualized him at the wheel of his Diamond-T truck, careening along narrow country roads under the strafing of Japanese aircraft.

Because of enemy planes our train had to travel at night, depriving me of an opportunity to see the countryside. Apparently sadness showed on my face.

"Don't worry," Miss Cheuk said. "We'll find you a fascinating job in Chungking."

I played with the word "fascinating" like a child with a toy. Had I for a moment realized what fascinating meant, what was in store for me before I would again see Kukong and the family, I would have demanded they halt the train. No, I would have leaped off, leaving my best dress and cherished suitcase behind.

As the gloom of darkness settled over the stateroom, Miss Cheuk continued to talk. I became aware of how really locquacious she was. She talked incessantly.

The train throbbed into the night; there was nothing to do but listen. Finally it dawned on me that she had chosen the curtain of darkness to break some news, to prepare me.

"When we reach Kweilin we'll be met by an Air Force Colonel," she said. "He is in love with me. Gloriously in love with me."

"What of Mr. Wu, your husband?" I nearly blurted, but quite sensibly bit my tongue. In the darkness she couldn't see my mouth agape. I marvelled at her audacity. Cheuk Sung-hai was truly one of China's most liberated women, along with the Soong sisters, one of whom was Madame Chiang.

"Because of the Colonel's great love for me, Chiang Kai-shek now has an Air Force."

A surprised sound must have escaped me. Allowing me a moment, she went on, "I am officially credited with that." She made no attempt to mask the pride in her voice. "You see, the Generalissimo only had a couple of derelict planes. The only Air Force in all of China was located at Canton under the command of General Chen Tsi-tong. I had been urging my Colonel to come over to the Nationalists and the General must have suspected something. Perhaps he heard a rumor. One night General Chen called all his flyers together and made a patriotic speech. Near the end he said, 'All of you who are loyal to me, stand up!' Everyone rose, to a man. But the next morning they all flew away, led by my Colonel. The darling panda. He really is in love with me."

She spoke the truth. When we reached Kweilin an Air Force Colonel met us. He was obviously deeply in love with Miss Cheuk. I sensed his desire to embrace her, but as we were there—his chauffeur, our manservant Ah-Fong and I—he did not.

The chauffeur drove us to a hotel and the situation became awkward. I felt so dreadfully in the way. My attempts to make myself inconspicuous were rather clumsy and made me all the more obvious. Miss Cheuk—we now called her Mrs. Wu—made no attempt to allay my discomfiture by asking me to go for a walk or on some trifling errand.

Still puzzled by her transformation to Mrs. Wu, I became aware that her title was not only determined by what others called her but in the way she referred to herself. She used marriage to the enigmatic Wu as a shield, to be picked up and put down at will.

On our second day in Kweilin Mrs. Wu came to me. "There's been a change of plans," she said mysteriously. "The Colonel is taking me to the airport. I'll meet you in Chungking."

The Colonel wept unashamedly. All my sympathies went out to him and it greatly embarrassed me to see him crying. Deeply in love with Mrs. Wu, his heart broke at the thought of her leaving. Although they talked in hushed tones I knew Mrs. Wu had told him she could no longer return his love; it was over. The hapless Colonel had mutinied against his commander and delivered an Air Force to the Generalissimo all because of her, and now she was leaving. He had every right to be angry. At the moment he displayed no rancor or bitterness toward Mrs. Wu. Heart-sick and sobbing he went to make arrangements for her flight.

Once the Nationalists had his planes, the Colonel, because he was a Southerner, found himself relegated to unimportant posts.

We continued to Chungking by bus, Ah-Fong and I. During the next several days he told me about Chungking, the capital city of Szechwan Province, "a place where the Ancients are alive." It was Ah-Fong's way of saying that civilization had not yet come to the city, people lived there much as their ancestors had centuries before.

"It's the best place for growing vegetables in all of China," Ah-Fong said, pretending to hold a giant melon in his hands.

He described in graphic detail the treacherous road down the mountains leading into one of the city's gates. By the time we started down the famous "Seventy-two Turns," he had me thoroughly frightened. Our bus tilted crazily from side to side as we negotiated the many hairpin turns. I swallowed one scream after another, exceedingly grateful the Japanese had not chosen that moment to attack.

Beyond the mountains, actually fierce little hills, the Szechwan countryside looks soft, lush and green. Orange, banana and evergreen trees cling to the same hillside and roses in bloom may be found every day of the year. Warm and salubrious in springtime sunlight, Chungking becomes cold and wet in winter when enormous blankets of fog smother the city, coating the streets with slime.

When we lived in Shanghai people sometimes spoke of Chungking as, "that place at the other end of the Yangtze," especially the sailors, who, after negotiating their gunboats through the narrow rocky gorges that almost strangle the river and make it one of the most hazardous in the world to navigate, forgot all about the safety of being tied to the docks and complained endlessly of the mud. On rainy days there was a great deal of mud despite the fact that one was inclined to think of Chungking as an indomitable city built on a rock. So sheer were the cliffs that the many tiers of homes seemed to be houses of cards balancing on matchsticks. In the vast panorama of homes splashed against the hillside before me, I could not see one devoid of stilts.

Our bus rolled through a gate in a wall many centuries old. Once the ancient wall ringed the city; now shacks sprawled beyond the wall in great profusion. Refugees were coming from every part of the land. As the wartime capital, Chungking was bustling. Soldiers were to be seen everywhere and gun fortifications dotted the perimeter of the city, but they were too sparse to be meaningful and provided only token resistance against marauding Japanese aircraft.

Between air raids, crowds choked the streets, each bent on the mission of greatest importance to him at the moment. The bus slowed for two coolies carrying a trussed and squealing pig suspended between them on a rod. The crowing of a rooster, proclaiming an insult to his dignity for being caged with a bunch of squawking hens, blended with the shrill shouting of hucksters and peddlers. An indignant woman yelled for a ricksha. In and out of a thousand twisted alleys they streamed, each with a similar purpose—to transact that one important piece of business before the next air raid.

A pale, squat man with a dirty gray turban trudged along with a bar across his shoulders from which an egg-filled basket dangled at each hand. A little girl squatting over a drainage ditch to relieve herself hunkered down at the sight of a basket coming at her and the man shifted slightly, gave a flick of his finger and the basket on one side of his yoke lowered slightly as the basket on the other side raised just enough to clear the girl's head.

"I'm glad you know the city, Ah-Fong," I said as we got off the bus.

We found a ricksha and I climbed into it, along with the luggage. Ah-Fong cheerfully trotted alongside, happy that he didn't have to carry anything.

There was the mark of antiquity about the city and I felt I had stepped into a place where time began—a city of filth, scattered, stacked and floating. Clothes were sweat-stained and dirty, and the effluvium rising from the sea of goat-ripe humanity was enough to insure total nausea, but vomiting would have been too pale a protest and altogether futile.

In her apartment, Mrs. Wu greeted me warmly. The apartment disappointed me. For someone of Mrs. Wu's obvious wealth and position I expected larger quarters. There were two small rooms and one bed. I saw at a glance that I'd be sleeping with her. Later I learned that Ah-Fong found a place at the back of the house.

"I'm glad you arrived," she said. "I've arranged a dinner party for some influential people..."

"I'd like to write a letter to my father," I said, "telling him that I arrived safely."

She smiled indulgently and waved me to a small desk and short legged straight-backed chair. I composed a letter telling Daddy how happy I was to be in Chungking and on my own. "It's much too soon to give my impression of the city and the Szechwanese," I wrote. Still hurt and irritated at the way Mother treated me, I didn't mention her specifically, but near the end of the letter I relented somewhat, adding, "Much love to the whole family."

By the time I dressed, four men arrived to take us to a restaurant. It didn't surprise me to see a general. Mrs. Wu was the type of person who would number generals among her friends.

"This is General Lee," Mrs. Wu said.

General Lee drew himself erect with ease, bowed and smiled. A Northerner with impeccable manners, he spoke in Mandarin.

"This is Dorothy's first day in the city. I'm trying to find her a job."

A curious light came into the General's eyes when Mrs.

Wu told him I spoke English. They exchanged comments I didn't understand. As we set out, Mrs. Wu enlightened me about Chungking.

"The city is a honeycomb of underground tunnels and caves. Centuries old, the caverns were formerly used by Emperors to store their wealth—and their concubines."

When she mentioned concubines the men nodded and smiled with approval.

"I'm surprised there are still restaurants open with all this bombing," I said.

"They get bombed, they get rebuilt. A little bamboo, a little mud and they're back in business..."

Her attitude seemed so carefree, so totally nonchalant, it made me think she lived somewhere else... but one can grow accustomed to anything.

Following her comment I studied the construction. With no steel for corner posts, bamboo had been used. Boards were not available so bamboo had been split, halved and quartered, flattened to form boards. Lacking nails, finely split bamboo had been used for lacing. To provide ballast, the flimsy structures were troweled with mud, banked and braced with mud, and finally crowned with a grass thatch to ward off rain. Due to incessant bombing the city was continually being rebuilt. Construction was temporary in nature, only designed to last until "next time."

At the restaurant, we climbed the steps to the second floor and found ourselves in a small room crowded with fifteen or twenty tables. As the hostess directed us to our table I recognized an old friend from Shanghai.

"Amoy Chang!" I cried, surprised and elated. "How wonderful it is to see you. What ever are you doing here in Chungking? I'm so happy to see you. I never would have imagined—"

For an instant there was a flicker of joy in his eyes, then his face clouded. "Do you know who you're with?" he whispered, leaning toward me in a little bow.

"No," I said dumbly. Who..."

"Shh! It's nice to see you," he said with stiff formality.

Whatever was wrong with Amoy? Didn't he want me to recognize him? Was he in some kind of trouble? "Let me have your address," I said. "I'll come visit you."

He shook his head. "No," he whispered. "Give me yours. I'll see you tomorrow night."

Was Amoy afraid of speaking English in a public place? I sensed it was more than that and quickly gave him my address.

Mrs. Wu cast impatient glances toward me. My absence had delayed the seating of a General—I hastened back.

"Who is that young man?" she asked.

"Just a boy who used to live on the same road as our family. I'm so surprised to see him here. I'm sorry. I guess I'm not very worldly."

General Lee nodded amiably. "One should always take time for old friends."

Mrs. Wu laughed and passed off the incident as if it never happened. In a few minutes, when I glanced over at Amoy Chang's table, I saw he and his friends were gone. Would I see the little professor again?

My thoughts were on Amoy the next morning until the wail of an air raid siren interrupted my breakfast.

"Jing Bao!"

I gulped the last morsels. Mrs. Wu hurriedly emptied her jewel box, covering her fingers with rings, her arms with bracelets.

Jing Bao means, 'to be alert.' To warn citizens of approaching aircraft, lanterns were hung on flagpoles placed on the city wall at strategic intervals. One lantern meant enemy planes were an hour away. Two lanterns indicated they were close and when both lanterns dropped it meant, "This is it." A long green sleeve signaled, "All clear."

We saw two lanterns as we ran to a large public shelter. As we sat waiting for the Japanese bombers to leave, Mrs. Wu said, "Dorothy, I must get you passes for all the shelters. There are several nearby. You should become knowledgeable about them."

Around us huddled the refugee masses from the four corners of China; those who'd fled the fall of Shanghai, those who'd come to form a new government, those seeking to capitalize on the collection of people by starting new enterprises. Daily they dug into the rock, enlarging caves and tunnels, stubbornly holding on—the hope of New China.

It became our custom to study language during the raids.

Mrs. Wu would drill me in Mandarin and sometimes Cantonese. Hearing our discussion, a small Szechwanese boy unacquainted with our dialect pointed a finger at me and blurted, "Mother, is she a foreigner?"

I was about to smile and say, "No, only half foreign," but when I considered it, the Cantonese were almost as alien to the customs and traditions of the Szechwanese as Occidentals.

During the next raid we found refuge in the Cantonese Club shelter, a cave reserved especially for people from Canton. Not as crowded as the public shelter with its standing room only, there were benches for our comfort which further enhanced the social club aura. The Cantonese delighted in having a status shelter. It reminded them that they were better educated, more progressive than the backward Szechwanese. After all, in Canton they had modern autos and streetcars. When an outspoken man observed, "Without us, Generalissimo Chiang wouldn't have an Air Force," Mrs. Wu nudged me covertly and we exchanged knowing glances.

"I wish he would use it more," groused another.

Bored with just sitting there, a Dr. Wong, a friend of Mrs. Wu's, began assisting with my lesson in Cantonese. Dr. Wong and his family were to play an important role in what would become a routine for Mrs. Wu and myself. She made an appointment to see him later in the week.

It was difficult keeping my mind on the study of Cantonese; I kept thinking of Amoy Chang, my friend from Shanghai. The way he acted had certainly aroused my suspicions.

At day's end when he hadn't called my worry heightened. What had happened to him? There was nothing I could do but wait.

All the next day I waited, greatly concerned for him. Towards evening, when a timid knock sounded at our door I knew it would be Amoy and rushed to answer.

He regarded me uneasily. "Shall we go for a walk?" he asked, looking about nervously.

"I can't get over seeing you here," I bubbled. "I've been worried about you all day. I kept thinking of Shanghai.

Remember how we use to race our ponies in the Chapei section?"

"Much has happened since we went riding on Scott Road Extension," he said soberly. "Do you know yet with whom you dined?"

"Mrs. Wu. General Lee. Of course."

"I can see you do not," he said, bitterness invading his voice. He raised his hand, extending his index and second fingers as one. "General Lee is right next to Dai Nup."

I knew dai nup meant bigshot but Amoy was trying to tell me something more.

"Dai Nup is chief of Intelligence. Next to Chiang Kaishek he is the most powerful man in the country. And nobody sees Dai Nup without first going through General Lee. Everyone who was at your table is with Intelligence."

"Spies?" I gulped, realizing now that his "Dai Nup" was in reality the dreaded Dai Li.

He nodded. "You're not a spy, are you?"

"*Me?* Of course not."

"I hope not."

His reaction was typical. A position in government was esteemed but if that position involved Intelligence it always evoked the same reaction among the citizenry—fear. "No wonder you didn't want to talk to me," I said.

"I'm not sure I should talk to you now. But what have I got to lose?" he choked. "I can tell you that I've become involved in the New Life Movement."

I knew a little about the New Life Movement, a youth corps similar to the Y.M.C.A. No, it was really more like the National Guard. Their main thrust was making do.

Amoy Chang would say no more. We turned and retraced our steps. When we were in view of the apartment he stopped.

"I will see you again but I don't know when."

Then he was lost in the shadows. I returned to the apartment alone.

Remembering what Amoy told me, I began to think it strange that Mrs. Wu didn't go to work. She had no office. Not that the daily air raids left much time for that. With the populace crowded into shelters much of the time it was amazing that the business of the city proceeded as well as it did.

Whatever lingering doubts I had about Mrs. Wu's connection with Intelligence completely dissipated during the next air raid. She took me to the Intelligence shelter. Everyone there worked in Intelligence. Mrs. Wu arranged to have a pass issued in my name so that I could use the shelter when she wasn't with me. How strange I felt carrying an Intelligence card, finding myself exposed to Intelligence agents. Didn't they know I could identify them?

Afraid to stare, I sat with bowed head, eyes on my sandals as Mrs. Wu rehearsed me in Mandarin. When the All Clear sounded we returned home.

Traffic in and out of Mrs. Wu's apartment reminded me of a steamship office where people called for tickets or a sinister back room where men came to place bets. Men constantly streamed in to see Mrs. Wu—young men, middle-aged men, old men, civilian and military men, but for the most part affluent. They would bow and smile, bow and smile again, beg a favor or ask Mrs. Wu to speak to someone in their behalf.

In China it is necessary to have someone intercede, to speak for you. Success is based on knowing the right people in the right places. One of the right people, Mrs. Wu thoroughly enjoyed holding court. She sat like a diminutive dowager empress, dispensing favors with an artful wave of her fan. When the fan fluttered impatiently it signaled the audience was at an end.

I mentioned influence peddling in my diary. "It's a wonderful solution for America's unemployment problem and President Roosevelt would do well to consider creation of middlemen. But perhaps America is not yet ready for the squeeze."

Two young men called frequently. Definitely Intelligence types, with slick black hair and furtive black eyes, they looked like they'd just walked off the set at Paramount. In imitation of Americans, they used only their initials. K.C. and J.B. weren't twins but I quickly came to think of them that way. I never saw one without the other. They regarded me with suspicion and I had the impression they were here to spy on us. I didn't trust them.

I hadn't told Mrs. Wu about Amoy Chang and now that I'd seen her friends I was more determined than ever to keep Amoy's secret. Not only because he would have wanted it, but because I had no inkling what his problem involved.

Four days passed before I heard his timid knock again. One look at his panic-stricken face told me he was still in deep trouble.

"Let's go for a walk," he implored. He looked around furtively. "I'm sure I was followed."

Craning my neck I saw only an old man carrying sticks and he didn't seem to have any interest in us whatever.

"What's wrong, Amoy?"

"You're like a sister to me," he said, calling me sister in Cantonese. "And I speak to you now as my sister. Some day you'll be able to return to Shanghai. I never will. Tomorrow I'll be shot for what I've done."

"Amoy. Amoy!" I cried, anxiously clutching his arm. "Why?"

He swallowed with difficulty, his eyes misty. "Tell my parents what I have done. The circumstances . . ."

"Yes. If I can. But what have you done? I don't know . . ."

"It all began with the New Life Movement . . . when I didn't approve of the way things were going. I wrote a letter critical of my commanding officer . . . and sent it directly to Madame Chiang. He wasn't following her policies at all. I should have known a mere private cannot write to Madame. My letter was intercepted."

A great sorrow clutched my heart.

He blinked. "If you do not see me by six o'clock tomorrow night you'll know I have been shot."

"Oh, Amoy! I can't bear it."

Shivering, he mounted a brave smile. "Well, twenty-three skidoo."

"Twenty-three skidoo," I got out over a lump in my throat. I don't think Amoy heard me; he was gone.

Greatly troubled, I couldn't sleep for worrying about him. Filled with melancholy, I agonized all the next day. Had there ever been such a long miserable day? Would it never end?

"Why so gloomy?" Mrs. Wu asked several times.

I shrugged and said, "I don't know."

By five o'clock I could stand it no longer and went out to wait. In my mind I knew Amoy was dead but I so desperately wanted him to be alive. How could I prepare myself for bad news? If he'd been shot I'd never hear from him again. I felt a strange emptiness and tried not to think of bullets spanging into his body, remembering instead all the good times we'd had in Shanghai. At six o'clock I saw him.

"Amoy!" I screamed joyfully, rushing into his arms. Through my tears I saw Mrs. Wu watching us.

"I had to come," Amoy said. "I had to risk it."

"You're safe! You're safe," I said over and over.

"Far from it. They decided to give me another chance. The least little thing . . ." He left it there, his face ashen.

"Amoy, you can't know how happy I am. I'm so glad."

"I must go. I only came to tell you." He nodded toward the door. "She's already seen too much—your friend who works for General Lee."

"Where can I contact you?"

"You can't," he said with sudden force. "I'll contact you." Then he ran away.

"Who was that young man?" Mrs. Wu demanded when when I returned indoors.

"Just a friend I knew in Shanghai. He means nothing to me," I added hastily.

"I can see that," she said with a laugh. "You do not lie very well. I'm not sure you'd do for a job."

"I-I mean," I stammered. "I've never even *dated* him. He's just a friend."

Explanations futile, I dropped it. Something more important came to mind. "When *am* I going to get a job? I'm getting tired of sitting around here."

"Patience is a great virtue." Mrs. Wu smiled. "It all takes time. Tomorrow I'm taking you with me on a business trip."

We started at an early hour. "Chungking has changed," Mrs. Wu remarked. "But the people do not."

The Szechwanese are short pale people who regard strangers with apprehension. The years since the Generalissimo made Chungking his headquarters had done nothing to allay their suspicions. "They never have been the friendliest people," Mrs. Wu said. "They would rather stare than speak."

Little Miss Cheuk—I hadn't thought of her as other than Mrs. Wu for days—was short like the Szechwanese, but dark, even by Southern standards. Here in the North she really stood out. I had a pale complexion—a tall white ghost to be greeted with inherent skepticism. Between the two of us we couldn't get it right.

"They're treating us like carpetbaggers," I said in Cantonese, but I don't think Mrs. Wu understood the significance of my remark.

What had been a sleepy little town of 200,000 perched on a cliff, pointing its nose into the rising mists of the Yangtze, had swollen to a diverse caterwauling city of more than a million. The city swarmed with military personnel and refugees from the South.

"More and more, people from the South are taking over businesses," Mrs. Wu explained. "The Szechwanese are naturally less than inspired businessmen. They lack imagination."

No match for the sharpies and slickers from Shanghai, increasing numbers of old line Szechwanese businesses were sold to foreigners. Adding insult to injury, the usurpers had taken to naming their places for their old home towns. We had a Shanghai Laundry, Nanking Grocery, Shanghai Dry Cleaners and Canton Tailors, all repeated many times as countless signs attested.

We stopped at the Central Bank of China. I expected Mrs. Wu to receive preferential treatment, perhaps from the chief teller, but I was taken aback when we were ushered into the office of the bank manager. A distinguished man wearing a western business suit, he greeted me in fluent English. "I'm happy to meet you. Are you enjoying China?"

"It would be much more enjoyable if I had a job," I told him.

He smiled blandly and Mrs. Wu dismissed me with a curt, "You'll excuse us, please." I withdrew, sadly realizing that the visit had nothing to do with my getting a job.

"What made you think you'd be working for the Central Bank of China?" Mrs. Wu asked reproachfully when she returned.

"I don't know," I shrugged. The bank manager had treated Mrs. Wu as if she could do *him* a big favor.

She seemed prepared to let the matter drop but I was not. "When *am* I going to get a job?" I demanded impatiently.

"Soon," she answered deviously. "But first we must leave the city. It's the time of the full moon."

"Full moon?"

"If you think the bombing has been bad so far, wait till there's a full moon. Then it's really hell."

There were advantages in utilizing Chungking as a command center. Not only because it was a rock fortress with countless caves and tunnels but because of the London-type fog that shrouded the city much of the time. Because of the fog there were fewer air raids from September through March but now that spring was here the Japanese Air Force would return with a vengeance.

"We're going to stay with General Yur," Mrs. Wu said.

General Yur Ying-kai lived in the San Tung section far removed from strategic targets. It took two and one-half hours over a narrow bumpy road to cover the fifty miles. His mansion was set in beautifully landscaped grounds dotted with roses, shrubs and citrus trees. Situated near the War College where the General was a student, his palatial estate became a popular social center for selected junior officers from the barracks nearby.

Usually officers received their appointments by political pull and graduation from a War College. General Yur was one of those rare people who had worked his way up through the ranks. A war hero, General Yur distinguished himself at the Battle of Nanking, usually referred to as the Rape of Nanking because of the brutally sadistic way the Japanese raped, murdered, and mutilated young women in a week-long orgy after the city fell. As a result of Nanking, General Yur had a stiff left knee and a large hole in the kidney area of his back. A pleasant, altogether handsome man, his face held an inherent fury. Eyes falcon-fierce, there was a certain rigidity at his jaw. The ferocity was in no way lessened by his hair style, a crew cut.

"I was saved by an American in Nanking," he confided when he learned I was from New York. "He found me unconscious under a bridge and carried me to safety. The doctors wanted to cut off my leg but I absolutely refused.

General Yur Ying-Kai as a one-star general when in War College.

Tell me, what good would I be without a leg?"

"I'm glad a countryman of mine was able to help you." My brain clouded and I thought my comment sounded as if I wanted to collect a favor. "It makes me proud for my country and humble for myself," I added.

"Come," said the General. "I want to introduce you to my young officers. Do you dance?"

"Yes."

"Splendid! They are dying to have someone teach them American dances. Everything now is copying the Americans. The guns, the planes, the clothes, the food. It seems they cannot wait to copy the American decadence." A laugh boiled from within him. "Is that a joke?" he asked seriously. "I thought I might try it on some of my friends."

"Yes, it's a fine joke. Especially from the viewpoint of a missionary."

The General slapped his side, laughing uproariously. "You return my joke with one that's better. I think I'm going to like you very much, Do-yur."

I withheld a blunt, "I already like you," and cast my eyes down demurely. "Thank you."

Moments after the full moon rose to the tips of the orange trees we heard bombs dropping on Chungking answered by the *wap-wap* of anti-aircraft batteries on the ground.

For the first time I experienced a feeling of detachment, a totally selfish feeling, and a voice rose within me, counseling, "Your time may come tomorrow, but it is not yet. Waste not these precious moments for they will not come again."

What had been a gathering became a party. Mah-jong players circled two tables but most of the young officers clustered around me, eager to have me teach them the waltz and fox trot. We played *La Paloma* over and over. Usually we alternated with an instrumental version of *Green Eyes*. The young officers were so attentive to me that they frequently forgot to wind up the phonograph.

"You've already had a lesson (one-two-three, one-two-three)," I would say. "Don't you think it's time to wind the gramophone? That's it. One-two-three, one-two-three."

Mrs. Yur, the General's wife, was from the South so theirs was an unusual marriage in many respects. A charming hostess, she directed the serving of refreshments, and boys in loose fitting white jackets with padded shoulders moved about, bowing and smiling, serving tiny cakes and tea.

"Frightfully British, don't you think?" the General said in haltingly bad Cockney English. He abruptly switched to Cantonese. "You'd think they invented tea," he laughed.

"No, only tea time," I said, enjoying his sense of humor. It was obvious we enjoyed each other's company.

"I wonder when the damn British will realize what is going on in China? They don't seem to care who wins the war out here. With Hong Kong you'd think they would care."

"They're diplomats, not fighters," I said brightly, repeating something I heard my father say.

"*Hao, hao*," General Yur said, which meant, "Good, good."

I knew my father's comment would be repeated by him. He waved a cautioning finger at me and laughed. I didn't understand the significance of his gesture, but later I learned he frequently left a conversation with a mystifying remark or gesture. I understood better at the end of the week when Mrs. Wu and I returned to Chungking.

"You needn't be so impressed with him," she said acerbically. "General Yur can barely write. If it weren't for the young officers helping him he'd never make it through the War College."

Gradually a new pattern developed in my life. Long and heavy seas of loneliness were punctuated by sudden squalls of activity but even these became routine. We constantly ran to a bomb shelter. When we returned to the apartment a steady stream of men visited Mrs. Wu. Mostly I ignored them as I hunched before the tiny desk and penned letters to Daddy and a few old friends.

Usually we conducted our business early, before the raids. We made frequent visits to banks and the procedure never varied. We'd be ushered into the manager's private office, the manager would bow and smile and greet me in English. Then I'd be excused.

Our weekly trip to Dr. Wong, whom we'd met in the Cantonese shelter, also became routine. The doctor was treating Mrs. Wu for something and after each treatment he invited us to have supper with him and his wife. Here I met General Chang Kai-min, commanding officer of all gendarmes in China. They were the military police, the best trained, the elite of the Army, and reminded me of U.S. Marines.

General Chang Kai-min achieved renown as a commander and was a famous calligrapher as well. Chinese picture writing fascinated me. Little did I realize that one day my life would depend on his calligraphy. Like the other generals I'd met, he was gracious and unusually kind.

The six generals we met when Mrs. Wu took me to visit a prison were also gracious but had more on their minds. How surprised I was to see one of China's most famous generals. I'd have recognized him anywhere. His likeness—distinctive long hair and goatee—appeared in countless photographs and on posters. My shock was no less than any young American would have experienced in finding General MacArthur in prison.

We visited each in turn. As we entered their cells they bowed low, almost reverently.

"Please speak to him," I heard one plead. "I cannot do it myself." Another simply begged, "Help me."

"I will do what I can," Mrs. Wu promised.

"Why are they in jail?" I whispered as we were leaving.

Mrs. Wu waited till we were beyond earshot to respond. "For displeasing the Generalissimo," she said. "For failing in battle. For delay in following orders. One burned his retreat before it was time."

It was customary, I knew, to fire a city before the advancing Japanese but the general had issued the order prematurely, before the population had sufficient time to flee.

A majority of the generals imprisoned were southerners but the Generalissimo's wrath went much deeper than the North-South hostility. Generals were accustomed to acting like governors or lords with absolute power within their districts and were not inclined to respond to the centralized Nationalist government of Chiang Kai-shek. It reminded me once again how close China was to the feudal system with power divided among various warlords. They caused Chiang

Kai-shek a great deal of trouble and he spent as much time bringing dissident factions together as he did in fighting the war.

"I never heard of an American general being locked up," I told Mrs. Wu.

"Your American government is more just," she said.

"But how can you help someone in jail?"

"There are ways." Mrs. Wu smiled. "There are ways."

Chapter Seven

The happiness I found at San Tung followed me to Chungking. Young officers from the War College stopped at our apartment and invited me to accompany them. Mostly we watched basketball games between various military units. As welcome as the visits were, my spirits sagged miserably when the young men left and I became wretchedly depressed. There were too many idle hours, too many hours confined in an air raid shelter. I had not come to Chungking to spend my time writing letters or fleeing to a rabbit warren.

"When am I getting a job?" I demanded of Mrs. Wu.

"Soon," she said, dismissing my plea. "I've been talking to General Lee about it."

What did General Lee have to do with my getting a job? Restless displeasure rising within me, I found it difficult to maintain the calm serenity expected of me. It had to be remembered that Mrs. Wu was supporting me. My father had only supplied my trip ticket. Being dependent on her heightened my discomfiture.

"Can something be done, please?" I said. "I'm getting weary of all this waiting."

Mrs. Wu smiled condescendingly. "Let me have some of your pictures so I can give them to General Lee."

"Why does he need my pictures?" When she did not reply I concluded the job required Intelligence clearance.

Within days the cycle of the full moon repeated and we again prepared for relentless round-the-clock bombing. Mrs. Wu arranged another visit to San Tung, and I looked forward to renewing acquaintances with the young officers. Flattered by their attention, I admitted in my diary that I enjoyed it.

However, at dusk, the time we'd chosen for our journey, the bombing didn't stop. Eighty Japanese planes kept up a seven hour marathon that reduced much of the city to rubble.

With the raid continuing from daylight into darkness the

Jing Bao lanterns on the city wall had not been lit. I failed to understand the wisdom of lighting lanterns to signal a night attack. If enemy planes could see the light of a candle, could they not see the light of a Jing Bao lantern? Of course the lanterns were lowered and extinguished when enemy planes were yet a great distance away. Actually there was no problem with individuals refusing to turn off lights during a blackout. When Japanese planes were still some sixty miles distant the superintendent at the main power generating station simply pulled the master switch, plunging the entire city into darkness. To have lighted a candle would have attracted the rifle fire of a patrolling gendarme. Thus the blackout was scrupulously observed.

The following day a messenger came for Mrs. Wu.

"Very bad," was all I overheard him say before they left.

At nightfall Mrs. Wu returned visibly shaken. "It was horrible," she said, her face pale. "We were lucky we went to the Intelligence shelter yesterday. Something went wrong with the ventilation in the public shelter and three thousand people suffocated. They were bringing out the bodies. It was terrible." She collapsed on the little sofa, utterly exhausted.

I hastened to make some tea.

She pressed the little cup to her lips and drained it. "Looters were everywhere. Soldiers were cutting off fingers to get rings, stealing watches, hiding jewelry in their leggings."

I was appalled.

"I can understand them not being able to resist temptation," said Mrs. Wu. "Government officials were shocked to find so much gold. I don't know why. We all take our valuables into the shelter..."

"They never pay foot soldiers."

"Two of the looters were shot."

"That'll teach them a lesson," I replied with ample sarcasm.

Of course Mrs. Wu didn't understand me. So much of the Chinese philosophy involved the 'ultimate solution.' Couldn't they grasp that dead men learned nothing? The problem had its origin in the overabundance of humanity. It was a matter of economics. As a commodity man had little value. And as for mere woman—

"I talked with General Lee," Mrs. Wu announced. "He seemed interested when I told him that you'd been in the Philippines."

"Really?"

"Yes, he did. Now tell me everything you did in Manila."

It didn't take long to relate my Philippine experiences. "Aren't we going to San Tung?" I asked.

"No. We've been bombed so intensely I think we'll have a couple days respite."

Mrs. Wu's prediction proved correct. We enjoyed two days without bombing. A couple sorties with sporadic strafing meant the Japanese were reconditioning their planes in Hankow or Ichang or wherever they came from. It couldn't have been the weather that kept them away because the skies were clear of clouds and fog free. During the two days much of the city was rebuilt. Life went on for the survivors.

We continued to visit banks and bomb shelters and made the weekly journey to Dr. Wong followed by a dinner with the doctor and his wife. My job prospects were no brighter; Mrs. Wu continued to put me off, evading my questions.

"General Lee is thinking about it," she said.

The despair of death and destruction, the loneliness of being away from my family, the loss of self-respect for not having a job catapulted me into a dark mood that even the sun's warm rays could not dispell. A brisk walk from our apartment, a cluster of trees that had miraculously escaped any sign of bombing became an oasis in which I attempted to cast off my gloom. Beneath the dappled leaves I prayed I'd soon waken from the bad dream. The constant bombing and death left me emotionally drained.

As the month wore on we again faced the prospect of clear skies and a full moon. This time our plans were carefully laid and executed well in advance. General Yur Ying-kai greeted us warmly. The General and his lovely wife, a union of North and South, were as genuinely fond of me as I was of them.

When classes at the War College dismissed for the weekend, young officers clustered around, begging me to dance. A number of them became remarkably good at the fox trot. I liked being with them...

A messenger came for Mrs. Wu.

"I'm being beckoned," she said, her face grave. "I must return to the city."

"What is it?"

"I can't tell you," she said, her face dark with worry.

She left without explanation and when she did not return I went to General Yur.

"I'm so worried. Whatever could have happened to her?"

He shared my apprehension. "I don't know."

"But..."

"Don't worry, Do-yur. My wife and I want you to stay with us."

Three days passed without word. Had Mrs. Wu attempted to give me a message? Hundreds of times I turned her last words over in my mind. "I'm being beckoned." Was there a hidden significance to the word "beckoned," a code I should understand, or was it merely one of the rare instances when she employed a usage I found unusual? No answers to my probing, I again sought General Yur.

"I can't stand not knowing what happened. I'm going into town to see if I can find out."

"No, Do-yur," he said, shaking his head. "That would not be wise."

"I do not think it wise to stay here and do nothing. Neither of us knows what has happened. I have to try..."

A frown creased his brow. "It would be better if you remained here with us."

"I must go. I must."

Unable to convince me he threw up his arms. "Very well, if you must. But promise me that you'll come back to us as soon as you have an answer."

"Yes."

His expression held little hope.

In a rickety old truck, open in back, I sat on one of the benches as we rattled toward Chungking. Other than myself, the passengers were blue-clad country people, Szechwanese who reeked of garlic and onions, an unbearable stench when added to the nauseating stink of gasoline. After a terrible journey, I arrived in the city dusty, dirty, tired and completely out of sorts.

Looking forward to a refreshing spongebath and a change of clothes I approached the apartment... My heart leaped to my throat. The apartment was gone, bombed into oblivion. *Mrs. Wu, Ah-Fong, you can't be dead! You can't be!*

Overcome with grief, I refused to accept what I saw. The neighbors found me, dazed and in shock, digging in the rubble.

"Come away."

"No. I have to see if there is anything..."

"Come..."

"I have to find her. I can't let the rats get her."

"None of the occupants were killed, Miss."

"Are you sure?" I cried. Hope surged in my breast. Could I believe her words? "Where are they? Have you seen Mrs. Wu?"

"No. I only know that no one was killed."

"*Hao*." Perhaps I could still find her. But where...?

Alone now, who could help me? Dr. Wong and General Chang Kai-min? The Commandant of Gendarmes had always been kind...

As I was running up the hill I drew up gasping, completely out of breath. A sudden panic seared my brain. As far as I knew neither Dr. Wong nor General Chang were aware of Mrs. Wu's Intelligence connection. Asking them if they'd seen her might jeopardize her life. More importantly, it could jeopardize my own.

What could I do? Was there no one to whom I could turn? Certainly I couldn't go barging into Intelligence. I didn't even know where Mrs. Wu made contact.

Slowly retracing my steps, I formulated a plan. I decided to wait for an air raid. If I couldn't find them—

Wandering aimlessly, I waited for Japanese bombers but the sky above the city remained clear. An hour passed. "Japs, where are you?" I cried in desperation. "You're always here except when I need you."

At length the Sons of Heaven favored us with their usual gifts from above. The air raid siren was still shrieking when I flashed my pass at the Intelligence shelter. I sat down and waited, hoping to to be noticed.

Presently two young men appeared, the sleek pair I had seen so often at our apartment. They sat down, one on each side of me, making me feel uncomfortable.

"Don't say anything, just listen," K.C. warned, barely

moving his lips. "Your friend has been arrested."

My eyes widened. They glanced about furtively and traded frowns.

"Why?" I asked dumbly, ignoring their warning.

J.B. looked at the ceiling and spoke out of the corner of his mouth. "She talked too much."

"Where is she?" I whispered.

Neither of them replied.

"Check into a hotel," K.C. said.

I felt something next to my thigh and reached down without looking. My fingers closed over a note J.B. placed in my palm. I nodded, pretending conversation with K.C. After a few minutes I nonchalantly tucked the note in my pocket.

Soon All Clear sounded and I left the shelter. A safe distance away I removed the note from my pocket. A hotel name, nothing more. I found the hotel, checked in and waited. They didn't come and at length I fell asleep.

In the morning they wakened me. They had few answers to my many questions.

"She talked too much," J.B. said again.

"Where is she? May I see her?"

J.B. and K.C. looked at each other. K.C. nodded. "I guess so."

As they escorted me across town I realized they had decided the day before to take me to her.

We stopped at an old presidio no longer fortified. A phlange of offices formed a compound encircling several bungalows. Mrs. Wu sat in a brightly curtained room surrounded by modern furniture. A maid had been assigned to cook, clean, launder and otherwise attend her. The bungalow wasn't at all like the cold and forbidding prison in which we had visited the fallen generals.

"I'm quite comfortable," Mrs. Wu said. "I have the freedom of the compound but I rarely go out." She shrugged in resignation. There was no fear in her face, no sign of anxiety.

"But why? What happened?"

"Save your questions, please. What about you, Dorothy?"

"I'm all right. Did you know our apartment was bombed?"

Intelligence Agent J.B.

Intelligence Agent K.C.

"Yes."

"There is nothing left. Nothing to salvage."

"I suppose not."

Her little apricot face became pensively sad. "I want you to do something for me," she said, urgency in her voice. Picking up a pen she scratched out a note and handed it to me. "Take this to the manager of China Bank. He will give you something for me. Go quickly."

At the Bank of China the manager greeted me with a cordial, "Hello, Dorothy," and small talk in English.

I handed him the note.

Color drained from his face. "Ahem," he got out. "Excuse me, please."

A curt nod directed me to his private office to which he quickly returned.

"Give her this," he said, placing fifty thousand Chinese dollars in my hand. "Put it in your pocket." Then he bowed, signifying the meeting was at an end.

With my hand closed over the money I hurried back to Mrs. Wu. She accepted the money without comment, ignoring the wide-eyed, questioning look on my face.

"What are you going to do?" she asked.

"I have been invited to stay with General Yur."

"Good. He owes me a big favor. If you need to, remind him of that. I've been acting on his request to transfer to the south . . ."

"He's very kind."

"Do not tell him that you've seen me. Do not tell him where I am."

"What shall I say?"

"Tell him I've been sent on a mission." Mrs. Wu rose, standing not five feet tall in her striped cheong-sam, coal black eyes flashing, face severe as her words came out deliberate, precise and clear. "Dorothy, if you tell him where I am I will have you killed."

My breath caught. "I-I won't t-tell," I stammered. Chest constricted, I managed, "Y-You can depend on m-me."

"Hao."

She pressed some money into my hands, barely enough for a trip ticket on the truck to San Tung.

General Yur met me. "I couldn't find her," I said. "They

told me she went on a mission. I'm to check again in a week."

"That's good news, Do-yur. Then we have no cause to worry."

I felt completely miserable lying to General Yur. Deeply ashamed, my eyes could not meet his.

"Yes," I agreed quickly. "I-I went to our apartment. It was gone. Bombed. Nothing left."

"That's unfortunate," he said with momentary sadness. He quickly brightened. "It's providence. Now you must stay with us."

I had no immediate worries. General Yur and his wife made me comfortable. A week later I again made the thoroughly disagreeable trip to Chungking. Knowing that I'd be bouncing along in an open truck loaded with farmers, I dressed accordingly.

"I have a mission for you," Mrs. Wu said when I arrived. She thrust a note into my hand. "I want you to go to the Central Bank of China."

This time I returned with sixty thousand dollars. What was she doing with the money? Since my last visit she had acquired some colorful new pillows, several quilts and two fancy silk dresses, but fifty thousand dollars worth? Of course, there was always the squeeze—bribes to be paid.

Mrs. Wu snapped her fingers. The maid appeared with a tall girl. "Here is someone I want you to meet. This is Su Ling."

We chatted pleasantly until conversation shifted to people and places in the Philippines. I remembered many of the places of which the tall girl spoke.

A curt nod from Mrs. Wu dismissed the girl. "Su Ling fouled up in Manila. *She* was sent home in disgrace."

She? It suddenly became clear to me. Mrs. Wu was recruiting me to take Su Ling's place in the Philippines! My brain reeled. *You've been trying to recruit me for a Philippine assignment all along. I want no part of this.* My face betrayed me.

Mrs. Wu read my rebellious thoughts but her face remained impassive. She called after me, "Dorothy. Remember what I said about not telling General Yur."

"I-I remember," I gulped.

Trapped.

Deceiving General Yur was like lying to Father. I tried to be blasé and nonchalant, as if Mrs. Wu's extended assignment was as natural as the oranges on his trees. My carefree demeanor failed to calm the knot twisting in my stomach. I lied. Lied! And in a week I would be asked to lie again.

Was there no way out? Time became an eternity.

To calm my fears, to get out of the house, I walked General Yur's enormous German police dog. We had not gone far when I noticed a strange looking soldier loitering nearby. He glanced back and forth, trying to make up his mind. Suddenly he ran up, pressed a note into my hand and fled into the grove.

From Amoy Chang, the note read, "I want to let you know I'm leaving Chungking. I don't know if I'll ever see you again. Take care of yourself."

I'd never heard of General Yur or San Tung when I last saw Amoy. How had he known where to find me? He—or someone—had been watching me. How else could his messenger have found me?

A great warmth circled my heart as I thought of Amoy Chang and remembered our horses racing . . . "Twenty-three skidoo," I whispered. I never heard of Amoy again.

Within the week I made another trip to Chungking, visited a different bank and carried fifty thousand dollars to Mrs. Wu. When I returned to San Tung, General Yur was waiting. He led the way, limping toward his study. Once inside, he whirled on me, his face mercilessly cruel, his eyes blazing. "Do-yur, you lied to me!" he shouted, shaking his fist in my face.

Completely dishonored, tears began to course down my cheeks.

"I know Mrs. Wu has been arrested," he stormed. "I know that she is in custody."

"How do you know?" I choked.

"Why did you lie to me?" he demanded angrily.

"Because she said she would have me killed if I told you," I cried, blurting out two or three words at a time between hysterical sobs. "I was afraid she would kill me." My tears became a torrent.

He was silent for a time. "She wrote some letters to my

young officers," he said, indicating several on his desk. "She told them to have nothing to do with you."

I remembered that none of the young men from the college had come to the house the previous weekend. There had been no walks in the garden, no mah-jong games, no dancing. So that was the reason.

"She said she picked you off the street working as a prostitute and warned them to beware of you. She threatened that if they continued to see you their positions would be endangered, their careers ruined."

"How could she do this to me?" I wailed. "How could she?"

He let me cry myself out. "I've been watching you," he said at length. "I want to help you."

"I don't understand her," I snuffled.

"Dorothy, I know you are none of the things she says you are. I am a fair judge of people and I want to help you."

"After living under your roof and lying to you? After all I . . ." I could not believe his kindness.

"What will you do now?" he asked.

"Return to my father," I said. "Father will buy my ticket. I'll wire him for money, ask him to send it at once."

General Yur assisted me in sending a telegram to my father and in a few days I had the money. This time it was I who asked for a private meeting.

"I want to see Mrs. Wu once more . . . to tell her that I'm leaving."

"That woman? I wouldn't," he advised. "What can she do for you except cause you more grief? You're asking for trouble."

"I have to get clearance. I can't leave the city without clearance."

"I know," he said dismally. "That could be a big problem. I will go with you to Chungking and help in any way I can. But I can not . . . will not see her."

General Yur and a young officer, Choi Kwok-yurn, who was fond of me, accompanied me to the city. Whether Choi had been asked by the General, selected by his fellow officers, or came of his own accord, I never learned. I was extremely grateful for his presence. On arrival in Chungking they promised to wait for me at a restaurant.

"After I see Mrs. Wu and get my clearance I'll be back," I told them.

Leaving them, I proceeded to the detention compound where I found Mrs. Wu sitting in her little cottage as usual. Neither surprised nor displeased to see me, her face displayed no emotion as we exchanged greetings. Then I flared, "How could you do that to me—writing all those letters? All those despicable lies!"

She made no reply. She averted her face.

"How could you turn all those people against me?" I raged. "I've had enough of your tyranny. I'm leaving this place and going home to Kukong. Back to my father."

A raw, touched nerve twitched at the corner of her mouth. She broke into tears. "Oh no, please don't go," she pleaded. "Please don't go. Forgive me for what I have done. I have been under such a strain. I didn't realize what I was doing."

"No, I'm going."

"Please don't. I'll make amends. Please don't go. You're my only link to the outside world. Without you, I cannot go on. I need you, Dorothy."

"I'm sorry," I said.

"There is no one else."

When she stopped crying I told her, "I'll need clearance . . ."

She turned away. "Don't expect me to help you."

"Then I'll help myself!"

Her voice became threatening. "You can't. Your pictures are on file with Intelligence. If you try to leave the city you'll be apprehended in twenty-four hours."

My face flushed with anger. "I've had enough of your threats and maneuverings," I shouted, turning my back.

"Don't forget all I've done for you. I brought you to Chungking. I took care of you. I gave you a chance to be somebody!"

"Goodby!"

"Don't go," she screamed. "I, Madame Wu, forbid it!"

Madame Wu? You must be having delusions. The title Madame is appropriate only for Madame Chiang Kai-shek. I stalked away, her pleas lost to my ears.

There was no turning back now. I had to flee the city before Mrs. Wu had me killed.

No time to lose.

I remembered General Chang Kai-min, Commandant of Gendarmes, with whom we'd so often dined. He had authority to give me clearance, but where could he be found?

Fortunately, some people on the street knew the location of Gendarme headquarters and when I arrived the General greeted me warmly.

"I need clearance to leave the city," I said. "I've decided to go home."

General Chang Kai-min reached for his brush. "Very well." In his renowned calligrapher's hand he began to write. "I'm sure your father will be happy to see you."

"I'd rather return to my father than go on some mission to the Philippines for General Lee," I babbled. "I didn't know Mrs. Wu was with Intelligence. I'm an American. I can't work for a foreign government."

General Chang's head snapped up, his hand jerked. His smile disappeared as color drained from his face. "I can't give you clearance," he gasped. "Not if you're working for General Lee! It isn't possible."

"But I'm *not* working for General Lee," I said, bursting into tears, cursing my stupid wagging tongue.

"I'm sorry. You'll have to see General Lee." He wrote out General Lee's headquarters address.

Heartbroken, I set out. Before I had gone far an air raid siren shrieked and I scurried for cover. "Curse you, bloody Japs!"

I found a shelter and when All Clear sounded I rented a ricksha.

Intelligence headquarters was located in a mammoth cave. From ground level I walked down three hundred steps to reach the bottom. A sentry halted me and gave me a curious look.

"May I see General Lee?" I asked, speaking Mandarin.

"He will not see you."

"He will see me," I said confidently.

"Wait," said the sentry.

He turned to talk with another sentry and I overheard the word, "Foreigner." If that's what it took to see the Chief of Intelligence, for once I was glad I looked like a foreigner.

A colonel came out and smiled politely. "What can I do for you?"

I repeated my request. "Just give the General my name."

The colonel disappeared and presently General Lee came out, smiling, bowing, extending his hand in an avuncular manner. "Yes, Miss Yuen," he said blandly. "Please come into my office."

I took a seat across the desk.

"We're sorry Mrs. Wu is in custody," he said gently. "Such things happen."

I nodded.

"She overstepped her power," he went on.

Like threatening to have me killed? I didn't care anything about Mrs. Wu just then. I thought only of myself. "It's time I went home," I told him. "To Kukong and my father. For that I need clearance. And I'd like to have my photographs back."

"Yes, of course," he said pleasantly. Opening the top drawer of the desk he took them out.

I was surprised they were so instantly available.

"I never did anything with them," he said. "We were aware of the situation. With Mrs. Wu . . ." He shrugged and rolled his palms. "I'll give you a note."

When he finished writing he handed me the note and my pictures. My heart leaped with joy. I gushed effusive thanks, ran up the three hundred steps and bounded into a ricksha for the return trip across town.

Soon I was back in the office of the Commandant of Gendarmes. General Chang looked at General Lee's note and nodded. Smiling, he wrote out a pass in his beautiful hand. "Miss Yuen is an overseas student returning to Kukong. Please extend her every courtesy."

With General Chang's gendarmes in charge of all inspection stations, ports of authority and military exits, the pass would be invaluable. I thanked him and raced across town again, wondering if General Yur and Choi Kwok-yurn still waited for me at the restaurant.

I found them at a corner table. "I didn't expect to see you," I said. "I thought you might have grown tired of waiting."

"We would have waited longer," General Yur assured me. "We were making arrangements to smuggle you across the river."

I held up the pass. "That won't be necessary."

"I'm glad," the General said with obvious relief.

He and Choi stayed until my bus arrived. As it squeaked to a halt my joy dimmed. I'd been expecting the same type of bus in which Ah-Fong and I arrived seven months earlier. I boggled at the sight of a dilapidated, flat-bed, open-air truck, the same kind used to transport farmers from San Tung to Chungking.

Suppressing my disappointment, I climbed aboard, the only girl with a group of crude soldiers. Waving goodby to General Yur, I hoped the soldiers would remember I was a friend of a General and not bother me.

Crossing the river, the truck swerved to negotiate the perilous seventy-two hairpin turns. I never looked back. There was nothing I wanted to see in Chungking.

Without a servant, I had to carry my own bags and prepare meals. I wished Ah-Fong was travelling with me again but I hadn't seen him since shortly before our apartment was bombed. Frightened to be with the soldiers, I sat with my face downturned and uttered not a word.

At nightfall the bus stopped. Because it was a rule that women never travelled alone, I encountered a problem. The inn only provided communal rooms and I certainly didn't want to sleep with four soldiers. I did what I had to do. One room had five beds. I rented all five, went inside and closed the door.

At dawn we resumed our journey and continued till midday when gendarmes stopped us to examine our passes. An officer heard me give them my destination. Later, he approached the spot where I sat eating my lunch.

"You look so frightened. I heard you talking. You speak Cantonese. I'm Cantonese. May I sit here and eat my lunch?"

We fell into Cantonese and he told me about his family. I enjoyed having someone with whom I could talk and when the journey resumed our conversation made the afternoon pass quickly.

At night I again faced a lodging problem. The hotel was so crowded I was unable to rent a room. However, I managed to get a bed in an open hallway.

"Don't worry," said an officer I found there. "I'll keep an eye on you."

I didn't trust him but there were no alternatives. Frightened and weary, I accepted my fate. Climbing into the bunk, which was more comfortable than the jarring truck, I soon fell asleep.

This officer, too, proved to be a friend and I was sorry I'd been so suspicious of him.

"Do you have anyone meeting you?" he asked when we reached Kweilin.

"No," I said.

"Do you have a place to stay?"

"No."

"Let me introduce you to my brother-in-law."

The brother-in-law, a man of influence, interceded in my behalf at the hotel and I was given a room. My luck changed when they told me there would be no space on the bus for at least four days.

"Four days? It can't be." *My money will never last that long.*

Again the brother-in-law interceded. Usually buses maintained a vacant seat for late-arriving dignitaries or government officials. With the brother-in-law's influence they assigned me the normally vacant seat. How relieved I felt to be continuing my journey! Without money I would have been in dire straits.

Before we reached Hengyang, armed sentries halted the bus and ordered us to transfer to a train. The conductor who met us did not speak Cantonese and my attempts to communicate with him in Mandarin aroused the attention of a cold-eyed tea merchant. The merchant's persistent stare left me disquieted.

The train moved slowly under cover of darkness. At three o'clock in the morning it stopped at a deserted station five miles from civilization.

"The tracks have been bombed. There'll be a brief delay . . ."

The tea merchant smiled at me with more than a casual interest.

I did not return his smile.

He bowed gently and smiled again. "May I help you? Do you wish to go to Hengyang? Is there someone to meet you? My servant can assist you."

I could not find it in me to respond.

"Do you have a hotel? A place to sleep?" he pressed.

I did not wish to talk with him but neither did I desire to stand in the darkened countryside alone. How could I carry my bag five miles?

"No," I said. "I didn't expect to stop here..."

"I have a friend," he went on. "She owns the hotel."

A chill ascended my spine. *It's only the night cold.*

His servant placed my bag on a pedicab.

When we reached the hotel, if a hotel it was, I saw two massive doors barred against the night. The tea merchant knocked impatiently and finally a woman came.

He introduced himself.

"Ah, yes," the woman said.

"Do you have a room?"

The woman glanced from him to me and back again. "Yes, we have a room," she said, an impish look on her large plain face. Obviously she thought we'd be sleeping together.

"I need a room for *myself*," I told her.

"Yes," the merchant asserted. "She needs a room by herself."

"Oh," the woman said, looking disappointed. "Oh. Very well, I have a client who's gone for the night. You may use his room. He won't mind."

She padded ahead of me, her bare feet slapping the floor. Men's clothing lay strewn about the room. Fortunately, there was no sign of a man. Only after I saw the door could be bolted from the inside did I agree to stay. When the woman left I shot the bolt and slept soundly.

It was late by the time I awakened and made my way to the main hall.

"Join us for breakfast," the woman called. "Your friend has already gone."

Just then the tea merchant walked into the room.

"I purchased your ticket for Kukong," he said, handing it to me. "But I do not go south myself. My business takes me to the west so I must leave you."

"Allow me to pay you," I said.

"By no means."

He continued to refuse until I said, "In my country a woman always pays her own way. Don't shame me. Please allow me to save face."

He accepted my money, accompanied me to the station and said goodby. I thought my traveling troubles were over.

The conductor directed me to a comfortable stateroom and pointed to an upper berth. A military man lounged there.

"Oh no!" I groaned in disgust. "Not again."

"So you have a problem," the conductor said with total indifference. "There's nothing I can do."

"You can get me another berth. Is there another woman on the train?"

"Perhaps."

"Would you see, please?"

We found a woman with a small child who was also assigned a stateroom with a man unknown to her. Together we persuaded the reluctant conductor to make a switch.

At length the train clanked and screeched to a halt in familiar surroundings. Was I really home in Kukong?

After all I've been through . . . I can hardly believe it.

The welcome at the station presaged the one I would receive at home. As I disembarked the Japanese launched a raid. I waited for the bombers to leave, then waited hours for my father to arrive.

"I'm so glad to be home," I wept as I rushed into his arms.

"Welcome home, Dorothy."

Mother's welcome was restrained, overshadowed by her disappointment in me. "When are you going to earn your keep?" she railed. "You spent your father's money coming and going. What have you got to show for it? Nothing! You never pay your own way!"

I hung my head in shame, choking back tears.

"When I was sixteen, I was on my own," Mother said. "You come slinking home, nineteen years of age and no job yet."

I turned my face toward Father, seeking comfort, but found none. He sat unconcerned, allowing my mother's raving to run its course. How I longed to run away! But there was no place for me to go.

"You impossible child," Mother scolded. "Are you going to get to work around here?"

"I'll try," I squeaked. "Yes."

Not one word did I tell Father or the family about what had transpired in Chungking. I didn't even tell them about Mrs. Wu. I was a failure, abject and complete.

My fears that Mrs. Wu would send a hatchet man gradually subsided. For six months I worked very hard. Not once did I venture into Kukong with its bustle and bombs. Finally, on a day when Father paid his troops and dispatched two trucks for their use, I summoned the courage and joined them on a happy trip to town.

We arrived at night and the city was dark. A single light hung in a giant arch where the two main roads intersected in the middle of town. As I stepped out of the shadows into the circle of light I came face to face with the two young men from Intelligence.

J.B. and K.C. looked at me.

I looked at them. My heart leaped to my throat. There was no place to hide. Didn't they know I had clearance? But how could I prove it? General Chang's elegantly written pass remained in my suitcase at home. I felt faint—numb—all life drained from me. Fear constricted my chest. "Y-You're n-not looking for me?" I stammered, my voice cracking.

"No," J.B. replied. "Would you like to work for us?"

My breathing resumed. New life surged into my lungs. *Work for Intelligence?* Everything within me recoiled. Rising above naked fear I heard myself blurt, "I'm not at all interested in the type of work you're doing."

"We understand, Do-yur," J.B. said.

His almost gentle tone prompted me to ask, "Is Mrs. Wu still in custody?"

"Yes," K.C. said, unsmiling.

Then they disappeared into the night, as if they had never been.

Chapter Eight

On my return to Kukong I began a season of disgrace. How keenly I felt my inadequacies. For years my education had been shamefully neglected and now I cursed my stupidity. An idle daydream—in New York I'd be intelligent—offered little solace. If I awakened and found myself in New York, I'd still be a grade school dropout.

"Really," I told Father, "there's nothing as important as a good education."

After a night of meditation he came to me. "It's time we thought about school again."

My pulse quickened and happiness warmed my heart. "That's wonderful," I said. With my education continued, I'd be able to get out of the house a few hours each day.

"A military school has opened across town," Father said. "I want you to enroll Gloria, Jack and Edna."

"And me?" I couldn't wait.

"No," he said. "Not now."

My dream shattered like a duck egg hurled on jagged rocks. Seeing my crestfallen look, he attempted to console me with reason.

"Your mother would be too lonely if we left her alone. She needs someone here who can speak English. In her weakened condition she needs the help of a full grown woman. We have to take care of her."

"Yes, Father," I choked, tears glistening in my eyes. After the expense of my Chungking fiasco, I dared not ask for another thing.

"When you were away your mother had a very bad time. We gave her dong quei but even that didn't help."

Believed to have great regenerative powers, dong quei is the dark meat of a black skinned chicken that, surprisingly, has white feathers.

"We took her to a mission hospital in Kukong," Father went on. "A British doctor said she has malaria—among other things. I really need you to be the woman of the house,

Dorothy. I'm depending on you."

I swallowed the lump in my throat and buried my sadness deep within me. As directed, I enrolled Jack and Gloria in military school but Edna was too advanced in her studies and it was necessary to find another school for her. Because the military school was distant, Jack and Gloria boarded there. Every other weekend they came home for the supply of clothing I had washed and ironed. On alternate weekends I took their clothes to school. It was a tedious heartbreaking ritual and I longed for the workfree days I'd known in Chungking. Completely unhappy, no joy sang in my heart.

The veil of sadness did not settle on me alone. The misery of war touched everyone. Sometimes the cackle of death came from guns held by our own troops. A colonel in charge of the Eleventh Repair Factory, Father's counterpart, was summoned before a military tribunal and condemned for appropriating trucks to his own use.

"I would like you to be with the widow," Father said. "They're strangers here. The family has no one. It would be a nice gesture on our part."

Although the Colonel had yet to be executed, Father was in no way disrespectful. On the contrary, pretending that the man was already dead prepared for the finality of judgment and helped to ease the burden. As Father requested, we walked to headquarters, Mother and I.

We joined a small cluster of people and watched as they led the Colonel out. His head hung in shame until he glimpsed his family. Encouraged, the Colonel squared his shoulders and raised his gaze in a moment of dignity before the blindfold slipped into place. The guns of the firing squad cracked and he crumpled.

I saw no dignity in his death. Amid the loud wailing of his family, friends went to the limp form and bore him away. Greatly comforted by our presence, the widow reached out and touched mother.

Mother impressed me with her courage. She had nothing to say about what we had seen. I wondered if she had been thinking as I had, that it might have been Daddy standing there. Using an Army truck to transport his family from Hsingning to Kukong and sending a truck to get Ah-Lau and the furniture had certainly been appropriating Army trucks to his own purposes. The thought sent a chill up my spine.

War presents grotesque and often interesting perspectives. A rock thrown into a pool makes a splash and creates waves, but we were so remote inside China that many shock waves dissipated by the time they reached us. One evening in December Daddy came home with some news.

"Sweetie, the Americans have joined the war."

"Oh," Mother said.

"The British too. It's a good thing you're not in Shanghai. The Japs have taken over the International Settlement and interned all aliens. Hong Kong is no longer in British hands."

"My word!"

"The Japs made a stupid blunder—attacked the United States." Father paused, his face expectant. "It was a stupid blunder," he repeated, standing there like a little boy waiting for Mother to respond.

"Attack?" Mother said. "They attacked the United States?"

It was not the question Father wanted but he spoke the line he had obviously rehearsed. "Can a stork swallow an eagle?"

"Attacked where?" Mother asked.

"That's a good comparison, Daddy," I said.

"I thought so too." He smiled. "If I were back in Shanghai I would give it to my friend who owns the newspaper."

"Where was the attack?" Mother persisted.

"Hawaii," said Father. "They bombed the naval shipyard."

"For a minute I thought it was California," Mother said.

"Not yet," said Father. "I don't understand how the Japanese can fight on so many fronts and not get overextended. With the United States in the war, the Japanese will divert some of the divisions facing us. They'll have to."

Father's hopes that the war would be shortened, that the situation would become easier for China, met with disappointment. Six months—even a year—after the United States entered the war, we failed to notice the least effect.

News that the International Settlement had been occupied heightened my concern for friends who remained. A number of my letters went unanswered but correspondence with Tiger dos Remedios continued uninterrupted. As a Portuguese citizen he hadn't been interned and continued to have the freedom of Shanghai. He reported on the welfare of friends and came to my aid when I asked for an English dictionary.

"Something must be done about my education," I wrote. "If I had a dictionary and studied it faithfully, at least I would sound intelligent."

Tiger responded, "Finding the object of your request is not one-tenth as difficult as sending it. The government prohibits the mailing of parcels."

I cursed the Chinese puppet regime installed by the conquerors. "Traitors! You're worse than the bloody Japs!"

Tiger found a way. I began receiving newspapers. Rolled in the first issue I found the yet neatly bound A section of a dictionary. In a few weeks the B section arrived. Eventually I received everything except XYZ. While the others were in school, whenever I could, I studied my dictionary.

Jack and Gloria arrived home for the weekend looking thin and pale. No one worried until I noticed they were listless and refused to go outdoors. I called it to Father's attention and in questioning them we learned their diet at military school consisted solely of rice and a few vegetables.

"They're starving," I said.

"Malnutrition," Father said at the same instant. "We'll have dong quei this weekend and when they go back to school I want you to pack a basket of food for them. I'm going to think about this, Dorothy."

As a result of Father's deep thoughts the soldiers built a new seven room house for us on the southern outskirts of Kukong, just across the river. A rather plain house, its seven rooms, including three bedrooms, a dining room, living room and kitchen, were luxurious to us. Like the others it had a wooden floor, but for the first time we also enjoyed a wooden roof.

Here we remained for more than two years while Jack and Gloria commuted and Edna walked to high school, a short distance down the sunrise path. A hospital on our side of the river was also within walking distance.

The location pleased Father. "Now we won't have to worry about getting you there, Sweetie. No more riding a truck into town to see a doctor."

"That's a relief," said Mother.

Knowing what it meant to flee a home in the face of an advancing army, we delighted in our two homes. Father maintained the one near headquarters and stayed there whenever he was unable to come to Kukong. For a time he had one of his favorite teakwood chairs in each house.

For Mother the hospital became a social center, a place where she could meet people who spoke English and hear the latest gossip. She couldn't wait to tell me about General Pan, whom she called Pun—not an example of Mother's perverse sense of humor. It merely illustrated variations in Chinese dialect. The General was known as Pan in Mandarin, Pun in Cantonese. The Chinese learned to cope with the fact that a name changed with the dialect. A map in Mandarin bore little resemblance to the same map printed in Cantonese. Wouldn't it be something, I thought, if people in Denver had a different name for New York? I smiled as I reflected that a lot of people did have different names for New York. Changing names was in reality no more unusual than the Chinese way of beginning a book on the last page or using a surname first.

"I think it's terrible," Mother said.

At that moment I saw two of General Pan's four wives walking ahead of us and knew precisely whereof she spoke. "At least he doesn't make all of them live together," I reasoned.

"Hmmmpft," Mother sniffed. "You don't understand. That's just his way of casting off the first wife."

General Pan's first wife—the old wife—lived directly across the road from our house. This marriage had been arranged by a matchmaker in accordance with ancient traditions.

"Perhaps you're right."

"I know I'm right," Mother said. "Actually, I feel sorry for them." She nodded in the direction of wives number two and three.

They continued to walk down the sunset path toward their house two miles away. A mile north of this location stood the home of wife number four.

I could hear the voice of a British nurse when Mother

continued. "Last year she was a servant in the General's home with no standing whatever. This year she's a wife. It's getting so a person doesn't know what to call her."

"Somehow I think you'll think of something," I said with a smile.

"There ought to be a law against it." Mother continued to vituperate as we entered our front door. "I think it's positively un-Christian."

Father spoke up. "I think that's the least that can be said about it." Home from headquarters, he sat in his favorite chair.

"Hi, Daddy," I said.

He smiled. "I knew she was talking about General Pan."

Accustomed to frequent gossip about General Pan's wives and the horrors of war, never in a week of fantasies could I have imagined the bizarre turn of events that would shock and sadden us all.

We had just undergone a massive air raid and I was in Au's store shopping when a man rushed in, wildly excited. "Did you hear the news?" he exclaimed. "Three of General Pan's wives were killed!"

I rushed home to tell Father.

He pondered a moment. "You must go and pay our respects. Offer General Pan our condolences."

I proceeded to dress in white, although light blue would have been appropriate. It didn't take long to walk two miles.

Spectators at the scene explained that wife number four and her child had come to visit wives two and three. When the air raid began everyone rushed for the shelter, a small earth-covered cave.

I pressed forward to the side of a bruised and badly shaken General Pan. "There wasn't room for everyone and when the wives and child were safely inside I threw myself under a tree. The bomb hit . . . right in the doorway." He broke down sobbing. "I was almost buried . . ."

Solemn-faced people stirred the earth around the giant crater, gathering up remains. The only identifiable part was half the body of the child. As people went about the grisly task, a mound of flesh accumulated in the yard.

A man ran up, tenderly carrying a hand. "I found it on my roof," he said, his face pained.

I hastened to make condolences to General Pan and left. Completely dazed, I doubted if he'd remember my presence.

A short time after I returned home we saw some coolies carrying a sedan chair, heading for the home of General Pan's first wife. In a state of collapse, General Pan had to be carried inside.

"Hmmpft. So Pun has no place else to go," Mother observed, directing a hard-jawed stare at the house across the road. "Serves him right. He never should have had four wives in the first place."

The cavity in the earth and the mound of flesh continued to haunt my mind. For a time I avoided the area, turning from the road before I reached the spot, but as the days went by the horrible memory faded to become just another tragedy of war. I would walk the sunset path again in a happier mood.

The dramatic upturn in my social life began with a surprise encounter. On the way to Au's store I heard, "Do-yur. Do-yur!"

Turning, I saw General Yur in the crowd and ran to him.

"General Yur!"

"Do-yur!"

"I can't believe it."

"I had to look twice to make sure my eyes weren't deceiving me." His crew cut glistened in the sunlight like a black hair brush.

"How good it is to see you! What are you doing here in Kukong?"

"Many of us who graduated from the War College have been sent here," he said. "You remember Choi, Wong and Ho. They're here. And several of the others."

"I'd like to see them again. I think often of the good times we had in San Tung. Your wife, how is she?"

"She is well."

"I imagine she likes it here. I recall she's from the South."

"Yes." He smiled. "She is a Southerner."

"Tell her hello for me. And tell her I remember her with gratitude. I owe you both more than I can ever repay. When I think of—"

He waved an aide aside, took a couple limping steps and

bent toward me. "I think of those days too. It isn't often that I offer to smuggle a girl out of the nation's capitol."

"Your transfer to the South—did Mrs. Wu have anything to do with that?"

"No," he said matter-of-factly. "I did that on my own. I'm glad that woman no longer touches my life. She's like a bomb with a short fuse. Totally unpredictable."

"Have you heard of her?"

"I do not concern myself with her." He read disappointment in my face and softened his tone. "The last I heard of her she was still under house arrest. You're still a friend of hers after all she did to you? Loyalty. That's a good trait, Do-yur, but it can be overdone."

"I suppose so. I should be very angry at her. But I can't help feeling sorry for her too. I wasn't being loyal. Only curious."

"Well, let us talk no more of her. We're having a party Saturday night and I want you to come. Your friends from the War College will be there. We'll have a fine reunion. Say you can come. Say you'll be there."

"Of course. If you tell me where it is."

General Yur gestured. "Along the river road. Not far beyond the place where General Pan's wives—" He broke off. "You can't miss it. I'm not going to tell the junior officers. Your presence will be a big surprise." He clapped his hands and rubbed them with enthusiasm.

"There is something," I hesitated. "If you ever meet my father or mother, they know nothing about what went on in Chungking. Only that I failed to find a job—"

"Don't worry. They'll learn nothing from me. What can I say? Your ideals were always the highest."

"Be sure to say hello to your wife."

"I will. I can't wait to see the faces of my officers when they see you." Smiling, he waved goodby.

On Saturday night I walked into the sunset. In the months that followed I would never walk home alone. The weekend parties, the nah-jong games at General Yur's home were as enjoyable as they'd been at San Tung, but there was a new dimension. A number of the young officers fell in love and wanted to marry me.

"But I don't love you," I told each of them.

"What difference does that make?" asked Choi Kwok-yurn, the most persistent of my suitors. "I love you and want to marry you."

On my frantic last day in Chungking, Choi along with General Yur had escorted me and plotted my escape. Had I been unable to obtain a pass he would have risked his career to smuggle me across the river. As a friend, I owed him much.

"You already have a wife," I said.

"That was arranged . . . a country marriage. It hardly counts."

"That's what you'll say when you take wife number three. No, good friend, I cannot marry you."

"Dorothy, with you I wouldn't need wife number three. Not ever. I can promise you a future now that I've graduated from the War College. It's like your West Point, you know. Everyone who graduates from the War College becomes a big success."

"I'm sorry. No."

"I know you won't marry me as long as I have another wife. That's the way of you Americans. I've thought about it . . . and decided. I'll get rid of my country wife . . . I'll divorce her. Then there'll be just the two of us."

"I couldn't ask you to do that."

"You didn't ask me. It was my decision alone."

"But I'd feel as if I had. In my country a woman of quality would never come between a man and his wife." I reached out and touched his hand. "You will always be my friend, Kwok-yurn."

"But I don't want to be your friend. I mean, I want to be more than your friend."

"Oh, you're so impulsive."

Kwok-yurn laughed. We both knew he'd try again.

Another officer whom I taught dancing at San Tung enjoyed walking the river road. Possessed of a curious blend of humor and logic, Ho Hon-si would have made a fine actor. A heavy shock of hair over a long thin face made him seem taller.

We stopped at a quiet place; the moon slipped behind a cloud.

"Dorothy," he said. "When I realize how many of us want

Ho Hon-si, one of Dorothy's ardent suitors.

to marry you I feel like a nameless foot soldier. There you are, calling the cadence, and we're all marching, marching, marching . . . right over a cliff."

"You can always fall out of line and stop marching," I teased.

"And miss all this delightful agony? I think not. Dorothy, you're so refreshing. So gay. Do you think I could stop seeing you? Me, a mere moth to your flame?"

"Ho Hon-si, you're so funny."

"The lady is laughing at me."

"I'm not laughing at you. You make me laugh."

"And you give me much happiness. Will you marry me?"

"No, Ho Hon-si. For the eighty-third time, no."

"Even when you reject me I cannot get angry. Is it any wonder we all love you?"

"If there were more girls around here, fewer of you would notice me."

"That's not true. You'd be noticed wherever you went. You have such presence. There's something about you that makes people want to do things for you. Have you not noticed how I open doors for you and give you other little courtesies?"

"It hasn't escaped me. I'm aware that all the officers treat me as an American, as a foreigner."

"No. We treat you warmly."

"That's what I mean. I am treated warmly, as you say, not like a Chinese girl. You just bragged how you open doors for me. You wouldn't do that for a Chinese girl."

"You've trapped me with my own words." He laughed and rubbed his chin pensively. After a moment of silence he said, "Ah, I see. We treat you special. A Chinese girl is ignored, treated in a more coarse manner. Not so special."

"Yes, and if I married one of you the special treatment would soon end. I'd be expected to become a traditional wife. That would create problems. Why do I want to make my situation worse? I've got enough trouble being a housekeeper for Mother. I know that here in China the bride is in reality the property of her husband's parents. After the wedding it's her duty to care for them, to prepare their meals, keep the house clean, bow and scrape, do all the mother-in-law asks."

"What you say is true," Ho Hon-si said soberly. "It's all very logical. That's why the parents of the groom pay for a big wedding. If they didn't acquire the services of the bride it would be a poor bargain. And they need someone to look after them when they are old. It is the tradition. If you marry me, I'll break the tradition. We'll have a house all our own, as is the American custom, and I won't allow my mother to order you about. I will continue to be courteous. Please reconsider. Marry me."

"Even if I was not afraid of being a servant to your family, we must remember we are at war. Have you not heard the ancient saying of a wise man, 'Marry in war, regret in peace?'"

"You sound like Lao-tze. Or Confucius. That's an old tale told by wives as they cluck over the fire. There might be some substance to it if I was in a foreign land and had a girl back home."

"Me Confucius? I'm just a dumb girl with very little education. Actually, if you brought me home to your family they would laugh at how stupid I am. They'd see at once that I have no polish. As for the old proverb, if you admit it might be true if you were in a foreign land, I can only say it's still true. The roles have just been reversed. It is I who am in a foreign land."

"Dorothy—"

"Although I have no one who loves me in America, I'm very grateful to all of you for making me look deeper than the scars in my heart. I have been thinking deep thoughts about it. Too much of New York lives within me and I feel that my far-away future, if there is any, is in America."

"Scars in your heart? You?"

"Yes, scars. I'm neither carp nor eagle. When I was in New York I was Chinese. Here I am American. There have been many scars along this lonely road. Ho Hon-si, you are the first to have looked so deeply into my heart. Truly you are my best friend."

"And I thought I was making progress." He laughed. "Looking deep into your heart... then you stab me with 'best friend.' Do you know what that tells me? I'm in last place. One does not marry his best friend. You'd marry all those other men before me. I'm sorely wounded." He playfully clutched his breast as if he had been stabbed.

"Ho Hon-si, the only way I would marry you is if my mother was so mean to me I could no longer live with her and ran away. If some day I come running to you and tell you that I am mad at my mother, you'd better marry me quick."

"That I promise. You'll have the fastest marriage ever seen in Kwangtung Province."

Although he was a close friend, there were things I hadn't told Ho Hon-si. In the quiet of my bed I thought deep thoughts. If my American background had muddied my hopes of ever becoming a happy Chinese bride, had not my Chinese background silted any chance of my ever becoming a happy American bride? I sighed, thankful that the problem rode a distant moon. It needn't concern me until I returned to America, or so I thought. How could I know American men would be coming to China?

"Sssst. Are you awake?" Edna whispered.

"Yes."

"Will you come to church with me in the morning?"

"Okay. If you'll help me scrub the floor."

"It'll ruin my hands."

"Then I won't go with you."

"Well, okay then."

Edna kept her part of the bargain and I attended the Episcopal Church, recently established after its leaders fled from Hong Kong. Attending often, I acquired another circle of friends, including May and Marion, Chinese girls who spoke English with a British accent. There would be a third circle.

Mother returned from a malaria treatment at the hospital and announced, "There's an American consular representative at the hotel. I'm going to see him and I want you to come along."

"I don't see why I have to go."

Mother's head bobbed in front of our faded mirror as she arranged her hairdo. She parted her hair down the middle and a roll extended from ear to ear in a sausage shaped crown. "You're twenty-one now. Although heaven knows you don't act like it. You need a passport. You've been listed on mine up to now—it's time you got your own. I know one ning for sure, I don't want to lose my citizenship. As soon as his war is over I'm getting out!"

No convincing required. I'd learned the importance of redentials.

During the long walk to the hotel Mother never lagged. 'he hotel manager directed us to a room and as Mother nocked I waited a respectful step behind her. A moist-kinned man opened the door.

"Are you the American representative?" Mother asked.

"He isn't here. Can you come back later?"

Despite the bad news, Mother enjoyed speaking with an merican. "It's a pleasure to meet you, Mister Smith."

"How would you and your daughter like to meet some merican soldiers?" Smith asked. "There's four here on R nd R. Go down the hall—no, on second thought, I'll take ou there myself."

Mr. Smith led the way and when he knocked on the door a oice from inside bellowed, "C'mon in, the gahdamned hing's open!"

"Fellas," Smith said as we stepped inside. "I want you to neet Missus Yuen and her daughter—" He stopped bruptly. The four men had their shirts out over their pants.)ne soldier's fly was unbuttoned and stood open in a V.

"Straighten up! Button up," Smith shouted. "These eople are Americans! They speak English!"

Completely aghast, four jaws dropped slack. Fingers aced to buttons. One man spun around, presenting his back s he tucked in his shirt. He yanked his belt to lock it.

"It-it's b-been months since I talked with a girl who spoke nglish," he stammered, face lighting up in a smile.

"Yer gahdamned right. Months," said the one I came to know as Cannon. "Jesus Christ! You almost caught me with ny pants down."

Mother extended her hand. "I imagine you boys are onely here. Would you like to meet an American family?"

"We sure as hell would."

Mother moved down the line. A man took her hand.

"Bob Yarano, Ma'am."

"Thank you, Ma'am. They call me Yogi."

"I'm happy to know you," Mother said. "When we have n air raid why don't you come across the river to our house?

It's only three miles and you'll be quite safe. We've spent two years there without mishap."

"I'm Lonnie," the fourth man said as he pumped my hand. "It's really Lonneman but everyone back home calls me Lonnie. You can too."

"Wow, Americans!"

"Yeah!"

"You want some wine, girly?" Cannon gulped. "I mean, Missus." He reddened—the last time I would see the cigar-smoking, heavy-drinking, hard-swearing Cannon embarrassed by anything.

"I think the gramophone needs winding," I said.

Lonnie kept staring at me as if in a trance. At length Yarano went over, wound it up, flipped the platter and carefully put down the needle.

Mother and I looked around and saw that Mr. Smith had gone.

"We don't want to interrupt your party," Mother said. "We only stopped by to say hello."

"Hell, you didn't interrupt nothin'," Cannon said. "You just made the party. Why in the hell don't you sit down and join us?"

"I'm sorry," Mother said. "We really must be going. I'll give you directions how to find our place." She drew a map and handed it to Lonnie.

"I wish you could stay," Lonnie said.

"Goodby." I waved farewell.

"We'll look you up."

"Poor boys," Mother said as we left the hotel. "They don't have a friend in the world."

"Gosh, they're big," I said. "Regular giants."

"That's the Americans!" The meeting had done Mother more good than a trip to the hospital.

I speculated on how ashamed the soldiers must have felt. Had I been caught as they were, I wouldn't have been able to face anyone for a week. I knew what it meant to be ashamed. Every day I had to scrub the floor, but I found a way to ease my shame. As the first sunbeams sparkled over the horizon I rose and completed the task before the family awakened. That way no one witnessed my degradation.

At sunrise, the misery of the floor behind me, I stepped out to scrub the porch, mop and bucket in hand. Four men lounged there, the Air Corps men we'd met the day before—Lonnie, Yarano, Yogi and Cannon. Startled, a scream tore from my throat. I dropped the mop and pail and fled inside.

I was completely mortified. How could I face them? They'd seen me with a mop and pail, looking like a coolie scrubwoman.

After an eternity of shame I opened the door a crack and peeked out. One of the men had spread the puddle of water and quickly finished mopping the porch floor.

Lonnie saw me. "It's all right. C'mon out."

"I'm too embarrassed," I whispered, my cheeks aflame. "I'm so ashamed that you saw me. I have completely lost face. I can't stand the thought of you seeing me. I—"

"Aw, that's all right. Don't worry about it."

"Shit," Cannon growled. "What's to get bent out of shape for? My old lady always scrubs the damn floor."

Some time passed before I realized that when Cannon said, "old lady," he was speaking about his mother. "How come you're here so early?"

"Early air raid," Yarano grinned.

"Yeah. When we saw you folks weren't up we decided to cat nap on the porch. I didn't even know you were here till you screamed."

"Yeah. We didn't see nothin'."

"That's the gahdamned truth," Cannon said. "We didn't see a thing."

With all the commotion the family soon wakened.

Members of the 76th Fighter Squadron, the men visited often, whenever they could get a Jeep and drive down from their base. Edna and I enjoyed riding in their Willys Jeep and we devised schemes to make them take us where we wanted to go.

With the coming of Christmas we wanted them to accompany us to the Episcopal Church. We overcame their reluctance by telling them about May and Marion.

"They're British subjects," Edna explained. "Their parents still live in the West Indies."

"I can talk Limey," Cannon said, chewing his cigar.

Lonnie looked at me. "I got mine. You can have the Limeys."

Bob Yarano and Yogi whispered back and forth. I overheard, "But what if one's fat?" and reassured them that such was not the case.

"What?" Mother exclaimed, regarding Cannon. "Are you going to church?"

"Hell, yes. I've been to church before."

Mother waved her arm. "Hmmft, if you go to church the roof will fall in!"

"She's got your number, Cannon," said Bob Yarano.

"C'mon. Let's go. I want to meet those Chinese Limeys."

We piled into the Jeep and arrived for the midnight service. Half way through "It Came Upon a Midnight Clear," we heard a resounding crash. The low balcony had collapsed. Constructed of bamboo the added weight of four American giants had been too much.

"I'm glad you girls were singing in the choir," Lonnie said.

"Dorothy's mother said the roof would fall in," deadpanned Yogi.

"Aw, shudup," Cannon growled.

When Mother heard of the incident she erupted in laughter. She particularly enjoyed Cannon.

Our family became theirs. They called my parents Mom and Dad, a mark of respect my father genuinely appreciated.

A few days later Mother handed me an invitation. "It's from a Missus Au. She's inviting you to a party. Who's Missus Au?"

"She runs a store," I said. "I shop there now and then. I didn't think she knew me well enough to invite me to a party."

"You're getting so popular around here it wouldn't surprise me if you got an invitation from Chiang Kai-shek."

Chapter Nine

A small woman with boundless energy, Mrs. Au charged around her store selling beans, rice and other hard-to-get staples. Had I known the store was a front for covert activities I certainly would not have accepted her invitation. Why I had been invited to one of her many parties remained a mystery as I crossed her threshold.

"Hello. Thank you for—"

"Ah, Miss Yuen. Welcome . . ." Mrs. Au went bounding toward the caterers who arrived with their collection of woks, utensils and dinnerware. Caterers supplied everything including tables, so even relatively poor families could host the thirty and forty course dinners we all loved.

My eyes fastened on a young American officer and I realized my presence had been requested because I spoke English, which would tend to make him feel more at ease. Mrs. Au would allow a proper interlude before bringing us together, all part of the Oriental mystique of making the obvious seem something less.

The American Captain fascinated me. Certainly he stood out in his uniform, but I would have found him attractive in the rough blue cloth of a field worker.

At first I thought he was like me—part Chinese. Mostly his eyes made him seem Oriental. Small, dark and satiny, half asleep under heavy lids, they squeezed shut to mirthful slits when he laughed. Hair like a midnight lawn swept away from his lofty brow as if blown by the wind. He had a lean handsome face. His gentle sensitive mouth revealed white even teeth whenever he smiled.

He's too pale for Chinese, I thought, and I remembered the Szechwanese were pale, but also short. This man was tall, fine boned, and there was a delicacy about him that his uniform could not conceal. Althought a Caucasian, had he been dressed as the others he could easily have passed for Chinese.

Was it my impolite staring that hastened Mrs. Au to act?

Approaching the officer, she led him toward me. Her introduction bogged down. Mrs. Au spoke only Cantonese and the American officer, it became apparent, spoke Mandarin. She forgot to tell him I spoke English.

"Hello," I said, relinquishing my advantage of being able to understand English without his being aware of it. I might have had some fun with him.

"Hello," he said tentatively.

"Are you enjoying the party?" I asked.

"You speak English!" he exclaimed, breaking into a warm and generous smile.

"I should. I'm an American citizen."

"I'm John Birch," he said, extending his hand.

"Dorothy Yuen." I laughed.

It was a forerunner, however mild, of the reaction I would receive whenever I met American military men. After an initial startled look came realization, followed by a feeling of euphoria as loneliness drained from their eyes. In the aftershock, a boisterous reaction, a sheepish look to mask the embarrassment of naked desire or the simple joy of kinship. The secondary reaction was never predictable; the initial reaction always was.

"Where are you from, Dorothy Yuen?"

"New York City. And you?"

"Georgia. Rome, Georgia. You've never heard of it."

"No," I laughed. "I never have. I can't believe you're from Georgia. You don't sound like a Georgia boy. I don't hear a Georgia drawl in your talk."

"You don't sound like you're from New York." He hesitated. "Actually I spent my formative years in New Jersey. A place called Vineland, and you've never heard of that, either. I went through grade school there, before we moved to Birchwood."

"Birchwood. I suppose that's another city I never heard of?"

"No. Birchwood is the name of our farm in Georgia." A cloud of sadness came ghosting into his eyes and quickly faded. "Let's not talk about me. What about you? What are you doing here? It's a long way from the sidewalks of New York."

"My father inherited a factory in Shanghai and we came

Captain John Birch, master spy.

over to be with him. It's lost now."

"With Shanghai, yes."

I told him about the year we spent in Detroit while Father studied at the Ford Institute.

"We're very much alike, you and I," he said. "Even our backgrounds, in many ways. My family moved around a good deal too. I was born in India."

Captain Birch and I got on famously. He did not take his eyes off me the entire evening.

There was something sepcial in the way the Chinese treated Captain Birch. He joined the many toasts but never drained his glass. Under certain circumstances this would have been considered an affront, causing a loss of face for the person who proposed the toast, but more than that, it surprised me that no one urged him to drink. A Chinese host or hostess spends most of his or her time exhorting guests to eat and drink, and guests continually exhort each other, especially during the toasts. Strangely, no one invited Captain Birch to participate in the finger game.

In the finger game, players face each other, make a fist and swing it out, quickly extending various fingers, calling out a number hopefully identical with the total number of fingers extended. A loud and boisterous game, the losing player is required to take a drink.

"Americans wouldn't understand the game," Captain Birch said. "They'd expect the winner to enjoy the free drink. Our entire philosophy is based on a capitalistic economy. Money."

"Seven," I shouted, shooting out five fingers. My opponent yelled, "Four," sticking out two fingers. I won and he had to take a drink. In China the purpose of the game is philosophical too. The game is designed to get the loser quite drunk.

"Five," I cried, adding to the merry din.

"Six," shouted my opponent.

With a total of nine fingers showing, neither of us won.

We didn't play the finger game long enough for anyone to get drunk but some of the guests were beginning to show the effects of all the toasts.

I felt Captain Birch's fingers on my arm. "May I walk you home?" he asked, his voice filled with authority.

"Yes..." Color rushed to my cheeks as I realized my blunder. It was I who should have invited him to our home. According to ancient Oriental custom a resident extends an invitation to a traveling countryman.

"I like a girl who can blush," he said.

We chatted pleasantly but before we had gone very far, our conversation took a serious turn.

"Do you attend church?" he asked.

"Yes. There's an Episcopal church in Kukong now. I sing in the choir. Not very well, though. I really can't carry a tune at all."

"I'll bet you do all right. Everyone can sing praises to the Lord. Everyone."

"We'd do better at it if we had a piano. Our church really needs a piano."

"I come across one every now and then. Maybe I could get one for you. I do a lot of traveling. I—"

He stopped mid-thought, awkwardly, and before he continued, he looked deeply into my eyes. His face became ominous, almost fearful, as if he dreaded his question would elicit a heartbreaking response. "Dorothy, does it matter to you that I'm a missionary?"

"No," I said nonchalantly, failing to understand why the question was of any importance.

"I'm Baptist," he said with obvious pride.

"When we get to my home, would you like to meet my family?" I said, making sure I wasn't forgetting social amenities again. "My mother, I know, would be delighted to meet you." I almost blurted, "She's always eager to meet anybody who can speak English."

He nodded agreeably. "I absolutely must see you again. I'd like to take you to dinner. Will you come out with me tomorrow night?"

"Yes." How kind it was of him to return my invitation so quickly.

Mother, of course, delighted in Captain Birch. So did my brother and sisters.

"Dorothy tells me you both sing in the choir," Captain Birch said when he met Edna.

"That's right."

"Maybe I can get a piano for you."

"Wowie!" Gloria cheered.

Within minutes Captain Birch had us singing hymns. As we raised our voices in song, our home became a cheerier place.

The following evening Captain Birch called me promptly, his face joyfully animated. Mother later remarked that he looked like a boy who'd opened a package and discovered a longed-for gift inside.

"I've heard of a restaurant on a boat," he said jovially. "A floating restaurant. I've never seen it but I would like to take you there."

"That sounds grand."

Almost elegant, splashes of red and gold with black accents made the restaurant a bright and happy place. A lovely white tablecloth almost caused me to wince. I knew how difficult it was keeping a tablecloth white. I'd washed ours a thousand times.

Captain Birch began to order and I listened in amazement. It's one thing to speak Chinese small talk, it is something else to order a complete dinner with instructions in flawless Mandarin!

"I hope you like duck," he said.

"Woh sil op will be most enjoyable," I said, hoping to hide my ignorance. In his presence I felt utterly stupid.

"You've really cast a spell over me," he said. "I've had nothing but you on my mind all day. In my business that may not be prudent."

"That seems hard to believe."

"Dorothy, do you know how really beautiful you are?"

A difficult question. I didn't think I was unattractive, but beautiful? The way he looked into my eyes, long and penetrating, left me disquieted.

"I'm confused," I said. "Yesterday you told me that you were a Baptist missionary but you wear a U.S. Army uniform. I don't understand . . ."

"I'll try to explain," he said gently. "I was a missionary before the war. Some time back they asked me to join the Army and I did. But I haven't stopped being a missionary. Besides, it provides good cov—" He broke off and began again. "You see, Dorothy, the work of the Lord is never done. I have in no way put aside my faith to join the Army. I travel with the Lord and hopefully He works through me—through all of us—to get His work done. When the war is over I'll be a full time missionary again . . . but I'm thinking of making some important changes. Have you thought about what you're going to do? With whom you're going to share your life?"

"Oh, no. I haven't thought anything about that."

"I'm facing my future with mixed emotions. There are days when everything within me cries out to return to Birchwood. But Birchwood is gone." He sighed wistfully. "At least the house. It burned down last September. They say the fire started from sparks from a train. When I received the letter from home I was heartsick. I'd put so much of my heart and soul into the place . . ."

"I can see that you loved it."

"Yes, I did. Still do," he corrected. "Although it's difficult to imagine it without the house. It was beautiful. To get to the house you went up a winding lane about a mile from the highway. You came upon the house nestled in a clump of trees. The hillside slopes down to the Ocmulgee River. Great domestic tranquility. I took that term from our Constitution. When Jefferson spoke of domestic tranquility I'm sure he was thinking of Monticello, but I found the same peace at Birchwood."

"I would like to see Birchwood."

"Would you really?"

"Yes. I wouldn't say it otherwise."

"I didn't mean to snap, if that's the way it sounded. I just couldn't believe what I was hearing. If I could only hope . . ."

Multi-faceted, when Captain Birch longed for Birchwood he was one person; when he thought about his missionary work he was another. And when he looked deeply into my eyes he became yet another. I perceived he did not know the latter person well, a stranger of whom he was unsure, who placed him in apprehension, someone he could not control. I detected another person, the Army person, but Captain Birch had not yet revealed him to me.

"I'm really surprised at myself," he said. "Do you know I've never told anyone how I feel about Birchwood? Until now, I've kept how I felt about the house buried in my heart. Miss Yuen, you have cast a spell. Do you know that?"

We enjoyed ourselves and many grains of sand fell in the hourglass. When we reached my home, Captain Birch stopped to visit the family.

"Don't forget about the piano," Gloria reminded him.

"Gloria!"

"I won't," he promised with a laugh. "If I find one you'll be hearing from me." He turned to me. "*You'll* be hearing from me at any rate." A boyish grin spread across his face. He turned to Gloria. "Dorothy can send the church address to me . . . so I know where to send the piano."

Gloria appeared satisfied.

I'm glad he didn't ask me to write the address then and there. It would have embarrassed me greatly, not being able to write it in Chinese. I needn't have worried, Captain Birch wasn't testing my intelligence. As I became acquainted with more American servicemen and learned of their wily ways, I realized that Captain Birch had finessed it well. If I expected him to obtain a piano it would be necessary for me to supply an address and for that I had to write him a letter.

"You will write me, won't you?" asked the Captain.

"Yes."

"Why don't you walk me down the path?"

I nodded and we set out.

"You will write to me . . . so I know where to send the piano if I find one?"

"Of course. I promised."

Suddenly his strong arms swooped down and caught me up. Drawing me close, he kissed me firmly.

"Captain Birch," I exclaimed in surprise. "I thought you were a missionary!"

He threw back his head and laughed uproariously.

Captain John Birch set a fine example. The next time Mother encountered American servicemen she brought them home.

"Dorothy, I want you to meet Jack Hartell and Willie Hershenfeld, radio operators with Twenty-third Fighter Control."

Willie gulped. "Wow. You're beautiful."

I found him totally unattractive but in the days ahead his compassion won my respect and I became attached to him.

My sister and I accompanied the radiomen to a nearby

restaurant. Edna watched them in amazement. "Do you always eat so much?"

"You're used to Chinese cooking where one pork chop is dinner for an entire family," Jack Hartell said. "At home I eat two, sometimes three, pork chops all by myself."

Willie Hershenfeld clasped his arms across his chest. "Ye gods! I never eat pork chops."

"You don't know what's good," Jack teased. "You ought to try it sometime, Willie."

"I probably have." Willie laughed. "Especially around here."

Aware that a secret communication had passed between these two friends, I did not understand the implication.

"I know a place that serves hamburgers," I said.

"You do?" they both said at once.

"Where?" Willie asked.

"It isn't far," I said. "Maybe we can go there next time . . ."

"Next time?" Willie said. "We're going there right now!"

As soon as we finished eating we walked down the street to another restaurant where Willie and Jack were introduced to a large ground-beef patty, deep fat fried and smothered in sweet-sour sauce.

"Now this is more like it," said Jack.

"I'm with you, Jack," enthused Willie. "I've got myself quite a girl here, haven't I, Jack?"

"You sure have, Willie. You sure have."

"My mother wouldn't believe this," Willie said.

"The way you tell it," said Jack, "she doesn't know there's anything west of New York. Make a note of this place so we can find it again."

"My girl will find it," Willie said, wolfing another bite. "Right, Dorothy?"

"Right." It was fun hearing New York talk again.

A couple days later, when I stopped at the radio shack, Willie and Jack introduced me to their stern-faced superior, Lieutenant Lynn.

"I've heard about you," Lieutenant Lynn said, no emotion on his lemon-puckered face.

Immediately intrigued, I asked, "From who?"

"From Captain John Birch. He told me to tell you hello. I

was going to look you up."

"Oh, do you work with Captain Birch?"

"We're in the same Army," the Lieutenant replied deviously. "He was very insistent that I send you his regards."

"That's nice of him," I said, remembering I had promised to write him but had delayed because I didn't know what to say. Completely in awe of Captain Birch because of his education, I knew anything I'd write would be stupid. What could I say to a man of his intelligence? Nevertheless, if I wanted a piano for our church I'd have to write...

Arriving home, I gathered paper, pen and my segmented dictionary in case I needed assistance in spelling, and went out on the porch. With my knees drawn up, forming a desk, I began, "Dear Captain Birch..." After writing three lines I scratched out what I had written.

I had ruined one sheet of paper and dared not waste another, so I thought very hard before I wrote:

January 19, 1944

Dear Captain Birch,

I am writing to let you know that we are all fine. Even Mother had a couple good days. We enjoyed your visit. Every once in a while one of us will remember the singing of hymns and Gloria will pipe up about your promise to look for a piano. I think she wants to be grown up like Edna and me. I am sending the address of the church in case you find one. I confess my father drew it for me.

Things are happening very fast here in Kukong. More Americans have arrived. I have two new friends, Willie and Jack. They visit our home all the time and take Edna and me out to eat. We are having a lot of fun. They are radio operators. They introduced me to their commander, Lieutenant Lynn. Was I ever surprised!! He said you had told him to give me your greetings. How nice it was that you thought of me. I sure was surprised.

I caught a glimpse of some other soldiers I thought were Americans. I suppose I will be meeting them soon. That is, if they are staying around here.

Please excuse my writing. I'm sorry I am not very good in English or in writing letters.

Your friend,

Dorothy Yuen

At least six weeks went by before I received a reply on stationery headed UNITED STATES ARMY AIR CORPS, which showed a pilot near a plane, his left hand raised to his goggles. I was happy to read:

Changsha
27 February 1944

Dear Dorothy;

Your kind note of the 19th reached here yesterday. Thank you for not waiting until my tardy one went to you. Just the word that you have not forgotten me means much.

Dorothy, you have not left my thoughts since the first night I saw you! You must be a witch,—a beautiful witch,—to cast such a spell. The reason I have delayed in writing (I did start several times, but lacked time to finish, then was dissatisfied with what I had written and destroyed the poor beginnings) is that I have been increasingly busy; since leaving Kukong I have been in Kweilin, Kunming, Changsha, Leiyang, and then back to Changsha day before yesterday. I expect to go north of the Yangtze River very soon, but will return to Changsha after that journey. I wish I were going to Kukong instead!

Glad to hear that your folks are well. I inquired as to pianos for sale in Changsha, and learned to my regret that a mission school here had sold two *before I arrived! If I can locate any more, I'll do all I can for you and Gloria.*

Am happy, too, that Lt. Lynn passed my regards on to you. I hope you're not seeing too *much of the American boys down there, Dorothy! I know this is a selfish thing that I have no right to say, but I am horribly jealous of those fellows who have opportunity to see you.*

Enclosed is a photograph made here in Changsha. I hope you will send me one (a snapshot will do) of yourself. I admit such a bargain would be entirely to my advantage,—to "swap" something ugly for something beautiful and rare. If you don't care to give me the pleasure of keeping your picture, feel free to keep mine, anyway, to scare the rats away!

Don't ever apologize for your English writing! I only wish I could do as well! Please write soon again; the address you used is O.K.

Please extend my best wishes to your family. Remember that, while I dare not hope for more than your friendship, still I want to be yours, as much as you will have of me, my lady!

P.S. Please don't call me "Captain Birch"
this is my name ------------------------------John.

A sigh escaped me as I put down his letter. Captain Birch was falling in love with me, like so many of the Chinese officers I'd met at the War College in San Tung and who had later come to Kukong. Military men always fell in love when they were away from home. It wasn't really love, I knew. I'd been through all that a thousand times.

"John," I whispered as I read his name. I read the letter again. "It isn't really love, John," I murmured. "It isn't love."

Chapter Ten

Whenever Mother encountered American G.I.s she invited them to visit us. The day she met the Navy Commander I heard them laughing as they came up the path, carrying on in the manner of old friends who had stopped too long at a tavern.

"This is Dorothy," Mother said.

"Hi, Babe," said the Commander, leering at me with X-ray eyes. A shirt collar that was too small sent his lapels out like wings. "Ma'am," he questioned. "Are you sure it's all right if Babe and I go out to dinner?"

"Of course," Mother said. "Dorothy has a lot of friends. I'm sure she'd like to have dinner with you."

I could see Mother thought he was a gentleman.

"Get your hat, Baby," the Commander called to me. He nodded once, slowly, as his eyes roamed over me. He turned to Mother and a short burst of laughter boiled out of his ample middle. "I probably shouldn't have told you that story coming out here."

"I enjoyed it," Mother said. "Do you know how long its been since I heard a good story? I used to have this friend Riley—" She broke off and shot a quick glance at me. Her voice dropped an octave. "He used to tell me some good ones."

"Say, didja hear the one about the traveling salesman?" The Commander stepped toward Mother and continued in a hoarse whisper.

Despite his subdued tone I managed to understand the phrase, "Out came the farmer's daughter." In a moment Mother threw back her head, rocking with laughter. "You're a real card," she shrieked.

"Is it all right if I smoke while I wait for Baby?" he asked.

"I'm ready," I said.

In the old section of town we found a café-bar and were directed to an intimate table for two. He sat there reeking of sweat and flatulence, blowing cigar smoke in my face. "I've got a good command. I run a tight ship, in a manner of speaking. There's room for a smart girl like you. Know what I mean, Baby?"

I gave him a sickly smile and eased back in my chair. The table was tiny and I didn't like the way his knees were touching mine.

"You wanna 'nother drink, Baby?"

"No, thank you."

"That's a good egg. Easy on the booze. Last floozie I got skanked with could drink a barrel. And she was nothin' like you. You got real class. Whatd'ya say, Baby? Do you want to come with me? It's a good deal for somebody." His arm went under the table.

"My mother isn't well. She needs me."

"What's wrong with her? She looked okay to me."

He touched the inside of my knee with a clammy hand. I gasped, almost yelped. "What are you doing?"

"Relax," he grinned.

"Remember you're an officer," I said, appalled.

He guffawed. "That's rich. Look, don't play coy with me, Baby. Not with an old lady like you got. She's been on the road. Now spin your legs back under the table."

"No."

"Have it your way, Baby. I like a challenge. Yes sir, lot of things come easy out here but you can't say I don't like a challenge. Pickin' plums can get to be old stuff. Your old lady tells me you an' another chick went up to Chungking for six months. They tell me that place rocks."

"Yes. The countryside is rocky and there are many caves. Most of them are used as air raid shelters. I think Chungking is the most bombed city in the world."

The Commander erupted with laughter. "That's more like it, Baby. I knew you were a live one. Waiter," he yelled. "Hit me again." He turned back to me. "You're my type, Baby."

"No," I flustered. "I'm not your type. I-I'm not even white."

"You're close enough to suit me. So your old man is a slopy, eh? It's not often you see a Chink married to a white gal. But you sure came out beautiful, I'll say that for you."

"My father is a colonel in Chiang's Army, in charge of repairs—"

"Yeah. Yeah, sure."

There was no way to speed up dinner but I certainly tried. His suggestion that we do a variety of things later fell on deaf ears. Reluctantly he agreed to take me home.

"This doesn't seem to be your night. Not mine either. Listen," he said, his face flushed. "Maybe I did get out of line with you there, Baby. I didn't realize you meant it about your old lady, but if that's the way you want to play it, it's okay, see?"

Before long we were at my front door. Putting his job offer out of mind, I was about to dismiss the Commander as well, but he followed me into the house.

He sidled over to Mother and repeated his offer. Smooth as a real estate salesman, his breath now reeking of Sen-Sen, he said, "Ma'am, I've been tellin' Baby here that I can give her a job for two hundred bucks a month as long as she wants it."

That was all Mother had to hear. At once she became a willing conspirator. "It's just the opportunity you've been waiting for," she exclaimed.

"No, Mother, it isn't. I'm not at all interested."

"What?" objected Mother. "Not interested? Here you've been complaining about wanting to get out of the house, wanting to get away from me and get out on your own. Now when a job drops into your lap you turn up your nose." Mother waved her arm in exasperation and turned to the Commander. "I don't understand her."

"Yes, Ma'am."

"Have you explained the job to her?"

"Yes, Ma'am," the Commander said silkily. "I told her about the money. The job isn't hard. Lots of time off. She'll be with me. No problem not being protected. I'll keep an eye on her, watch her like a hawk."

"There," Mother said.

"No, Mother. Can't you see?"

"She's a stubborn one," Mother said with a shrug. "When she gets this way she won't budge. Let me talk to her." She passed a wink that I detected. "You stop back tomorrow."

"Okay," grunted the Commander, lighting a cigar and shoving it between his teeth. "I'll be back tomorrow but that's the last chance. I'm leavin' this burg."

"What are you waiting for?" Mother demanded when he had gone. "When I was your age I had already supported myself five years."

"Oh, Mother!"

"Don't 'oh mother' me! Sitting around here, having your father support you—you ought to be ashamed of yourself."

"*Mother,*" I pleaded. "Can't you see what he wants? Don't you understand *anything*?"

But Mother heard only his unctuous, "Yes, Ma'am, no, Ma'am."

"He wants to give you a job," she stormed. "It's the first decent offer you've had, and girl, you're going to take it. Tomorrow when he comes back for an answer, you're going to give him an answer and that answer is yes."

"Who's going to help you with all the housework?" I shot back in desperation.

"Edna's getting old enough to take your place. Don't get the idea that you can't be replaced. It's time I tossed you out of the nest."

"But do you have to throw me to the wolves?"

"Hmmfpt. You wouldn't know a wolf if you saw one. A nice officer like that. Pleasant . . . courteous—I don't know what more you could want."

Mother refused to listen and launched a tirade only Father could withstand. Knowledge that malaria affected her reason afforded me neither comfort nor escape. Where could I turn?

A knock on our door catapulted Willie Hershenfeld and Jack Hartell into my problem. I turned to them, panic-stricken.

"I don't want to go with the Navy man," I burst out after I explained my predicament. "He only wants to get me into bed. I'm not that kind of girl."

"I know it," Jack Hartell said. "From the first day I met you there was no doubt about that. When you walked in the front door I saw a halo over your head."

"Don't worry," said Willie. "I have an idea. There's still a chance. We need a translator. We'll go back and have a talk with Lieutenant Lynn. Maybe we can get you a job."

At that moment Willie's chiseled features looked truly beautiful.

"We really do need another translator," Willie insisted.

"Don't tell me," Jack said. "Tell Lieutenant Lynn."

"I'm going to. I can't stand to think of her with Navy brass. God!" His face contorted as if he'd just bitten into a quince. "Let's tell Lieutenant Lynn now."

"We don't have a thing to lose," Jack said.

"Right."

I quickly changed into a clean dress. "How do I look?" I said nervously.

"You look fine," Jack said. "Come on."

We started for the radio shack and when they attempted to comfort me I became all the more tense. What work had I done? I had no experience. Fear of rejection gripped me, threatening to freeze my will. "I'm scared."

"Don't be," Willie said. "Stand straight and tall. Don't speak unless you're spoken to. When you do speak, do it with confidence."

"I-I'll try—"

"Just a hint of a smile," Jack Hartell suggested.

Shivers raced up my spine as we went before the Lieutenant. Fortunately Willie and Jack did most of the talking.

His face stern and rebuking, Lieutenant Lynn listened thoughtfully. "Oh yes," he said. "You're the friend of Captain John Birch."

"Yes . . ."

"Okay. I think we can use you."

My shoulders sagged in relief. A heavy sigh escaped me. Remembering what Jack and Willie had said, I sucked in a deep breath and stood erect.

"Dismissed," Lieutenant Lynn said, a hint of a smile touching the corners of his hard mouth.

Willie and Jack were smiling broadly as we stepped outside.

"We did it!"

Overjoyed and grateful, I kissed them both.

Paralyzed with fear, I reported for work, the third member of the downstairs translating team. "I don't know what to do."

"Don't worry," said a young Chinese man with the Christian name of Robert. "You'll catch on in no time."

"Right," said the young Chinese woman assisting him.

As radio messages came in we translated them into English, phoned them up to Willie and Jack on the second floor and they and Lieutenant Lynn relayed them to headquarters. The communications concerned troop movements, locations of trains, aircraft and even ox carts—anything that moved. Military vocabulary in two languages baffled me but with the help of my new Chinese friends I learned quickly. I also learned that we three were not allowed upstairs.

"Off limits," declared Robert.

"Why, for goodness sake?"

"The mysterious way of Caucasians," Robert said, deadpan. "They think they have something up there that we don't have down here."

We all laughed outrageously.

"We could sabotage their transmitters," I suggested. "Perhaps that's what they're afraid of."

"I don't even have the energy to destroy this one."

I soon developed radio proficiency and managed a shift of my own, allowing Robert to have some time off.

On a Sunday morning, during a lull, a bird colonel came in with a lieutenant colonel. "I'm Dick Wise," he said. "This is Chuck Hunter. We're looking for Captain Lynn."

"Just a minute," I said. "I'll tell him you're here."

I notified the recently promoted Lieutenant Lynn, now Captain Lynn, and he called them into his office.

After a time the colonels came out, paused, gave me the once-over and said goodby. Had I known that Colonel Richard Wise would become an important figure in my life I might have reacted with more than indifference. Momentous relationships, like a good stew, often begin with a pot of cold water.

Willie and Jack appeared, conferred with Captain Lynn and went on a mission into the country with nothing more than their transmitters.

Willie . . . my feelings for him grew as steadily as the foliage on a plum tree. How long my head would have remained oblivious to the murmurings of my heart had not Captain John Birch chosen that day to make a visit, I can only guess.

His appearance was always a surprise. Captain Birch knocked on our door and swept in on a whirlwind of enthusiasm. "Have dinner with me, Dorothy," he said. "I only have a few hours. Where I'll be tomorrow you wouldn't believe."

At once I abandoned my plans for the evening. "Yes, Captain . . ."

"You must call me John. I thought we settled that in my letter. You did get it?"

"Yes—John."

Reaching out, he took my hand. He gave no thought to releasing me and we continued down the path hand in hand.

"You can't imagine how many times I read your letter, Dorothy."

"And I yours. There is a beauty in the way you write. A formal way. Perhaps a better word is dignity. I enjoyed your letter so much. Especially the part where you said, 'My lady.' It reminded me of your home in the South. I could almost see your family."

He laughed. "A picture of women wearing gauzey blouses and crinoline skirts in an antebellum mansion? That's not quite Birchwood."

I furrowed my brow. "Antebellum? That's a word I don't know. I couldn't possibly—"

"Another reason I like you," he said with gusto. "There's absolutely no pretense with you . . . in your letters or in person. You're fundamental. So you remembered, 'My lady.' Tell me, did you think of it in the formal sense? I mean, did you—?"

"I just thought of being your lady."

"You did?" he exclaimed with obvious delight.

"Yes."

"That's wonderful. I'm sorry I couldn't get a piano for your church. My lady," he mused. "Hmmm . . ."

As we dined I studied him. Much about him reminded me of my father. He had the same chin, the same high forehead, an elongated face not quite as narrow as Father's. Their noses were not dissimilar, but there the comparison ended.

Where Father was retiring and always carried a trace of sadness with him, Captain Birch was dynamic, outgoing and possessed such a keen mind that he could have simultaneously played two opponents at chess and beaten them both. His mind leaped from topic to topic with the resilience of a bouncing ball. He gazed at me intently, absorbing me, yet I was not disquieted. Once I had thought he was of mixed blood like myself but now I saw he had moved so deeply into the life of China that I had to remind myself that he was not Chinese.

"A penny for your thoughts," he said smiling. "*Our* thoughts."

"I was thinking how completely you've accepted the culture of China."

"You're very discerning . . . a person of depth."

"Oh . . ."

When we had eaten we walked to a secluded spot near the river.

"I'm glad you're a serious person, Dorothy. You'll be able to appreciate what I'm about to say. As a missionary I know that marriage is a serious undertaking." He paused to study my face for reaction and finding none he went on. "It means commitment; the commitment of one life to another for all time, like vines intertwining, from the earth where they receive sustenance, all the way up—" He raised his arm skyward "—to Heaven."

His conversation raced toward marriage, a topic I did not wish to discuss. "Birchwood," I said to change the subject. "How you love that place! Some day I must see it."

"You shall. Strange," he mused. "After talking together people sometimes don't understand each other."

I nodded, unable to follow him.

"We talked," he said. "We talked some more and I thought she—" He broke off and managed a pained smile. "Dorothy, can you come to grips with China? I mean, really understand it?"

"I thought I had. Perhaps if I could better understand the language. The *languages* . . ."

"You do very well. I find it so easy talking to you. There's no wall between us. You're not pulling in another direction. In you the east and west have blended. You understand—"

"John," I said with sudden force. "You've been speaking about another woman! Oh. Forgive me," I said quickly. "I had no right—"

"That's okay," he said, reaching out. "I *was* thinking of someone else, something that's over. She couldn't commit herself to my way of life. You're very perceptive. When I'm with you my guard is down. I've got to watch that." He chuckled. "I wrote how you bewitch me. Now I'm not casting you in a harsh light, I'm only thinking of the way you affect me . . . an extremely compelling effect."

"Really?"

"At night when I'm out there, you're constantly in my thoughts. That's all I have . . . my thoughts, meditation and prayer. Your face comes to me out of the mists. Today, when I saw you again, I couldn't believe how well I had fixed your image in my mind. I had your picture correct to the most minute detail, the way your curls fall about your face, the dimple in your cheek—do you know the Chinese call a dimple a 'wine hole'? Your wonderfully understanding eyes. That sounds gauche—I should be telling you how beautiful you are—and you *are*. There are so many things I want to tell you that I really don't know where to begin."

"You could tell me what you do—out there."

"That's terribly secret. Of course, with your work in the radio shack, you know by now that I'm involved with communication. I move around a greal deal. I've been up north with the Communists, with the Nationalists, behind enemy lines—"

"I didn't know that," I said.

"There's danger in this business. One never knows when he might say too much. Well, Miss Yuen, I've told you a secret of mine, now you must tell me a secret of yours. A really deep, dark secret."

Pondering a moment I remembered how Tiger dos Remedios was sending me a dictionary in installments, concealed in a newspaper, so I told him that.

"Bravo," he said. "I like the intrigue involved there. Studying a dictionary. No wonder, my lady, that you have captivated me. You not only dazzle me with your charm and beauty, but with your intelligence. No wonder I have fallen in love with you."

"John—"

"I wish we could be together more. I curse this war, what it does to people and their lives. But we must go on. We are in a conflict we dare not lose. I'm jealous of Lynn and the others in the radio shack, being with you every day while I'm out in the field, remote and distant. They have the advantage of proximity. I hope it does not become an unfair advantage."

I failed to understand the word 'proximity' but didn't confide the fact to Captain Birch. One such admission in an evening was enough. Later I would consult my dictionary.

"I would never be unfair to anyone," I said.

"I know."

We talked for a time of his home in Georgia. He was enthusiastic at the idea of showing it to me. The way he described it, Birchwood was a peaceful spot, a place I would enjoy.

Again he abruptly changed the subject. "Dorothy, do you believe that the Lord taketh away but the Lord also giveth? I'm glad I have found you. It is so easy to confide in you."

"There is no mountain between us."

"I know I have no right to ask for your affection but when I go out into the field I will take you along in my heart. There is something I want to give you so you will remember me." He reached into his pocket and brought out a badge about the size of a twenty-five cent piece, bearing the emblem of the Flying Tigers. "Mine once, now it is yours. It isn't exactly a fraternity pin and this certainly isn't the campus of Mercer College in Macon, but the bond I share with these men transcends—here, let me pin it on you."

When he had it pinned to my chest he held me at arm's length for a moment, admiring his work, then he drew me near and kissed me. "I love you," he whispered.

I returned his emotion and at length he released me. "There," he said, well pleased. "You are pinned to me."

"I don't think I should wear it," I said. "After all I am not a Flying Tiger. The military will object—"

"Tigress," he corrected. "And forget the objections." His expression went somber. "I have traveled the length and breadth of the land. I have seen the tiger and heard its mighty roar. If you roared, I'm sure it would be beautiful. You shall be my tigress. I think you're the finest tigress in all of China."

Exhilarated, Captain Birch placed his arm about me and we walked happily homeward. After he had kissed me again and made his farewell I noticed that Mother was up and stirring. I asked her about a growing uneasiness.

"Mother, does the phrase, 'pinned to me,' have any special significance in America?"

"What do you mean?"

"Captain Birch gave me a Flying Tiger pin and said I was pinned to him. I was just wondering—"

"It doesn't mean anything to me, Dorothy. I suppose it's something those military boys have dreamed up. The way they come out with things, I can't understand them half the time."

My dictionary defined proximity as being near. Captain Birch suggested that someone near would have an advantage. I pondered the nearness of Willie and needed no deep thoughts to realize that with each passing day my eyes found him more handsome. Unattractive to me at first, it was getting so that the harp within my breast and the harp within his were being plucked to the same tune. He was a lovely man, exceedingly kind and compassionate. How could I continue to work at the radio shack and not lose my heart to him?

Likewise, how could I continue to see the outrageously handsome Lonnie and not fall in love with him, this man who would rather take me for a lonely walk than share me at a party? A wave of happiness coursed through me whenever I saw him arrive in the Jeep.

Father warned me about becoming too deeply involved with Willie Hershenfeld. Father looked further over the horizon of my future and became disturbed by what he saw. Of course, he opposed anything that might lead to my leaving China.

On my day off from the radio shack Father summoned me, I assumed to counsel me about my continuing relationship with Willie. Alone in the room, Father slumped in his chair.

"I've sent the others away," he said, despair lining his lean thin face, his eyes sunken and filled with anguish. He motioned for me to sit down. "Dorothy," he said, his voice strained. "An owl has come to rest in my pear tree."

I knew an owl was an evil omen. According to legend young owls devoured their mother. "Pear tree?" I said. "I do not understand about the pear tree."

"A pear tree," Father said softly, "is the symbol of long life, of purity and justice."

My head came up sharply. What evil news was he about to reveal?

His hands came across the table. "Here is all the money I have. On this paper I have written of my other assets."

"Why, Father?"

"Do not interrupt. Listen closely, for there is great pain in my heart and I have no desire to tell it twice. I have written instructions for things to be done when I am gone—if I do not return."

Questions bombarded my mind but I listened intently, gloom already rushing into the depths of my being.

Father raised his gaze, averting his face slightly to stare past me toward some object in the distance. "I-I have been accused," he got out. His eyes met mine fleetingly. "You remember the colonel of the Eleventh Repair Factory? It-It's the same—"

"*No*," I exclaimed fearfully, a vicious claw twisting my insides. "Not the firing squad!"

"Who can say? It is in the hands of the gods."

"For using an Army truck to transport your family from Hsingning? For dispatching a truck to the faraway river to pick up Ah-Lau and our furniture? For this they are going to shoot you?"

"No, my daughter." He smiled wanly, warmth coming to his eyes. "Those things were permitted a person of my station. The care of my family comes with the dignity of my rank. They said I sold spare parts for my own gain."

"What?" I cried, incredulous, fighting distress and anger in my voice. "How could they?"

"I am not guilty of what I have been charged."

"You can't be charged if you are not guilty."

"The bird chooses its tree, not the tree the bird. There is nothing more to be said. I must go to headquarters now."

Through tear-filled eyes I watched him depart. As he reached the door he stopped and turned. He looked at me calmly, as if he was about to take a walk of the least consequence. "Dorothy, I love you," he said. "Tell the others that I love them."

"Father!" I cried out.

Stunned, I stood frozen for a moment. Then I broke into a run, sobbing as my brain searched for a solution. Instinct more than reason had sent me in the direction of General Yur. My lungs burned and screamed for breath. I halted. Crazy fragments spun back and forth across my mind. The terrible crack of firing squad rifles—the victim's body jerking, sagging helplessly into death. I blotted it out, choking back my tears. This was no time for weeping. How completely Chinese Father was! So coolly composed. Inside, fear must have been twitching through him like wires. *What do you expect, idiot? To have him act like a Spaniard?* Right at the end, how American he was as he said, "Dorothy, I love you. Tell the others that I love them." Damn the Chinese and their final solution. No sense. I ran again. *What are you going to tell General Yur?* I had no answer, even when I reached his home and found myself in his presence. I made a great effort to be the daughter of my father.

General Yur's smiled greeting, "Hello, Dorothy," changed abruptly as he sensed my mood. "You're in trouble," he said, sobering. "How may I help you?"

"It's my father," I said, coming directly to the point. As I blurted out the facts his brows came together like the wings of a duck hawk and his jaw became rigid. "I know he is not guilty of these things," I said. "This man who refuses to allow his vehicles to make a trip to Kukong until there are many reasons—whose troops cannot use vehicles except once a month, on payday. How many times I have heard him say, 'Every ounce of gasoline is a drop of blood for China.'"

"Your problems are never small ones," he said gravely. "I have little power with military justice. But I will look into the matter. Go home and don't worry. I will see what I can do."

I returned home, no joy within me. I plodded through the next day at the radio shack feeling lifeless. Even Willie, who knew nothing of the cause of my melancholy, was unable to cheer me. It was not until Father returned home and called me aside, saying, "You may return my money," that the black cloud was dispelled and I inhaled a happy breath.

"I'm so glad!" I said. "What happened?"

"Upon close investigation it was found there was no evidence against me."

"I had faith in you," I said.

"It will not be necessary to tell the others of this," Father said.

"No," I agreed happily. "It will not be necessary." However, I realized it would be necessary for me to thank General Yur. I faced Father, bowed as a smile brightened my face and said, "It is observed that the owl has flown out of your pear tree."

Father clasped his hands together and bowed, joining my play. "Come, let us share a pot of tea and speak of happier times."

"Yes," I said. "Let us speak of New York."

He frowned slightly. "Those were happier times?"

"We were at peace," I reminded him.

"You're developing a quick mind," Father said, nodding with approval.

The leached-out tea in our pot had grown cold when Mother entered. "Dorothy, Ho Hon-si is here to see you."

Always correct with Mother, Ho Hon-si developed a mischievous grin, little more than a twinkle in his eyes, that told me, "If I could just get your Mother mad enough at you, Dorothy, I would have you as my wife."

We went for a walk and before we strolled very far he said, "I had to tell you my good news. I'm now a colonel."

"Congratulations. The tangerines of your New Year are hanging high and bright."

"It has been a fortunate year for me," he acknowledged. "Just being with you would guarantee that."

"Oh, stop it," I chided. "Enough old China games."

"I didn't start it," he said gleefully. "You and your tangerines."

For a moment he allowed me to simmer in my kettle of embarrassment.

"I have other news," he said, his tone suddenly serious. "About the dark-haired American with the dog—the one who calls on your sister."

"Oh?"

"When he leaves your house he stops to visit the girls on the sampans."

I could not mistake his meaning. The surge of refugees into Kukong, along with American troops, made our town an attractive place for harlots and prostitutes, a number of whom had set up a flourishing business along the river. Nor could I mistake to whom he referred. Edna had but one frequent visitor, an American of Italian descent. The dog Ho Hon-si mentioned was a chow puppy our family had given Edna's friend Gilbert.

Arching my eyebrows I asked Ho Hon-si, "Are you watching our house?"

"Not exactly. The sampan girls are under surveillance. We follow the paths where they lead."

"I thought maybe you were jealous," I teased.

"Of course I am," he said. "On that subject, you're not mad at your mother, I hope.

"Not enough to run to you." I smiled.

"Seriously," he said. "I wish you wouldn't run around with the Americans. They'll only get you into trouble."

"Don't worry," I said smugly. "I can take care of myself."

"I hope so," he said, a bantering quality in his voice. "But if you can't, remember I am always around to pick up the pieces. Are you *sure* you're not mad at your mother?"

"Yes," I laughed.

Ho Hon-si bowed. "Now that I've shared my good fortune, I must return to work."

"Thank you," I said, aware that the real reason he had come was to warn me about Gilbert.

Anger simmering within me, I planned a course of action. Rather than involving Mother or Father, I stationed myself at the door at a time when I expected Edna's friend to call. Seeing him, I went out and accosted him in the front yard.

His greeting was friendly. Mine was not.

"I'm going to ask you not to see Edna any more," I said coldly.

"Why not?"

"It has come to my ears that when you leave our house you stop to visit the girls on the sampans."

"What if I do?" Gilbert said. "That's no concern of yours."

"Quite right. My concern is only for my sister."

"My seeing her is none of your business."

"I'm making it my business. I don't want you to see her."

"Let *her* tell me that."

"No, *I'm* telling you that. She's too young to know what she's letting herself in for. She's only a high school girl."

"She's old enough to know her own mind. I'm going to ask her."

"You shall not see her. No!"

"Well, I *will* see her."

I placed myself squarely in his path. "You're not coming into our house again. We invite only guests of good character."

"What's wrong with my character?" he yelped. "I'm going in to see Edna right now. She can tell me to go if she wants. Only Edna. Not you."

"You can push me aside," I said tersely. "But if you do, you'll be making explanations to Intelligence. How do you think I learned where you went?"

"Intelligence?" he gulped. "Bitch." He turned away, muttering. "Damn slopies. We ought to let the Japs have you!"

Wretched from the encounter, I knew the worst was yet to come—the wrath of my sister. A teenager and completely infatuated, Edna would be neither understanding nor forgiving. Nevertheless I reasoned with her, withholding none of the facts.

"I don't believe you," Edna said bluntly. "You didn't send him away."

"Yes, I did. Look, it's already an hour past the time he was to be here. I told him never to come to our house . . . never to see you again."

"How could you?" Edna stormed, eyes glaring defiance before tears flooded her cheeks. "You're so bossy. You're not my mother."

"Somebody has to look after you," I countered. "Mother isn't able to do all the washing and ironing, see that you look neat, see that you're fed, worry over you when you're out with some G.I."

"You have no right," she choked, her voice thick with tears.

"'Right' is why I did it. What Gilbert's doing isn't right and he certainly isn't right for you. Edna, you deserve a man of high quality—"

"But I *love* him," she sobbed.

"You only think you do. Time will pass. Time will heal the wound in your heart."

"Gilbert isn't like that. He's wonderful. They're all lies . . . lies you're telling me! I can't believe that about him. He wouldn't!"

"He would and did. He was followed. There is no doubt about the facts."

"I hate you!"

"Hate me if you like. I won't allow my sister to stumble blindly into his clutches. After he steals your love you'll be nothing more than a sampan girl to him. When the war is over he'll run home and leave you with a child."

"You have no right." She waved her arms; her body trembled with anger. "I'm going to him."

"Edna," I said coldly. "Listen! If I can't have your promise not to see him again I'll have to tell Mother and Father and let them deal with you. If we leave it between us there will be no lectures and no punishment. No restrictions. You'll be free to choose more wisely."

"You've ruined my whole life! My whole entire life! I'll hate you forever. How could you possibly understand? What do you know about love? You treat love as a joke, to be spread around like cards among players, with none getting enough to be important. Gilbert means everything to me!" She reached for a handkerchief and blew her nose.

"I know how you feel," I said, putting my arm around her consolingly.

"Don't you touch me," she screamed. "I never want to speak to you again!"

Brokenhearted, she cried herself to sleep, refusing my efforts to comfort her. Edna continued to sulk for a week and would not speak to me unless we were in the presence of my parents.

On a weekend when we had visitors I went to Edna with an invitation. "Lonnie and Cannon and some of the guys have come down from the air base. There's a grown-up party in town and you may come with us if you wish. There'll be dancing. It's a chance for you to show how mature you are."

Edna made no response but I could tell she was weighing a decision.

"Make up your mind," I said. "It's your decision. Go or stay." Then I used a word I'd just learned. "It's immaterial to me."

"All right," she said. "I'll come."

"Okay. Get the lemon out of your face and come on."

I prepared the guys. "Edna is a wonderful dancer."

"Great."

"Yeah, I guess she's growing up," Lonnie said when Edna appeared.

"Other guys may want to dance with you," Yogi reminded her. "Just remember you're with us."

"Damn right," Cannon said.

Lonnie kicked the Jeep in gear and we roared off. I sat relaxed, bantering with him, exchanging pleasantries, little realizing that this would *not* be just another party.

After a fifteen minute drive we arrived at a sturdy pre-war home. The party occupied the entire second floor. In a whirl of gaiety, Chinese students from Lingnam University, relocated after the fall of Hong Kong, played mah-jong with American G.I.s. Money changed hands across plain round tables. In an adjacent room dancers spun to uptempo rhythms from scratchy five-year-old records.

"Play that Bluebird again," someone said.

Edna, feeling very grown-up and pleased with her popularity, no longer despised me. As I walked toward her, the downstairs door popped open and gendarmes with drawn weapons charged up the stairs.

"You're all under arrest," the gendarmes shouted. "Don't move!"

I had to move. I couldn't be caught and compromise Father's position in the Army. I fled to the bedroom and hid in a closet. Behind me a gendarme scolded, "Gambling is illegal. Dancing is prohibited by the New Life Movement."

The gendarmes continued their search and a stern-faced trooper discovered me cowering behind the door. He directed me out with a curt wave of his bayonet.

Across the room the raid leader ranted, "Making merry while China burns! You should all be ashamed."

They bound our wrists and presently two dozen of us were tied together with a long rope. In the line of offenders I saw students, Chinese military personnel including a colonel, and several women, one of whom was heavy with child. Menacing us with weapons, the gendarmes ordered us to march to their headquarters.

Looking around, I saw Edna clutching Cannon's arm. I guessed what happened. At first sign of a raid she had gone to him. The gendarmes wouldn't touch American troops or anyone with them. Why hadn't I thought of that? I could have kicked myself. Why hadn't I used my head?

Lonnie and Yarano stood by helplessly and watched me being led away. Raising my eyes I called to Edna. "Get Ho Hon-si."

We were humiliated in the street.

Several hours into the night as we huddled in detention I heard my name called in Chinese. I went to the guard, who nodded for me to exit. There stood Ho Hon-si, resplendant in his new colonel's uniform.

"I'll take charge of the prisoner," he said brusquely. He returned the guard's salute. "Follow me." Not till we were outside and out of earshot did he relax.

"So you can take care of yourself," he chided. "I told you not to get involved with American troops."

I chose the alternative of silence.

"I don't know what I ever saw in you," he fussed. "I wouldn't want a wife of mine to be a common criminal. Dorothy, Dorothy—" His head went back as he laughed.

"Thank you for getting me out."

"Why didn't you tell me you were going to that place? I would have told you not to go. We planned the raid for days. You and the Americans you hang around with are a constant embarrassment to me. Now there's one thing you *must* do."

"Yes?"

"In the morning you must see my commanding general and tell him what I have done for you."

"I will."

"I suppose I can release you now. I shouldn't. I should never let you go."

"Thank you, Ho Hon-si."

On my way home I stopped at a midnight bakery and purchased a peace offering for Mother, some of her favorite custard tarts.

As promised, in the morning I went to Ho Hon-si's

commandant and explained the details and also succeeded in obtaining the release of my friends from Lingnam University. As they were being discharged they were extremely angry with me.

"If you have the influence to have us released now, you should have done it last night," they charged. There was nothing I could say to appease them. None of them ever spoke to me again.

When I left home, Mother, content with her tarts, still had no knowledge of the raid. There was no doubt in my mind that she would know when I returned.

"Well, it's finally happened," she said, launching a scathing tirade. "You finally landed in jail. I always knew you would."

"It was all a mistake," I said.

"I knew the police would get you sooner or later. Ever since I saved you from jail for starting fires in the streets of New York."

"You saved me?" I retorted. "That's not the way it was. You were hanging out the second story window shouting, 'Take her away. I don't want her!' Some saving that is. If the policeman hadn't had a kind heart I would have been arrested. No thanks to you."

"That's not the way I remember it," Mother said, her face an indignant mask. "You always were able to wrap men around your finger. Some day, my girl, you'll find out that trick won't work. And speaking of work, I need some help around here. Go and help Edna."

I found Edna washing dishes.

"You used your head," I told her. "I only wish I had done as well."

Edna returned a smile of appreciation. Certainly she must have felt pleasure at seeing me humbled but she resisted every impulse to utter unkind words. Still, it was too early to forgive me for sending away her beau. Perhaps she never would.

Her words, "You don't know what love is," flung at me in anger, returned to haunt me and I wished with all my heart that she was right. However, every time I analyzed it, I realized I *was* in love in a limited way with the dashing Lonnie, with whom a simple conversation became a delight, but more—helplessly—with Willie. Even now I saw his countenance before me, a heroic face of carved teakwood the artisan had forgotten to sand, a face that when the smoothness of youth disappeared, would be craggy, almost Lincolnesque. Of course I was in love. Otherwise why would my heart race so wildly at his touch? I had a feeling of falling through space with nothing to grab. Could I blame it all on proximity? Was it too late to heed Father's repeated warnings?

Soon I found myself in Willie's arms, listening to his voice in my ear. My fingers tingled to the sensation of muscle beneath his shirt and my breath quickened as I felt his hands on me, gentle in their awkwardness.

"Darling, darling," he said, completely enraptured. "I love you so much."

"Willie, I-I—" My protest died as his lips covered mine.

In the comfort of his arms I felt my strength ebbing, my heart racing, my cheeks flushing. "Willie—" I murmured, gently pushing against him to signal my desire for release.

He tried to kiss me again but I turned sideways in his grasp. "Not so much."

"You can't know how much you mean to me." A smile spread across his face. "Darling, do I have a surprise for you!" Reaching into his pocket he came out with a jewel box and flipped open the lid. The sun's orange rays caught the green jade and it became a little robin's egg in the nest of his hand.

"It's beautiful," I gasped.

"It's an engagement ring," he beamed. "I love you and want to marry you."

How could I answer him? "Willie—I don't know what to say."

"Say yes."

"B-But—"

He swept me off my feet and closed my mouth with a kiss. Under the turmoil of my heart I was powerless to resist.

"Stop—" I gasped finally.

"I can't wait to take you home to Mother," he said.

"I'm glad you remembered her," I said, eager for conversation. "It may make what I have to say a little easier."

"Say what?" he said hopefully.

"I can't marry you now."

"I didn't mean right this minute," he said, undaunted. "We can wait—"

"Willie, listen," I gripped his arm to get his full attention. "This is wartime. You're in a foreign country. You shouldn't think of marrying anyone so far away from home."

"But I want to."

"I know," I whispered. "You want to fall in love. It's natural that you should. In wartime love comes easy because you're lonely. Love is a convenient place to turn. Love found in war is temporary, not something that will last. I haven't been able to meet your family. What if your mother doesn't like me?"

"I'll make her like you."

"Don't talk nonsense." I snapped shut the cover of the jewel box. "Your mother is a strong-minded woman from what you've said. But that's not what I'm trying so desperately to say. Don't interrupt—please. If I married you and we went to New York, to your home, back to your friends, you would soon tire of a wife who was so foreign, so unlike your family—a wife with a background and culture so different that even poets have said the twain shall never meet. Then you'd reject me. Willie, darling, can't you see the insurmountable odds against success? It would be something else if we were both in the United States six months. That would be different." I extended the jewel box. "It's very beautiful, but I can't accept the ring now, Willie."

Crestfallen, he turned out of the sun and a dark shadow moved across his face. I pressed the ring box into his hand. At first he hesitated, then with reluctance he took it. "I'm not giving up," he said determinedly. "Your handing back this little package in no way diminishes my love for you. I love you and I mean to have you, even if it means waiting until we both get back to the States. I've written my mother all about you—described you to the last detail. She's going to be pleased."

"I haven't heard such a dream since my uncle smoked opium. She'll say, 'Willie, have you gone mad? Have you lost your senses? Get ahold of yourself.' She'll put in an urgent call to the American Red Cross."

"God," Willie cried. "Was there ever such a woman as

you? I just absolutely positively love you!"

He was about to kiss me again but my stiffened arm prevented him. "Haven't you heard a thing I said?"

"My heart hears only what it wants to hear," he said. "And no dumb war is going to stop that."

"If the war doesn't stop it, I must. It's my fault you fell in love with me so I must teach you to fall out of love. This weekend I expect some friends to call and if they do, I won't be with you."

"Oh," he said, his voice hollow and empty. "That bunch of crew chiefs again?"

The next two days I reinforced what I had said. On Saturday, when Lonnie and the group arrived, there had been a change. Yogi was not with them. Considering that life in wartime is subject to sudden and dramatic upheaval it surprised me that the group had remained intact this long. In Yogi's place sat a young man with hair the color of corn in the sunlight.

"We brought you a little ol' country boy from Pennsylvania." Lonnie chuckled.

"Chicken plucker," Cannon said, chewing his cigar.

"Evans City is so small," Bob Yarano quipped, "and so tough, even the town rat left."

"This is Fred Ifft," Lonnie said finally.

"Hello," I said, extending my hand. He tossed his head, a heavy mane of golden blonde hair flipped back over his ear and settled like a sheaf of grain. There was a quiet air of self assurance about him; whatever Fred Ifft would start, he would finish.

"Dorr-thy," he acknowledged in his heavy rolling Pennsylvania twang.

I loved the way he said my name.

"I'm stationed in Kweilin," he said. "I came over to visit the guys and decided to tag along."

Lonnie kept giving me sidelong glances as he drove. I'm sure he thought I was paying too much attention to Fred Ifft.

"Have you lived here long?" Fred asked.

"A couple of years. Why?"

"I was in headquarters the other day and happened to overhear some scuttlebutt. The Japs are mounting a big summer offensive and this sector is a prime target. Of course, if you've been here a couple years, maybe the Chinese army can hold it."

"I hope so."

A casual conversation, easily forgotten under normal circumstances, I remembered it a month later as I listened to the thunder of Japanese cannon coming closer. Fred Ifft had not been speaking idle gossip.

Father made the decision for us to move. "This time you'll not wait until the Japs are charging down the nearest hill. Go while the trains are still running."

Willie Hershenfeld came over as we packed.

"Oh, my God, you're leaving," he said frantically. "I've got the duty shift tonight. I don't know if I can get there to see you off." He ran about the room getting in the way.

"We'd better say goodby here," I said.

"This place is like Grand Central Station."

"Do you think the railroad station will be any better?"

He drew me aside and we collided in a kiss. "I'll move heaven and earth to see you off. Dorothy, I love you. We can't end it like this. Maybe I can come up to Kweilin to see you."

"Perhaps this is the end. I will remember you with great warmth in my heart."

He turned to leave. "I'll try to be there," he called back to me.

Night settled in as Father and two of his men transported us to the station. We boarded the train at once. With our quantity of suitcases and bundles there was barely room for the five of us in the stateroom.

Saying goodby to Father had become a ritual. He pressed a paper into my hand. "This is the address of my friend in Kweilin. He will look after you. Now Dorothy, take care of your mother and the children. You are responsible. I'm counting on you."

"Yes, Father."

"I have to go now," he said. "We have to get back."

The train was about to leave and there was no sign of Willie. I stationed myself on the loading platform between cars, peering into the gloom for a sight of him. People moved and huddled in the shadows of the station, each wrapped in their own sorrows.

I heard him before I saw him. "Dorothy! Dorothy! Wait!"

He came running and I caught his arm as he jumped aboard.

"Made it," he said breathlessly. "Jack covered for me."

I found myself enclosed in the strength of his arms.

His voice sang in my ear. "I love you so much I can't bear the thought of us being apart."

I felt his body trembling against mine. My eyes moistened and my voice thickened in my throat. "I don't want to leave you either," I got out.

"Will I ever see you again?"

"I hope so."

"Without you life is going to be nothing. Nothing!"

"Don't say that, Willie."

The train lurched, threatening to throw us off balance but we clung to each other more tightly.

"Tell me you love me," he pleaded.

"I do love you," I whispered, unable to hold back a rain of tears.

The train began to inch ahead.

Willie released me and fumbled in his pocket. Out came the jewel box. "You wouldn't take this as an engagement ring," he gasped. "Your birthday is coming up in a few weeks. Take it as a birthday present."

"I can't!"

The train was gathering speed.

"Yes, you can. You just said you loved me."

"I know. But we can't marry—"

"Take the ring."

"Willie, we're moving."

"I know it. Take the ring!"

"You've got to get off!"

"Take the ring!"

"All right!"

"I've got to go. One more kiss." He drew me close and pressed his lips against mine. Almost too hard. "I'll love you forever," he said, preparing to jump. He flung himself from the train. "Write—" I heard him shout over his shoulder as his words were swallowed by the rush of air and the click-clack of cars moving over rails.

Chapter Eleven

The train chuffed into Kweilin, a teeming city surrounded by grotesque mountain peaks and rocky outcroppings not unlike the badlands of Dakota. Located in the rice-rich Kwei Valley, the city boasted a large modern railroad yard and two air bases.

When we disembarked I approached an American soldier wearing a black brassard with the letters MP.

"Excuse me. Do you happen to know Fred Ifft?" Fred, who'd come to visit with Lonnie and Cannon, was stationed at one of the bases.

Utterly astonished, the soldier did a double take. His mouth opened and slowly closed. "Y-You speak English," he got out. Finally—"I-I don't know any Fred Ifft."

"He's stationed at an air base here," I said. "Perhaps you could get a message to him."

"At the air base?" he said dumbly. "I could try to have him located. Yeah, sure. I'll be glad to help you. If you give me your address—"

"Tell Fred that Dorothy Yuen has arrived." I copied the name of Father's friend and the address where we expected to stay. The MP folded it carefully, gave me a broad smile and placed it in his breast pocket. Walking away, he turned to look once more at Edna and me. "American girls," he said wonderingly.

The next day a Jeep screeched to a halt at the home of our host. Fred Ifft and several of his friends from the air base stepped out, accompanied by a Chinese guide.

"Dorr-thy," Fred carolled in his Pennsylvania accent. "I got your message." His hazel eyes sparkled beneath his tousled cornsilk hair.

"I'm happy to see you. I was hoping you would get my message. You should have seen the startled look on the face of the military policeman when I spoke to him."

Fred laughed. "Well, Dorr-thy, you have to realize that in this entire place there are less than a dozen girls who can speak English. And that includes our nurses."

While the others were plying the family with candy bars filched from K-rations, I drew Fred aside. "Do you think I could get a job at the air base?"

Fred's face lit up. "Shore."

"I worked as a translator for Captain Lynn. I really need work—"

"Leave it to me. I'll get you a job as a secretary."

"A secretary?" My mind boggled. I couldn't possibly be a secretary. I didn't know typing, shorthand, or office procedure. "I'm not sure I could—" I broke off, hoping I had not offended. After all I had requested his help.

"Don't worry, Dorr-thy. I'll take care of everything."

Fred Ifft was as good as his word. The very next day he was back.

"I got you an appointment. All you have to do is go down and talk to the Colonel."

"The Colonel? I can't—"

"Yes, you can. I told the Colonel that you can't take the job right away. It's all arranged. Tomorrow you see Colonel Wise."

"I'm afraid—"

"Afraid? Dorr-thy, if I can face him, so can you."

"You went in to see the Colonel? For my sake?"

Fred put on a beatific smile. "Shore did."

I took his arm. "Tell me what happened."

"Well," he said, his face animated. "First I went to the Sergeant Major—Pepin. 'You know about any jobs for a girl?' I said. 'Does the Colonel need a secretary?' 'No,' the Sergeant Major says. 'We don't need anybody.' 'Yes, sir,' I says, waiting my chance, and the minute Sergeant Pepin isn't looking I sneak in to see the big brass. I walk right up to Colonel Wise and toss him a highball (that's a salute). 'I have a friend who's looking for a job,' I say. 'Do you need a secretary?' 'Maybe,' he says. 'You wouldn't happen to have a picture of her, would you?' he says. Well, I had your picture in my wallet, one of those you gave me in Kukong. I hand it to him. He looks at it, smiles and nods his head. 'Have her come see me tomorrow,' he says. Just like that. It's all set."

"But I don't know how to be a secretary—"

"Don't worry, Dorr-thy. Everything will be all right."

With Fred Ifft's assurance, I kept the appointment trembling with fright as I approached the Colonel's desk. Finding the courage to lift my eyes I recognized him at once. Colonel Wise had come to visit Colonel Lynn one Sunday morning when I was on duty in the radio shack. He had noticed me then and he was watching me now.

He smiled genially. "So we meet again," he said. "I understand you're looking for work."

"Yes," I gulped, feeling his deep-water blue eyes burrowing into me. "I-I was thinking of something in administration."

He had a particularly handsome face with a firm, resolute chin. His lower lip turned down in an incipient pout that never reached fruition; the upturned corners of his mouth all but neutralized the petulance.

"What *can* you do?" he asked, his eyes showing fatigue. They were baggy from lack of sleep.

"I can't do much," I confessed. "But I'm willing to try."

"Can you type?"

"A little. Only a little," I fibbed.

"That's fine. I understand that you're not ready to come to work."

"I-I have to get the family settled. By the end of the month—"

"All right. We can wait a couple of weeks. When you're ready, let me know. I'll send a man to get you."

"T-Thank you," I mumbled.

Outside Fred Ifft waited.

"What am I going to do?" I exclaimed. "I can't type. What *am* I going to do?" Already I was frantic.

Fred's palms flew up like two tranquil doves. "Don't worry, Dorr-thy. I'll take care of it."

Less than twenty-four hours later he appeared, carrying a typewriter.

"I had to make it look official," he grinned. "I liberated this typewriter and this official Army manual—*How to Type*. I also brought a ream of paper. The manual explains everything. You won't have any trouble, Dorr-thy. All you have to do is practice. You'll learn how to type in no time."

Fired with Fred Ifft's enthusiasm and confidence, I pinned the accompanying chart on the wall before me and sat down to learn the keyboard: *A-S-D-F J-K-L-*.

The instructions stated a student should be able to type without watching the keys, a particularly disheartening requirement. I spurred myself to greater effort and ran page after page through the machine, filling both sides. My head throbbed to the clatter of keys. Every time I stopped to examine what I had written I shrank back in disgust. Would I never learn? A sudden thought made it easier. I wouldn't try to master the numbers. Numbers weren't required for correspondence. Why would the Army Air Corps need numbers? If a random number appeared I could always peek at my fingers.

Two weeks into my agony over the keyboard, Mother came and interrupted my practice. "We can't live on greens and water," she said, her brow furrowed with worry. "You'll have to go to your father and get some money."

Kukong still had not fallen. The collapse of the city, imminent when we fled, had somehow been averted by a stiffening of our defensive positions. Accordingly, Father hadn't joined us as he planned.

"We'll try to hold out till you get back," Mother said.

Counting and recounting our dwindling money supply hadn't solved the problem. For once I agreed wholeheartedly with Mother. We had to have money and the best way to get it was from Father. I prepared to make the trip.

As I boarded the train my thoughts centered on two items I carried with me—a chart I had drawn of a typewriter keyboard and a letter. I knew the train would be darkened most of the way to prevent its detection by Japanese aircraft. Still, there might be instances when I could study. The second item, an anxious letter from Willie's mother, had recently arrived, forwarded from Kukong. "We have picked out a nice Jewish girl for Willie," she wrote. Before starting my journey I had answered, "Don't worry. The matter is already settled. I have refused the engagement ring."

A heaviness settled in my heart and I was sorry, not for myself or Willie, but for his mother. Brought up to believe that as the twig is bent so is the tree inclined, she would never be able to comprehend that the Willie who went off to war was not the Willie who would return. As a lamb does not lie down to sleep with tigers, in no way would she be able to select a wife for the Willie I knew. I foresaw much trouble between them.

An air raid greeted my arrival in Kukong and I went directly to Mrs. Au's store.

"Would you send Father a message telling him of my arrival?"

"Yes, Miss Yuen. As soon as we can."

I sat down on a heap of rubble to await him. I passed the time pretending to practice typing. The movement of my hands astounded onlookers and I'm sure some of them thought I'd lost my mind.

The thunder of guns rumbled down from a leaden sky hanging over the city like a wet gray blanket. Ribbons of smoke, black and forbidding, drifted over the tops of buildings and the acrid smell of burning oil and rubber assaulted my nostrils. Somewhere nearby a bomb had made a direct hit.

Father materialized out of a group of plodding refugees.

"How is your mother?" he asked.

"As well as can be expected. About the same."

"And little Gloria?"

"We are all fine. Edna and Jack too."

"Good. I brought all the money I could scrape together on short notice." He handed me a wrapped parcel. "Tell Mother I'll be with her as soon as I can."

"The city—will it fall soon?"

"Who can say? I can't understand where the Japs are getting all the equipment." He looked around furtively. "I cannot desert my post. I must go back."

"Take care of yourself, Father." I embraced him with great feeling.

A surprised look came into his face. His eyes searched mine briefly. "Goodby, Dorothy." He left as he had come. Our harried exchange lasted barely five minutes.

Raindrops stippled the pavement. I hesitated. Hours remained before my train was due to depart, ample time to see Willie. I walked to the radio shack.

Jack Hartell greeted me with unrestrained joy. We hugged and kissed.

"Dorothy! Dorothy, I'm so glad to see you."

"I'm glad to see you too." I looked around. "Where's Willie?"

Jack shook his head. "He's not here. After you left he became terribly depressed. Despondent. He asked for extra-hazardous duty in the field. He's out there somewhere with his transmitter—"

"Oh—!"

"It's what he wanted." Jack shrugged and spread his hands in helpless resignation. "There was nothing I could do, Dorothy. I said everything I could—"

"I know."

"What could I tell him?"

"You don't have to explain, Jack." *A wonderfully sympathetic man.*

Jack brightened at once. As soon as he could get a break we swung out into the drizzle to seek a place to eat. We found a small café and sat quietly, pleasantly, two good friends, as if there was no war and time had neither beginning nor end. Yet the end came. All too soon Jack had to get back.

Outside, the night sky strained the rain into a heavy mist. I decided to wait at the train station. Had I realized what news awaited me I would have returned as soon as I concluded my meeting with Father. People were shaking their heads and crying, some staring blankly into space. No line stretched from the window.

"No tickets," said the officer who stood in the place of the ticket agent. "The train has been confiscated by the military. No civilian passengers will be allowed."

"But I have to get to Kweilin," I protested.

"No civilians."

My brain numb with fright, I wandered aimlessly till conscious reasoning returned. Halting, I took a deep breath and forced fears of being stranded in Kukong, a woman alone, into the far recesses of my mind. Initiating a plan of action, I ran out, yelling for a ricksha.

"Headquarters, please," I instructed. The sands were running in the hourglass. Desperately I hoped that my friend Colonel Ho Hon-si would be able to help me. *What will I say to him?* I dared not tell him I'd gone to visit the Americans.

He'd bristle and blow with indignation. No, I'd tell him I'd returned to see Father...

At headquarters, relief flooded my troubled mind. Ho Hon-si sat in his office. His uniform appeared slept-in.

"Dorothy," he acknowledged in a weary voice. He listened to my tersely stated problem and said, "I think you're in luck. Do you remember General Zung? You met him several times at San Tung. He's now in charge of troop trains. Perhaps he'll make an exception for you."

"Would you write a note on my behalf?"

"I'll do better than that. I'll take you there myself. I've been wanting an excuse to get out of here."

En route to the station Ho Hon-si asked abruptly, "How are you getting along with your mother?"

"Fine." I cuffed him playfully.

He gave a tense laugh. "That's the first fun I've had in days."

"Then I'm glad."

"When I think of the joy you could give me in my lifetime—which shall not be—the tragic loss of all China is pale by comparison."

I fell silent. At the station, soldiers ran and shouted in confusion. How could they possibly all get on the train?

We were directed to an office where Ho Hon-si explained my plight to General Zung.

The General's heavy head moved from side to side. "There's no space, Dorothy," he said apologetically. "However, there's one possibility. A small roomette has been assigned to General Fong. Perhaps he'll be willing to share it. I'll ask him for you."

"Thank you."

I had met General Fong only once when I was in Chungking. It had been said he had an eye for girls. I prayed that General Zung or Ho Hon-si would tell him that I was not that kind of girl.

"General Fong says you are most welcome," General Zung reported. "But there's just one thing—"

My fingers clenched. "Yes?" I held my breath, balancing on the edge of fright.

"The train only goes to Hengyang. You'll have to switch

to another train there."

A sigh of relief kicked the props out from under my shoulders. "Thanks again," I said.

Troops clustered like flies on mooncakes atop hopelessly overloaded railroad cars, and in open boxcars soldiers had standing room only. I squeezed my way to the roomette. General Fong nodded as I entered and remained seated. He, too, seemed tired. There was no way to know if my friends had spoken to him about me but he remained a perfect gentleman. He spoke only of the day when the war would finally be over. "How nice it would be," he mused, "to sit on the bank of a lonely stream, waiting for some fish to come and attack the hook."

As he lapsed into silence, my mind looked into my book of memories and I thought of Mrs. Wu in her prison cottage. But for her and my introduction to Chungking and San Tung I would not have been acquainted with military leaders. It was comforting to be the friend of so many generals.

Perhaps I should have expected the news I received in Hengyang but again I was caught off guard. The train to Kweilin had been commandeered by Chinese and U.S. Air Force troops.

"I must get to Kweilin," I said frantically. "It's urgent. Who do I see?" Frustration and fatigue gnawed at my bones like an angry dog. Already I heard the hiss of steam from an impatient engine.

"I'm an American and I must get to Kweilin!"

"An American? Then you'll have to see the Americans."

"Where?"

"In a hotel across town. The train isn't leaving for a while," said the Chinese officer.

"But it will by the time I get back."

Seeing no alternative, I hailed a pedicab.

At the hotel, the Lieutenant, a short, swarthy, sour-faced man, regarded me with suspicion. He rubbed his prominent nose in annoyance, his only desire to be rid of me. I kept talking. At length he broke down. "All right," he said in a bored voice. "If you don't mind sharing a roomette with some men, I'll put you aboard."

"A group of Americans?"

"Yes. Take it or leave it."

My only chance. Americans are civilized. "I'll do it."

The Lieutenant rose and tugged at his jacket. "I have to go to the train anyway. You can ride with me if you like."

I murmured, "Thanks." At least I wouldn't miss the train.

At the railroad station the Lieutenant pointed to a car and I started down the tracks. I saw no way to board. A tight cluster of men huddled in every entrance; corridors were jammed. Steam whistled from the engineer's testing. My pulse quickened to a puff from the engine. Panic rising within me, I ran to my assigned coach, my hand drummed the side. "Excuse me," I shouted. "I'm assigned to this car and I can't get aboard."

"Grab on," someone said. Arms reached out and hauled me through the window. The men were delighted.

One of the four declared, "I haven't spoken to an English-speaking girl for so long that I've almost forgotten how."

"I'm Whitey," said a platinum-haired youth.

"Dorothy Yuen," I responded.

"You're a friend of Willie Hershenfeld and Jack Hartell," he exclaimed, his face animated.

"Why, yes," I said with surprise. "How did you know that?"

"I'm with Twenty-third Fighter Control too. We radiomen talk about you all the time. I've heard a lot about you."

"Really? All good I hope."

"Positively wonderful," he said, his body moving to the train's gentle sway.

Before long most of us encountered a problem. With corridors blocked, and the waiting room outside the toilet packed with troops, for all practical purposes we were without a toilet. My companions solved the problem by standing on the platform between cars to relieve themselves. However, my anatomy didn't avail me of that privilege.

Seeing me fidgeting, Whitey offered a solution. "The train's so loaded down, it almost stops going up hills. Jump out."

The men lowered me out the window. In the darkness I squatted behind a bush, and ran as fast as I could as the train began gathering speed.

"C'mon, Dorothy," they cheered.

Catching my arms, in a whirl of gaiety, the airmen pulled me aboard. They were very kind, which reduced my embarrassment.

"I wish the trip was longer," said one.

For my part, I was glad to get to Kweilin. The liberated typewriter awaited my attention. After exercising it for a couple of days, on July Twenty-ninth, I summoned the courage and sent a message that I was ready to report for work the next day.

Hope rising within me, I waited for a driver to take me to Yang Tong Air Base.

Lieutenant Willett, the tall lanky man I'd seen in the office the day I applied, arrived with a Jeep. He loaded my things while I made my goodbys to the family. When we reached the base he drove to a small building at the edge of the runway.

"This is your billet, the place where you'll stay," he said. "You'll be living with nurses."

He carried in my footlocker and introduced me to two young women. Apparently three others were on duty at the base hospital just beyond the narrow mountain range that snaked along the edge of the field.

"Hello," one nurse acknowledged, tight-lipped.

"Hello," said the second with utter indifference.

Was my reception by the plaster-faced pair indicative of what I could expect from the others? Because the two were inclined to be cold and uncommunicative, I didn't belabor attempts at conversation and started for my assigned room to hang out my clothes. Before I closed the door I heard, "What's *she* doing here? She isn't even military."

"Hell," scoffed the other. "She isn't even white."

I didn't wait to hear any more and slammed the door.

Busily unpacking, arranging my things, I heard the screech of brakes as a Jeep skidded to a halt out front. Looking out, I saw two men I would later know as Colonel Tex Hill and General Casey Vincent. The horn beeped, they waved their arms and called out.

Both nurses ran to meet them. The racing of the engine and the squeal of tires drowned out their giddy voices as the Jeep darted forward. One nurse flung up her arm and I heard an airy giggle before the Jeep changed gears.

I resumed unpacking. Within minutes the air raid warning shrieked. Running out, I looked around. Were there caves in the mountain behind me? Did I need clearance? A pass? Ahead of me stretched the runway—I couldn't go there. I stopped, turned, ran a few steps and hurled myself to the ground. WHY HADN'T THE NURSES TOLD ME ABOUT THE AIR RAID SHELTER? The first thing people did when visitors arrived was point out the air raid shelter. I heard the roar of a plane. One of our B-25's, a Mitchell bomber, coasted through a gap in the peaks. Eyes wide in terror, I saw a Japanese bomber on its tail, following it home. A Japanese bomb came hurtling down. Frantically I pressed my cheek into the earth, fingers straining. *Woom!* The earth trembled. *Woom!* Too close—only a few hundred feet away. *Woom! Woom! Woom!* A string of explosive madness stitched down the field. Knuckles straining white, my fingers became talons, holding me to the quaking earth. Vaguely conscious of a woosh of air, I heard a rain of steel fragments thudding behind me.

It was over in seconds. Down the field our B-25 landed safely. My stomach wrenched free of the evil hand clutching it. Fury rose within me, steam searing, exploding in my throat. "Bitches!" I screamed, completely enraged. Kicking wildly, I pounded the earth with both fists. "Bitches! You should have told me about the air raid shelter!" My body racked to uncontrolled sobbing.

Dazed, shaking with fright, I stumbled to my quarters and collapsed on the bed. Tears flooded my pillow. I cried myself to near exhaustion, feeling desperately alone and rejected. Before I fell asleep I realized I hadn't eaten. The nurses hadn't informed me where I was to have my evening meal, either. "You white bitches," I cried before another deluge of tears.

In the morning I tried to face the nurses without glaring.

"Oh, hello," one said tonelessly.

"Hello," said the other.

"Hello," I croaked over the fury knotting my throat.

"She doesn't say much, does she?" I heard one say as I turned to go.

"Probably doesn't know how," said the other in a voice loud enough for me to hear.

Their treatment didn't put me in a state of mind conducive to starting a new job. Lieutenant Jim Willett called for me and as we started for the crude wooden office building I debated whether I should complain about the nurses. I decided not to mention the incident.

"Is there a place to eat around here?" I asked.

"Mess hall," he said.

"Perhaps we could stop—"

"The Colonel is waiting to see you," Lieutentant Willet said. "He'll explain your mess privileges." He opened the door and marched me to the desk of Colonel Wise.

Already terrified, I stood shivering as the Colonel's cold blue eyes searched me.

"Dorothy, your personal life is your own," he began. "You're a civilian employee of the Army Air Corps. Although a civilian, you are nevertheless considered an officer and entitled to eat in the officers' mess. I understand that you've already been assigned a billet in the nurses' quarters. Nurses are officers."

And bitches.

"Any questions?"

I swallowed. "Yes," I managed. "Can't I eat in the enlisted men's mess?"

He hesitated, perplexed that anyone would ever want to eat with enlisted men. "Yes . . . I guess so," he said slowly. "If you wish."

At the far end of the room I sat down at a typewriter and allowed my eyes to roam, to photograph a scene I would long carry with me. A stark wooden building with plain floor, ceiling and side panels, the room had neither central heating nor lighting. Lacking partitions, I could see everyone. On my left, about half way down, lanky Lieutenant Willett bent over his desk.

On my right, far down and facing me, sat Colonel Richard Wise, West Point trained and born to lead. As governor of

Colonel Richard H. Wise.

Virginia, his great-grandfather had signed the order to hang John Brown. Commanding the Third Sector, Colonel Wise was responsible for logistics for nineteen air bases.

As if in his shadow, at the next desk, sat Lieutenant-Colonel Chuck Hunter. Lieutenant Ed Cabelka, who had volunteered to come to China from a post in Africa, and Sergeant Moore completed the row.

My desk stood in the center at the end of what might be considered the middle row. Directly in front of me, at the only other desk in line, sat Master-Sergeant Shirley, whose back could be a comfort.

Presently Lieutenant Cabelka came over. A tall man with a gently triangulated face, the little black moustache stuck on his upper lip didn't move when he talked. "I want you to type an endorsement on this."

"I-I don't know what an endorsement is," I flustered.

"An endorsement," he said didactically, "is a terse, usually one-line response to correspondence, indicating approval, or disapproval or whatever action is taken. It's typed on the bottom of a communication, headed by the words 'First Endorsement.' Unless it's a Second Endorsement. The signatory officer signs above his typed name, rank and command authority."

"Yes," I mumbled, spinning the letter he handed me into my machine. I felt all eyes on me. I was suddenly uncomfortable. Perspiration broke out at my armpits. A hot nervous spasm flashed across my back, congealed at my shoulder blades and burned there. Sitting erect, I squared my shoulders, inhaled deeply, clamped my jaws together in determination and began to punch haltingly at the keys. Holding my breath, I decided to hazard a look. Not one error, not even two—the result was total chaos, as mad as if a gibbon had danced a gavotte on the keyboard. Cabelka's name was mangled.

"Cavelka? My God!" he exploded. "You didn't even leave a margin. Don't you know anything about margins?" He rushed back to his desk, groped around in a drawer and came back with a procedure manual. "The first thing you have to learn is to leave proper margins. Read this manual. It'll tell you all about margins and spacings. The Air Corps is fussy about form."

"I think her form is fine," Sergeant Shirley intoned soto voice.

Lieutenant Cabelka ignored him. "You don't know how to type. Okay, you're going to learn. I want you to type this endorsement until you get it letter perfect and I don't care if it takes all day. When you get it right, we'll cut it out and paste it over this—this—this—" He flung up his hands in disgust and retreated to his desk.

The cut-out-and-paste procedure prevented me from ruining official correspondence. I studied the manual and learned the requirements for margins, but I soon encountered a problem not listed in the manual. Seeking help, I went to Sergeant Moore, the lowest ranking member of our group.

"Sergeant Moore, I need help—"

His face twisted as he erupted, "Just because you're the only girl here, if you think you're going to get special attention, forget it. You're not."

"B-But—"

"Don't think we're going to do everything for you."

"I only—"

"I haven't got time to answer your questions." He slapped down a sheaf of papers and began to read.

I hadn't reached my desk when he released a parting shot. "Do your own work. Don't ask me to help you."

Sergeant Shirley stared in utter disbelief.

Lieutenant Cabelka frowned. He rose and walked to my desk carrying a typing manual like the one I had at home.

"This should help you," Cabelka said gently. "Now, Dorothy, if you need help, you come to me. Don't worry about things you don't understand. Right now I want you to keep practicing. This is your first day and you're nervous. In a couple days—"

I clung to his words as I floundered, ready to sink for the third and final time.

My decision not to learn the numbers of the keyboard had been a mistake. Everything about my work involved numbers. Endorsements used numbered abbreviations for the 14th Air Force; 23rd Fighter Control. Men flew P-38s, P-40s and B-25s. We needed 25,000 gallons of gasoline. We dropped 500 pound bombs. During a certain period we destroyed 12 locomotives, 87 railroad cars, 164 trucks, 29 bridges, 193 sampans. 7500 enemy troops were massed at—and the crazy code, Abel, Baker, Charlie, Easy, Fox, George, instead of the letter of the alphabet and the chock-a-block abbreviations such as ComServPack for Commander of Service Forces of the Pacific, drove me to distraction. In an alien jungle, I flailed through a territory foreign to me.

Having had neither supper nor breakfast, by the time midday arrived I was ravenous. Sitting down to a quiet meal would be a pleasant respite from the tension of the office...

I walked to the officers' mess and opened the door. The moment the men saw me a cheer went up. Officers whooped and hollered, applauded and stamped their feet. Betty Grable wouldn't have received a more tumultous welcome. My feet froze to the floor and I was powerless to halt the column of red that rose in my neck and flooded my face with a rosy glow.

Embarrassed, on the verge of tears, I didn't know where to turn. A loud voice within me cried, "Run." As the alternative was starvation, I decided to stay. My eyes found refuge in my tray. Could I possibly eat the double portion of everything I'd been served? Clenching my teeth, I held my chin up and found a seat. Too dazed to know precisely where, I mouthed banalities. "But I'm not a star," and listened completely dumbfounded to some officer saying, "Out here you are."

A sea of faces continued to stare. I tried desperately to eat with poise. Really there was no way it could be done. I settled for not wolfing my food.

The ordeal over at last, I returned to the office. Hearing a loud voice I hesitated.

"I don't give a damn if she can't type," someone said loudly. "She stays."

Although I couldn't identify the voice, when I entered I'm sure Lieutenant Cabelka had been laying down the law to the rude and impertinent Sergeant Moore. Eyes lowered, I went to my desk.

Colonel Wise raised his head. "Ma'am."

Leaping up, I hurried to his desk and listened to

instructions. I went to carry them out but by the time I reached Sergeant Pillsbury's desk in the adjacent wing my mind blanked.

"Oh God," I fumbled. "The Colonel sent me to get a Special Order but I'm so nervous and distraught I can't remember a thing."

Stan Pillsbury, the sweet adorable man, leaned forward and touched my hand in an avuncular manner. "Don't worry, Dorothy," he said softly. "I'll help you."

A professional librarian from the New York City library, Pillsbury had been charged with maintaining our files. He popped his head into our office. "Colonel, what was the subject of the Special Order you wanted?" Returning, he pulled the order and allowed me to carry it to Colonel Wise in apparent triumph.

As the shadows of night crept in to curtail our activities, I ruefully looked at the cardboard box near my desk. An empty cigarette case overflowed with wastepaper, a monument to my mistakes.

Lieutenant Cabelka came by and nudged the container with his toe. "Tomorrow only half a case of Lucky Strikes." He smiled and I wondered if he would ever trust me to place a message from General Chennault in my typewriter, instead of having me type the endorsement on a separate sheet and paste it on the initial letter.

I remembered that hunger is cured by food, ignorance is cured by study. Or as my father said, "Patience and a mulberry leaf will make a silk gown."

Eating in the officers' mess became unbearable. After a couple days I tried the logical alternative. The reception I received from the enlisted men was equally tumultous. How I detested the adulation! Couldn't they just ignore me? Was there no place I could eat in peace?

Part of the problem originated with Twenty-third Fighter Control. The platinum-haired Whitey with whom I shared a roomette on the train from Hengyang had announced my arrival on the radio and if I could believe the rumors filtering around the base, the radiomen of the Twenty-third were spending about as much time carrying on about Dorothy Yuen as they were on official communiqués.

"I'm tired of eating eggs all the time," I complained within earshot of a freckle-peppered, red-haired Irishman from Boston. "All this commotion—I can't stand it."

"Leave it to me, Dorothy," Sergeant Denehy said. "Next time you want to eat alone, you come see me."

"Okay. Next time," I said firmly.

"That's a deal," he agreed.

At the appointed time he led the way to a secluded spot in a storeroom piled high with crates. There we dined in peace on K-rations. I liked the pork and beans and nearly developed an addiction for matzo balls.

Red Denehy raised a stubby finger in warning. "Don't say nothin' if you like it here. Let the enlisted men think you're eating with the officers and the officers think you're eating with the enlisted men. Man," he exclaimed, the fire in his eyes matching the flame in his hair, "This is putting my life in jeopardy. If they caught me they'd kill me."

"Really?"

Seeing my concern he quickly said, "Naw. That was just a manner of speakin'." A grin spread over his broad face. His head went back and an Irish tenor laugh boiled forth.

We continued to dine in secret.

Ten days had passed since I arrived on base. As I appeared for work on the eleventh day Colonel Wise called me to his desk.

"Let's step out back," he said curtly.

Out back was nothing more than a plowed area. Already frightened of him, I knew he had something to say he didn't want the others to hear. The stern look on his face meant trouble.

He stopped pacing and turned to me. "Dottie, you remember I told you to consider yourself an officer. Maybe I didn't make myself clear. An officer has certain responsibilities along with the honor. It is his honor that must be upheld at all times. Even before duty."

"Yes, sir."

"Let me say again, what you do with your personal life is your own business." His voice became brittle. "Still we positively cannot have enlisted men in your quarters!"

My mouth dropped slack in dismay. "Enlisted men in my quarters? I *never*—"

"It has come to me on authority—"

I felt my fingernails biting into the palms of my clenched fists. "I never did—"

"*High* authority."

Tears sprang into my eyes; all courage washed out of my spine. My shoulders sagged and began to shake to uncontrolled sobs. "I never had any men in my quarters," I choked, fingers unclenching. "When someone calls for me I'm always ready. I watch to see him come up the road and go out to meet him. The only man who was ever in my quarters was Lieutenant Willett the day he dropped me off. He carried in my footlocker. He was gone within a minute."

At once the Colonel's tone softened. "I believe you," he said. He waited for me to stop crying. "I'm sorry—"

His hand went to his rugged chin as a pensive frown furrowed his brow. "I'm beginning to see daylight. Yeah, I get it. You're not very happy living with the nurses, are you, Dottie?"

"No," I sniffed.

"Please forget what I said to you. I was given wrong information."

I dabbed my eyes.

"Come." He touched my arm for an instant and we started back to the office.

No sooner were we inside than Colonel Wise called Lieutenant Cabelka. "This is another one of Casey Vincent's deals," he said. "I'm sure of it. Dottie is cramping the boy general's style with the nurses. Otherwise he wouldn't be feeding me this bullshit. I hate to play into his hands and give him what he wants, but I want you to find a different place for Dottie. We'll put a stop to them spreading those God damn rumors. I want her out of there."

"Now?"

"Right now."

"You're a lot of trouble to me," Cabelka grumbled. There was no malice in his face as he went out. When he returned he said, "I found a place for you in the officers' headquarters of the Twenty-first Photo Reconnaissance Squadron."

I moved into barracks directly opposite the hospital on the opposite side of a narrow mountain range that threaded along the edge of the field. Assigned to a corner room, at first the men liked having me. However, they hadn't anticipated what the presence of a woman would mean.

"You sure slow our speed," one officer complained. "We're used to running around here nude. Or maybe in a towel."

Toilet and shower facilities were located in a large room and every time I locked the door the entire battery went out of commission. It made me so self conscious I began to use the ladies' restroom in the base hospital across the street. Formerly when I encountered a nurse I'd receive little more than a sterile, "Hello." Now I heard, "Good morning, Dorothy."

May the salt of a million tears pour into your wounds.

I tried not to disrupt the officers' routine. To avoid monopolizing the toilet at night I kept a chamber pot in my room, less embarrassing than encountering a gentleman clad only in a towel. I slept soundly.

The *blam-blam* of anti-aircraft guns startled me to wakefulness. Quickly I realized we were in a raid. Leaping up, I threw open the door. The men had gone. Major Leo Brown, who had the adjacent room, was supposed to knock on my door to awaken me. He hadn't. The whir of machine guns and thump of bombs emanated from the airfield side of the mountain, about five hundred feet away. I'd be safe unless the Japanese miscalculate. I decided to stay.

When I accosted Major Brown in the morning he gave me a sheepish look. "I didn't remember you till I was halfway up the hill to the shelter. Then I was too scared to come back."

I arched my eyebrows. "Really?"

"Yes."

He never forgot again.

Having me billeted with the officers of the Twenty-first Photo Recon proved to be a costly decision for the government. For every reconnaissance photo they shot from their P-38s they snapped one of me. Overnight I became the pinup queen of the base. There were no scantily clad shots, leggy or outrageous photos. They were content to photograph me casually leaning against a B-25 or sitting on a crate of ammunition. I'm reasonably certain that members of the Twenty-first were selling the photographs or trading them for favors.

In a few days Lieutenant Cabelka lifted the ban on placing

original correspondence in my typewriter. The humiliation of typing a correct endorsement on another sheet, cutting it out and pasting it on a letter had ended. Not only did I type orders, the officers barked commands and I had the responsibility of composing the orders. For letters the officers no longer needed to prepare a hand written draft. Colonel Wise would say, "Send a letter to the base commander. Tell him—"

My responsibilities increased. When a plague of dysentery immobilized a number of Sergeant-Major Pepin's crew, I was assigned to fill in for them and placed in charge of the files. Privy to classified information, I couldn't avoid learning a secret the officers were keeping from the Air Force high command—that we were running a brothel.

"I know it's not by the book," Colonel Wise remonstrated. "Still I can't have the entire base laid up with the clap. All the tarts, hookers and prostitutes in China seem to be concentrated here in Kweilin."

"Every other one is an enemy agent," Cabelka interposed. Our 'Button your fly and button your lip' campaign hasn't shown results. If Doctor Shaner examines the girls from the Bamboo Club at least it'll keep things under control."

Because the base was some distance from town, the men flocked to the nearby Bamboo Club.

"Any trouble enforcing the Off Limits edict for Slit Alley?"

"No," Lieutenant Cabelka said.

"Well, round up the girls from the Bamboo Club and have Major Shaner examine them. That's the best I can do."

Later, at lunch, I learned from Sergeant Denehy that Slit Alley was an area north of the bridge where the VD rate was so high it had been declared Off Limits.

"Lot of good that does," Denehy scoffed. "So the guys can't go there. What's to keep the broads from mincing over to the Ledo or the Red Plum? Or the Central Café?"

"I can understand how the boys feel," I said. "Every time they fly out they know they might not come back."

"They don't give a damn. If they did, more of them would come to Supply and get a pro-kit."

"Maybe it's a good thing the Colonel doesn't go by the book. It's a problem for him."

"You think *he's* got trouble? Listen, what about me? I go to confession and Father Buckley says, 'What are you gonna do now?' 'I'm going back to Supply and hand out contraceptives,' I tell him." Sergeant Denehy tilted back his head and laughed.

Truly the devil had left his mark in the red haired Sergeant Denehy. He watched me munching on my favorite part of a K-ration.

"Dottie, if you don't stop eating those things you're gonna turn into a matzo ball."

I enjoyed being with the men, sharing their lives, helping them combat the constant tension of the base. From the time they learned of a mission the men tensed and became quick to anger. Fear grated over their nerves like a heavy-handed bow sawing across violin strings. Not until fighters and bombers touched down after a mission did relief flow across frayed nerve endings. As the first returning plane became a growing dot in the sky everyone on the base rushed out and started counting. Over clutched breathing and heavily beating hearts one could almost hear the chant, in reality a prayer—"Six . . . Seven . . . Where's eight? There he is! Eight . . . Nine!" A sigh of relief. "That's all of them." The men would slap each other on the back, plan to have a drink and—

We girded ourselves for bad news but were never able to prepare for it. Ken Kesterton took off in his P-38 on a photo recon mission. Unable to gain altitude he aborted the mission and attempted to return to the field. The P-38 plunged . . . exploded. Sirens shrieked, fire engines and ambulances roared to the glowing ball of flame . . .

Sorrow engulfed me. Mule-kicked, I hunched over, weeping.

The previous evening Ken had called me to his room nearby. I couldn't forget his face as he handed me a 'Dear John' letter from his girl back home.

"Dear Ken. Relax. I'm married."

There were many new names and faces. Some men I would meet once and never see again. Captain Sweeny, a cocky fighter pilot, brought news that my friend Lonnie had rotated home on points. "Do you know that sonofagun had a scheme all set up to smuggle your family out on military aircraft? He would have done it too, if he hadn't been shipped."

"That's Lonnie," I said. "I'm glad he could go home. His mother will be happy to see him."

"Not to mention his wife."

"*Wife?* I didn't know Lonnie was married!!"

"Oops! Damn. I shouldn't have said anything."

"Yes, you should."

Captain Sweeny walked away with an amused expression. If there was any humor in it I couldn't see it.

With death a constant companion, humor on the base often became grisly. For days the biggest joke concerned an enlisted man killed when his still exploded behind the barracks. Our Chaplain, Father Buckley, joked about writing a letter to the family telling them the man had been killed in the line of duty.

Pressure from advancing Japanese units increased and air raids intensified. In our office we tried to bring order out of confusion. Returning from an errand, I saw Lieutenant Cabelka waving his arms.

"I don't know what he expects," he said in a high-pitched voice. "He appears out of the blue like a phantom and wants me to get everything ready on a minute's notice!"

"May I help you, Lieutenant?" I said.

"I'm going to need a case of cigarettes to pay his radio operators. And I'm going to need some CN. I can't pay them in gold. He expects me to pay in advance. Doesn't he know that's prohibited by Army regs?"

Cabelka scooped some papers off his desk and handed them to me. "There's no use fussing about it. All right, Dottie. I want you to type up the request, the voucher and disbursement forms. I'm going to payroll."

"Yes, sir."

I understood some of Lieutenant Cabelka's problem. CN was Chinese National Currency in which non-Americans had to be paid. Gold simply meant American money. Every time we made a payroll, Lieutenant Cabelka had to take American greenbacks to the local black market and change it for CN. There was no other way to do it. Most Chinese radio operators took part of their pay in American cigarettes, which they otherwise couldn't obtain at any price.

I read the order. My head snapped. I stopped typing. *Captain John Birch.* "Is John Birch here?"

"Ask Lieutenant Cabelka."

Before long Lieutenant Cabelka returned with a bag of CN. "I hit it lucky," he said. "A newsman on the base gave me the same rate as the best black market operator downtown. He's running a money changing racket, but why should I care as long as he gives me the same rate?" He placed the sack of money on his desk.

"Is Captain Birch here?" I asked eagerly. "I mean, on base?"

"Yes. He went down to eat."

"I have these forms typed, all except the dates. They'll have to be falsified in some way so we can make payments in advance. May I take a break? It's important."

"I'll fudge the dates. A break? Okay. Haven't those cigarettes gotten here yet?"

"Not yet," I said over my shoulder as I hurried out. Outside, I broke into a run. Reaching mess hall I looked around. I had to see John.

"Have you seen Captain John Birch?" I asked, out of breath.

"You just missed him," said the mess sergeant. "You know what he did?" he exclaimed. "He ate one meal including dessert. Then he started over and ate another whole meal."

"Where did he go?"

"I dunno," he said. "Maybe he went down to fighter headquarters."

I ran to fighter headquarters and couldn't find him.

"Maybe he went to pick up medical supplies."

A sergeant heard me. "I'm going over there in a Jeep. Hop in."

At the dispensary a medical technician said, "I haven't seen him."

I decided to return to the office but had to wait for another Jeep. Frustrated, I fussed, "I'm wasting valuable time!"

Finally I caught a ride. Racing into our office, nearly out

of breath, I asked, "Has Captain Birch come in yet?"

"Back and gone," Lieutenant Cabelka said. "You just missed him."

"Oh damn! I wanted to see him!"

"Maybe you can still catch him, before the plane takes off." Lieutenant Cabelka ran out with me at his heels. "No you can't," he said. "They've started to taxi—"

Seeing the plane moving down the runway I spat some newly acquired cusswords.

Lieutenant Cabelka observed my crushed and forlorn look. "Let's get a cup of coffee. I didn't know you knew John Birch."

"We're good friends."

"I'd say a little more—"

At the mess hall Cabelka drew two cups of coffee and slid one across the table.

"So you know the living legend."

"Yes." I forced a smile.

"We have to keep the lid on about John," he said soberly. "Can you imagine some correspondent getting the scoop on him? He's one of the biggest heroes in the Pacific."

"Really?"

"Really. The man is absolutely fearless. He's behind enemy lines half the time. The other half he lives with the peasants. Do you realize every time one of our planes gets shot down the peasants take what's left and put it on ox carts, horseback, railroad cars and the plane gets back to the nearest base. Eighty percent of them fly again. That's all John Birch's doing. More importantly, when a flier is downed, the peasants don't finish him off with a pitchfork like in the early days. Those who survive the crash get back to us safely. That's the work of John Birch. He set it up. Of course, the CBI patches the fliers wear help. Dozens of guys are going to come out of this with a whole skin because of John Birch. I hope someday they realize it."

"I'm glad you told me. I don't know how the guys will find out . . ."

"Maybe when the war is over somebody will write a book about him. Working the way he does may not be as dramatic as shooting down enemy planes, but it's a hellova lot more dangerous. Just one tiny slip—"

I shuddered. "Well, no one knows . . ."

"And probably never will. Folks will remember Colonel Doolittle's raid on Tokyo back in forty-two, and maybe they'll remember Doolittle was forced down inside China, but will they know it was John Birch was saved his butt and got him out? Hell, no. The American public will never hear a damn thing about that." He applied a flame to his cigarette and inhaled deeply. "Or the fact that I have to float our entire Chinese payroll through the black market. I finally found some use for a newspaper correspondent." His shoulders shook as he laughed at the irony of it.

"We'd better be getting back," I said.

Cabelka nodded. "Efficient little Dottie, that's you. Since Colonel Wise started calling you Dottie the whole base has picked up on it. Incidentally, the Colonel likes you."

"Really?"

"He had me put through a raise for you. I'd say that proves it."

"A raise? Me?"

"Oh, c'mon, Dottie. Don't you know the influence you have over him?"

Chapter Twelve

"Sergeant Moore won't be back," Lieutenant Cabelka said, twitching his little black moustache. "That ought to make you happy, Dottie. He always treated you mean."

I raised a questioning eyebrow.

"Moore fouled up," Cabelka explained. "Casey Vincent's Intelligence reported the Japs still sixteen miles from Paoshan. I told Moore to send a message, 'Do not—repeat not—blow up the base.' He snafued—left out the 'not.' Wing communications thought the message looked odd and contacted me before sending it. Fortunately I was able to straighten it out. I told Moore he could stick around and get court martialed or transfer the hell out. He grabbed the transfer. He won't be bothering you any more, Dottie. God—we're losing bases fast enough the way it is."

We certainly were losing bases. As the Japanese Army surged down through the interior, Hengyang fell and we lost Lingling. Kweilin stood in the path of the Japanese assault and at Yang Tong Air Base we'd been on evacuation alert for days. The nurses and the wounded had already left. Newspaper correspondents Clyde A. Farnsworth and Teddy White popped in for final stories.

"You're not going to let Dottie stay?" Lieutenant Willet questioned.

"Hell, yes," bellowed Colonel Wise. "She's been at war seven years. You don't see her cowering behind a desk or pissing in her pants every time a bomb goes off around here. Which is a hellova lot more than I can say for some of my officers and men."

"A girl who's worked at headquarters? Do you know what the Japs would do to her? You can't trust the Chinese Army. If they break and run, we'll have Japs up the ass in twenty minutes."

"Tell me something I don't know. Give me a couple American divisions." The Colonel turned to me and his expression softened. Sometimes, as now, in a tense situation when he had things under control, a wry smile formed on his lips and a twinkle came into his eyes. "Are you still going with us, Dottie?"

"Yes," I nodded. "I want to stay with the outfit. Unless my father doesn't get here . . ."

Since the fall of Kukong Father hadn't been able to make his way to Kweilin. If he didn't arrive before the evacuation my first responsibility was to my family. Colonel Wise understood that.

Ripping a sheet of paper out of my typewriter I winced and my hand instinctively went to my shoulder.

"Still hurt?" Lieutenant Willett asked.

"A little," I said. "Actually it looks worse than it feels. I'm all black and blue." Earlier I had been out with Fred Ifft and Harry Bratty, a former streetcar conductor from Philadelphia. They'd given me a crash course in firing a variety of pistols, carbines, automatics and machine guns.

"Well," Lieutenant Willett said, a smile pushing a look of amazement off his face. "I'd rather have you with us than against us."

My work nearly caught up, I went to the Colonel's desk. "Colonel Wise," I said. "May I have a couple hours off? My family must be frantic seeing everyone else leaving and not knowing when they're going. I'm sure they're worried—"

"No word from your father yet?"

"Not yet. I taught my sister how to phone me but I haven't heard. I'm afraid Mother—"

"Sure, Dottie. You go ahead."

As I passed through the streets I saw shop owners boarding up their stalls. Some pasted patriotic swatches of red and black on the boards to encourage resistance. Others had daubed on red and black paint. Most used paint to post dramatic price cuts. Items G.I.s would buy were marked down a half or two-thirds. Amidst the posting of bargains were signs hung by some of the prostitutes. "So long, boys." A couple girls had even signed their names. It was part of the evacuation madness.

City sanitation services were suspended. Dead and dying accumulated in the streets, many the victims of a cholera epidemic. The stench burrowed into one's nostrils and clung there. People with death on their faces trudged toward the suburbs or crowded into the railroad station, one of the most modern terminals in all of China. There, activity exceeded the frenzy on the base as engines puffed back and forth, assembling trains. Inside the station men shouted and waved their arms to determine priorities—which equipment or which people would be allowed to depart.

Rumors were rampant. "The Japanese are wearing Chinese uniforms," an old woman asserted.

"Our soldiers caught some of them and shot them," added another.

I knew the rumors were untrue. Our intelligence reports indicated the infiltrators were members of the Chinese fifth column.

Reaching home, the family clustered around me. "No sign of Father yet?"

"No," Mother replied, her face ashen. "I'm worried sick. People are leaving much earlier than they did in Kukong. As if they know something."

"I heard the last train is tomorrow," Jack said excitedly.

"No," I said, calming him with a wave of my hand. "Trains are going to run until the last minute."

"You think old General Ironpants can hold the line?" he interrupted.

"A long time yet." Actually I had no idea how long General Chang Fa-kwei could hold out up north.

Gloria and Edna inclined worried faces. "Have you heard anything about Daddy?" Gloria whimpered.

"No."

"Is it true Chiang Kai-shek had some of his generals shot?" Jack piped up.

"Where did you hear that?"

"In the street."

"Stop worrying," I said. "Just calm down. The Japs are at least fifty miles away. Maybe more. And stop listening to street talk. Remember I work at headquarters and we get reports from OSS and our reconnaissance men take pictures. If things get critical I'll let you know. I may even have some guns—"

Jack's eyes widened. "For sure?"

"Yes," I said quietly.

"Boy!"

"How are we going to carry all our things?" Mother asked.

"You won't be able to. You'll have to leave what you can't carry."

"I hate to do that—your father's chairs—after bringing them all this way..."

"There's no other choice."

"We must depend on you, Dorothy."

"I have to go now," I said. "Don't worry. Father will get here."

Desperately I prayed that he would. I had my heart set on going with the men of the Fourteenth Air Force. It was exciting, thrilling, to be with them and I enjoyed being part of the war effort. Certainly I didn't want to be left behind.

It surprised me how well informed my family was. I smiled to myself as I realized I had succumbed to a military idiosyncrasy—the feeling that only the military grasped the situation. In reality the facts were there for anyone to see.

The Chinese Sixty-second Army had been swallowed up in a week as the Japanese churned through the hills toward the Chuanhsien Pass, the strategic gateway to Kwangsi Province. The Ninety-third Army had been assigned to bottleneck the Japanese there. A ragamuffin army, the Ninety-third had pillaged government rice stores at Liuchow before going to the pass. According to American OSS reports the Ninety-third was so disorganized that one field commander didn't know where the next unit was operating. Some men had Chinese rifles, some had Russian. They either had no ammunition or the wrong ammunition. Old distrusts between commanding generals and Generalissimo Chiang Kai-shek surfaced and flamed into hostility. The Ninety-third retreated from the pass without firing a shot, whereupon the Generalissimo ordered the commander shot. By then it was too late. The Japanese strategy was simply to push on south to join forces sweeping up from Indo-China, giving them a road from North China all the way to Singapore.

At Yang Tong we were on evacuation alert for two weeks before the order came down to leave. Men hastily packed their gear and I typed a frenzy of last minute orders. We were ready to go when Colonel Wise received an urgent message.

"Rescind the order," he said. "We're staying."

"Hell, it was only a dress rehearsal," Lieutenant Willett muttered. We were all showing the strain.

Lieutenant Cabelka swore. The landing strip at Paoshan, which he'd saved from destruction earlier, had to be destroyed, the planes stationed there diverted to Chihkiang.

Air raids increased in intensity. Instead of using lanterns to signal the approach of enemy aircraft as had been the custom in Chungking, we used large red balls. One ball went up, then two. In those final days we never had a three ball *Jing Bao*. Everyone knew when the second ball went up it was only minutes before we would be under siege. Nobody bothered to raise the third ball. Our fighters roared off the runway to prevent being bombed on the ground.

Bombs rained on the city and fires broke out with volcanic fury, glowing red, then abating, black smoke billowing in the autumn sky, forming an enormous cloud. It hung like a pall, waiting for a *kwang mo* wind, wide and endless, adding its acrid smell to the already overpowering stench of death.

Surprisingly, Chinese telephone lines were yet operational but there had been no word from Edna. Where was Father? Why hadn't he arrived? I feared the worst. With heightened anxiety I had grave doubts that he would reach Kweilin before we departed.

When Edna finally called there was so much interference on the line we had to yell at the tops of our lungs to make ourselves understood. I asked Edna to repeat what she said so there'd be no mistake.

"Father—has—arrived! Father—has—arrived."

"Good," I hollered. "*Hao*."

No message could have cheered me more. I was happy that Father was safe but I was even more delighted that I could stay with the outfit.

Edna's message reached me in time. The very next day we were ordered to abandon Yang Tong and retreat to Liuchow, our nearest base to the south. Despite hectic conditions that threatened to disrupt procedures, the transition went smoothly. Bomber crews were sent to targets and ordered to return to Liuchow or alternate bases, allowing them to continue their runs without interruption.

Fighter pilots had their own transportation . . . it was mostly a matter of allocating them to other bases.

During the last minute rush, a UC-64, a high wing monoplane, dropped in.

"What the hell does he want?" roared Colonel Wise.

Lieutenant Cabelka checked and returned faintly amused. "He came to pick up Casey Vincent's flush type toilet. I don't know why not. It's the only one in the area. The damn thing's probably an art treasure."

"Then it ought to go to the Smithsonian," Colonel Wise growled.

Actually it was flown to Luliang where General Vincent had his new headquarters.

"Dottie, can you run these papers over to fighter control?"

"Yes, sir."

I was half way there when someone cried, "Look out, Dottie!" The warning came almost too late. The bullet spanged into the building before I flung myself to the ground.

A sniper, concealed somewhere distant, kept pecking away. His rifle must have been equipped with crude iron sights because he wasn't hitting anything. Cursing, I scooted around the corner on my hands and knees and ran out of the line of fire.

I saw Major Huang, a Chinese liaison officer who had been ordered to stay with us to the last, scolding one of his guards.

"My shoes are gone," he screamed, punching his guard. He wrenched the man's rifle out of his hands and began beating him with it. "Idiot! Imbecile! Bring back my shoes or you're a dead man."

Pale, shaking with fright, the soldier scurried off to seek the Major's shoes. He must have known death was imminent. He had already lost his weapon, an offense for which Chinese infantrymen were frequently shot. Certainly he had nothing more to lose.

Later Lieutenant Cabelka told me the sentry's life had been spared. He had come back with six pairs of shoes, one of which belonged to Major Huang. However, the Major had retained all six pairs.

Shortly after my return Captain Earl Gibbens came into

the office to ask Colonel Wise a favor. "Let me have Dottie for a while."

The men conferred briefly, then Colonel Wise nodded, smiling. "Just don't get her blown up," he cautioned.

"Would I do that?" Captain Gibbens asked. "C'mon, Dottie."

As I followed him to a Jeep he explained, "There's more than five hundred buildings on the base that have to be destroyed before we leave . . . and I want you to get in on the fun."

In each building demolition crews had placed a gasoline drum. Captain Gibbens halted the Jeep in a line with the open doorway and handed me a .45-caliber automatic. I fired once. Gasoline gurgled from the hole in the drum, spread across the floor, sending up fumes. The Colt bucked in my hand again, exploding the fumes, igniting the building. Flooring the Jeep, Captain Gibbens raced to the next shack where I took aim. Now and then a thatched roof would heave into the air with the explosion, then settle gently into the flames. Little tongues of liquid fire sometimes ran down the roof from the apex to the eaves, dripping off the roof to burn in hot little patches on the ground. Some of the buildings took fire slowly, others were gone in a crimson flash. After a moment, evil black clouds belched forth from the petrol.

"Anybody can hit 'em sitting still," Captain Gibbens teased. "How about trying a little wing shooting?"

"Okay."

"On this row I'm not going to stop. You shoot each can once. Then I'll circle and you can light 'em off on the second pass."

He drove slowly on the initial run. Even so I had to snap a couple of shots at some of the drums. Increasing his speed on the second pass, some of the buildings failed to *wump* behind us.

"You missed, Dottie," he laughed.

"They're not so easy to hit when you're speeding."

Not until I got behind the wheel and raced the Jeep did he understand the problem.

"I see what you mean," he said.

Captain Gibbens had the last word. He touched off

targets we'd missed with a few well-aimed shots from a carbine.

We retained a number of fighter planes for air cover but as the sun was sinking Colonel Wise dispatched the last wing to Liuchow enabling them to get there while it was still daylight. Demolition crews placed thousand-pound bombs in the runway, wiring them in clusters of three. Out came fuses; into nose cavities went C compound. When detonated, the blasts made thirty foot craters fifteen to twenty feet deep.

Veteran ordinance officer First Lieutenant Norwood Wilson, whom the men called "Whiskers," led the demolition crew. A high stakes poker player, Whiskers carried a brief case containing more than one thousand American dollars and two gold wrist watches. He ran into a building, fused a hundred pounder and ran out. He drew up short—he'd forgotten his brief case! Before he could turn, *Woom!* His brief case was blown to smithereens, the money incinerated in the same instant.

His shoulders sagged, his arms went limp. After a moment he yelled something appropriate, drew himself erect and ran to fuse the next bomb.

As the sky became dark I could see silhouettes of demolition crews frantically working in the eerie glow of headlights. Men fired into partially filled gas drums while others rushed around with torches. The rows of flaming buildings and shacks lit up the area with the brilliance of noon. Suddenly we heard a crackling sound, like a string of Chinese firecrackers.

"Who forgot to remove the ammunition?" Lieutenant Willett demanded as bullets popped and slugs whined in all directions. Tracers arched left and right lending a festive touch to the tragic row on row destruction.

"Mount up," someone commanded.

The thirty vehicle caravan moved into the hills—trucks, command cars, Jeeps and an ambulance. Colonel Wise, Lieutenant Cabelka and C.K. Wong were in a Jeep bringing up the rear. Cresting the hill, I turned for a last look at the bizarre scene in the valley below, the campfires of some monstrous pow-wow.

I saw the Colonel's Jeep draw up with a flat tire. Men

from the truck ahead, armed with machine guns, swarmed out to stand guard until the spare tire could be bolted in place. We lost sight of them but it wasn't long before the Jeeps, with Colonel Wise at the wheel, raced up and down the length of the convoy like a shepherd dog herding a flock of sheep.

Despite the despair and tension of the moment, Colonel Wise enjoyed driving the Jeep. Most of the men loved Jeeps. More versatile than the hotrods they remembered from their teenage years, the men could "express themselves" in a Jeep. A Jeep was a symbol of home . . . perhaps of a childhood they never had.

A hundred miles out we came to a river. A pontoon ferry, pulled back and forth across the stream by ropes, allowed only two vehicles to cross at a time. The convoy came to a standstill.

Colonel Wise galloped up in his Jeep. "What's the bottleneck?" he asked as he reined up and dismounted. "If the Japs catch us bunched up like this there will be hell to pay."

Anxiously we craned our necks, staring at the clouds.

Lieutenant Willett explained the problem. "We're crossing as fast as we can."

A sergeant ran up. "There's an earthen dam down the stream a ways. If we blow it maybe the water level will drop and we can drive across."

"Blow the damn thing," Colonel Wise ordered.

The men placed a land mine in the center of the dam. Crouching behind the vehicles we heard the mine thump, sending yards of earth skyward. Clods rained down on us as water gushed through the rupture. When the water dropped to the level of the hubcaps, one Jeep slowly started across. It reached the opposite shore safely, then all the vehicles followed.

In another thirty miles we arrived in Liuchow and began the task of setting up new headquarters. At dawn, as if we had planned it for days, a wing of our fighters roared off the runway to engage the enemy.

Chapter Thirteen

When our convoy arrived in Liuchow we had no place to stay. Base facilities were already overcrowded, but Colonel Wise solved the problem. Clutching the wheel of his Jeep, in a near standing position, he waved the convoy into a turn and we followed him into the city where he appropriated a two story hotel.

A fairly modern structure, the hotel sat on an old-style compound surrounded by a wall. Chinese sentries were immediately placed at the gate and hotel workers joined army cooks carrying in supplies. Separate mess and sleeping quarters were set up for officers and enlisted men, and Colonel Wise assigned me a suite of my own. The retention of key hotel people made getting settled easier and at once boosted morale.

"Casey Vincent doesn't have a thing on us," Lieutenant Willett declared as a group of us assembled in the newly established officers' mess. "Do you know we have flush toilets?"

"Yeah."

"Don't tell Casey. He might come back from Luliang."

"I'm going to miss your daily briefings with him," I said. Sometimes the men joked about Casey Vincent but I knew that deep inside they appreciated having a general who was only twenty-nine years old.

Lieutenant Cabelka rubbed his moustache with a knuckle of his index finger. "How does it feel to be a prisoner of the Japanese?" he asked wryly.

Seeing our quizzical expression he continued. "Sure. We have to be prisoners of the Japanese. Teddy White jumped the gun on filing his dispatch. We were in Kweilin days after he had the base destroyed."

Colonel Wise emitted an oath.

"Teddy had some deal cooked up with Casey Vincent," Cabelka explained. "After the control tower was wired Casey was suppose to fly over and set off the detonators with a well-placed burst. The tower detonators were to be synchronized with a row of thousand pounders in the runway—one big grandstand play. I guess Teddy wanted some pictures of the whole thing going up, but demolition couldn't wire it that way. The deal fell through."

Colonel Wise swore again.

"Isn't that terrific?" scoffed Lieutenant Willett. "Casey Vincent and Teddy White all alone on the base after everyone else had left with the Japs closing in. Hell, not even a schoolboy would believe that!"

"A schoolboy *would* believe it. That's the stuff heroes are made of."

"Bullshit."

"Precisely."

"That's what's wrong with some of these correspondents. They make heroes out of the wrong people."

"Why in the hell can't they send us somebody like Ernie Pyle?"

Cabelka drained his cup. "The feedback I'm getting indicates that Teddy is saying that he and Casey hung around after we left."

"Man, there wasn't anybody there when we left. Could they have been hiding at Ehrtong?"

"Did you see anybody over there?"

"No."

"Well, that's your answer."

"You're the base historian, Cabelka. Straighten it out."

"I can't. It doesn't fit into military history. What do you think I'm writing, a Hollywood gossip column?"

"That's what I thought," Willett said sourly.

"Dottie," Colonel Wise said. "I'm making the hotel our headquarters. I want you to stay here and man the phones. We'll have to go to the base a lot. If none of us are around, you're in charge."

Being on the phones was not so much a matter of initiating orders as it was repeating instructions I had been given. Because a substantial part of my work involved locating persons or things, a joke developed. "Dottie, see if you can find some of the bases we lost."

Experience should have taught me by now that after every move I would encounter old friends. The awesome finality inherent in parting made reunions occasions of great joy. It startled me to see Jack Hartell come into the hotel.

He smiled genially. "Still in communications?"

"Jack," I cried, ripping off the headphones to embrace him. "How did you know I was here?"

"I got my ways," he said, an impish gleam in his eyes. "I checked up on you."

"Really."

"Are you kidding? Your name is all I hear on the radio. Dottie Yuen is leaving Kweilin. Dottie Yuen is enroute Liuchow. Dottie has arrived." His chuckle died and his face cleared in anticipation of the question he knew I'd ask.

"What do you hear from Willie?"

"He got back from his mission with a whole skin. When Kukong fell he was pulled back to headquarters for reassignment. He must be about ready to point out for home. That's what most of us old timers are doing—stacking up points so we can go home."

"It's sure good to see you."

"Gotta go," he said. "I'm on duty. See you later."

"We'll get together."

"As Willie would say, 'Right.'"

"Right."

Soon I was hugging another Jack—my brother. Father managed to get the family on a hopelessly crowded refugee train and after arriving in Liuchow they came to visit me. They all looked thin. Mother's dress hung on her bones like a sack.

"I've never been through anything so miserable in my life," Mother said, making a dreadful face.

"The conductor sold the toilet for one gold bar," Jack exclaimed, wide-eyed. "Nobody could go to the bathroom."

"People went where they lay," Mother said. "What a stink! The smell alone was enough to kill. I never want to go through that again."

"It really was bad," Edna said. "We were human sardines in a sauce of filth. I hope the conductor is happy with his gold bar. We sure had to suffer for his greed. When I saw all the pots and pans and buckets hanging on the train when we got on, I didn't realize we'd be using some of them for potties before we got through."

"There was a ricksha on top of one car. And a pig. One boy hugged a rooster all the way to Liuchow. Some woman had a baby—"

"Ten people died." Mother sighed wearily.

"They had boards and canvas slung under the cars over the brake rods and people were hanging on under there," Jack said, still wide-eyed.

Mother sighed again. "Even when the train stopped people refused to move. They were afraid they couldn't get on again. It was terrible."

"Gloria," I said. "How are you?"

"Fine. Can I have some candy bars out of K-rations?"

I clasped both hands to my cheeks. "We can't talk about that here," I said softly. "If you don't say any more about it I will see what can be done."

Before they left I raided the commissary and gave each of them a treat. They cut short their visit because the phones kept me busy.

The phones ringing incessantly reflected the command post's importance, but my second floor suite became more popular. The officers brought in a detachable belly tank containing fifty-five gallons of one hundred ninety proof alcohol.

"Your room is absolutely the best place to put it," Colonel Wise said. "Who would think of looking for it there?"

Whenever the officers wanted to drink they dispatched a room boy to my door. He came padding in with bottle and hose in hand. Inserting the tube in the tank, he sucked on the end to siphon out the alcohol. A clumsy lad, he always burned his mouth.

"Sorry, Missy. Sorry, Missy," he spluttered as he raced to the sink to spit.

"Won't you ever learn?" I scolded.

It became my custom to have a glass of water ready for him. The entire sucking and spitting routine annoyed me, and to further heighten my discomfiture the room boy sometimes knocked while I was asleep. Couldn't the officers keep their booze in their own quarters? The belly tank took up half the room.

To some extent I managed to even the score. I decided to share the alcohol with the enlisted men.

"If you can find a bottle and a hose," I told Jack Hartell, "I'll fill it for you."

"That's great, Dottie."

Soon I was filling bottles for Sergeants Musto, Denehy and Korowski.

"The price is right, Dottie."

"You're a real friend."

Being a friend of Sergeant Korowski became a hazardous occupation. Unwittingly, he placed me in a situation that generated serious consequences. Even I didn't know when it happened.

Jack Hartell raced up to the hotel in a Jeep. "I came as quick as I could, Dottie," he said breathlessly, his face tense and red. "You're in big trouble. I know it was your voice coming over the air. Where were you broadcasting from? What were you doing on the radio?"

"Radio? Radio? I wasn't on any—"

"Yes, you were. I recognized your voice. God, it was critical. We were talking down a gut-shot tanker. The pilot was shot to hell and the tanker was coming in for a belly landing. Your voice kept coming on, 'No, I can't go out with you tonight.' Every time an officer came near I made static to cover your voice, but God, I couldn't cover it all. 'I already have a date tonight,' you said. Where the hell were you broadcasting from, Dottie? They're going to chew you up on this."

Stunned, my hand flew to cover my mouth as my jaw dropped. "No," I cried as realization whipsawed my brain. "I know—"

"Where were you? How did you get on the air?"

"It all went on the air? I can't stand to think—" Swallowing hard, I tried to compose myself. "I-I went for a walk with Sergeant Korowski. He asked me aboard a B-25. 'Go to the tail gunner's section,' he said. 'Put on the headphones.' He stayed up front. 'How about a date tonight, Dottie,' he said. 'No, I can't go out with you tonight,' I said. We were kidding around that way a long time. It all went on the *air*? I can't stand it. How did it happen?"

Jack shook his head. "That damn Korowski. He didn't have it closed off. He threw the intercom switch too far. Listen, I'm on duty. I've got to get back. The guys can only cover for me so long. If the brass comes to me I'm gonna know nothin'. You're in big trouble. Maybe you can say it was an accident. Let Korowski answer for it."

I nodded ostensible agreement but my heart knew I could not blame Korowski. My guilt was as great as his. A great turmoil boiling within me, I fumbled my way through the next phone call. What was I to do?

Major Frank Gleason of OSS stopped and I gushed out my problem to him. He ran his hand through his flame colored hair and nodded. "You're in big trouble all right. Is our date still on for tonight?"

"Yes, but—"

"Let me see what's being done—find out how much trouble you're really in."

"Would you please? I can't—"

"I'll look into it."

In his mid-twenties, Major Gleason headed our counter-spy activities. Once I accompanied him to a secret room in the city where we met four beautiful girls, two Eurasians like myself and two foreign nationals. Beyond a pleasant greeting I spoke to them sparingly; I didn't want to know anything about their spying activities. Lately Major Gleason directed the dynamiting of bridges as we fled.

He called for me, his face grave. "You're in trouble, Dottie. I just came from a meeting with the big brass. They know all about it. One asked, 'Who was the female on the air when we were trying to bring in that cripple?' 'There's only one girl on the base,' said another. You're about as popular as Tokyo Rose. Your number is up."

Panic stricken, I could only think in my confusion that I didn't wish to take Colonel Wise down with me. I bolted for his room, the surprised voice of Major Gleason trailing after me.

"Dottie, where are you going?"

My knuckles still drummed his door as Colonel Wise came to answer. "May I speak with you?" I blurted.

Surprise flooded his face. "Yes. What—?"

"Colonel Wise, I'm in big trouble," I flustered. The whole sordid story rolled from my lips like marbles from a can.

"Uh-huh." He nodded soberly, his hand went to his chin. "Yes—well, thanks for telling me. Have a nice evening,

Dottie." The corners of his eyes crinkled. "I'll take appropriate action."

"Thank you! Thank you," I bubbled, feeling immensely relieved. "I couldn't stand it having you mad at me."

His eyes twinkled and the petulance went out of his lower lip. "Enjoy yourself, Dottie. Have a nice time."

"Thank you," I said again, reaching out and pumping his hand. Only after I had started down the corridor did I realize what I had done. I spun around but the Colonel's door had closed.

"Colonel Wise is going to put in a word for me," I said with elation as I returned to Major Gleason.

Part of the burden lifted from my shoulders, I barely noticed the two dozen tarts who continually hung around our gate waiting for the men, shouting, "You say how much—one time."

"I know a decent café," the Major said.

My mind was not on food. I kept thinking that with Colonel Wise's help I might get off with as little as a severe reprimand. "I sure don't want a black mark on my record," I said aloud.

"Is that all you can think of?" Major Gleason complained as we sat down to dine.

"I can't help it. I'm worried."

"Relax."

He kept saying, "Relax," but I couldn't. As we were completing our meal he lifted his head and smiled. "I think it's time I leveled with you. The brass doesn't know anything about your broadcast."

"What?"

"Aw, I made that up," he said. "I was only fooling you. Having a little fun." There was a satanic gleam in his eyes.

"Fun?" I exclaimed before violence erupted within me. *"Fun?"* Rising, I pounded the table with the flat of my hand. "Frank Gleason, I'm so damn mad at you I-I—" I shook a clenched fist in his face.

He threw back his carrot-crowned head as uncontrolled laughter boiled from his depths.

I sat down and thumped the table with a fist. "You make me furious! Is it true that all redheads have the devil in them? You're as bad as Sergeant Denehy. No, worse. A lot worse!"

Dorothy Yuen

"I think it's hilarious," he chuckled. He just sat there and laughed, waiting for my anger to subside.

I was annoyed with Colonel Wise too. He could have warned me. Men and their practical jokes. I was still apprehensive and on guard a few days later when the Colonel gave me an assignment.

"Dottie, there's some females at the end of the runway. I want you to go over and get them—find rooms for them. This is a helluva time for them to drop in. Don't they know we're on evacuation alert?"

I detected a trace of frivolity in his manner but his expression remained serious. Not particularly upset at their presence, Colonel Wise appeared more concerned for their safety. I wondered, why is the Air Corps sending WAAFs or WAACs at a time like this?

The "females" (and males) I found at the end of the runway were Hollywood stars—Jinx Falkenburg, Pat O'Brien, Ruth Carrell, Jimmy Dodd, Harry Brown and Betty Yeaton.

The troop put on a show in one of the hangars and the men were absolutely thrilled. Afterwards the entertainers came to the hotel where I had officers double up to make room for them. Pat O'Brien went off to bend elbows with newly found friends, while officers crowded around Jinx and stared with adoring eyes.

At midnight, when I showed Jinx to her room, I told her, "The enlisted men feel bad about your being with the officers. 'Officers get all the breaks,' they say."

Jinx halted. "I have no way to get to the enlisted men. If you can get them together, I'll talk with them."

Running to the enlisted men's wing I began pounding on doors. Some of the men told me they slept raw so I dared not enter.

"Come and meet Jinx Falkenburg," I yelled.

"Stop kidding," said a sleepy voice.

"No. On the level. C'mon, wake up," I pleaded.

At last someone in shorts stumbled into the corridor. "Oh, it's you, Dottie," he said groggily.

"Wake up the guys," I said. "It's an order. Anybody who wants to meet Jinx, follow me."

Men never dressed more hastily. They clustered around

the tall and willowy Jinx, admiring her fine featured face, the hair that cascaded to her shoulders. The two dozen homesick men kept her in conversation until two in the morning.

"Dottie," one of the men said, "You can wake me up any time."

"If I had something like that waiting for me back home—"

"I thought you did, George."

George issued a one word epithet.

One of the men thanked me with a thumbs up salute.

It was too dangerous for entertainers in Liuchow, so we sent them out the next morning. Once they were airborne I set out on a project of my own. With evacuation imminent I needed to get my family on the first convoy, an arrangement requiring permission of the transportation officer.

Major Bull was a slightly built, thoroughly unpleasant man who parted his gray hair in the middle. Glaring at me through round eyeglasses, he displayed some of the irrascibility that earned him the nickname, "The Bull."

"Out of the question," he bellowed. "We can't take civilians on a convoy. This is a military convoy. Strictly military."

"Yes, Sir."

Despite his curt refusal he had unwittingly supplied me a plan of attack. With a speech well rehearsed, I went to Colonel Wise.

"They're all American citizens," I said. "Mother, Edna, Jack, Gloria. As the senior American officer around, I think you owe some responsibility to them—to help them if you can. They're destitute."

"What about your father? Can't he—"

"He's an ally, married to an American. He wants to go on the convoy too."

"A foreign national. That's a little more difficult."

"He's really a member of the family—"

"It's a little unusual—"

"Americans. They need help!"

"Very well," he said. "I suppose it would be permitted in an emergency. All right, I will give my permission." He jangled the military phone and instructed Major Bull to make a truck available for the family. "Send a driver out to pick up their possessions."

Although I did not witness the Major's reactions he found a way to vent his indignation. "No dogs," he decreed, when he learned the family had a chow. "I'm not going to allow dogs on the convoy. No dogs!"

Back to Colonel Wise I went. "Major Bull won't let us take our dog. The Chinese Army always has dogs—"

"A *dog*?" he erupted.

"Yes. A nice chow dog—all white. It's really a wonderful little dog. Part of the family. I just love it. It won't take up any room at all."

"Dammit to hell, Dottie! What do you think I'm running? A kennel?"

"It's just a little thing. A puppy."

"Oh, all right. Take the damn dog. Only don't bother me!"

With the matter of the convoy settled there would be time to visit a friend in the residential section. Less than four hours earlier I learned that Livia Lung was in the city. Livia and I had become acquainted in Kukong and I wanted to see her before we left.

When I arrived at her home she and her family were preparing to flee to the hills, hoping to find refuge in a remote mountain cave.

"You can't take Livia with you," I remonstrated with her brother. "Don't you know what the Japs do to girls like Livia?"

"What else can I do?" he said, spreading his hands helplessly.

"They're sure to send out patrols. If they get her—"

"We don't have wings," he said, his face drawn and pale.

"There's a chance," I said, grasping an idea. "I might be able to get her on the convoy with my family. I'll ask Colonel Wise. Can you stay here till morning?"

"If you think there's a chance. But we can't wait any longer. The risk is too great."

"I'll get in touch with you. Wait for my message."

I knew I couldn't see Colonel Wise until morning. As expected, I found him having an early breakfast. I slid up a chair and greeted him in a gentle voice.

"Good morning, Colonel Wise."

"Good morning, Dottie."

"This war sure is terrible," I said tentatively.

"We all get sick of it," he agreed.

"Bad times makes being a friend all the more important."

"Yes," he replied absently, reaching for his cup, raising it to his lips.

"I have this friend, Livia Lung. It's important that I help her."

"Uh-huh."

"The Japs will get her unless I get her out on the convoy with my family. It's real important—absolutely vital—"

Colonel Wise gulped. Choking on his coffee, he slammed down the cup in a paroxysm of coughing. "God dammit, Dottie. What the hell do you think this is? A tour bus?"

"B-But she's such a frail thing," I stammered. "Delicate and beautiful. She can't live like an animal. She'll die. The things she's taking with her won't fill a bandana. She won't take up any room at all."

"No."

"I can't bear to think what will happen to her if the Japs catch her. Do you know what the Japs do to a girl like Livia? I mean, do you know?" Sniffing, tears formed in my eyes.

"Yes, I God damn well know," he growled, exasperated, his eyes glaring blue flame. "Okay, she can go—but hear this. This is it! No more family. No more dogs. No more girlfriends. No more anything." He pounded the table, his face livid. "I've got a war to fight. You're going to cost me my eagle. How did you ever get into my outfit? Can't you go over to Chennault, Stilwell, MacArthur—anybody?"

"I-I'll get you a fresh cup of coffee."

He regarded me sheepishly as I returned. "I'm sorry about the cusswords, Ma'am." Immediately he was glowering again and I had no doubt that I had exhausted his patience.

"Thank you, Colonel."

He shook a warning finger at me. "Do you always get your way? There's a limit to some things—" With a sour and disgusted look he waved me away. "Now get the hell out of here." He had given up on me.

Originally it was intended that a six by six truck dispatched to the Yuen family would transport both the family and their possessions. Unlike the Chinese who traveled light, the Yuens packed everything they owned, filling the truck completely. An irate Major Bull was forced to allocate a second vehicle, an ambulance.

Overcome with gratitude, Livia Lung bowed, saying, "I'm so grateful."

Mother picked up on it. "This is wonderful, Dorothy. I'm so proud of you. When I think of that wretched train and all its filth this ambulance is like heaven."

"Stop," I pleaded. "You're embarrassing me. I don't want to be conspicuous. I don't want the officers to notice."

Father bent forward and whispered. "A messenger came for me during the night."

Following the direction of his inclined head I saw a man lingering outside the gate. I recognized him as an employee from Father's factory in Shanghai. He had long been in Father's command.

Father's imploring eyes asked the question before he could find the words. "Is there some way he can accompany us on the convoy?"

"I don't know," I said, remembering that the man was one of those who had built several homes for us at Kukong. I dared not approach the Colonel. Could I face the wrath of The Bull?

"All aboard," a sergeant commanded.

I ran over to the Major. "Major Bull. Major Bull, Sir. My father has just received an urgent message. His runner is here. Can he come aboard the convoy?"

The Bull's evenly parted gray head snapped up imperiously. "Of course not! We can't take Chinese nationals on this convoy. It's absolutely forbidden. Against regulations."

"Not even a little way?"

"Out of the question."

At that moment Colonel Wise came by. "What's going on?"

"She wants me to take a Chinese national," Major Bull supplied.

The Colonel wheeled on me. "You again! God dammit, Dottie. What is it this time?"

"A runner, a messenger," I blurted. "Came for my father during the night—big surprise—didn't know he was coming. Been together for years—practically a family member."

"God dammit, get him aboard. And get the God damn convoy out of here!"

"Move it," the Major said.

"Move out," cried a sergeant.

The man from the factory came running as Father held the ambulance door open. The convoy was moving.

Waving goodby to the family, I was distracted by the *me-ee-ow* of planes zooming overhead. One of our new P-51 Mustangs was in a dogfight with a Japanese Zero.

"Get him!" I yelled.

As the aerial combat shifted I ran around the corner to watch. The Mustang came streaking down, all six of its fifty caliber machine guns spitting. The more maneuverable Zero rolled on its broad wings, peeling off to right rudder, throttle on full, diving into a loop, intending to climb out on the Mustang's tail.

Deprived of a kill by last second evasive action, the Mustang burrowed up into a cloud. In a moment it came roaring out, screaming down on the Zero, engine straining under full power, guns hammering.

"Get him," I cried, jumping up and down. "Get him!"

Suddenly I felt myself bowled over, held by strong arms that carried me into a nearby trench.

"God dammit, Dottie. What the hell are you doing?" Colonel Wise scolded. "Standing out in the street. You don't even have on a helmet!"

Behind us a row of bullets from the planes kicked up dust. The Zero began to emit a thin pencil line of smoke that became a heavy black ribbon. Its engine never faltering, the plane began losing altitude in a graceful arc, then began to plummet. It went down over a nearby hill. A boom sent up a dark mushroom cloud.

"Atta way!" I cheered.

Colonel Wise looked at me, sadly shaking his head. A grin spread across his face and a twinkle came into his cold blue eyes.

"Dottie," he said, continuing to shake his head slowly.

As I looked into his eyes I saw they were really very warm.

"Do you want to get yourself killed?"

"No," I said, dusting myself off. "But if you keep using me for football practice, I'm liable to get hurt."

"Dottie," he murmured.

I turned in the direction of the convoy but they were out of sight. My family would be departing the column at

Kweiyang because Father had been ordered to Chungking. His orders were vague and in all likelihood the Chinese Army would not have missed him had he dropped out of the war altogether, but Father was patriotic.

I need not have been concerned about bending the rules and putting my family on the convoy. The next time I saw Mother she told me that when the column was three miles out of Liuchow trucks and Jeeps began stopping for assorted tarts, prostitutes and girlfriends who had stationed themselves along the route. It was all prearranged. Not to be deprived of all creature comforts, our men were leaving Liuchow in style.

The order for us to evacuate was given the next day but the base was socked in by an early winter fog, placing us in grave danger. The Japanese might overrun the base before we could get our planes in the air. Shelling increased along with sniper fire.

"Don't leave the phone," Colonel Wise ordered. "I need you here as long as possible. And I want to know where you are every minute. The first three foot opening in this soup and out you go."

Within hours the clouds parted and a Jeep rolled up to the hotel. "Get in," said the crew chief of a C-47.

"You speak English," he marveled as we sped toward the plane.

"Don't all Americans?" I asked.

"Yes, but—but we don't see many girls, I mean—"

Aboard the plane I seated myself in the cargo area and presently the co-pilot came back and introduced himself. "The Captain wants to know if you'd like to come up front."

"Yes, Lieutenant."

They were exceedingly happy to be speaking with an American girl and we had a fine time. Several hours later, as we approached Kunming, the Captain said, "Put on the headphones and request landing instructions."

"I don't know what to say."

"I'll tell you."

He briefed me.

The airwaves cracked with incessant chatter and abundant static. Adlibbing a little, I spoke into the mike. "This is

Flying Tigress on C-forty-seven, ATC, approaching field. Request landing instructions, please."

Immediately everything went silent.

After a long pause the Captain said, "Do it again."

I repeated the lingo. "Request landing instructions, please."

The network remained ominously silent.

At length I told the pilot, "You'd better do it. I'm not getting a response."

"They probably think you're Tokyo Rose." He chuckled and took the mike. The moment he completed his request the entire network came alive. The crisis was over.

"What if General Chennault was standing in Operations?" the Lieutenant asked, looking worried.

"What if he was?" the Captain said nonchalantly.

After touchdown I went directly to my assigned billet and never learned if the Captain took any flak for putting me on the air.

Chapter Fourteen

A half dozen glasses clinked together over the table. "*Kampei*," I said.

Attempting the Chinese version of "bottoms up" some of the others managed, "Gambay," or "Gumbuoy."

"Dottie," an amused Lieutenant Cabelka said with a wry smile. "You should have seen Willett here. There we were, the last two planes out of Liuchow—" He raised his palms to represent the planes. "A DC-3 takes off ahead of us and Willett says, 'How come I never get to light off any buildings? You guys always have all the fun. I want to light off something.'"

"Shut up," Willett growled, giving Cabelka the evil eye. "I don't want to hear any more about that." His face soured.

"Now we *must* hear it," I said.

Cabelka chuckled. "Like I said, we were boarding the last plane. 'Go light off the latrine,' Colonel Wise told him. Willett goes over and applies a torch to one corner. Just then the old Chinese Revenge catches up with him. The side of the latrine is only smoldering so Willett figures he has time. He pops in and sits down. Suddenly—*pow*! What happens, the fire snakes into the pit below. The oil down there flames up against Willett's butt; he lets out a scream and comes tearing out with his pants flopping around his ankles."

"Aw, shut up about that!" Willett scowled.

"He got the latrine but the latrine got him first."

We guffawed and snickered, enjoying Willett's discomfiture.

Colonel Wise, who had been silent, banged down his glass. "This place is chicken—" He broke off as his eyes found me, as if he had only now become aware of me.

Startled, we turned our faces toward him. "Lieutenant Cabelka," Colonel Wise said firmly. "I want you to pass the word that the officers and men will have to get used to saluting again. We're in Chennault country—China headquarters for the big brass. Get the word out." He rose and walked off in a thoroughly discontented mood.

"That's surprising coming from a West Pointer," Jim Willett observed. "You'd think he'd go for all the spit and polish."

"He prefers to get things done instead of going by the book," I said.

"He's getting a lot of heat from the top," Cabelka explained.

"I wonder what's bugging him? It can't be the uniform requirement."

"I'm with him. This base *is* chicken shit."

Since coming to Kunming our group had suffered a noticeable drop in morale. They didn't appreciate the emphasis on military regulations amid the uncertainty and ill fortune of war. Formerly we were in the Third Sector, but there wasn't enough left of it to be retained as a separate command. As a result, Colonel Wise took command of Sector One as well as the Sixty-eighth Service Group which had the responsibility for supplies and personnel west of the one hundred third meridian. Absorbing bases from the inactivated Third Sector into our new command, we were once again charged with logistics for nineteen bases.

Lieutenant Cabelka read the list aloud. "Namyung, Anshun, Mangsheh, Szemao—" He stopped. "Paoshan? I thought we lost that." He made a check and reported. "What do you know, it's another Paoshan."

"I hope we have better luck with this one," I said.

"Than the other little walled city? Yeah. This one is bigger. I think I'll send Captain Earl Gibbens over there to shape things up." As Colonel Wise's deputy, Cabelka had uncommon authority.

There were many personnel changes. Major Bull became base commander at Siuchwan; First Lieutenant Norwood Wilson was placed in charge of Tsingchen.

War news remained bleak. Since leaving Liuchow our base at Nanning had fallen. However, loss of another base did not have as dramatic an effect on our office as the November 20, 1944 issue of *Time*. As soon as early copies hit the newsstands officials in the pentagon fired off inquiries to General Chennault and by the time the ripple reached us it had become a tidal wave. We could hear the General raving as Colonel Wise held the telephone receiver away from his ear.

Hands shaking, his face drained, the Colonel replaced the phone and sat stunned. After a moment of shocked silence, color began to flow back into his features. "He wants to court martial me," he got out. "I don't know anything about burning a million gallons of gasoline. Damn!" His color heightened; slow movements accelerated as he leaped to his feet. "Cabelka! I want to get to the bottom of this. Get me a copy of that magazine!"

Lieutenant Cabelka managed to obtain a transcript of the offensive portion of an article that concerned our systematic loss of bases:

> *The dreary process began all over again at Liuchow, 100 miles to the southwest. Colonel Richard Wise, commanding the Third Sector, China Air Service Command, worked around the clock to get out all the men, equipment and supplies which he had worked the year around to get in—up to 3000 planeloads flown over the costly Hump route; a million gallons of aviation fuel, torturously accumulated and stored, now impossible to save.*

"Me destroy a million gallons of gasoline?" Colonel Wise raged indignantly. "We never *had* a million gallons. Who the hell wrote this crap? Teddy White? I ought to deck him."

"I don't think it was Teddy White," Lieutenant Cabelka said soberly. "Anna Jacoby was hanging around the hotel. She's the only one who had access. I had her type up some things for me. She's a fantastic typist—she really rattles things off."

"Rattles off God damned lies, you mean. I'll kill her!"

"You okayed the dispatch," Lieutenant Cabelka said blithely. "After Third Sector passed it, her dispatch had to be released by headquarters of the Fourteenth."

"I didn't pass it. Not a million gallons. God damn! We never had a million gallons. If I ever get my hands on her—"

An amused smile formed on Cabelka's triangular face. "I'll dig into the fuel consumption records. We couldn't have burned much over five thousand gallons."

"What are you laughing at, dammit?"

"I think it's funny."

"Well, I don't. This could cost me my eagle."

"I've got the fuel consumption charts. Want me to call Chennault? Take 'em over?"

"Hell yes. Get him off my back."

Cabelka chuckled softly, took the reports and went off to convince General Chennault that the gasoline consumed when Liuchow was destroyed was more like five thousand gallons. Much later Colonel Wise encountered Anna Jacoby and confronted her with the wrath of a million dragons. Taken aback, she nevertheless offered to produce her notes, maintaining that her editors, unable to read her shorthand, had inadvertently added two zeros to her report. Colonel Wise was less than satisfied with the explanation.

The explosive clash between Colonel Wise and General Chennault fresh in my mind, I was approaching a state of panic as I went to see the General about a personal problem. "You've seen dozens of generals," I told myself, attempting to cast off fear and replace it with courage. "This will be no different." Totally unconvinced, it turned out my first formal meeting with the General wasn't at all like the others.

At headquarters I got as far as an aide. "Is it possible to see the General?" I asked.

"He's always got time to see a pretty girl," his aide quipped, a mischievous sparkle in his eyes.

The aide had revealed no secrets. General Chennault's reputation, his love for China and China's girls, was well known. I had already observed him at a party and knew what they said to be true.

Seated at his desk, General Chennault looked up wearily, his eyes widening as he saw me.

I studied his face. His eyes were narrow, covered by thick arched eyebrows, his nose long and probing. A pugnacious jaw came jutting out beneath a straight slash of a mouth. Much revered by the Chinese, who called him Chennote Chiang Chung, the General had so often looked trouble in the eye and stared it down that his face wore a resolute expression even in repose. The Chinese had another name for him—"Old Leatherface." His leathery, weatherbeaten skin came as a result of open cockpit flying.

Like the Americans, the Chinese venerated their heroes with diminutives, usually employing the prefix, "old." In our office I had sometimes heard the General called "Old Hatchetface."

"I'm Dorothy Yuen," I said, introducing myself. "I've been working for Colonel Wise since Kweilin and I'm hoping you will help me."

"If I can. First I have to hear what it is. What's the problem?"

"It's my grandmother," I said. "She's trapped behind enemy lines and I want to get her out. We need a plane. Can the American Air Force help?"

He cleared his throat as if he had bronchial trouble. "It's extremely dangerous landing behind enemy lines."

"Grandma says there's an air strip near where she lives. She sees American planes coming in and taking off all the time. It has to be a secret strip—"

"Where did you hear that?" he recoiled. His face became grave, then pensive.

"Grandma was able to get a message to my father. He's a Colonel in the Chinese Army. I received Father's letter from Chungking yesterday."

His eyes narrowed. "I don't know of any landing strip. Show me where it is on the map." He swiveled around, rose and went to a map dominating the wall behind him. "Show me where."

"In Honan Province. Right there," I said, pointing to the spot where the hidden air strip should be.

The General blinked. "We have no landing strip in that area. There must be some mistake. We have nothing there."

"But Grandma saw them—"

"Could be," he said, speaking loudly for he was slightly deaf. "Maybe the Japs are using the field. They might have painted our emblems on some of their planes for a surprise raid. I wouldn't put it past them. I'm sorry. I can't help you. I would if I could but we have no strip there."

"Thank you, anyway," I said sadly.

Outside the sky was darkening, the gloom of night sweeping down over the mountains as I directed my steps toward the mess hall. I had listened to the words of General Chennault. His statements were definite, his denials emphatic, yet, somehow, I could not believe him. Why did I doubt him, I wondered. Was there something lurking behind his grim visage that his words could not conceal? Still, what did it matter? Nothing could be done. General Chennault had given his answer.

I became aware of footsteps behind me and tensed. On a shortcut to the mess hall, I didn't wish to encounter anyone in the darkness. The footsteps continued ominously. Approaching the mess hall door I turned to see who had been following me.

"Captain Birch!"

"Dorothy!"

"John—"

"It's good to see you," he exclaimed, finally releasing me from his embrace. "I didn't know you worked for the Air Force." His face warm with delight, he swept off his overseas cap and opened the door for me.

"Then you probably don't know how we missed each other in Kweilin by less than a minute."

"When was that?"

"A couple of months back."

"Oh-h-h." His face went long and sad for a moment. "If I'd known that I'd have been blue for weeks. Seeing you again is wonderful. I've been hoping against hope that somehow I would see you again. After Kukong fell, I was worried."

"We evacuated by train. Later Father joined us in Kweilin."

How handsome John looked in his khaki uniform, but thinner, I thought. We found a table in the corner of the mess hall and when he had satisfied the initial ravages of his hunger he asked, "Dorothy, what's troubling you? When I was following you—of course I didn't know it was you—I sensed it was someone leaning into despair . . . and now your mind keeps moving elsewhere . . ." His hand came over to cover mine in a consoling gesture.

"It's Grandmother—she's behind enemy lines." I told him about my visit with General Chennault. "I can't understand his denying the existence of the air strip. Not after Grandma saw it with her own eyes. It has to be common knowledge in the area."

"General Chennault is concerned about security. Maybe the strip is no longer being used. Things change rapidly out here."

"I'm so worried about her."

"Perhaps I can help. I will if I can. When we've finished eating we'll go somewhere and look at a map. You can point out the location, then I'll see what I can do. Right now if you'll excuse me I'm going back for a second helping. Would you like me to bring you something?"

"No, thanks."

Captain Birch walked to the serving area and returned with enough food for another meal. He stopped and looked at me before he seated himself. "My lady, you're as lovely as I remember."

"I'm surprised—"

"That I remember you? You shouldn't be. You've often been in my thoughts and now that I have found you again I'm going to make sure that you don't escape me."

His two meals took him no longer than I spent with one and soon we were in the barracks I shared with eight other girls. At the moment none of the eight were present. Captain Birch spread a map and brought me near with a wave of his hand. "Show me where your grandmother says there's an air strip."

I indicated the spot on the map. "Here. Right here."

"Uh-huh. Yes. I've been to Chengchow several times. I'm acquainted with Honan." He turned to face me. "Don't worry, Dorothy. I'll rescue your grandmother for you."

"You say that so easily..."

"It won't be easy."

"I hope you can rescue her. She's a nice grandma."

"When I rescue her how shall I contact you, Dorothy? I may not be able to bring her where you are."

I thought for a moment. "Bring her to any air base and ask for Colonel Richard H. Wise."

"Fine. All right."

"I just remembered. She has bound feet, little feet no longer than my hand. She can't run for a plane."

"I understand."

"She's a Baptist, you know."

"Imagine that! That's wonderful. The Lord works in mysterious ways. I'll be all the more dedicated. Come, tell me all about her." He began to fold the map.

"I never saw a silk map before," I said. "Where ever did you get it?" The map was printed in four colors.

"At Liangshan Air Base, from Ong Hong June." He smiled as he sang the name.

"A famous Chinese topographer?" I was proud of myself for knowing the word.

"No," he said. "Captain Ong is with American Intelligence. I think he said he was from Arizona. Actually he gave me three." John finished folding the map and handed it to me. "Here. I want you to have it. Silk maps are very practical. After wading a stream they don't fall apart like paper."

"Thank you. I'll remember that the next time I wade a stream. Are you sure you want me to have it?"

"Yes. I still have two others."

"I will treasure it."

"I hope it will make you think of me. Whenever you look at it you will know that I am somewhere in China thinking of you."

"Really?"

His shoulders shook as he laughed. "You're precious. Do you still have my Flying Tiger pin?"

"Yes. Of course, I never wear it. I don't believe the others would understand..."

"You're right. There are so few girls out here that the men can talk to that they're literally starved for conversation. I'm sure you'd rather be friends with them all instead of being pinned—"

"I'm not entitled to wear it. I'm glad you understand. I do try to be a friend of all the guys. Quite often at Kweilin and Liuchow for example, I was the only woman in the outfit. I feel some responsibility..."

"A sense of mission. Wonderful!" His lean face brightened and he looked rather like a teenage boy. "I'm learning a lot about you, Dorothy, and I like what I find."

"I'm learning about you too." We sat down side by side. "They told me you rescued Colonel Doolittle. Tell me about that."

"There isn't all that much to tell."

"Tell me anyway. I'm interested."

"I was only doing my patriotic duty—"

"Yes. Go on."

He took my hand and held it gently. "All right. It happened in western Chekiang Province along a river. You really want to know?"

"Yes. Please."

"A friend of mine had to get to Shangai and I took him as far as Sing Teng and was returning to Shanjao when I stopped to eat. I docked the boat and was sitting in a little restaurant when someone crept up and whispered, 'Are you an American?' I nodded and he said, 'Follow me.' Follow me—that's Biblical. The man led me to the river, actually not far from where I'd left my boat. There, hiding in a sampan, was Colonel Jimmy Doolittle. He'd been forced down after leading the raid on Tokyo—this was back in forty-two. April, I think. I helped get Colonel Doolittle out safely, also some of the other flyers who ran out of gas or parachuted down. That was some raid. You know, they had no place to land. They were just told to bomb Toyko and head for China. One thing led to another and before you know it I was involved. I mean *involved*."

"What you did was certainly important."

"They made a movie about the raid. '*Thirty Seconds Over Tokyo*.' I'd like to see it some time. I wonder how they decided on thirty seconds? It had to be longer. Tokyo is the world's second largest city. Perhaps they meant critical time over the target."

"I also realize how important is the work you're doing now."

"We can't talk about that."

Just then an air raid siren shrieked.

"*Jing Bao!*" I cried, rising, attempting to pull away my hand.

"Let's do something daring," he said calmly, refusing to release me. "Let's stay right here. Actually I think it'll be quite safe, unless the night-time precision of the Japanese has dramatically improved." He laughed heartily.

I nodded agreement and we sat there in the darkened barracks, Captain John Birch and I, holding hands, speaking Cantonese, practicing a few words of Mandarin, sharing thoughts in English, probably the only persons on the base not in an air raid shelter except for the men manning anti-aircraft batteries around the perimeter. We could hear the steady *blam-blam-blam* of the batteries over the boom of nearby bombs, the dull thud of distant shells.

His leg was warm and reassuring against mine and our free hands moved to join the hands that linked us, forming an even stronger bond.

"What are you going to do in the future?" he asked. "Have you given any thought to your life?"

"When all this is over? Yes, I have. What are your plans, John?"

"I think I'm getting back on the track. For a while I was running down a dead-end street. Just because you like and admire someone very much, it doesn't necessarily follow that that someone has the same goals in life or that they are willing to share—"

"I know. Sometimes I've been unable to return the affections some of the men say they have—"

"It can be rather painful. An outpouring of love, aspirations for the future, the joy of sharing—suddenly, a realization that the feelings aren't returned or shared, then loneliness."

Listening to his words I realized he had fallen in love but now it was over. Somewhere in China there had been another girl; I was sure of it. "I'm happy you know what you want," I said.

"Actually that's the problem—trying to fit my private desires in with my calling. What about you, Dorothy? Have you decided yet whether your real life is in the United States or here in China?"

"More and more I keep thinking of New York. Perhaps if I returned for a visit—I mean, if I could *feel* New York—I might know then that my heart really belongs here in China. I know I love being with the Fourteenth more than anything. It's the most exciting thing I've ever done. And there's a lot of gaiety."

"You're looking at a dream, my lady. Not reality. When the war is over the excitement will be gone. Men will return to their wives and sweethearts. Many already have. Hey, there's the All Clear!"

"Yes."

"I want you to think about your future, Dorothy. I think there will be a happy future for you here in China, with the right man."

An incipient laugh rose in my throat. "You're fun even when you're serious."

Holding hands, we talked far into the night, dreaming of a time we could not see, a future that lay far beyond the next air raid. Then it was time for him to go.

"I've had such a nice evening, John."

"So have I. And I wasn't haunted by any ghosts." He laughed as he rose, continuing to hold my hand as we walked to the door. He drew me close and in a voice as hushed as the wind rustling oak leaves I heard him murmur. "Dorothy, I don't know anyone I enjoy being with as much as you."

I felt his lips on mine and in the swirling passion I dared not think of a tomorrow with this man. As my legs lost their strength I knew such a thing was beyond my reach. This was war time.

He faded into the night from which he had appeared. As I reflected on his words I realized how preposterous it was planning a future. With Captain Birch ghosting all over China, materializing behind enemy lines with the same ease in which he appeared at headquarters, there was no way of knowing if we would ever see each other again. To sit in a darkened barracks, looking beyond our immediate situation, was utterly absurd. At least it would have been, but for hope—and faith.

On the map John had left with me I was able to track the progress of the war. At headquarters news was uniformly bad. We continued to lose bases.

"Dammit," fumed Colonel Wise. "I wish we had a division of American infantry. If we only had some ground support—"

Suddenly the Colonel exploded, "Good God! Of all the damn stupidity. Look at this! The Chinese Army had

Dorothy in CNNRA jacket.

fifty-three thousand tons of ammunition hoarded near Tushan. Two dozen warehouses full! Major Gleason got in there minutes before the Japs overran the place and blew it up right under their noses. If I had an army in the field half as efficient as OSS I'd have something. Nearly twenty thousand tons of it was dynamite."

"That's bizarre," Cabelka said. "I wonder why the Chinese didn't use it?"

"Bizarre? It's stupid. How in the hell can an army lose fifty-three thousand tons of ammunition and supplies? Who's in charge of their logistics? Didn't anybody know about it?"

"Somebody must have if Frank Gleason got wind of it."

"But to lose that much ammo—"

Sergeant Stan Pillsbury spoke up. "In the last war an entire command was lost—completely forgotten. If the ammunition was cached for use in their civil war the misfiling of a single document could have effectively removed it from consideration for any other purpose." A former New York librarian, Stan understood the paper bureaucracy.

"Hell!"

A bundle of energy, Colonel Wise had difficulty dissipating his frustrations. Frequently he accepted too much personal responsibility instead of passing it down the chain of command. I was particularly pleased to learn that he planned an inspection tour of the Burma Road. A few days away from Sector headquarters might relax him.

On December 22nd, the Colonel, Major Maurice Hollman, Lieutenant Cabelka and American Vice-Consul Richard M. Service set out in a command car for Mangshin, 880 kilometers distant, in Yunnan Province.

During their absence I looked forward to enjoying the many Christmas parties around the base, but the parties proved to be a problem. With only a dozen girls available I found it impossible to dance. No sooner had one airman placed his arms around me than another cut in. We only had time for a hasty exchange of words and before long my attempts at conversation were reduced to inane repetition.

The inspection group returned from Mangshin on the 29th and reported that the Burma Road was capable of handling increased truck traffic; good news, because supplies were sorely needed. Colonel Wise went to his desk immediately and began sifting through intelligence reports.

"How's our base at Tushan?"

"Almost completely evacuated, Sir, according to radio from Kweiyang. The belly tank factory at Kweiyang has been ordered here to Kunming..."

"A mobile engineering crew has been dispatched to Paoshan," Lieutenant Cabelka reported. "The weather is so bad I can't get supplies into Suichwan."

"Look at these reports," Colonel Wise said gravely. "Chinese intelligence is completely broken down in the Kweiyang area. And Chinese troops are in a state of utter confusion. I'm worried about Suichwan. We may have to pull Major Bull out of there."

"I don't think you should do that," I said. "I think you should leave him there. Send him forward. If he could just glare at the Japs—"

"What?" he demanded sharply. Slowly his features drained of rigidity, his mouth turned up and a rifle-report of laughter rang out, attracting all the eyes in the office. He slapped the desk with his hand and his body shook with glee. "Send Bull forward... to glare at the Japs..." He continued to laugh, as if he'd been hoarding it for weeks. "Now I know why we keep you around," he chuckled. "You're precious!"

It was good to hear him laugh. Although it lasted only a minute it had a salutary effect on the entire office. Lieutenant Cabelka approached him with a problem that was easily solved. They decided to send additional personnel to Louhuanping even though orders had been received to stop construction at the base.

"We can still use it for fighter staging operations," Cabelka said.

That night the Japs bombed Yunnanyi Air Base, destroying two A-3 refueling units that were badly needed at Paoshan.

With the new year a letter arrived from May and Marion Shim, friends I'd met at church in Kukong. Before the city fell the girls managed to flee and were now in a village near Namyung. The last line of their letter held a poignant plea. "Can you help us? May and Marion Wilson."

Wilson, I assumed, was the name the family acquired in amaica, probably the name of an early employer. Chinese eople sometimes did that in colonial countries.

Of course I had to help May and Marion. At a time when ie Colonel didn't seem harried, I put on a confident smile nd strode to his desk. How I wished I could make him ugh, but that only happened when I didn't try.

"Colonel," I said. "I just received a letter from two dear iends from a village near Namyung."

"I was just thinking about Namyung. We've got ieutenant Irwin Mohr over there."

"Is there any way they can be flown out?" I shifted my eight to my other leg. "It's been more than a month since iey wrote the letter and I know there's been trouble in the rea..."

The Colonel's chin came up. His upper lip appeared very ide as the corners of it drew down over his petulant lower. nstantly there was reaction. "God dammit, Dottie, what do ou think I'm operating here, a shuttle service?"

"No, sir."

"Do you realize that's nine hundred miles?"

"B-But there's a constant stream of planes to headquarers. Everything seems to come here..."

"Namyung is in danger. The Japs are moving all around iere. We'll have to blow the runway any day." He lit a igarette. "Mohr hasn't got time to go looking—"

"The girls won't be hard to find." I remembered how annon used to call them 'The Chinese Limeys.' "They speak nglish with a West Indies accent. The village isn't all that ir."

"I'll look into it. But I can't promise anything. I'm going leave it up to the discretion of Lieutenant Mohr. If he ants to risk his bar it's all right with me."

"He will if you ask him."

"Yes, yes," he said irritably, taut lines forming around his yes. "I said I'd look into it. Ma'am, haven't you got some ork to do?"

Retreating to my desk I knew that under the circumstances there was nothing else I could do to aid May and Marion. Bases continued to fall. The irascibility of Major ull did not save Suichwan. An order was dispatched to

blow the runway at Namyung. There was no way to tell
May and Marion had been found before the base wa
destroyed. I continued to worry.

Colonel Wise called Lieutenant Cabelka to his desk
"Look at this," he declared, his finger tapping a photograph
"The Japs are freezing to death in their cotton uniforms. Se
how they're stripping bodies to stay warm. Look at the ice o
the trees. Everything is coated with ice. It's a cryst
wonderland. They can't live off the land. They're run tw
hundred miles past their supply point. The Japs will stop o
their own. The Itchy-bitchy offensive is over. They'll neve
get to Kweiyang. I'd bet on it."

"I almost would . . ." Lieutenant Cabelka said slowly.

"Logistics," the Colonel said. "It's Napoleon at Waterlo
all over again. Major Hollman won't have to evacuat
combat material from Kweiyang."

A brilliant tactician, Colonel Wise liked to attack
problem directly. Sometimes he could be almost too direc
Approaching the office a couple days later I became aware o
an amalgamation of voices. As I entered I heard the Colone
shout at General Chennault, "You'll have to give me that i
writing!"

General Chennault's face froze, the muscles in his nec
tightened, his jaw jutted out pugnaciously. He wheeled an
stalked out, his back stiff with anger.

Cabelka, sporting new captain's bars, bent down over m
desk. "That wasn't very diplomatic," he said in a hushe
voice.

The incident was recalled later in the club. Jim Willet
who had also acquired captain's bars, offered an opinio

"One reason Wise is rebellious is that he's not in line fo
Brigadier General."

"He wants to make Bee-gee so bad he can taste it."

"Casey Vincent went home last month—maybe there
room for a new star."

"Not the way Wise tangled with the Old Man."

"Casey was getting old," Cabelka said with a laugh. "H
celebrated his thirtieth birthday a couple of weeks before h
left. Remember Casey mouthing off about Chennault? 'Th
Old Man is war weary,' he kept saying. 'The flight surgeo
ought to relieve him.' That's one thing, giving an opinio

behind his back. Our fireball Colonel rears back and yells to his face, 'You'll have to give me that in writing!' There's a big difference."

"He's his own worst enemy."

"See the difference?" Cabelka persisted. "The subtle difference in diplomacy?"

"Subtle? Like a chop in the mouth!"

"I still like his style. Let's drink one for the Colonel."

"To the Colonel. A man who can't accept mediocre work. Or mediocre thinking."

"Or mediocre drinking."

"That's for damn sure."

"Gambay."

"Gambay."

Not only the Colonel had a problem. All of the men were drinking too much.

The order to evacuate Namyung had already been given when we received a radio message from Lieutenant Irwin Mohr. He found May and Marion but with the airstrip at Namyung destroyed it was too late to fly them out. He'd taken the girls with him in a Jeep over treacherous mountain trails to Kanchow in an attempt to catch a plane there, but on reaching Kanchow the base was in flames. They'd gone on to Changting and were ready for take-off when he received last minute orders. He put May and Marion on a 32nd Troop Carrier plane with twenty British soldiers and took another plane to Chihkiang.

Several weeks passed before I saw Lieutenant Mohr and heard him exclaim, "Thank God for last-minute orders. I'm sure glad I didn't get on that plane. May got the last parachute. I wouldn't have had one."

As I waited for May and Marion now, I asked one of the men to calculate the ETA and went to headquarters to see if the girls would arrive on time. The staff eyed me with indifference, their faces suspicious, as if they would call the military police at any moment. At bases where Colonel Wise had been in command I'd been accepted by the radiomen. Here in Kunming no one knew me. I couldn't even get inside General Chennault's control tower. Feeling rejected and helpless, I returned to Sector headquarters and asked a friendly sergeant to help me.

"I'll see what I can do, Dottie." He jangled the phone an
asked for a report. He listened, put down the earphones an
frowned. "The plane is lost."

My breath caught. "Shot down?"

"No. Lost. They don't know where they are. They'r
flying around in circles."

In a few minutes I urged the sergeant to call the towe
again.

"No more news," he said. "Maybe it's compass deviation."

"How come every time one of these farmers turne
navigator gets lost it's compass deviation? If it was dayligh
at least they could see the haystacks. You know some of thes
guys navigate by haystacks."

"They'll be all right, Dottie. Want a cup of mud?"

"No, thanks."

"It might be a long night."

"I know."

After a bit the sergeant was on the phone again. "No wor
yet? Listen, call me back as soon as you hear, will ya? Th
Colonel is interested. Roger."

A half hour ticked by.

"You sure you won't have a cup of Joe?"

"Maybe. Oh, all right. Why not?"

I took a puckering swallow and nearly gagged at th
acidity. "Standard Air Force coffee," I muttered.

Presently the caffeine assaulted my frayed nerves
whipping them to a frenzy. Why didn't the phone ring
Where was that plane? What was happening?

The phone rang and my spine went rigid.

"Sector," the sergeant said laconically. I saw his hea
snap. "They're running out of gas and are gonna ditch?" H
turned to me and blinked. "Bad news, Dottie."

"I heard."

"Maybe they'll hit the silk," he said hopefully.

May and Marion parachuting down? I couldn't eve
imagine it. A curtain of gloom settled over me as I trudge
back to the barracks.

We received no news at all, not even the report of
crashed plane. My heart was heavy and I despaired of eve
seeing my friends again. Three weeks passed; February wa

nearly gone when I heard that two English-speaking Chinese girls were on a plane coming to Kunming. May and Marion. Had they been injured? I forced the thought out of my mind.

Tense and anxious, I waited for the plane to taxi to a stop. The hatch came open. I saw them and breathed a sigh of relief. They were walking. We hugged each other and everyone spoke at once. Finally I said, "What ever happened to you?"

"The Jeep ride over the mountains with Lieutenant Mohr was terrible. My heart was in my throat half the time." Marion's eyes widened and she clapped a hand over her mouth.

"No, no," I said impatiently. "Not the Jeep ride. What about your flight?" I turned to May. "What happened to the plane? Tell me all about it."

"Well," May said. "The first thing I knew about it, they took the plane up to twenty thousand feet and had us check our parachutes. 'Buckle up,' the crew chief said. I thought he was kidding. 'We don't know if we're over enemy territory or not,' he said. 'So when you land, don't call out. It could be the enemy. Wait for daylight.' Then he threw me out. My scarf was torn off. Suction ripped off my shoes. I yanked the ripcord, the chute came open and shook the daylights out of me."

"We're so light," Marion interjected. "They were afraid we'd get caught in the slipstream and smash into the tail."

"I landed in the snow," May said, "with no shoes. After a minute I realized I was unhurt. I wrapped myself in the parachute and waited for morning. When the sun came out I spied someone in the distance. I stayed perfectly still and waited. Fortunately it was a British soldier. Soon there were others. We met some Chinese—we weren't in enemy territory after all. I tried to communicate with them but their dialect was different. They were strange people in a remote area. They didn't even know there was a war on! Little by little we regrouped—everybody except Marion—"

"I came down over the next ridge and they couldn't find me," Marion said.

May shrugged. "We had to set off without her. Luckily we found her. The next day we were passing through a little village and a small boy came running up, wide-eyed. 'We also have a girl who came out of a bird!'"

"I sprained my ankle," Marion said. She still favored it.

"It's a wonder you didn't break a leg," I said. "I'm sure glad to see you both. It's a lucky thing Lieutenant Mohr didn't get on the plane. Did you know May got the last parachute? By the way, what did he mean when he said you were conservative?"

The girls looked at each other. A knowing glance passed between them but they made no response. They followed me to my quarters where we continued our reunion. Eventually they obtained jobs on the base.

I noticed a pattern developing in my life. Momentous changes occurred at the beginning or at the end of a month. Captain Cabelka and my pistol-shooting friend, Captain Earl Gibbens, had been sent to open a new base more than two hundred kilometers away, near the Indo-China border. They returned near the end of March.

"Am I glad to see you," Colonel Wise said as he greeted them. "We're all set to transfer out. To Chanyi. The base up there needs shaping up and I've been elected. I'm sending you two on ahead."

By his manner Colonel Wise invited a question and Captain Cabelka flashed him a quizzical look.

"I just got wind of a plot to rob my staff," the Colonel said. "They want Gibbens and Cabelka, but I'm going to transfer you out before they can get you. Right now. When headquarters discovers that you're already at Chanyi I doubt if they'll call you back. I'm glad I still have a few friends over there." The Colonel quick-glanced at me. "Dottie, cut the orders." He turned back to the men. "Unless, of course, you'd rather ship out of my outfit..."

"No, sir!" they roared in unison.

Within two hours the Captains were aboard a weapons carrier jolting their way toward Chanyi. A couple days later the rest of us boarded a C-47 we called the "Thunderhead Special." The plane had flipped over in a storm while we were stationed in Kweilin. Colonel Wise had the wings replaced and before we evacuated Kweilin he'd sent the plane ahead to Liuchow. Despite its well-dented fuselage, we'd been using the Thunderhead Special ever since. Having been officially "destroyed," the plane appeared on no official records.

"Dottie, this is the life," Colonel Wise proclaimed as he took out his aluminum cigarette case and lit a cigarette off the butt of his last. "I'm gonna have to account for this plane some day," he mused. "Maybe I can do what Captain Cabelka did. You know he destroyed two trucks on paper and gave them to the Chinese Army as we fled Kweilin."

I nodded. Actually we were involved in two wars—the real war and the one fought on paper. One frequently bore no relation to the other.

The Colonel smiled. "Cabelka made the trucks go away. I have to make this plane appear. I'll talk to him about it. I'm sure he'll come up with something. There's more than one reason I picked him for my deputy. He's great on tactics and he knows how to move paper. It's the army that moves paper most efficiently that wins." An amused laugh rolled out of his depths. "I've even got a couple lieutenants to fly this bucket."

In high spirits as we winged toward Chanyi and the challenge of a new command, I once again thrilled to the majesty of flying, realizing that somewhere, far below, in a remote area behind enemy lines, my grandmother waited and prayed.

Chapter Fifteen

A cargo plane that made it over the high Himalayas, called the Hump by our pilots, came lumbering out of a leaden sky and hit the surface of the runway hard like an overstuffed goose and went careening, brakes shrieking, to the far end, threatening to overshoot the apron and catapult over the dyke into the river beyond. For its size Chanyi was extremely busy. A record number of planes had landed since we arrived, bringing in much needed supplies. Our air superiority was growing. Unable to replace the planes destroyed by the Fourteenth, the Japanese presence in the sky was dwindling.

Although I had been with the staff for some time I was surprised by the increasing confidences the men shared with me. As I listened, they told me of their hopes and fears, their innermost thoughts, their indiscretions with women. Why were they telling me these things? Undoubtedly it had something to do with my being the only woman with whom they could communicate. Perhaps I was a mother figure for some of them but I believe most of them looked upon me as a sister. We were very close at Chanyi; we became a family.

However, we did not have family toilets. There were three tents, two for the men and one for me. How I hated going to the latrine. As I minced back and forth to the tent I felt very conspicuous. Were all the men watching me? Thin tent walls were hardly soundproof and I attempted to time my functions with the roar of aircraft engines. If only to get away from a frightfully embarrassing situation I was pleased with the news Captain Cabelka brought me.

"You can start packing, Dottie. We're moving out." He placed a stack of files on my desk. "Cut orders for all of us to Peishiyi."

"Peishiyi? That's wonderful," I cheered.

"I thought you'd like that," he said, smiling. "I know your family is in Chungking. Maybe you'll get a chance to see them."

"I hope so. How does Colonel Wise feel about the transfer?"

"He's optimistic. There ought to be a lot more action in Peishiyi."

We were in high spirits as we boarded the Thunderhead Special. This time we were not fleeing the enemy. We were leaving the base intact, running more efficiently than when we arrived. Things were shaped up. Our mission had been accomplished.

A month to the day after arriving in Chanyi we landed at Peishiyi. The base was only thirty-five miles from the wartime capitol and the first time I heard that someone was driving a Jeep to the city I hitched a ride. The road was rough and bumpy and it took us well over an hour.

Here I was in Chungking, city of intrigue, a place that evoked dark and evil memories of Mrs. Wu and failure. I had been an uneducated child of eighteen then, but now with the maturity of four more years and a confidence learned by being with the Air Force, I faced the city unafraid. I would not seek out the haunts of yesteryear. Nor would I recognize them if I saw them. The past belonged to a little Chinese girl. I was an American now, a member of the Fourteenth, seeing Chungking for the first time.

It was impossible to ignore the fact of Chungking's rapid growth. Stilted shacks and ramshackle structures clung to the slopes as if their proudest achievement was to defy gravity.

The family was delighted to see me. Moments after I exclaimed how much Gloria and Jack had grown since I saw them last, Edna drew me aside, her face anxious, her voice frantic.

"I can't stand Mother. She's after me all the time. You know, like she did with you. Remember the way she was?"

A sigh escaped me. "How can I forget?"

"The harder I work the more difficult she becomes. All I hear is, 'When I was sixteen I had a job. I was out on my own. Look at you—you're eighteen and still laying around the house.' What can I say? I've got to get away."

"What does Father say?"

"When I reminded him that when you were eighteen, you came here to Chungking alone, he gave me one of his all-knowing nods and said, 'That is true.' Daddy won't object if I get a job."

I grimaced as I remembered my fiasco with Mrs. Wu. My mind lingered on the past for a moment and I heard Edna saying, "Besides, I'm nearly nineteen. Dorothy, can you get me a job at the air base?"

"I-I don't know," I hesitated. It was an important decision. Did I want a younger sister at the base? Was she ready to meet the world in the person of the Fourteenth? Still, if she remained at home she wouldn't be any more ready a year from now. She had to learn sometime. And if she was at the base with me I would be able to keep an eye on her. "I don't know. I'll ask Colonel Wise. It's up to him."

"You *will* ask him?" she pressed.

"I will see what can be done." I knew too well that her situation at home was really hopeless.

"Dorothy, I'll be eternally grateful."

Edna was excited at even the remote possibility of coming to Peishiyi. Naturally I lost no time in taking up the matter with Colonel Wise.

"I didn't know there were any more like you at home," he said soberly.

Had it not been for a sudden chuckle from Captain Cabelka who overheard my request I would not have been aware that Colonel Wise was beginning a cat and mouse game with me. I returned my averted eyes to his face briefly.

"At least this request won't get me court martialed—I don't think. You're beginning to show promise. On that basis I suppose I can take a chance on Edna."

"Thank you."

"I don't know if I can stand two of you pressuring me. How long before Edna comes in here demanding that I hire her sister?"

My hands clasped, I made a phony bow and said in a squeaky voice. "It is in the hands of the gods."

The Colonel chortled and cleared his throat. His eyes narrowed. "No. It is in the hands of Mother. When Edna gets here have her report to Sergeant Pillsbury. He's an extremely patient man. We'll see if your sister can learn filing."

"Yes, sir."

"And one more thing—"

"Yes—?"

"She can't ask me anything. No dogs, no frogs, no nothin'!"

"Right."

Colonel Wise need not have worried. The next time I saw Edna I had some instructions of my own. "You're going out into the world before you're ready," I said, regarding her with a steely stare. "You're going to be the second woman on the base. That involves a great deal of responsibility."

"But I'm almost nineteen. Next month—"

"No," I snapped. "You're eighteen. And that's what you'll tell them. It sounds better. And listen, young lady, there are some strict terms."

"Anything, Dorothy. I'll do anything."

"You will not do *anything*. First of all you will obey all the rules and regulations of the United States Army Air Corps. And when you're with the men you will not allow them to touch you below the shoulder or above the knee. If they try, you make them stop immediately. Understand?"

"Okay."

"And when you go out with the men you'll be in by eleven. No exceptions."

"But—"

"Further, what I say goes. I've asked the Colonel not to speak to you about this, but technically you're in my charge. What I say is final. One word from me and you're off the base."

"I'll be good, Dorothy. I'll try very hard. No job can be as bad as Mother."

I nodded agreement. "You'll be working for Sergeant Pillsbury, an extremely intelligent man. Learn all you can from him."

I knew Sergeant Pillsbury would watch over Edna like a mother hen but that did not quell my fears when the work day was over. I fretted and worried every night until eleven. It was weeks before I felt comfortable about Edna going out with the men but gradually I was confident that Edna had learned to take care of herself.

The road to Chungking grew more familiar but no less bumpy. My drivers made no attempt to avoid the pigs and chickens that foraged in our path. Wary pigs evaded the Jeep but sometimes I would hear a dull thud and looking back I'd see a ball of feathers fluttering itself to death, rolling like a tumbleweed. Frequently a youngster would dart out of nowhere to retrieve a dinner.

While shopping I glimpsed General Zung and stopped to thank him for allowing me to board a train at Kukong the time I had gone to visit Father. He acknowledged my gratitude as we exchanged pleasantries.

"You know Big Brother is here," he said.

"No. I didn't." Big Brother was the name some of the officers used for General Yur Ying-kai. "General Yur is here?"

"He's at a hotel not far from here."

"I'd like to see him again."

General Zung accompanied me to the hotel and after saying he had brought a surprise, he departed.

General Yur nodded toward a woman who peeked into the room. "This is my wife."

The lady was not the wife I had met earlier—she had to be his country wife from the marriage arranged by his mother.

General Yur wore a gloomy expression. His eyes were heavy lidded. A shadow came across his face as dark as his closely cropped hair.

"Forgive me," he said. "I'm in a melancholy mood."

"I thought you looked troubled."

"It's my mother." He sighed wearily. "The doves have flown; she is ill and will soon meet her ancestors. It is the duty of a son to be with her at this critical time—" He broke off as his voice caught. Eyes misting, he went on. "She is in Hunan, behind enemy lines . . ."

"The area is yet free?"

"Yes, Do-yur. But it has been isolated from us. It will require a plane . . ." He sagged heavily into a chair.

"The Fourteenth Air Force has many planes."

"And a goose has wings," he said hopelessly.

"I will see what can be done." I raised a cautioning finger. "My influence is not great."

"I will be most grateful for whatever you can do."

General Yur was in a better mood when I left him to return to Peishiyi. At the base I went at once to Colonel Wise to seek his assistance.

He was strangely calm. "Dottie, that's a twelve hundred mile round trip."

I was certain the Colonel was going to refuse.

"If he was an American general there might be something we could do. But a Chinese national . . ."

"He is a dear friend who has often helped me." I dared not tell the Colonel that I had been mixed up with Chinese Intelligence and Mrs. Wu's covert activities. "Colonel," I said with deep emotion. "I owe my life to him. Without his help I would not be here." Could I tell him that General Yur had saved Father from a firing squad?

"He saved your life?"

"Yes."

"I can't drop everything I'm doing right this minute. I have a war to fight." The sleeping tiger was awakening in his voice. "You know what you're asking me to do is patently illegal. Dottie," he said, his voice poised for a roar. "You're going to get me court martialed."

"Yes sir," I said quickly. "I mean, no sir."

His hands sliced up and down sharply. "I'll have to arrange something. I can't just go winging down there. I need an excuse. It has to look good."

A couple days later the Colonel called me. "Ma'am." I went to his desk to await instructions.

"It's necessary that I make a trip to Hunan," he said with a lopsided grin. "Tell your friend to get ready. Now I don't want him on the base till I'm ready to take off. If he's conspicuous people might start asking questions. I'll taxi over to the runway near the road, then he can climb aboard. And one more thing—"

"Yes?"

"I know he has servants and aides. He can bring a couple of them but not the whole God damn Chinese Army. Understand? I'm only flying a C-47. I can't take the whole kit and caboodle."

I couldn't wait to tell General Yur the good news. As soon as I could I went to the city. When my driver dropped me in front of the General's hotel I was so excited I forgot my purse in the glove compartment.

General Yur was delighted, his eyes sparkled beneath his bristling crew cut. "Do-yur, when you are here magpies build nests at my front door. Truly you are a child of the Lan Hua."

"You have meant more than an orchid to me," I said, nodding formally, almost bowing.

"Come," he said. "Let us share a pot of tea." He did not invite his country wife to join us.

Later, as my driver called for me—a sergeant who had been out on the town—I looked at once in the glove compartment.

"My purse. It's gone," I cried in dismay. "I had nearly three hundred dollars in it."

"I'm sorry, Dottie. If I'd known you left your purse in there I'd have taken it with me."

"Not your fault, Sergeant." I was disgusted and angry with myself. Everything I'd managed to save since coming to work for the Fourteenth was gone. In my mind, in the depths of my sorrow I visualized myself pushing a bag containing three hundred dollars across a giant ledger marked, "Owed to General Yur." Of course, the loss of my purse had nothing whatever to do with General Yur. It was specious reasoning to ascribe the loss to a debt I owed him, but the rationalization, however illogical, made my loss easier to bear. A mere three hundred dollars would not have extinguished the debt I owed General Yur.

At the appointed time of departure, General Wise's well-dented plane taxied to the end of the runway, preparing to take off. A car rolled out of its place of concealment toward the plane. General Yur stepped out, saw me, bowed very low to thank me again and limped toward the hatch as fast as he could. There was no ramp and it was difficult for him to get aboard. He grimaced in pain as he twisted his stiff leg, the limb that had been badly injured at Nanking. A couple of aides scrambled aboard after him, the hatch closed and the Thunderhead Special revved and began to roll.

With the prop-wash tousling my hair, a warm feeling came over me. I was thoroughly happy that I had at last been able to do something for General Yur.

On April 13th, Captain Cabelka left for Washington, D.C., then on leave to his home in Wisconsin. We didn't expect to see him for about two months. His absence increased the work load around the office and I was glad my sister had come to work. She proved to be a great asset when her mentor, Sergeant Pillsbury, suffered one of his recurring bouts with malaria.

The hospital was situated behind headquarters and one afternoon I popped in to visit him. I could see him through a break in the curtain.

"Sergeant Pillsbury. How are you—?" My jaw dropped slack. He had a roommate. "John!" I cried in wide-eyed surprise. "What are you doing here?" How thin and pale Captain Birch appeared!

"Malaria," the Captain said weakly. "I'm all right."

"You know each other?" exclaimed Sergeant Pillsbury.

"Yes," we said.

A discerning man, Sergeant Pillsbury read much into my reaction and after a few moments excused himself so I could be alone with John.

"Dorothy, I'm so glad to see you." His hand came out to touch mine.

"And I you. This is such a wonderful surprise."

"Seeing you is the best medicine I can get."

"You've allowed yourself to get run down. What you need is a vacation. Out here all this time... you've certainly earned a vacation. Why don't you go on leave... to Georgia?"

"I can't. Not until this war is over." He managed a weak, almost rueful smile.

"Yes, you can. For many men the war *is* over—they've been rotated home. You've been here since long before the war. You're overdue for a vacation. It's richly deserved."

"My heart cries out to see Birchwood but I can't go. Who else would do my work?"

"Who's doing it now? Surely the war can do without the Phantom Mandarin for a few weeks."

"That's just it," he said soberly. "It can't. My people can't," he amended. "In too many places I'm the only link. No one else can speak with the people. I'm their only liaison. I've got to get out of here. I can't be wasting my time waiting for a relapse that might never come."

"Or that might return with a vengeance."

"About your grandmother," he said, changing the subject abruptly. "I haven't forgotten my promise. I'm working on it. The strip she is near is seldom used . . . only when we have to drop in a new transmitter or supplies. It's going to be touchy but some of my friends are working on it."

"Grandma will be happy to get on this side of the Japanese lines."

"Don't worry, Dorothy."

"Why not? You said it's going to be touchy. Somebody has to worry. Just like you needing a vacation. Really, you ought to go home on leave . . ."

A dimly adventurous sparkle took shape in his eyes. "Tell you what. Let's get this war over, then we'll go back to Birchwood together. You can be my guest."

"That day might not be far over the horizon."

"I know," he said. "Have you noticed the way our troops are pouring up through Italy, across France? When Germany collapses the Allies can concentrate on Japan."

"It's time for me to go—"

"You can't possibly know how much seeing you has meant to me, Dorothy. Please come back and have dinner with me."

"Very well."

"Good. I'll be expecting you."

I did return for dinner and in the following days I saw Captain Birch at least once daily, usually twice, and on some days three times.

"Have you thought about your future?" he asked.

"Have *you* thought about taking a vacation?" I retorted. "About going home to Birchwood for a visit?"

"I thought we had been all through that," he said with measured impatience.

"So we have. I think we are at an impasse. Still," I said, pointing a scolding finger at him, "I think you ought to take a vacation."

His face became coolly composed, his voice impassive. "I may not ever leave China." As if surprised at his tone he covered his intensity with a nascent smile. "Perhaps one should not pay that much attention to voices in the mists. I'm sure it's not a premonition."

"John . . . what do you mean?"

"My lady," he said abruptly. "Do you believe in ghosts?"

"Of course not."

"I thought you might not. I hope you won't think any less of me if I tell you—"

"Think any less of you? Nonsense! I recall once before you mentioned ghosts. I didn't understand but I didn't question you. Do you really believe in ghosts?"

His voice lowered to a whisper. "It isn't a matter of believing or not believing. I've heard them on many occasions..."

"You have? Tell me about it, please. I'm fascinated." I found it passing strange that such a learned man would believe in ghosts.

"One night I was in a deserted house, resting, when I heard footsteps. I went to investigate but there was no one there."

"Perhaps someone came and left..."

"No. I heard noises. I looked and there was no one there. I was alone. The ghost was the ghost of a Chinese military man. That wasn't the only time. The look on your face, Dorothy. You don't believe me."

"It isn't that I don't believe you. There may be a more logical explanation. I know you must be constantly on guard. Could it have been a dream? In that ephemeral zone between wakefulness and slumber, could it have been a dream?"

"No."

"Perhaps it was your imagination...your imagination playing tricks on you."

"I thought of all of these things. Perhaps if I had just heard a sound... but I lashed myself alert. I walked around. Then I heard voices again. It wasn't battle fatigue and I certainly didn't feel that my sanity was threatened."

"Of course not."

"Hah," he chortled. "I wonder what my mother would say if I told her I had heard ghosts. Or my father?"

"They'd be distressed."

"Possibly. But I think they would rather hear of my experiences than not. They are very understanding parents and I'm indebted to them for bringing me up in the Christian faith, inculcating Christian virtues."

"I'm sure they're proud of you. They have every right to be."

"You can tell that to them when you meet them."

"I certainly will."

Captain Birch laughed. His lean face retained a grin. He was in a happier mood.

"It's time for the movie," he said.

We picked up our stools and went to join the others. When the last reel flickered out and the screen again became a white bedsheet he walked me to the door. With a quick embrace he brushed a furtive kiss along my cheek.

"Until tomorrow."

His high spirits were not maintained. On my next visit he seemed worried and I spoke to him about it.

"I know," he said. "I'm trying to chain my wildly racing heart. The mad thing is going completely out of control but I'm going to stop it if I can. During the past days we have grown extremely fond of each other. I see love in your eyes, written on your face . . ."

"But John—"

"Please, let me finish." He reached out a silencing palm. "I know you've tried to stop as I have. I remember a couple times when I spoke of Birchwood . . . you took pains to emphasize it would be a nice place to *visit*. You've attempted to avoid looking into the future, the subject of marriage, as have I. We're both caught up in something we're powerless to control."

"We can't think of a future. This is war time."

"That's what my mind tells me. But my heart—that is something else again. I recognize the signs. More than a year ago, I was growing fond of a cute lassie, a British Red Cross nurse. Then it became painfully clear that her future could not be with me. The problem was averted. But with you, Dorothy, I can't take the chance. Our backgrounds are too much alike, the blending of cultures . . ."

Sergeant Pillsbury darted his head around the corner. "Hi. Am I interrupting?"

"No. You're just in time. We were discussing what good friends we are. I think your timing is perfect."

"What are you going to do after the war, Stanley?" John asked.

Sergeant Pillsbury turned to me and said emphatically, "I shall resume my studies of library science."

"That's good," Captain Birch nodded. "And you, Dorothy?"

"I'm not sure," I said, looking John in the eye. "I'm going to wait until the war is over to decide.

"You'll make some lucky man a wonderful wife, Dorothy," Captain Birch said.

"That she will," returned Sergeant Pillsbury. "Of course the selection process may take some time. She probably dates a dozen different guys every week.

"Oh?" John said seriously, a dark shadow of concern moving across his face, ending in a frown. "You'll have to tell me all about that."

"I've already said too much," replied Sergeant Pillsbury. "I hope you didn't take it as an insult, Dottie. With all the guys on the base I should have said at least two dozen. Captain Birch, you should see this girl dance."

They continued to banter until it was time to take my leave. I did have a date that evening and when I saw Captain Birch again we resumed the conversation as if there had been no parting.

"Dorothy," he began. "Quite apart from what you plan after the war, do you think you could stand being a missionary's wife? There is a tremendous challenge for a Christian woman...and I still think you'd make a wonderful helpmate."

"I-I don't know, John..."

"I've watched you—your dedication, the way you get on with people. I've even observed a sense of mission, of responsibility."

At that moment a pilot stuck his head into the doorway. "Hey—Dottie! Dottie's here, gang."

Within minutes we were surrounded by eager upturned faces and the men began to relive their war experiences—not the battles, but happier times.

"Dottie, do you remember that party in Liuchow, when the Colonel had too much to drink? He was standing there, as if on a dime, three sheets to the wind..."

After the story there was a cackle of laughter and another immediately began.

"There was Chennault with this little Chinese gal. How the hell was I to know? He wasn't wearing any stars. How was I to know who he was?"

Enjoying myself immensely, I happened to glance at Captain Birch and saw displeasure had hardened his face. He turned and his eyes met mine fleetingly, then wavered as he averted his face, pretending to be interested in the speaker, but he had not been able to conceal his injury.

"Yeah," one of the men went on. "I remember back in Kweilin. This was before the Bamboo Club burned to the ground. I was going—"

"Knock it off!" a voice commanded. A male nurse approached. "Knock it off. Get back where you belong. This is a hospital."

"Yes, sir."

"We sort of forgot—"

"Dorothy," Captain Birch called as I was about to go.

I hesitated and his hand came out for mine and held it. "Goodby, Dorothy. Thanks for everything."

"Bye-bye, John," I carolled easily. "See you later." It was not until I was outside that I was aware of a haunting quality in his voice, something ominous. Without further thought I shrugged it off and returned to my duties. How could I have known that he was speaking with finality?

His somber tone meant more when a messenger hand delivered his letter.

9 May

Dear Dorothy:

I don't know why I'm writing this; maybe it's because I have failed to find an opportunity to speak with you alone in the last few days.

It makes little difference now, as I expect to leave Peishiyi in three days, but until then, please don't waste any more of your time coming to see me. You see, dear, your visits have come to mean too much to me. I'm afraid I'm falling in love with you, and this I intend to stop.

Even if I thought I had a chance with you, I should still want to stop running the risk of looking into your eyes. You want a life of city lights, gay parties, many friends, and much excitement. I want to find my pleasures where sunlight dances on grassy meadows, where blue mountains tower into the sky, or where ocean waves break on moonlit beaches. I prefer a few old friends to many new ones.

I should have learned my lesson a year ago, when after leaving Kukong, I wanted you so badly I couldn't sleep. In spite of my intention not to see you any more, I guess I'll always have a perverse longing to see you again,—it's a queer life, isn't it?

Anyway, Dorothy, I want always to be your friend. If ever you can use my help in any way, please command me.

Forgive me if this note seems to you foolish or annoying. God bless you and keep you.

Good-bye,
John

P.S. I shall always be grateful for the kindness you have shown me the past two weeks. J.M.B.

As I read his letter my hand began to tremble. How could he say that? How could he? Sorely wounded, anger surged within my breast as I struggled against tears and triumphed. How could he know so little about me? I didn't want a life of city lights, gay parties and many friends. I wasn't like that. How could he say such things?

Unconsciously I had run several paces in the direction of the hospital but I drew up short to the realization that John no longer wished to see me. Starting at the beginning I read his letter again. My sudden spur of mindless anger subsided to the return of reason, calming the torrent of my injured pride.

Shaken, I watched a lonely sun melt into a distant rocky skyline, feeling that a certain future had slipped away from me. The loneliness of life and its recurring shadow moved over me just as lengthening shadows from the dark and distant bluffs spread over the land. I was unwanted.

In deep introspection I felt that Captain Birch was miserable too, reacting against forces that threatened to separate us for all time. My heart was in turmoil. I had to see John again.

Sleep did not alter my decision. Mid-morning, I ventured

to the hospital, hoping he would be alone. As I approached his cubicle he saw me. His head came up sharply and he stared as if slapped. "Didn't you get my let—" He broke off, his smile at first pained.

"I couldn't stay away," I got out over a tight lump in my throat. "I-I'm not going to let you banish me so easily."

"I don't want to—"

Instantly we were in each other's arms, trembling, clinging to each other. His gentle voice fluttered in my ear. "Darling—I can't let you go. I've been so miserable—riddled with guilt for sending you away. It's been agony. I'm so glad you're here!"

My heart lifted and I remained silent, waiting for him to find the words I knew would be carefully selected. "Dorothy, I'm not sure we can—or should—go on this way. There are dangers—"

"I know. One who rides a tiger cannot always get off. But if there is no danger of falling off, would it not be wise to carefully consider a course of action before leaping off?"

"Yes. Excellent. Let's talk about it. You first."

"You said you wanted to be friends, but your letter tore at my heart. You wounded me and I became angry. John, you don't know me at all. Where did you get the idea I wanted a life of city lights and gay parties? I'm not like that. You hurt me."

"I'm sorry if I hurt you," he said with compassion, his great brow furrowing. "Perhaps I'm wrong but that's the way I see you . . . carefree and gay. You're always in a light and airy mood. You're so popular with the guys, how could I think of you other than the life of the party?"

"I've been spreading myself thin. Very thin. But that has nothing to do with my future."

He sat down and drew up a stool for me. "Well then, tell me, what would you like?"

"I don't even want to live in a city," I said. "If I could, I'd like a home in the country . . . near a stream. On the hillside there would be an orchard . . . cherry trees . . . apple . . . plum. And birds—larks, thrushes, magpies. And children. A couple cows for milk, a hive of bees for honey . . ."

His palms went up, as if to silence me, his eyes widened in

amazement. "Except for the specifics, do you know what you just described?"

Before my lips could form, "No," he finished, "Birchwood! You just described Birchwood! I'm overwhelmed."

"Really?"

"You've certainly given me something else to think about, aside from my own future."

"I know you have been thinking about it deeply, John. I realize you have some special ideas about being a missionary."

"Have I ever. I'm not sure my family will understand. It may mean making a break with the missionary society. It's not that radical—my beliefs have not changed—but I'm unalterably opposed to some of their methods. You know, they send missionaries out here who can't even speak the language."

"You speak it well."

"When I learned Mandarin my tutor accompanied me wherever I went. My introduction to the language was intense. It wasn't just 'hello' or 'thank you,' which is all some of these so-called missionaries know. I wanted to learn the language, be able to write it. I intend to be an intense missionary, to live among the ordinary people, to speak their language. I'm a little tired of these missionaries who live the comfortable life. They sit around in a mansion, in splendor, right in the middle of poverty and they expect to teach Christianity." He stopped as he saw my bemused expression. "Ah . . . I guess I've been carrying on, but I'm enthusiastic about my ideas, Dorothy. That's why asking any woman to share my life would involve tremendous obstacles. Offering you a comfortable life might mean compromising my principles. I care for you so deeply that I can't think of offering you anything less than a comfortable life. It's a strange world."

"I'm glad we're friends again."

"That's certainly the understatement of the week, sweetheart."

"I'd better go. Otherwise Colonel Wise will think *I'm* a patient."

"Goodby, my lady . . ."

It was not goodby. I saw Captain Birch often the next two days and on the final afternoon when he was released to resume his covert activities he walked me to a grassy knoll overlooking a valley. We seated ourselves beneath a large tree, absorbing the tranquil beauty. Actually it was beautiful because Captain Birch was there.

"Darling," he said at length. "My thoughts have been with you constantly. There is no way I can get you out of my mind. There may be a hundred reasons why I shouldn't ask you to share my life, but the minute I start to list them my heart finds two hundred reasons why I should. Dorothy, I've come to a decision. My mind is made up. I'm asking you to marry me."

"John," I said helplessly. "I-I thought we—"

"I can't go on without you. I may be a missionary but you will give me courage and hope. And sustenance. There is no longer any way that we can't be—"

I pressed a finger against his lips. "Friends."

As I lay in the grass his face loomed above me against the soft blue heaven. "John—" I murmured, before he closed my lips with a kiss.

"Don't ask," I gasped. "I'm not sure—"

"Darling, darling, this is the happiest moment of my life! I love you. I adore you. I can't go on without you. There's nothing else we need. Say that you'll marry me, Dorothy."

He was kissing me and kissing me so that I couldn't say anything. My wildly racing heart wanted to cry out, "Yes," but I could not forget that we were in a war. He saw I was trying to speak. As he released me I rolled away and sat up.

"Captain Birch," I said, putting out a restraining arm. "I've asked you not to propose to me. I thought we had agreed not to spin ourselves into a coccoon of passion. You're so impetuous. You want an answer. Surely you must know what my immediate answer must be. Don't make me give you the answer. If you make me say it now the words may forever haunt me. And if I said them they would not be the words of my heart. They would not be true."

"Oh darling—" He was kissing me again.

"Please,—we must stop, John. It is a time for reason. A solid future requires a solid foundation. You told me that after leaving me in Kukong you couldn't sleep for wanting me. If your feelings have not waned in these years—I think they have matured—we are in no danger of the future. Even now there is talk of the war ending. It is no longer a matter of if but of when. We can be patient . . ."

"I suppose so."

"This time when you are alone beyond the outposts of the enemy I hope you will not lose any sleep, but will remember me and know that for now I am your very closest friend. We have often met despite the war. Surely we can find each other when there is peace. That is, if you . . ."

"We shall. I promise it, my lady. God has sent you my way, I'm sure of it. I was afraid that you would say no. Afraid that I would feel wretched. Although I did not hear what I wanted—" He broke off. "Dorothy, I love you so much."

The sun's warm rays filtering through the leaves dappled the turf with their shadows. I squinted up at the sun.

"It's time to go," I heard him say. He helped me to my feet.

"I know. But I have a favor to ask."

"I'm yours to command."

"Would you go ahead? Let's say our goodby here. I want to remain and meditate . . . remember this moment."

"Of course."

He held me in his arms. "Goodby, Dorothy. Just remember that I love you."

"I love you, John."

Had I told him I loved him? Had someone spoken the words for me? Still feeling his lips on mine, my legs lost their strength and I sagged into the grass. I watched him go, his stride long and loping. Then abruptly he turned. Flashing a boyish grin, he waved, shouting, "My lady, you have not heard the last of Captain John Birch!"

Laughing, he ran down the hill and was soon lost from sight. A plane whirred off the runway, followed by another, and another. Rising, I knew that for today my decision had been the correct one. There was still a war on.

Not more than ten minutes after I returned to the office Sergeant Pillsbury thrust an envelope at me.

"Captain Birch wanted me to give you this."

Quickly I tore open the thick packet. There was no message, only American currency.

"Three hundred dollars!"

"He felt badly about your purse being stolen."

My head came up sharply. "I never told him about that."

"I did," Sergeant Pillsbury said quietly. "We were just talking... and I happened to mention it."

"Gossiping, you mean."

Sergeant Pillsbury shrugged. "Not really. It's a surprise to me too, him giving you the money. I only mentioned it casually."

"What am I going to do?" I said awkwardly.

"Enjoy it. What else?"

"He's such a dear..."

Sergeant Pillsbury nodded over a knowing smile and returned to the file room.

My old routine had been shattered. Captain Birch had monopolized most of my time during the past two weeks and now I found myself wondering what I would do during my lunch break. Passing telephone central I engaged a signalman in conversation.

"That looks interesting," I said. "I've never operated a switchboard."

"You haven't? C'mon Dottie, sit down here. I'll show you."

"Are you sure it's all right, Sergeant?"

"Heck yes, I'll show you how to run it."

Presently a call came through. Responding as instructed I put through the call. Immediately after it was completed there was another. "Let me speak with the duty sergeant," commanded a voice heavy with authority.

"Oh my goodness, Sergeant. It's your C.O., Captain Dell."

The Sergeant took the phones. "Yes, that was Dottie," he said. His face drained, there was a tightening in the muscles of his throat, and I knew he was receiving a dressing down. He pulled the plug with an affected gesture and turned.

"Uh—this is a classified area," said the Sergeant, his cheeks flushed. "Y-you're not supposed to be here."

"I hope I didn't get you in trouble."

"That's okay, Dottie. It's time the Captain noticed me." He sniffed and forced a smile.

It had been my custom to report at once to Colonel Wise whenever I thought I had done anything that might reflect on his command. However, Captain John Dell reached him first.

"That girl who works for you," Captain Dell charged. "Do you know what she was doing? Working the phone switchboard! That's a sensitive area. It's classified. I want her reported!"

Colonel Wise emitted a short dry laugh. With a supercilious reproving look, like a grandfather staring over spectacles to scold an errant yet beloved grandchild, the Colonel said slowly, "Don't be silly, John. Dottie is cleared for Top Secret."

"Uh," the Captain shrugged. "I was just doing my job."

"No doubt about that!"

Captain Dell nodded stiffly as he stalked past me in the doorway.

Colonel Wise looked up as I entered. "One thing about your sister," he mused. "She didn't cause me any trouble."

Edna was no longer with us. A quick study, she had transferred to the Chinese American Composite Wing, an integrated group where American pilots taught combat skills to their Chinese counterparts. The CACW had flown to Chihkiang taking Edna with them; once again I was the only woman on the base.

Since early April, when elements of the Fourteenth supplied coordinated support for the landing, Colonel Wise had been vitally interested in Okinawa. He had grown fond of saying, "Only three hundred miles to go," the distance from Okinawa to Japan.

From my station I had a profile view of the Colonel bending over his desk, studying reports. A bell jangled and he scooped up the phone. He listened a moment and his face took on a perplexed look. "Two Chinese women—an old lady and her daughter? Asking for me? Hell, I don't know any old Chinese woman and her daughter. Tell 'em to get lost. Where did you say they were? Chihkiang? How would I know anybody over—?"

"Colonel Wise, Colonel Wise," I exclaimed excitedly. "That must be my grandmother!" I ran to his desk. "Colonel—"

"God dammit, Dottie, what are you saying?"

"I didn't have a chance to tell you—"

"Hold on, Sergeant. I'll call you back." The Colonel put down the phone. "Now what the hell is this?"

I ran it past him quickly. "I didn't think it would happen so soon. Captain Birch is trying to get Grandma out. If they made it she was to report to any air base and ask for you." I was wide-eyed and breathless.

"My God, Dottie, what are you going to pull next? This is top secret intelligence! What am I supposed to do. We can't transport Chinese nationals and I can't leave them standing on the runway in Chihkiang."

He phoned base operations. "Ah—Sergeant, tell control over at Chihkiang to make the ladies comfortable and . . . ah . . . as inconspicuous as possible. And get my plane ready. At once!"

Colonel Wise turned to me. "I have to get them out now. The sooner I do the fewer will know about it. Dammit, Dottie, this is the living end! You're going to get me court martialed . . ." As he was going out the door he turned to bark instructions. "You know what we're going to need when I get back—just like with General Yur, only in reverse."

Colonel Wise flew the Thunderhead Special to Chihkiang and returned the same day. No sooner had the plane touched down than I approached with a Jeep and my favorite driver. Up till now I could only guess which of my aunts was with Poh-poh. I saw it was Auntie May. Racing past the amenities with a terse, "Not now," I helped Grandma into the Jeep. As we lurched forward I directed a furtive look at the cockpit. The Colonel was smiling.

Less than a minute after touchdown we were off the base, bumping down the road toward Chungking, scattering chickens in every direction.

I told the Colonel about our glorious reunion. "Grandma is very happy. She has asked me to convey her thanks and to ask if there is anything she can do."

"She might come and visit me if I land in the brig. Dottie, this is absolutely the last time."

"Right."

Within days bombers were flying out of Okinawa. The Fifth and Seventh Air Force, also utilizing recently siezed Philippine bases, continued hammering at Japan and

Shanghai. The China skies had been swept clean of Japanese planes.

"Do you realize we haven't shot down a plane in aerial combat for six weeks?" Colonel Wise said. "We're moving to Chungking. The end of the war is imminent."

In Chungking we were little more than unpacked when rumors mounted. Some reports were utterly fantastic.

"One bomb. A whole city gone," the Colonel said in amazement. "Hiroshima gone. Nagasaki gone. We've done it."

At that moment Captain Cabelka came running in. "Japan is suing for surrender!"

The Colonel's eyebrows went up majestically and came down with indulgence. "As I was saying..."

Chapter Sixteen

Turning into the Chaling House Annex, a merry din in my ears, I swung up the steps past the "OFF LIMITS" sign at the foot of the stairs leading to the third floor which I occupied alone. The sign was to remind the staff that they were restricted to the two floors below. As I stepped out on my balcony a turbulent sea of humanity surged through the streets below, overflowing the square, laughing, cheering waving flags and bottles, celebrating the end of hostilities The war was over!

Jeeps and command cars moved at a snail's pace or not at all. The tires on two Jeeps were flat from overload as Chinese youths swarmed over them, shouting, "*Ding Hao*," to their American friends, saluting them with a thumbs up gesture

Ding Hao. Yes, we are number one, I thought with a rising bitterness I could not understand.

Firecrackers popped endlessly. One five-hundred-foot string supported by bamboo poles sounded like runaway machine guns in a battle dance.

I understood the unrestrained outpouring of joy but I could not share it. I watched the crowd with detachment, as if watching a play, and wondered how many shared my loneliness, the loneliness of a plaintive flute playing solo counterpoint to this bedlam.

After a short time in the war, for most Americans no more than a couple years, they would be going home. There was no home to which I could return. War had given my life meaning and direction. What would happen to me now? Where would I go? Floundering aimlessly, my rudderless ship had no safe harbor. Without war, what was the purpose of my life?

The officers had gone to a glittering banquet at the embassy. Already I had seen an eagerness in their faces. Something electric peaked in their voices when they said "Home." Their thoughts were with wives and sweethearts. In spite of the way our lives had been entwined, there would be no place for me in their future.

It was over.

From a distance I heard the endless reverberation of a giant gong which reminded me of a Buddhist temple. From there a short step led to thoughts of a missionary. Why the need for mental gymnastics? Of course I would think of Captain Birch. I wondered, would it be possible to be a missionary's wife?

A sudden chill breeze cooled my face and I heard loudly, "No. It's too late." I spun around to see who had spoken and saw I was quite alone. It must have been my own voice, or a thought so fervent in my mind that it registered as a voice.

More firecrackers exploded below and I marveled at the incongruity of it all. Here I was standing in the midst of what might be the greatest celebration in the twentieth century—it was going on world wide—and I'd never felt so lonely, so alone.

At length I withdrew and went down to find someone with whom I could talk. The room boys were all drunk. Presently Captain Cabelka returned, picked up his servant and put him to bed with a bucket near his head.

The entire next day the young man kept apologizing, "So solly, Suh. So solly, Suh." He lost much face because he'd been served by his master.

Our presence in Chungking may have been justified—certainly it could be explained on paper. In early August a new unit, the Northern Sub-Depot, had been created, with Colonel Wise commanding, Major Earl Gibbens as executive officer, and Captain Cabelka as adjutant. Northern Sub-Depot distributed in transit supplies to bases north of the Yangtze River, operated Lushien Air Base, and supplied Peishiyi, responsibilities which had up to now been handled by the 12th Air Service Group. Colonel Wise also commanded the 12th.

In a general way we separated command functions by our locale. When we were in Peishiyi we operated as the 12th Air Service Group; in Chungking as Northern Sub-Depot. However, if we wanted something done, orders had to be carried out by personnel of the 12th because Northern Sub-Depot existed only on paper and had no warm bodies other than Wise, Gibbens and Cabelka. If the paperwork maze separating the two units became a tangle, no less confusing were the instructions we received from above.

Ironically, as the war drew to a close, General Chennault was relieved of command of the Fourteenth Air Force, succeeded by General Charles B. Stone. After conferring with General Stone, Colonel Wise came back shaking his head in disbelief.

"Stone wants us to maintain a thirty-day level of supplies. God dammit, Gibbens, that's contrary to purpose! We're only an in transit depot, not a permanent storage facility."

Major Gibbens bridled. "I've got enough problems at Lushien. Supplies are backlogging—we can't use a radio because of the terrain and a letter takes three weeks. I have to fly in and out with orders. Since we moved inland a year ago our troops haven't had replacement uniforms. They're starting to look like the Chinese Army."

"Tell me about it," retorted the Colonel. "With the war over, people on the other side of the Hump have turned everything off, right when I've got explicit orders to build up a thirty-day supply!"

"Captain Willett is pushing things through Lushien as fast as he can," Gibbens went on. "The problem is whether to move the clothing from Lushien to Liangshan by air or water. I've got the Twenty-four fifty-ninth Quartermaster Truck Company picking up supplies at the river at Wanshien and hauling them to Liangshan, but have you seen those six by six trucks lately? The damn road's a killer. We lose half the trucks to broken springs, half to blowouts. Forty percent are deadlined."

Colonel Wise pondered. "Vehicles aren't needed for combat any longer. I'll pull some out of the field. You can strip 'em for parts, but they're war-weary too."

On the way to Peishiyi, Captain Cabelka reiterated, "We still have this problem with Base Section Number Five. We've just about blown a ream of paper trying to nail down their responsibilities."

Actually the problem should have been presented in Chungking because it concerned Sub-Depot, not the 12th Air Service Group.

"Try radio," the Colonel advised. "See what CASC has to say."

Surprisingly, we received a prompt reply from headquarters of China Air Service Command. "Northern Sub-Depot is charged with command and operation, but not administration, of Base Section Number Five."

"Well, that clears everything up," Cabelka snickered. "Command and operate, but do not administrate."

"Now what the hell does that mean?" asked Major Gibbens.

"Dottie," said the Colonel, "I have to attend a policy conference in Chungking on the Twenty-fourth. Headquarters—China Theater. Make sure everything dovetails."

"Yes, sir."

We were relieved when the Colonel returned from the conference saying that Northern Sub-Depot would continue under the command of CASC. Then we discovered both our truck companies had been reassigned to the 10th Air Force.

"Radio headquarters," the Colonel said disgustedly.

CASC radioed back at once correcting the order.

"Hmm," Captain Cabelka mused as he read a report. "I see China Theater is allocating one C-Forty-seven from the Three hundred twenty-second Troop Carrier Squadron to the Twelfth Air Service Group."

Everyone laughed uproariously. The C-47 was the Thunderhead Special the Colonel had been using ever since Liuchow.

"I wonder if we could use it for Sub-Depot?" Major Gibbens said with a whimsical smile.

"Not by a damn sight," Colonel Wise said. "The transfer order reads Twelfth Air Service Group. I don't want any screwing around in this command. (Excuse me, Ma'am.)"

Major Gibbens cleared his throat. "I've ordered the Twenty-four fifty-ninth Truck Company to cut down their ground speed. They're breaking too damn many springs. We're out of boats—the river is running high on account of the monsoon. I don't see how we can get sufficient tonnage for September."

"September?" raved the Colonel. "Hell, I'm still working on August. And I don't have any men."

On August 29th, in the role of Commanding Officer of Northern Sub-Depot, Colonel Wise flew to Chihkiang to raid the personnel of the 12th Air Service Group which he also commanded. Before he left, he said, "Dottie, I'm sending you on an important mission to headquarters."

Briefed and ready, as I waited on the apron for a plane to take me to Kunming, an intelligence officer approached me and said, "Dottie. John's been killed."

"John who?" I said.

"John Birch."

Stunned and speechless, agony jarred my brain. I felt cold, as if all my blood had drained from me. Dazed, I staggered on board. As the plane soared off the runway I found comfort in the roar of its engines, a muffling blanket closing out the world, leaving me to my sorrow. I stumbled through my mission at headquarters, little more than a robot, and when it was over and I looked back it was difficult to believe that I had been to Kunming, much less accomplished anything. I felt that I had been in a vacuum.

I proceeded to intelligence to see what could be learned. At first there was only fragmentary information. Captain Birch had left an air field in Fowyang, Anhwei Province, and had not reached his destination. Intelligence officers shrugged sympathetically saying, "Sorry, Dottie. That's all the news we have." How could I know they would soon grow tight lipped and begin to withhold information?

By the time Colonel Wise returned from Chihkiang we received information that Ankang Air Base was to be closed in the immediate future. Captain Cabelka radioed Ankang and directed the commander to retain sufficient personnel to operate the base until further notice.

Ankang set the pattern. Bases that had so laboriously been assembled and supplied now had to be liquidated, men and material allocated to remaining bases. We moved to Liangshan where Major Gibbens presented a problem.

"The Three-hundred-fiftieth Service Group is being redeployed to a new area and they're dumping all their equipment right here."

Colonel Wise conferred with his officers. "All right. Ship it on to the Three hundred first Air Depot Group in Kunming."

Not long thereafter instructions issued from CASC. "No material is to be turned in by any units until a Standard Operating Procedure is established."

Unpacking, I came across the silk map Captain Birch had given me. It felt soft and smooth to my touch. Instinctively I placed it against my cheek and imagined I felt John's cheek against mine. My heart ached. John had received the map here in Liangshan from a Captain Ong. Ong Hong June. John had sung the name.

I sang it now. "Ong Hong June." The map was home . . . I quickly blocked out the agonizing thought that John would never come home, forcing it out of my mind. But I couldn't stop thinking. The map reminded me of many pleasant meetings with John, coincidental meetings, always a surprise. I'd grown accustomed to his surprises but that in no way prepared me for the shock I would receive here in Liangshan, a surprise that originated with Captain John Birch.

Liangshan resembled a bee hive—units criss-crossing in transit, the material of war suddenly useless, stockpiling, being redeployed. Office space became available only after several combat units departed. It wasn't until the tenth of September that I completed the Northern Sub-Depot historical report for August. On the last page of Captain Cabelka's chronicle I typed, "Captain E. Cabelka was relieved from the above duties in preparation to being returned to the 12th Service Group for duty as group adjutant."

"But you're still here," I said.

He smiled laconically. "It's just a paper transfer."

Captain Cabelka remained attached to Sub-Depot and didn't serve with the 12th Service Group at all, another case where the facts and the records had little in common. Yet, the truth would out. The final lines of the report caused me to erupt in a sharp thunderclap of laughter.

"The status of the Northern Sub-Depot continued to remain obscure throughout the month."

Captain Cabelka checked over the six page report. "Pretty good, Dottie. Let's knock off for today."

"Mail call," a voice sang out. "Mail call."

"You're certainly late."

"No," the corporal laughed. "I'm early for tomorrow."

With the war ending my mail diminished to reasonable proportions. For a while it seemed as if half my spare time was spent writing. There were four letters for me. I flipped through them and froze. One letter was from Captain John Birch.

Could he be alive? A startled cry rose in my throat and I found myself running to my quarters, racing blindly, the clop-clop of my sandals on the macadam keeping rhythm with my wildly beating heart. My senses returned. Of course John couldn't be alive. He'd written the letter before...

Gasping for breath, I wrenched open the door and heard it slam behind me as I stood trembling, hands shaking, fumbling, unable to open the envelope. At last I had the paper out, unfolded, and began to read.

13 August 1945

Dear Dorothy:

Thanks lots for your kind letters of June 25 and July 13, just received. Sorry to hear about the heat and ill health in your family; trust things are better now. The summer here fell far short of last year's heat, and I am in excellent health, a little thin, and very sunburned from swimming in a river that flows by my station, and from taking several long motorboat trips on business. (Did you know I have a captured Jap boat? I'd like to take you riding in it!)

Perhaps I can find a way to see you soon again; the radio for the past three days has been loud with rumors of Japan's imminent surrender. Please keep me informed of your whereabouts, dear. I have been unable, out here in the plains, to keep up with the new APO's; does your change to # 271 mean that you have moved again?

Thanks for the word from May and Marion. Please give them my best wishes. I think of them quite often (but not so often as of you).

It really begins to look as tho this long terrible war will soon be over. Yesterday, Sunday morning, I held a church service here, thanking God for bringing us to the eve of victory. All the men in my station attended excepting one operator who could not leave his transmitter.

I believe I shall visit my family as soon as I can, then return to China (possibly the extreme western part) to resume missionary work. Some people want me to stay in the army as an intelligence officer, but I can't escape from the conviction that God has called me to the other.

Please write me whenever you can.

Affectionately,
John

"John..." I choked, helpless before a deluge of tears. Sorrow stricken, I flung myself across the bed, my body racked with paroxysms of sobbing. "John," I cried. "Why? Why did it have to be this way?"

Sharp pieces of memory flooded my mind. His face came into focus, a lean face with a gentle boyish smile. "My lady," he had said. "You have not heard the last of Captain John Birch."

His word were prophetic; I held his letter. My fingers were at once careful, my touch delicate. The letter had to be preserved.

Sniffing, blowing my nose, I rose, moved to my writing box and read an earlier letter. "I want to find my pleasures where sunlight dances on grassy meadows, where blue mountains tower into the sky, or where ocean waves break on moonlit beaches." His words were beautiful. I could not control my emotions and a new wave of tears washed down my cheeks, like ocean waves breaking on moonlit beaches. "Oh John," I sobbed uncontrollably. "There is no sunlight dancing on grassy meadows now."

When my tears showed signs of abating a sudden realization halted the dizzy thoughts swirling through my mind. I hadn't even thanked John for saving Grandma. I should have—

Overcome with remorse, I collapsed on the bed and lay sobbing until exhausted, until I was once again able to master my emotions.

In the depths of despair, the same questions continued to bombard my mind. Who? Where? Why? As I composed myself I knew I'd have to find answers for these questions. I had to know the truth.

With renewed zeal I questioned men assigned to Intelligence. There were the usual shakes of the head and stoic responses. "No news." Perhaps my persistence made one officer feel sorry for me. "Dottie, the government has clamped a tight lid of secrecy on the whole incident."

Incident? An incident related to top levels of diplomacy. What made it an incident? This wasn't just another death in the course of war. The war had been over two weeks by the time news of John's death reached us. When *had* he been killed? Had he been captured as a spy? There was no way I would accept silence; I would learn the truth no matter how terrible the details.

Not to be deterred, I turned to another source—Chinese Intelligence. The Chinese wouldn't be concerned with an information blackout imposed by the Fourteenth Air Force, the Embassy or the Pentagon.

My efforts to teach a young liason officer the fox trot ingratiated me with him and I didn't hesitate to request a favor in return.

"Those who sent Captain Birch to aid your people now need the help of the people he served," I told him. "The people of the villages..."

He nodded agreeably. "Perhaps it would be possible to make inquiries."

In due time the young officer reported. "Some say it was a stray bullet."

"Do you believe that?"

His face was impassive as he slowly shook his head from side to side. "No more than I believe he was killed masquerading as a Japanese."

"John wore the garb of peasants. He wouldn't be mistaken for a Japanese. That's absurd."

"Not for certain minds. There are those who find it a convenient way to divert attention. After all, who'd care if one more Jap was killed, even ten days after the war was over?" He rubbed his hands to illustrate. "It is regrettable." He made a little bow. "And quickly forgotten."

So the war was over when John was killed. Ten days.

"Yes, what you say is true. No one would care if another Jap was killed."

He then used a phrase I didn't comprehend. After explanations back and forth I understood him to mean "highway bandits." His voice became emphatic. "The bandits are enemies of the Kuomintang."

"Communists," I said.

He nodded. "The area is a stronghold for these bandits. There is too much silence in a village near Hsuchow. It is said a Chinese officer accompanied Captain Birch and his party but there's no record. The mission may have been important to the Americans, but to China . . ." He shrugged and left it there.

My search continued. Agents in the field knew little, but I decided someone in administration, someone who had an opportunity to read reports as they came in, would be a fertile source. The constant transfer of personnel resulted in the fortuitous replacement by a man with access to secret files.

After I found Lou it took a bit longer for him to follow my subtle hints and find me. "Dottie . . ." he asked. "W-Would you like to go out and have a couple drinks? I-I mean . . ."

His reluctance had nevertheless afforded me a longer time to study him. An enlisted man, Lou reacted negatively to command authority. He considered officers' orders abrasive. In my opinion he could be manipulated by stress. Following my suggestion, he took me to an out-of-the-way gin mill.

The afternoon sun had faded, rendering remote corners of the club dark. It was little more than a dive. We skirted a panting yellow dog lying on the floor and Lou continued to a table in the corner, covering his insecurity with swagger, pretending to be very suave. Maybe it was the way he thought officers acted.

As the waiter brought our drinks I glanced at mine and reacted. "That's not a sour high," I exclaimed indignantly, raising my voice. "Don't you know the difference between a whiskey sour and a sour high?" I allowed a nascent fire to blaze in my eyes.

Lou's palms came up, as if to shield himself from my sudden fury. "It's okay. It's okay," he said with a nervous patting motion designed to soothe both me and the waiter. "I'll keep it. Bring her what she wants."

At the waiter's reappearance my smile was genuine. The ploy had succeeded. Lou was starting with two drinks to my one. "I'm sorry," I said soothingly, reaching out my hand to touch his. "It's just that people keep taking me for granted. I've started to stick up for myself. A couple duty stations back I was helping a sergeant friend on the switchboard and his C.O. reported me to the Colonel. The Colonel sure set him straight. 'She's cleared for top secret!'" I allowed a giggle to escape. "I can hear him yet."

"The C.O. got chewed by the Colonel? That's great," he chuckled. "Are you really cleared for top secret?"

"Sure."

"Is that a fact?"

"Yeah. I was working as a top secret translator at Kukong long before it fell. We'd get radio messages from operators in the field, monitoring everything that moved. That's where I first met Captain John Birch. After handling his calls I finally met him. He came into the shack one day."

"So that's where you met Dog-Sugar-Eight."

"Uh, Dog-Sugar-Eight. Right!" Recovering quickly, I hoped my split-instant hesitation had gone unnoticed. Actually I hadn't known Captain Birch's secret call letters and to my knowledge had never talked with him on radio. "He came over to our house . . . made a real hit with the family . . . tried to find a piano for the church. He was quite a guy."

I kept talking, reminiscing, spewing out a wealth of irrelevant information.

"We really shouldn't be talking about Birch," he cautioned.

"Why not? It's all ancient history. You'd think the government would be more interested in catching black market racketeers. We had a foreign correspondent running a money changing racket in Kweilin. Do you know we ran our payroll through his black market, converting gold to C N?"

He made no response and presently excused himself for the restroom. In his absence I ordered another round of drinks, telling the waiter, "Don't forget to put something in them." I poured mine down a crack in the wall and was cradling the empty glass as Lou returned.

"I was hoping you'd come back. I was getting lonely."

"I didn't think I was gone that long."

"You left me to drink alone," I said, waving the empty glass.

He reached for his and took a couple deep swallows.

"I remember the days in Kweilin," I went on. "Do you know we paid Chinese operators with American cigarettes? Captain Birch would swoop down on the base and I'd have to scurry around looking for smokes."

"I suppose many of his operators were Communists."

"Communists, Nationalists, anybody he could get..."

"You know, he shouldn't have trusted the Communists," Lou said. "He was warned... but he kept saying he could deal with them."

"Captain Birch was successful. In the early days our fliers would get axed. After he went out among the peasants we got them back."

"Yeah, but you can't trust the Communists. I knew they'd start up again as soon as we settled it with the Japs. The Commies were stashing bullets all along. We'd give them three, they'd fire two and save one, or fire one and save two. Damn Communists—they killed him."

"Why? How?" I held him with my eyes.

He leaned forward and lowered his voice. "Cap'n Birch was with a small group, mostly officers—one Chinese Lieutenant. They were heading for Hsuchow when they were halted by a Communist roadblock. Cap'n Birch objected, saying something like, 'You have no right to stop an American military detail.' The Reds thought it over and let the group pass. A little later there was a second confrontation. Cap'n Birch and the Chinese Lieutenant left their group and walked into a village to talk. While they were gone the Red disarmed the rest of the party. Before long the disarmed men heard a couple shots... but they didn't see anything. According to reports from villagers they found two bodies full of bayonet holes. They were about to bury Birch when the Chinese Lieutenant stirred back to life. They say he survived but he's dropped out of sight. Most of the reports are hearsay... what the Chinese Lieutenant told the villagers while they nursed him back. The killing was deliberate. The Commies had him there in the village a couple of hours before the order came down. None of the other Americans were killed. They were finally released..."

"I wonder who they are?"

"Funny thing. They were never named. Not in the stuff I read."

My further questions generated little information. Reasonably certain the well was dry, I said, "You know, we're getting into recent developments. I think we ought to knock it off. You never know, the waiter may be with OSS—or a Red."

"You're right. I'd hate to be put on the carpet for a loose lip. But that's one thing... I've never had. A loose lip."

"Right."

"Karl Marx and his dialect-ical material-ism," he said thickly. "Damn Communists!"

"You sure know a lot about communism."

"S-Studied it in col-lege. I been to college. I got a lot more col-lege than some of these damn officers who give me—orders."

Although not all of my questions had been answered I could be content with what I had learned. During our final days in Liangshan as we were closing the office, Captain Cabelka happened to mention John. "He was quite a guy."

"I don't suppose I ever will get over it," I said sadly. "I'm grieved that the Communists killed him."

"I knew they would," Colonel Wise interjected as he walked up behind us.

"You what?" I demanded sharply.

The Colonel's eyebrows went up at the sudden intensity in my voice. "During the last few days of the war I tried repeatedly to get him out of that area. I knew the minute the war was over the Communists would kill him, but I couldn't reach him. Captain Birch worked with us but he was never under my command. He didn't work *for* me."

"How did you know they would kill him?" I pressed.

"Once the war with Japan ended civil war would resume. Only a fool would think otherwise. John knew all their agents. They couldn't have a man running around who could identify all the operators. He had too much influence with the peasants. He could speak with them, eat with them, live with them. And there was the religion thing. There was no way the Communists were going to let him live."

"I wish I had known sooner," I said. What more could I say?

We flew to Chengtu and were successively stationed at Chihkiang, Hsinching and Tsingchen. It was the season of jubilant trees adorned in reds and golds, and as the leaves fluttered down, wrinkled and brown, to be trampled into the earth, we received orders to proceed to Shanghai. It had been two months since I stood on a balcony in Chungking, melancholy because the war was over, depressed because there was no future for me. Ever since, a vague feeling within me had kept the war alive, but now as I returned to Shanghai I realized it had finally come to an end. The Fourteenth Air Force would go on and I would go with them. Optimistic about my future, I couldn't wait to see my old home, the Bund, the harbor with its pungent aroma of oil, fish and sweat, where gulls stood in the sky waiting to catch a ride on a passing cloud.

Chapter Seventeen

Life in Shanghai became a microcosm of the chaos I had known during the war. After a few days in a cramped room I returned to 1412 Yu Yuen Road to help Father open the house in which Mother and we children had lived before going inland. Father had come from Chungking alone and before a week passed my sister transferred in with her wing.

Edna had plans of her own. "I'm not ready to live here," she said. "Mother will be coming home before long. Have you noticed the little houses around the base?"

"Of course," I said. The Japanese had constructed a cluster of tiny homes surrounding Kiangwan. The little homes were neat and clean and rent through the U.S. government was reasonable.

"It would be fun having a place of our own... and we could get a maid," Edna suggested.

"All right," I agreed. "I'm ready for a bit of extravagance."

What a pleasant surprise it was to find that our friends May and Marion, whom I had last seen in Kunming after their harrowing parachute escape, lived only a few doors away. Having my sister and our friends near at hand helped me over the turbulence of being detached from the command of Colonel Wise. The Colonel's assignment—training Chinese troops to take over American responsibilities—had been completed and I was sent to assist a Colonel Kinsey. My new job was not unpleasant; neither was it inspiring. After two months I was thoroughly delighted to be assigned to Colonel Wise again.

The Yuen family spent a lonely Christmas, with three of us in Shanghai, the remaining three in Chungking. However, we were barely into the new year when an exciting idea promised a delayed Christmas for us all. Captain Jim Willett offered to fly to Chungking to get Mother, Gloria and Jack.

Colonel Wise expressed an interest and became part of the plan. He and I drove to Kiangwan, parked the Jeep at the end of the runway and waited. Before long we saw Willett's plane break out of the haze, come gliding down smooth and level, bounce once and coast to a halt.

Colonel Wise sent the Jeep racing forward before Captain Willett cut the props. Parking on the off-tower side, the Colonel hurried to the hatch. When it came open his head jerked in surprise. For an instant he froze in the open hatchway, recovered, and slammed it shut.

"Willett!" he screamed. "I want to see you!"

The Colonel came running back to the Jeep, his face livid. "Good God! It's not your mother and brother and sister. The plane is full of women and kids."

"Who . . . ?"

"How would I know? How the hell are we going to get them off the base?"

"Oh, my goodness!"

Captain Willett approached with an easy long-legged lope. "What's the problem?"

"Jim, where the hell are your brains? The inside of that ship looks like a Chinese whorehouse. Women . . ." The Colonel paused. "I'm sorry, Dottie. I didn't mean that about Chinese you-know-what . . . your mother and all, but I'm so damn mad at Willett here." He resumed his tirade. "You've put us in a helluva spot. How the hell are we going to get them off the base? Where did you find them all?"

"Dorothy's mother had a friend . . . and she had a friend. I had a friend . . ."

"God dammit, I don't care how they got on, the question is how are they gonna get off? I have to think. Jeeze! All right. Trot your ass back there and tell them to stay put till we come back. We have to figure out something. Anybody who gets off that plane before we get back will be interned as a prisoner of war. Tell 'em!"

"Colonel," I said. "The war's been over for months."

"I don't care."

Captain Willett sauntered back to the plane, attempting to appear nonchalant, as if maybe he'd forgotten his flying scarf. Really I don't think he'd given any thought to how he was going to discharge his passengers. In a few minutes he returned. "Well, what are we going to do?"

"Wait till dark, that's for God damn sure," growled the

Colonel. "It wouldn't be so bad if it was only Dottie's family. They're American citizens, but you went and brought a whole load of Chinese nationals. How are we going to get them off the base? Hell, man, you could lose your bars . . . and me my eagle. I hope you told 'em to keep those kids quiet."

"I-I did," Willett said.

The Colonel shot him a withering look.

It seemed like hours—it *was* hours—before the night became sufficiently dark to attempt a rescue. By now we'd acquired a command car in addition to the Jeep. With Willett following in the Jeep, Colonel Wise drove the command car up to the plane and opened the hatch.

Immediately Mother appeared in a storm of ill temper. "Dorothy! What took you so long?"

"Not now, Mother."

"Do you realize how long we've been waiting?" Her voice took on a cutting edge. "We had to use a helmet for a potty. The plane was becoming another refugee train."

"*Not now*, Mother," I said sharply. "Later. Shut up or we'll all be arrested. Do as you're told."

"American citizens in the Jeep," commanded the Colonel. "Now I want it quiet."

With the children stashed underfoot, hiding beneath robes and luggage, we started forward at a smart pace. At the gate Colonel Wise hit the brakes, tossed the sentry a crisp salute and roared in his finest West Point manner, "Colonel Richard M. Wise, Commanding." He reeled off some elaborate command authority. "Official convoy of two vehicles. Military personnel . . . American nationals . . . civilian Air Force employees. Is that button on your collar open?"

"N-No sir. Proceed."

"Look sharp, Soldier."

Already we were moving.

Upon reaching home I explained it all to Mother. I expected a salty retort, at least a pointed comment about the stupidity of base regulations, but she surprised me completely. She tilted back her head and laughed.

Not many days later Colonel Wise approached me in the

office. "Dottie, they're allowing officers to bring over dependents. Would you complete these forms? I'm sending for my wife and kids. It'll take a while to process and I'd like to get the ball rolling."

"Of course. I know you'll be glad to see them."

"I'm looking forward to it."

The Colonel returned to his desk and soon Willett, Gibbens and Cabelka huddled around him. Over their banter I heard someone say, "Let's make Dottie a proposition."

I directed a censuring look in their direction. The Colonel's palms came up to silence the laughter. "This is on the up and up, Dottie. No hanky-panky. As you know, we've acquired a home and we want you to move in with us and run the place. Edna too. It won't cost you a thing."

"I don't know if I can trust you," I said fussily, including them all in my gaze. I still didn't feel completely at ease with American humor. "My job won't evaporate?"

"No," Colonel Wise said, seeing my concern. "This has nothing to do with your Air Force job. We need you to run the house, give instructions to the servants, keep things organized. You speak their language..."

"Edna and I have a maid..."

"Bring her along."

Edna was invited to see the home and after one look she was ecstatic. We told our maid to start packing.

The officers' home was on Avenue Joffe Lu, in the French Concession near the American Consulate. Formerly the residence of a wartime traitor and profiteer, the mansion towered as a castle behind eight-foot walls. A gateman presided over arrivals and departures. Inside the walls on spacious grounds nestled a three car garage and a formal tea garden.

"How many servants?" I asked.

"Only ten," the Colonel grinned. "With your girl, eleven."

We became accustomed to elegant living. One of the servants was an accomplished tailor, another a gourmet chef. We indulged ourselves with flaming desserts—our favorite was Baked Alaska. Our parties were gala affairs and Mother, a frequent guest, thoroughly enjoyed the ballroom floor. We were "in the groove," according to the new American idiom. Edna and I found all the post-war jive talk rather bewildering.

In this idyllic setting the weeks slipped by quickly. The only contention that arose concerned the medal. The Air Force wanted to award me another medal.

"It's not that I don't appreciate receiving a medal," I explained for the seventeenth time. "I certainly do appreciate it and I'm honored, but why can't they mail it to me like they did the last one?"

"This one is more important," said Captain Cabelka. "The other one was for civilian service. This one is for *meritorious* civilian service. Superior service . . ."

"I'd prefer to have it mailed."

"That's no way to be decorated, Dottie," Colonel Wise remonstrated. "Receiving a medal in the mail is like getting a letter. That's no way—no way at all."

"But it's what I'd like."

"You talk to her, Gibbens."

"Why not, Dottie?"

"I'm not going to walk up there in front of—everybody. All that cheering, foot stomping, catcalls . . ."

"It won't be like that, Dottie. It will be dignified. All the big brass will be there. Probably General Wedemeyer, General Stone, General—"

"*Wedemeyer*? Oh no!"

"Aw, c'mon, Dottie."

"No!"

"I could order you," the Colonel said.

"I won't go," I said stubbornly.

"She's got you there, Colonel. As a civilian, it's within her rights not to attend the presentation."

"Who asked you to get involved?"

"You did."

"Dottie," the Colonel fumed. "If you weren't indispensible . . . if we didn't need you so darn much . . ."

Their cajoling spilled over to the office where Sergeant Stanley Pillsbury was asked to speak to me.

"Dottie," Sergeant Pillsbury said. "I went through an awful lot of work doing the research, compiling the biographical data, the narrative, writing the citation . . ."

"I appreciate it, Stanley."

"Look at the record. China Air Service Command, Sector Three; Sector One; Twelfth Air Service Group; Northern Sub-Depot; Fourteenth Air Service Group . . ."

"No thanks. I'm not going."

"Not even to get a medal with a silver wreath?"

"No."

"Listen to this, Dottie. Here's the way the General will read it. 'Miss Yuen's duties required her to become familiar with organization, policies and principles and to develop a detailed knowledge of administration, personnel, and logistical matters in which she had no previous training or experience. She acquired and constantly increased this knowledge by study, by unusually keen observation, and by a very retentive memory. She demonstrated great adaptability and initiative during enlisted personnel shortages by taking over various administrative tasks ordinarily performed by trained enlisted men. During the difficult and dangerous days of the withdrawal from East China, she set a high example for civilians and soldiers alike by her cheerful demeanor and devotion to duty through excessively long hours. Her calmness under frequent enemy day and night bombing and under threat from enemy agents and snipers was common knowledge of the command and an inspiration to all. Of her own volition this civilian employee remained on duty in Kweilin and Liuchow until the final—"

"Stop!" I interrupted, waving my hands.

"Well, that's what it says."

"It's very nice, Stanley, and I appreciate all the hard work you put in it. But I can't. I'm not going to listen to any more of this and I'm not getting up on any reviewing stand in front of the whole Fourteenth Air Force and that's final!"

"I understand, Dottie."

I remained adamant and refused to attend the ceremonies. Like the first, the second medal promptly arrived in the mail along with the citation which I could read in private without embarrassment. A medal from the Republic of China, bearing the likeness of Generalissimo Chiang Kai-shek would take longer—twenty-nine years longer.

"We really have come to depend upon you," the Colonel said later at the mansion. He and I were there alone, except for the servants. He was sitting in what had become his favorite chair, fondling a glass, a cloud of blue-gray smoke from his cigarette coiling above his head.

"I was just thinking," he said, slowly exhaling. "Looking back . . . you know, I'm feeling like Urbanowicz."

"Who?"

"You don't remember Group Captain Withold Urbanowicz?"

"No."

"He was out here in Forty-three. A Polish officer—Free Poland. He became a legend. Flying out of London, he made seventeen kills before they packed him off to our Pentagon. But he was like a third thumb there and eventually he came out here with Chennault. He checked out in P-40s, went up and made a kill the first day. He'd never fly a mission; he'd go up alone, sometimes tagging transports. Always alone—searching. He made ten or eleven kills out here before going home. Always searching . . . searching. I feel like that tonight. Searching . . ."

"You're just down."

"I need a drink." He rose, went to the bar, poured some bourbon in a glass and kissed it with a splash of water. Returning to his chair he sat down heavily. "I should have earned a star," he said suddenly. "I should have made Bee-Gee."

"Yes," I agreed. It surprised me to hear him talking about himself. He never did.

"I would have, if I'd been commanding a fighter group. But somebody had to push through the bullets, bombs and chow. The Fourteenth compiled a fantastic record. During nineteen forty-four, in aerial combat alone, our kill ratio was seven point seven to one. Nearly eight to one. I'm proud of being part of that. It was our logistics that kept things going when we were losing base after base. Logistics."

"The men all respect you . . ."

"I hear what you're saying." He smiled wanly. "I guess I *am* down."

"You'll feel better when your family gets here."

"They're not coming," he said abruptly.

"Not coming? But I thought . . ."

"My wife wrote she would only come without the kids.

Without the kids," he repeated morosely. "It was just a ruse. She knew what I would say. I told her not to come alone. It was one of her tricks. She doesn't want to leave her boyfriend."

He took out his aluminum cigarette case, removed the rectangular cap, shook out a cigarette, placed it between his lips and flamed it with his lighter.

"You know," he said through a puff of smoke, "I've really become accustomed to having you around."

"Just don't call me comfortable," I said, laughing. "One of my boyfriends did that."

"You still going with the sailor?"

"Not since Chungking."

"Major Cullen Brannon?"

"I see him sometimes. You have no objections?"

"Oh no," he said quickly. "None. I was just making conversation. Or trying to. You know, Dottie, you could have anyone in the Fourteenth—" He broke off, left it unfinished. "What's wrong with this," he continued, making a circular gesture, indicating the room, "is that it has to end. Before long Captain Cabelka will be returning to the States. Willett won't be far behind him."

"And you, Colonel. What are you going to do?"

He laughed. "Somehow I wish you hadn't asked."

I left him then and as I moved down the spacious hall I heard him utter a melancholy one-word expletive.

As Colonel Wise had predicted, in June Captain Cabelka returned to the States, as did Captain Willett. Our days at the mansion were over. Edna and I watched our maid pack, then the three of us went home to our family. For a short time Edna and I reigned as spoiled royalty.

Mother didn't object to us having a maid. "With you prima donnas back, somebody has to do the work."

Nevertheless, the maid had to leave, mostly because the only place she had to sleep was in Gloria's bedroom, to which Gloria objected. Edna hated to part with the maid. "Just watch," she said. "Mother will start ordering us around again."

At the office the career of Colonel Wise took a surprising turn. Secret orders arrived from the State Department detaching him from the Air Force and assigning him to General Chennault. Chennault was coming back.

Replacing Colonel Wise, a man arrived who smoked thick black cigars and rested his feet on the desk most of the time. I wasn't pleased with him because he urged me to spy on other secretaries. Fortunately, a new opportunity arose.

In early Autumn, Colonel Wise summoned me to the Cathay Hotel. "I want you to come and work for us," he said. "We're starting Chennault Air Lines."

"A job not with the Air Force?" I asked. "But—"

"This will be better. You'll be chief secretary." His eyes sparkled. "Have you noticed the acres and acres of supplies building up around Shanghai? Tractors, plows, and foodstuffs as far as the eye can see. It's part of the United Nations relief organization. There has to be a way to get these supplies inland where they're needed. So we're starting an airline. C'mon," he said, eagerly leading the way. "I want you to meet the Old Man."

He ushered me into the next room. "General, this is the girl I was telling you about. You remember Dottie."

Chennault's leathery face cracked into a grin. "I'll say I do." He squinted to appraise me. "Didn't you come to see me once?"

"Yes."

"I thought so. Something about a hidden air strip . . ."

"It was there, all right. Just where Grandma said. Captain John Birch located it and got my aunt and grandmother out."

"I'm glad," Chennault said. "Too bad about Birch." His face became stony, his eyes narrowed to slits as his jaw went jutting out. "I wish I'd still been here in command of the Fourteenth when that happened. I'd have sent a squadron of B-25s over and blasted the Communist son-of-a-bitches and that would have been that."

"The Generalissimo would have been delighted."

"That he would. But it's water over the dam now. Dottie, we'd like to have you with us."

"Dottie," Colonel Wise interposed. "I want you to take applications for pilots. Make sure they have their green cards . . ."

"I'd better resign from the Air Force first," I said.

There were no further formalities. Presiding over the birth of an airline proved an arduous task. As midwife I watched the pangs of birth and experienced the joy of seeing the squalling infant take nourishment, make a few faltering steps and grow. Correspondent Clyde Farnsworth arrived to take charge of publicity. An old friend, Colonel Chuck Hunter, also joined us.

"Dottie," he declared. "I still remember the first day you came to work for us in Kweilin."

"You had the desk next to Colonel Wise," I remembered.

"And Cabelka had to teach you typing."

"He did not—I taught myself. But Ed was kind."

"Dottie," he said, initiating what would become a favorite pastime whenever Old China Hands met. "Let's get together and talk about the good old days."

"Okay."

Later, in a little café, Colonel Hunter reminisced. "I've been out here a long time." He gave his coffee a stir. "I was here in Shanghai before the Generalissimo had an Air Force. General Chen Tsi-tong wanted to be emperor, remember? He was virtually king of Kwangtung Province. I was there the night he got up in front of his pilots and asked them to pledge their loyalty. The very next morning some Colonel led them off with every last plane, taking them over to Chiang Kai-shek."

"I roomed with the girl who engineered that—the Colonel's lover."

"The hell you say!"

"Her name was Wu—or Cheuk."

"Well, I'll be darned! Chen Tsi-tong blamed his misfortune on the fellow who read the forecast of his prayer stick in the temple. The stick scratched a sign in the sand and the poor interpreter read the sign as opportunity. 'Don't lose the opportunity.' He should have read it as 'Don't lose the planes.' It's the same symbol—opportunity and planes."

"Yes," I nodded. "The symbol 'gay.'"

"Perhaps it was a face-saving device. So Chen would have someone to blame?"

"Who can say?"

"Then was then and now is now. I know one thing. I neve
thought I'd get into a hush-hush operation like this. After all
the war is over."

"This? Hush-hush?" Perplexed, I furrowed my brow.

"You don't know, do you? I didn't think so Remembe
OSS?"

I nodded.

"Well, you'd better know this Chennault Air Line
operation is being funded by the CIA."

My breath caught. Immediately I remembered the secre
orders that had come for Colonel Wise from the Stat
Department. "If that's the case," I said, "the less we say abou
it the better."

Chennault Air Lines changed its name to conform to it
United Nations-UNRRA purposes and we became CNNRA
Air Transport, which was further abbreviated to CAT
Supplies which had accumulated on the docks began to
move inland.

I continued working long hours, forgetting the clock
hiring pilots, supervising a secretarial staff, coordinating a
myriad of things with unnumbered bureaus and agencies o
two nations, frantically trying to outdistance fleet-foote
minutes in the race of time, dragging myself home late
sleeping fitfully, dragging myself back to work, gulping
coffee, losing all track of the days, growing
weary . . . wearier . . . then suddenly one night my feet lagge
so that I doubted whether I could reach home. Staggering in
the front door, I faltered and collapsed on my bed. Weak
barely able to raise my head I was seized with a terrible chil
and lay shivering, unable to find warmth.

"It looks like malaria," Mother said, covering me with a
quilt. There was no comfort in the cover, nor in the second
My frozen bones shook. I was exhausted.

Struggling on the borderline of consciousness I heard my
youngest sister ask, "She isn't going to die, is she?"

"No," Mother said. "No, she isn't. Now go away."

Mother's words were not reassuring. Her tone frightene
me. I felt Mother's hand trembling on my wrist.

"You're going to be all right. . . . Sandow! Get a doctor
quick."

At that point I fainted.

Some time later, through the turbulent mist I made out the face of Dr. Wong slipping in and out of focus. The room was shifting, spinning crazily. "She's completely anemic," he said in a voice a mile away. "She needs a transfusion."

"Is she going to die?" Gloria asked again.

"No!" Mother said.

"Ah," smiled the doctor. "You're coming back to us." His smile remained in focus.

"I'm so cold," I said through chattering teeth.

"That's normal," Dr. Wong replied. "You will feel warmer as soon as you get some blood. We must get you built up."

I nodded agreement. "I have to get back to work . . ."

The doctor shook his head. "Not for a while. It would be better if you waited until you can walk." He turned to Mother, still shaking his head. "These world builders. Do they not know that Shanghai was not built in a day?" Again he regarded me. "I would lose face if I returned with blood and you were not here."

They held a hushed conference and I managed to hear, "Yes, I think she's going to be all right."

A week after my crisis I felt warm and well enough to return to work. Colonel Wise took one look at me and declared, "My God, you're thin!" Cupping his chin in the palm of his hand he allowed his eyes to move up and down. "You've lost so much weight you're in danger of losing your skirt."

I had already solved the problem by wearing a belt under my skirt over which I'd hung a ridge of folded handkerchiefs.

"Dottie, I've made arrangements for you and Edna to have physicals at the base. There's a Navy doctor there."

"Don't I have a choice?"

"No," he said, his voice gentle but firm.

"I'm feeling fine . . ."

"Good. Then you won't have anything to worry about."

Four days after our examinations Edna and I returned to the base hospital to receive the reports. A Navy doctor came out and said to Edna, "You have a clean bill of health." Reaching into a large envelope he removed a giant negative and held it out for me to see. "There's some spots on your lung here." He frowned. "I'm not ready to make a definitive diagnosis until I have a consultation. I want you to come back."

On my next visit he made a diagnosis. "I'm sorry, Dottie," he said. "You have tuberculosis. I advise you to seek treatment immediately."

"What should I do?"

"Go to the United States. I think a sanatorium can cure you. The main thing is to get it arrested."

"Thank you," I mumbled.

The doctor had given it to me straight, without a build-up, without double-talk or adornment. The news hit me clean, like a sniper's bullet. And like a sniper's bullet it took a few minutes for shock to set in. By then I was outside.

"I do *not* have T.B.!" I cried out. "I don't *want* T.B.!"

A horrid affliction, T.B. rendered lungs decrepit, made young bodies old inside . . . and finally outside. How many days did I have? How much time before I became a coughing emaciated hag?

From deep within me tears began to well, rising as a tide. "No," I admonished myself with resolute determination, clenching my fist. "You will not cry." And I didn't.

"Go to the United States," the Navy doctor had said. How could I go to the United States? I couldn't burden my family with that now, not with Christmas coming, our first Christmas together since the end of the war. Family expenses were mounting . . .

Trapped, I felt myself losing composure. I had to do something. I did what I always did when threatened—launched into action. Foolishly, I ran. There was no way I could keep my date with Major Cullen Brannon. At his quarters I penned hasty regrets and slid my note under his door.

My life ruined, my feet raced again. Gasping, chest heaving, I labored for breath. Fright snick-snacked through me. Breathless, I gulped for air. I couldn't breathe! Why all of a sudden? There hadn't been anything wrong with my lungs before.

It's all reaction. You'll be okay if you settle down. Relax. You're not going to die until tomorrow. There is great joy to be found in this day. I walked slowly, inhaling deeply, savoring all the aromas in the air.

Could I smell the flowers, I wondered, when I got really bad? I did not return to work.

Having decided that life had to go on, I arrived at the office promptly the next morning. Before an hour passed Colonel Wise approached, his gaze penetrating. "What's wrong, Dottie? You're not yourself. I've never seen you like this."

As soon as I poured out my bad news he launched a counter-offensive. A cable message was dispatched to our former flight surgeon, Major John F. Shaner, who now had a practice in St. Louis. "Make arrangements," Colonel Wise told him. "Cable us back."

My friend Major Cullen Brannon stopped by. "Why didn't you tell me?" he chided. "I had to hear it from the doctor. He saw me sitting in the mess hall with a long face after getting your note. 'Isn't it too bad about Dottie?' the doctor said. He proceeded to tell me the bad news. Why couldn't you . . . ?"

"I just couldn't," I said. "How come the doctor told you? I thought ethics forbid . . . isn't a patient's condition supposed to be confidential?"

"You're public property, Dottie." The Major smiled wanly. "You belong to the Flying Tigers . . . the Fourteenth."

Around the office—UNRRA, CNNRA, CAT—procedures disrupted as plans were formulated.

"You're going back to the States," Colonel Wise said.

"I-I can't. How . . . ?"

"Leave everything to me."

The Yuen family celebrated Christmas and New Year's Eve approached. Colonel Wise and I had gone for a horseback ride along Yu Yuen Road, an early morning excursion that had become a twice a week custom. The ride completed, we accepted Mother's invitation to join her at breakfast. As we prepared to leave, Mother said, "Dorothy, I want you to take good care of yourself. Keep your chest covered."

My eyelids raised. "Yes, Mother."

"I had a dream about you last night. You had a breathing problem. Be sure to bundle up and watch your lungs."

"All right."

The Colonel shot me a quick sidelong glance as we exited.

"She doesn't know you have T.B. You haven't told her, have you?"

I gave him a painful shrug. "I can't..."

"You won't be able to put it off much longer..."

"I know..."

With every hour it became more difficult to tell the family. At last, when I could no longer contain my anxiety, I blurted, "Mom, I've got T.B. I have to go to the States."

The family gave me wonderful support. My brother and sisters hugged me. "Just when we're finally together," Jack lamented. "Now we're going to be separated again."

"Cheer up. I'll be back as soon as I can."

"Forget it," Mother said. "You stay in Saint Louis. I'll meet you there. I'm getting out of China as soon as possible."

"But Sweetie," Father pleaded, the hurt puppy look coming into his long thin face. "My future is in China."

"You can stay here if you like," Mother said. "I'm fed up. I'm going home. I'm going."

I studied the determination in the faces of Mom and Dad. I had seen their resolute expressions before and realized it was just a matter of time before my parents separated, Mother to return to the United States, Father to remain in his beloved China.

As suddenly as I received the disastrous news I was caught in a whirlwind of good wishes. My friend, Major Cullen Brannon, who planned to return to Albany, Georgia in the near future, asked for special orders so he could accompany me.

"I pulled some strings," he said as he told me the news.

Officers and men chipped in money. I was overwhelmed. "There's so much! I'll never be able to take it out of the country."

"Don't worry, Dottie," glowed Colonel Wise. "We thought of that. It's all arranged. We cleared it with both embassies. Don't ever worry about money. There's more where that came from."

How could anyone expect all the wonderful treatment I received from these men? Although I might be gravely ill, I faced 1947 with optimism and hope.

Already there had been publicity. A United Press release in a Shanghai newspaper of January 5th stated:

Yuen family seeing Dorothy off for the U.S. when she was stricken with tuberculosis. (Left to right) Gloria Yuen, Edna Yuen, Lillian Yuen, Dorothy, Colonel Sandow Yuen, Jack Yuen.

Overcome by sadness at leaving her family and friends, Dorothy prepares to leave China.

UNHAPPY HOMEGOING FOR WAR HEROINE

A young woman who used to play hide and seek on New York sidewalks, sometimes hiding with other kids amid the shadowed pews of the Hungarian Catholic Church in Eleventh Street, has set out today upon a strange, unhappy return to America.

Monday, January 6—The North China *Daily News:*

FORMER FLYING TIGERS SECRETARY LEAVES

China *Daily Tribune:*

DOTTIE YUEN, HONORARY G.I., WHO RETURNS TO U.S. FOR T.B. TREATMENT, IS ALSO WAR CASUALTY

A crowd came to Kiangwan to see me off. As a CAT photographer lined up the family for a picture Colonel Wise stood to one side, quiet, very proper, not showing any emotion.

"I'll send money to bring you back," Dad promised.

Mother gave me a box of candy and flowers. "I'll see you over there, Dorothy."

"Be sure to write me," Edna said.

"I will. You too. And you too, Jack."

Jack's eyes brimmed with tears. He gave me an emotional hug.

"Gloria, take care . . ."

"Oh, Dorothy . . ." she choked.

I was desperately trying to be brave, trying to be gay and smiling, but my eyes were misting over. A lump rose in my throat. Blinking through tears I started up the ramp, feeling awkward in the parachute harness.

I felt Major Brannon take my arm . . .

As we continued our journey the attention of the press astonished me. There was a photograph in the Honolulu Advertiser with the caption HOME AFTER 12 YEARS.

San Francisco *Call-Bulletin*, January 8:

GIRL ENDS 3 YEARS SERVICE IN CHINA

Petite Edith ("Dottie") Yuen, 24, veteran of three years service with the U.S. Army in China as a civilian employee, rested here today at the end of a 10,000 mile "flight for health" from Shanghai.

Associated Press:

DOTTIE YUEN ARRIVES IN SAN FRANCISCO

Bundled in a pilot's furlined jacket, 24 year old . . .

San Francisco:

FLYING TIGERS' 'DOTTIE' COMES BACK TO U.S.

Fabulous Girl to Get Medical Aid

The heroine of the Flying Tigers was back on American soil today on her way to a St. Louis, Mo., sanatorium, where she will undergo treatment for tuberculosis. . . . They set her down at Fairfield with loving care, for she is a legend to the men of the American, as well as the Chinese, Air Forces.

Scripps-Howard Newspapers

HEROINE OF 'FLYING TIGERS'
REACHES U.S. ILL WITH TB

St. Louis:

SHE HELPED THE FLYING TIGERS
NOW THEY HELP HER

The darling of the Flying Tigers has returned to the United States at last. For three years Dottie Yuen braved bombs and sniper fire to work with the handful of American airmen who challenged Japan from Chinese soil. Now, she is here to battle a more insidious foe—tuberculosis.

Back in the U.S.A.

St. Louis *Post-Dispatch*

*SHANGHAI GIRL, CITED BY U.S.
HERE FOR MEDICAL CARE*

Treatment for 'Mascot' of Flying Tigers Arranged by St. Louis Surgeon.

Miss Edith Dorothy Lillian Yuen, Chinese-American "mascot" of the "Flying Tigers" through three years of dangerous work which undermined her health...

Some reports to the contrary, I had traded my fur lined flight jacket for a long coat by the time we landed at Lambert Field. Dr. John F. Shaner was waiting and as I came down the ramp he took my extended hand. We blinked as flash bulbs popped.

"You didn't know I was traveling with a star, did you?" Major Brannon quipped.

"With what I've been hearing," said Dr. Shaner, "I'm beginning to get that idea. At least I recognize you."

He continued to talk as we made our way through a crowd of reporters. "Which is more than I can say for the Flying Tigers I see in the movies."

"I hear we're a pretty rough outfit," I laughed.

"How are you feeling?"

"Fine."

We made our way into the coffee shop. While reporters fired questions at me Dr. Shaner talked with Major Brannon.

After a few minutes Dr. Shaner nodded that it was time to go. "They'll take good care of you at Mount Saint Rose," he said. "I have some excellent doctors assigned to your case."

He waved farewell as Major Brannon and I seated ourselves in a taxi. I heard the Major instruct the driver, "Ninety-one-oh-one South Broadway..."

Chapter Eighteen

As we approached Mount St. Rose Sanatorium a statue of Christ, larger than life, spread its arms in compassionate welcome. I directed my gaze above the imposing brick structure for a last look at the blue-gray Missouri sky. In the fastness beyond the office, black and white robed nuns scurried along the corridors, but the matronly nun across the reception desk employed a paucity of motion as she completed the admissions questionnaire. Impatience rising within me from her incessant questions, I longed for the easy manner of reporters. Suddenly she closed the ledger, placed it aside with meticulous care and dispensed a measured smile.

"You may go to your room now."

Her pronouncement was also a command for someone to bring a wheelchair. A glance at the bulky chair confirmed that it was the last thing I wanted.

"I've just traveled twelve thousand miles," I said. "I'm sure I can walk to my room."

"This is where your journey ends," the nun said with authority. Her smile failed to thaw the frigid determination behind it.

Distressed and humiliated, I obeyed her command and allowed them to wheel me to a room where I was disrobed and placed in bed. Major Brannon was permitted a brief visit so he could purchase some of the things I needed. He left and returned with a stack of pajamas, a toothbrush and other personal items. We talked until a nun told him to leave.

"If there's anything else you need," he said, "let me know. I'll be staying at the Coronado Hotel."

Smiling, I waved farewell, realizing that our next meeting would contain the sorrow of parting. In the past months we had grown fond of each other and I knew what he intended to say, but I would have to tell him we had no future together. He confided that going home always saddened him and it distressed me to add to his burden.

Presently a nun arrived with a tray and I started to swing my legs out of bed.

"Oh no," she said. "You can't get out of bed. You're not allowed out of bed."

"For anything?" I asked, dumbfounded. "Not even to go . . ."

"Not even for that," she said curtly.

The final indignity.

As the sun hid over the western horizon, with the gloom of night approaching, a dark cloud settled over me. I had never felt so alone. If I was a casualty of war like the newspaper stated, I wanted to be with the guys . . . not stuck away in some remote corner of the world called St. Louis, with neither family or friend, where nurses and attendants in their strange black plummage treated me like a vegetable.

Too quiet. Not even the chirp of a bird penetrated the windows closed against the chill of winter. I heard the faint sound of a car protesting its way through the gears, gathering speed. Then I heard the drone of B-25s rising off the runway one by one, and a P-40 in a screaming *me-e-e-o-ow* diving down on a Zero just the way Chennault instructed, engines straining, machine guns hammering, sending a Son of Heaven down in flames. We'd shown the ill-fated Japanese. We'd gotten even for all the bombing, the strafing of junks and people along crowded highways. I remembered falling on my face in a wet and muddy rice paddy . . .

"I said I'd get even," I choked. Out of the depths of loneliness and despair a tide came rising, relentless, warm and salty. What had it all been for, the last dozen years? How many times had I felt the hot breath of bombs? If I was going to be a casualty of war, why couldn't it be swift and sudden? It would be better if a bomb landed at my feet. Then it'd be over in a flash . . .

Trembling, sobbing, all the pent up hostility and anger and frustration of a dozen years surged through me. Helpless before the deluge, I raised the flood gates wide.

The *click-clack* of heels sounded in the corridor and a black-robed nun entered. Seeing only her white face against the darkness I felt her hand touch my shoulder.

"You must not cry, Miss."

"I'm all right," I blubbered. "I just *want* to cry."

"Don't be sad. You mustn't cry."

"I'll be all right when I've cried it out . . . when I'm washed clean."

"No. You must stop crying. You have to save your strength."

Unable to console me, she asked, "Do you need a bedpan?"

"No! Just go away and leave me alone. I'll be fine in the morning."

She withdrew to a fresh monsoon as I flung my arms across the pillow and allowed myself to be carried along with the surging current.

Presently soft footsteps came padding into the room. Turning, I made out a figure in white. As I rolled over on my back an arm came out and the light over my head went on, blinding me for an instant. As my eyes grew accustomed to the light I saw the face of my enemy, staring down through coke bottle bottom glasses. Large buck teeth filled his smiling Japanese mouth. In that electric moment of recognition, the revulsion of a decade seared across raw-tipped nerves and ran twitching through me like wires. I wanted to scream, kick, lash out . . .

"Hello," he said. "I'm Doctor Ohmoto."

I regarded him in stony silence.

"Miss Yuen, you really must stop crying. It's bad for your condition."

"I'll be all right in the morning."

"Would you like me to give you a sedative?"

"No."

"You're all upset from the trip and the strange surroundings. It's important that you get plenty of rest. I want you to get a good night's sleep, so I'd like you to have a sedative . . ."

"B-But . . ."

"I'm going to prescribe a mild sleeping pill . . . and I want you to take it."

I nodded. When they brought a tiny medicine cup containing a two-colored capsule I regarded it with suspicion. The face of the nurse reassured me. Reluctantly I brought the cup to my lips. Maybe the doctor was American-Japanese like I was American-Chinese? I gulped the pill. Words came into my mind of their own volition. *Dorothy, the war is over.*

There could be peace. As the days went by, Dr. Ohmoto and I would become friends.

Major Brannon came the next evening to say goodby. "It's going to be lonesome for the both of us these next months," he said, sober-faced. "But I think you'll be cured sooner than you think."

"I hope so."

"I'm sorry I've take up so much of your time when you need rest..."

We stumbled through the awkwardness of breaking off a relationship. The carefully selected words we planned remained mostly unsaid. "Try not to have a dismal homecoming," I said.

"I'm glad I talked to you about that. I wrote you a letter—I'll mail it later."

It's never a joyful occasion when a man hears his lady friend will not marry him. We left it like that—over, but not really over. The broken strand could be respliced if either of us desired to make the effort. In a few days I would receive his letter on buff colored stationery, written on that last afternoon before he came to see me.

"Sweetheart—" the letter began. "Although I will see you tonight I want to put down a few thoughts for you to remember me by." So he had known before he came what my answer would be. By the time he penned the third page his style had become formal. "Your strength of character has been a source of inspiration to all who have known you."

It pleased me that we had been able to part on good terms... we would always be good friends.

There were other letters. With all the publicity, I received an outpouring of cards and letters. My room was banked with flowers.

"Who *is* she?" I heard someone ask as they passed my door.

A nun came running in. "There's a long distance call for you. You can take it at the end—"

"You mean I can get out of bed?"

"Just this once. We'll make an exception."

Without a phone in my room, I had to run down the hall.

Pressing the receiver to my ear I heard a familiar voice.

"Hi. This is Lonnie."

"Lonnie," I retorted. "I'm so mad at you! Why didn't you tell me that you were married?"

"Well," he said, groping for excuse. "If I had told you, you wouldn't have gone walking with me. Isn't that right?"

"That's right."

"This is some greeting, Dorothy. I'm not sorry. We had something beautiful. I'm not ashamed of anything I did. My wife could have looked over my shoulder the entire time. I'm not sorry."

When I reflected on it later, neither was I sorry. As Lonnie said, "We had something beautiful." In war beautiful moments are rare. I regretted being sharp with him. However, I mentioned what a dear friend he was to have telephoned and I promised to keep in touch.

In a few days I received permission to leave my bed. A visitor arrived looking rather unkempt. Unshaven, his hair mussed, he wore a long, black, loose-fitting overcoat and a curious smile. My eyes widened at the sight of him. He grinned and said, "Hello, Sis."

"Bobby Roloson! How did you find me?"

"Like somebody is shoving a newspaper under my nose asking, 'Isn't this your sister?' So I took a couple days off and here I am."

"Are you still in New York?" I hadn't heard from my half-brother in years. Addresses changed and we'd lost each other.

"Like yeah, Sis. I'm married. I'm in the shingle and roofing business. How's Mom? The kids?"

"Fine. Everyone's fine. I think Mom is coming back. It might take six months or a year. The red tape is fantastic."

"Groovy."

"You talk funny."

"Just plain New York talk."

We visited as much as we could and at the end of the day Bobby returned to the big city. Before he left he said, "When you get out of here, Sis, I want you to come and live with us."

I was delighted Bobby had found me. Now that we had each other's address, we could reestablish family ties. That evening I wrote Mother telling her about Bobby's surprise visit.

My treatment continued. The first sputum test had been positive, but after that they were all negative—the guinea pig didn't have to die. It wouldn't please me to kill a guinea pig for every test.

Certainly one of the benefits of having a disease is learning all about it. I acquired a new vocabulary, including such mystifying words as 'streptomycin' and 'pneumothorax'—the procedure whereby a needle was inserted between my ribs and air pumped into the pleural cavity to collapse the lung. My twice a week treatments gradually diminished to once a week.

The original mountain of cards and letters quickly dwindled, along with the flowers. I was cheered by a letter from Shanghai dated February 26, bringing me news of the office. "Two new planes have arrived from Manila. It was good to see our emblem and CAT painted across the side." A friendly greeting, the letter closed with, "I hope that after six months you will be completely recovered and we will look forward to seeing you out here again. Most sincerely, C. L. Chennault."

The General's letter focused my attention on a decision I would have to make. Should I return to China or remain here in the States? It was something I had to decide before being released. It wasn't like the other problem I had—whether to write to the parents of Captain John Birch. I could keep putting that off. A dozen times I decided what I would say and each time I abandoned the idea. Sometime I would send John's mother the Flying Tiger emblem, the silk map and some of the other things John had given me but I couldn't do it . . . now. I couldn't bring myself to tell her what we had meant to each other. The more I pondered it, the closer I came to deciding that I'd present it rather low key, if at all. I would write a letter some day . . . eventually.

Then an old friend stopped to see me, bringing a whole new dimension into my life.

"Hello, Dottie."

"Colonel Wise," I cried. "What are you doing here?"

"I'm on the way to Princeton . . . to see the family. I'm

oing to be stationed Stateside."

Although it was springtime he already wore traces of a ummer tan. I saw an almost angelic refinement in his eatures, a gentleness superimposed over masculine good ooks.

"And then?"

"Washington, D.C. The Pentagon." His eyes sparkled nd his petulant lower lip relaxed in a smile. "How are you oing, Dottie?"

"Very nicely. The doctor says if I continue to improve as I ave, I'll be released in August."

"Wonderful!" Relieved that I was really all right, his look f compassion became venturesome.

"I've coming for something else," he said with a rapturous rin. "You!"

My mouth became an open oval.

"Don't look so surprised. I've loved you for a long time. Being away from you has made me realize it. You can't know ow much I've missed you these past four months. I can't get long without you . . . and I've decided not to try."

"Really, I couldn't come between a man and his wife."

"You're not."

"You haven't divorced?"

"Not yet. But I'm . . ."

"I just couldn't break up a marriage."

"You haven't. This has been coming a long time."

"Just the same, folks will say I broke you up. That's what hey will say and I couldn't bear that. It would be my fault."

"It won't be your fault."

"I can't help feeling this way. You can find out for yourself vhen you get home. Talk to your mother. You'll find out vhose fault . . ."

A boyish smile washed over his face without touching the lueness of his eyes. His hand closed over mine. "You don't ave to decide anything right now. There will be plenty of ime to think it over. I'm going east now and in a few weeks 'm coming back. The next time I see you, Dottie, I'm going o ask you to marry me."

Excitement rising within me, I heard him add, "I'm not going to take no for an answer."

He looked into my eyes intently. He started to leave, then

wheeled and gave me another long penetrating look.

My mind was awhirl. All the old vague agonies, th loneliness of life was swept away as my heart soared to a ne potential. All the troubled years of life were slipping awa like a moon into the sea. I went out to enjoy the sunset.

It was a grapy dusk, the pink hues fading to purpl beyond the stately new leafed trees. Their lengthenin shadows faded as gray streets turned dark. A ribbon o smoke from a nearby home began drifting on a gentle breez that stirred the tree tops. The air felt crisp, but sweet like th first bite of an apple. At my feet spring flowers breathe goodnight, still bowing farewell to a vanished sun.

Staring into the dark mystery of the future I let the word form on my tongue. "Mrs. Richard H. Wise." It was a ste not to be taken lightly. He was somewhat older.

The hoot of an owl came out of a nearby tree, ominou and eerie. I stiffened, turned and listened again. Was it a evil omen? Furrowing my brow, I drew my back erect i decision and squared my shoulders. There was always an ow lurking in a pear tree somewhere. It could not be denied tha the owl selected the tree, but the tree usually remaine standing long after the owl had gone.

I knew what I would do. I had said "no" for what seeme like an eternity. Now it was time for me to say yes. As started to go inside I heard the rustle of wings. I was sure th owl had flown from the tree. I never looked back.

TWICE DEAD — LB601KK $1.75
Larry D. Names — Novel

Did Lee Harvey Oswald die in 1959? Reporter Tom Regan finds evidence that this may be the case, and he follows the lead on a trail that takes him to the core of the conspiracy to assassinate President Kennedy—and to the brink of death!

THE PRO — LB647 $2.25
Bob Packard — Novel

Golf was more than a game to Doug Austin—it was the way to get off the assembly line, the way to get rich, the way to get away from his wife, and the way to win glamorous Melinda Long. But for Doug Austin, the high life only meant he had a long way to fall!
Setting: Pennsylvania, Las Vegas, the pro golf tour, contemporary.

MILLIE & CLEVE — LB615 $2.25
Jess Carr — Novel

Prohibition hadn't changed anything in the hills—moonshiners and the law still kept up a fast-paced competition. Cleve was a deputy sheriff who wanted to be the best sheriff Edison County ever saw, but he was in love with Millie—and she and her father were already at the top of the moonshiners' heap!
Setting: Southern United States, 1920's

PROMISE ME ROMANCE — LB607 $1.95
Jeannie Sakol — Novel

A public relations agency on the verge of success in London, a variety of wealthy and handsome lovers—Margaret Sturtevant had everything a modern woman wants, but all she really wanted was a chance to give it all up and be a housewife for the man she loved!

DAUGHTER OF CONQUEST **LB646 $2.25**
Robert E. Mills **Historical Romance**

Isolated within the French colony in Cairo, Louise Rouland longed for an adventure to relieve her boredom. Martin Braddock, an American engineer, joined Napoleon's expedition to Egypt to have a part in history. When they met they knew their fates were one, but adventure, history, and Napoleon's ambition stood between them!

THIS SPLENDID LAND **LB638 $1.95**
Chet Cunningham **Historical Romance**

The Breckenridge Saga concludes with Jed and Jeannie building their new ranch in Texas into an empire. As the ranch grows, so do the passions of those on it, and Jed's tempestuous affair with the Mexican beauty Teresa leads to an armed showdown, with the whole future at stake!
Setting: Texas Panhandle, 1840's

DESTINY AND DESIRE **LB639 $1.95**
Lorinda Hagen **Historical Romance**

Orphaned Letitia Cooper got a sudden opportunity—to go west and live on her uncle's ranch. Before long, he'd been killed, and someone was out to get control of the Sierra Lorena spread. Two men stood at Letty's side, but one of them wanted to kill her!
Setting: Nevada, 1867